D1274285

The Intimate Hour

The Intimate Hour

Reuben Fine, Ph.D.

AVERY PUBLISHING GROUP INC.
Wayne, New Jersey

Copyright © 1979 by Avery Publishing Group, Inc.

All rights reserved. No part of this publication may be reproduced, stored in a retrieval system, or transmitted, in any form or by any means, electronic, mechanical, photocopying, recording or otherwise, without the prior written permission of the copyright owner.

Library of Congress Catalog Card Number: 78-067412

ISBN: 0-89529-023-5

Designer: Rudy Shur

Typesetter: Roslyn M. Sydney

Printed in the United States of America

To my patients,
who allowed me to enter their private world
and help them

Contents

Preface   v

PART I.   *Introduction*
          The Experience of Psychotherapy   3

PART II. *The Case Histories*

   1.   Sally, the Promiscuous Woman   23
   2.   Harvey, the "Schlemiel"   54
   3.   Alice, the "Normal" Woman   82
   4.   Jim, the Drifter   105
   5.   Holly, the Abandoned Woman   118
   6.   Sheldon, the Frightened Boy Genius   144
   7.   Gloria, the Reformed "Easy Lay"   162
   8.   Peter, the Addicted Physician   189
   9.   Beverly, "Evil Incarnate"   216
  10.   Frank, the Man Who Made a Pact with God   239

PART III. *Discussion*
          A Review of the Ten Cases in the Light of the
          Analytic Ideal   271

GLOSSARY   308

INDEX   311

Preface

In the sciences of man, psychoanalysis represents the greatest intellectual adventure of the twentieth century. Though not quite a century old it has already revolutionized psychiatry, transformed psychology, created an entirely new spirit in the social sciences, helped hundreds of thousands of people find the way to a happier life and brought about a spirit of optimism in psychotherapy that had never existed before.

Yet in spite of these enormous changes, it is difficult to convey to the average educated person what someone goes through when he is psychoanalyzed. Usually the process is either glamorized Hollywood style, or condemned by its enemies. Sober factual case histories are hard to find. Even Freud, in more than half a century of continual treatment, only published one complete case history.

In this book ten case histories are presented. My goal has been to show the essentials of what happened to these ten individuals, without getting lost in a mass of detail, or resorting to needless technical jargon. After all, when a person comes to a psychoanalyst for help, the question is: how is this help given, and with what effects?

When the question is put in this way, it becomes possible to describe the results of many psychoanalyses, even those of many years' duration, in a fairly brief outline. Psychoanalysis is not a miracle cure. Yet it has shown itself to be by far the most effective way of helping human beings with their troubles. How this assistance is given, and with what consequences, are the essential questions that I have kept in mind throughout.

The case histories have been rather arbitrarily selected from my files. They cover the range of problems that people bring to psychoanalysts and other professionals, from schizophrenia to marital discord.

Still, if the people involved are looked at carefully, it soon becomes clear that very few correspond to the traditional picture of a psychiatric patient. In fact, only two of the ten would have gone to a doctor a hundred years ago, and no doctor then would have had any technical tools with which to help them. Psychoanalysis is an entirely new idea, even though the names of its practitioners are old. For all practical purposes, the great upsurge of psychoanalytic treatment can be dated from the end of World War II.

No material has been revealed that is damaging to any of the individuals described. For obvious reasons, the cases have been slightly fictionalized, yet broad outlines faithfully recapitulate what actually happened.

I wish to express my thanks to Mr. Rudy Shur and Dr. Gary Belkin of the Avery Publishing Group for their consistent encouragement in the preparation of the manuscript.

Reuben Fine

New York

January 29, 1979

PART I
Introduction

The Experience of Psychotherapy

Medical cures are easy to understand, even if the underlying biochemical processes remain a mystery. Not so with psychotherapy. Patients get better, but how, why, when, or for what reason are all hard to pin down. A considerable reorientation of ordinary thinking is needed.

THE NATURE OF "NORMALITY"

To begin with, it is necessary to take a closer look at what is meant by "normality"; the quotation marks already highlight the fact that it is more of a fiction than a reality. The cultural image of normality is the person who never worries, functions effectively at his or her job, is happily married, has no deep troubles, is rarely ill, and then only for good medical reasons, such as infection, and is never unduly ruffled by the ups and downs of everyday living. Merely putting down these characteristics on paper serves to show how rare such people are, if they do exist at all.

But it is necessary to show the world a normal front, keeping a stiff upper lip. In this way a gap is created between the

3

public and the private selves. Sooner or later everybody becomes aware of this gap, and then handles it in different ways. There ensues a defensive process, whereby the individual wards off from others, and often from himself, the unflattering, sometimes totally self-demeaning, feelings that he has deep down inside.

What do people do about this gap? Mostly, they keep it secret and suffer. As Thoreau said more than a hundred years ago, most men lead lives of quiet desperation.

Suffering is disagreeable. So in their desperation men have always turned to somebody for help. The only trouble was that before Freud no valid help was to be had.

To be sure, the Greeks, as in so many fields, had made a start. The Sophists, from the fifth century B.C. on, who were incorrectly despised by later generations, began to experiment with various forms of psychotherapy. Breaking away from the older reliance on magical charms, Gorgias urged persuasion, arguing that words have the power to take away fear, banish pain inspire happiness, and increase compassion. One of his followers, Antiphon, set himself up near Corinth to treat the grief-stricken by means of "discourses"; by informing himself of the causes of the affliction he unburdened and consoled his patients. Sounds almost modern.

But the enlightenment of the Greeks was followed by a long dark night of the human soul. From the Sophists to Freud no progress whatsoever was made; if anything, nineteenth-century psychiatry never fully attained the insights and even techniques of the Greeks. Instead, men turned to faith healers, mesmerizers, magical charms, dream-book interpreters, religious fanatics, and assorted other specimens in the search for relief from their pain.

The French revolution ushered in a period of great hope for mankind. Yet its emphasis remained on a reorganization of the political and social structure; it had no real insight into the nature of emotional disturbance.

Hope led to the faith that somehow the brain of the "deranged" person was affected. The greatest exponent of nineteenth-century psychiatry, the German Wilhelm Griesinger, pontificated that "mind disease is brain disease." The idea went back to the Greeks. The mind, like the physical universe, was seen as a kind of machine. Psychology was suspect, viewed as a form of charlatanism.

The conviction that any kind of emotional suffering must be due to some bodily affliction persists to this day among most people, including a large percentage of the medical profession. As a result the terminology in use follows established medical language; we speak of "neurosis" (inflammation of the nerves), of "illness," of "symptoms," and the like, although in a very real sense these terms have long since become obsolete. It is not surprising that the consequence is one of large-scale confusion, which is only gradually being dispelled.

THE PRE-FREUDIAN "PATIENT"

Who went to a psychiatrist a hundred years ago? (Freud lived from 1856 to 1939; his major discoveries date from the 1890's.) Only a few of the most obviously deranged persons. The term "psychiatry" did not yet exist. Some physicians set themselves up as "neuropathologists" but their scientific knowledge was zero, and their treatment techniques completely haphazard. In the modern sense there was no treatment before Freud. There was only custodial institutionalization, mostly for life, since few of these patients ever really recovered their sanity. The less seriously disturbed, who could not be hospitalized, had nobody to go to, except for a rare handful of humane physicians, ministers, or other counselors, who by the force of their own mature personalities could offer some relief to the distressed.

The division into those who had to be hospitalized and those who did not was virtually the only function the nineteenth-century psychiatrist could perform. Psychologists in the modern sense did not yet exist; the few who did were college professors or researchers mapping the geography of the five senses.

Because of the lack of scientific knowledge, the patient of that day was a bizarre, deviant, aberrant individual whose symptoms were totally baffling to the medical profession which tried to treat him. The treatments available were hit-and-miss procedures, with little rhyme or reason to them. In the social scale, the psychiatrist (then still referred to as a neuropathologist or alienist) was next to the bottom of the ladder, just above the ship's doctor. The number of patients who went to psychiatrists was minuscule. In the larger scheme of events the psychiatrist played no significant role.

While the situation has undergone a drastic change because of the Freudian revolution, the older images of the psychiatrist and his patient still persist. In many communities the person who sees a psychiatrist is still viewed as incurably violent, a danger to the surrounding "normal" folk. Even in a city as sophisticated as New York it is sometimes difficult for a psychiatrist to find an apartment because of the neighbors' fears of what his patients might do. It is only gradually that the altered situation is sinking into the public consciousness.

THE CONTEMPORARY PATIENT: TEN CASES

The ten cases selected, more or less at random, for this book, present a cross-section of the patients who currently visit mental health practioners (psychiatrists, psychologists, social workers). Before discussing what their therapy meant to them, it will be useful to review in brief outline what they were like when they first came to treatment.

The Promiscous Woman

Sally was a promiscuous woman who had literally thousands of sexual contacts. She was severely depressed, frightened, and suffering from nightmares all the time. Then she fell in love. It was the conflict created by the love affair that brought her into treatment.

The "Schlemiel"

Harvey, the last of six children, was dubbed by his mother her "twelfth abortion." Naturally, this crushed his self-esteem, leaving him an easy prey to any woman who wanted to manipulate him. Anyone knowing him would have called him a typical "schlemiel," (a yiddish word for an unlucky gullible person). It was the urging of a friend who saw how poorly Harvey was functioning that brought him into treatment.

The Normal Woman

Alice had always been known to her friends and acquaintances as one of the most normal, best-adjusted women around. No one knew that she was deathly afraid of sex, and in fact suffered pain during intercourse. Her sexual frustration was covered over by a conventionally "good" marriage. It was only when she experienced some pleasure in an extramarital affair that she found the courage to come to treatment.

The Drifter

Jim had drifted through life, not knowing who he was, where he was going, or what he was doing. For a while he had been a homosexual, then gave that up, and led a celibate life, without either male or female companionship. At thirty-eight he had almost no friends, no women, and no clear-cut career goal. He came to treatment ostensibly to get some vocational guidance, though once the analyst suggested therapy he accepted it readily enough.

The Abandoned Woman

Holly experienced what so many women go through: her boy friend jilted her. The result was, as with many others, a severe depression. That a psychotherapist was available to help her understand her depression and get over it was the real novelty.

The Frightened Genius

Sheldon, a seven-year-old boy, had one of the highest IQ's ever recorded. At the age of seven he had a reading comprehension of fourteen, and had memorized the entire subway system in his area of the city. Nevertheless, he was dreadfully insecure and unable to communicate with other people. At first he was sent for "speech therapy" because of the lack of awareness on the part of the authorities that his speech problems were due to his fears. It was only when he ran out of the auditorium alarmed by the showing of a picture of an accident that therapy was undertaken. Even there the opposition of a quack physician-friend, who favored a bizarre physiological theory, had to be overcome.

The Reformed "Easy Lay"

In her adolescence Gloria was the town's "easy lay." She would have sex with anybody and everybody, in sordid hotel rooms, in any available bedroom, even sometimes on the street in a dark alley. Neither VD nor pregnancy, both of which occurred several times, interfered with her promiscuity. Nor did any of this precipitate her into therapy.

Finally, she married a man with whom she settled down and reformed completely. A child was born, a son, who became the apple of her eye. Understandably, the sexual attachment to the son became strong, and both mother and son developed problems. But only the difficulties of the son led her to undertake therapy.

The Addicted Physician

Drug addiction has emerged as one of the greatest problems of our time. Subsequent historical research has shown that it has always been a problem, among virtually all peoples, at all times. Only the drug has varied with technological advances.

In the present case, the patient, a physician, was addicted to methadone, a synthetic derivative of morphine created by the miracles of modern medicine and biochemistry. Underneath the addiction lay an ocean of terror which had been with him all his life. But treatment was undertaken only when he could no longer function at his medical practice.

"Evil Incarnate" — The Treatment of Insanity

Beverly had passed beyond the bounds of ordinary eccentricity and would have been considered "crazy" by anyone who met her. Among other delusions she was convinced that anyone she touched would immediately be destroyed. Her history showed several hospitalizations, several courses of shock treatment, and treatment with about ten psychiatrists with whom she had failed to make any significant progress.

Finally she found one psychiatrist with whom she fell in love, and he brought her back to a modicum of functioning. Unfortunately, he had to leave town on three days' notice because of personal problems of his own, and this precipitated another break. Now she came to see herself as evil incarnate, unworthy of human attention. Even a hospital, she thought, would see her as unfit for their institution.

It is one of the triumphs of modern psychoanalysis that in spite of the severity of her symptoms, they could be made intelligible, and a sensible form of psychotherapy could be used to help her.

Religion and Neurosis: The Man Who Made a Pact With God

In his adolescence Frank began to suffer from peculiar and terrifying states of panic. Although religion played no significant role in his life, in an effort to get over these panics he made a peculiar arrangement with God. The pact was that if the Almighty would get him over his panic states, Frank would never have sexual intercourse with a girl before marriage.

For a while this pact served to calm him down. Then it began to lose its effect. Although he held on to the agreement with God, he also entered psychotherapy to help him with his fears.

THE SHIFT IN THE PATIENT POPULATION

Merely enumerating the above ten cases, typical of modern practice, in such brief outline serves to demonstrate what is becoming increasingly evident: there has been, especially since

World War II, a marked shift in the patient population. Of the above cases, only one, Beverly, technically classified as a schizophrenic, would have gone into treatment even fifty years ago. What would the others have done? Committed suicide, taken to drink, vegetated, drifted on aimlessly, died prematurely, or who knows what. The course of human existence is not easily predictable, but of one thing we can be reasonably certain: when emotional problems set in, they tend to get worse as time goes on.

A recent best seller, which popularizes the findings of modern psychoanalysis, refers to the predictable crises of existence. Life is indeed a series of crises, each of which requires all the resources of the individual for their mastery. When an early crisis has been improperly mastered, later problems become all the more difficult. Each new problem brings more despair in its train, until finally for a large number of individuals some disaster overtakes them, leading to irremediable disease or death.

It is because of this realization that the patient population of the average psychotherapist has shifted from the acutely disturbed to the more or less normal. America has been called the most therapized community in history. Yet this is to be seen as a sign of progress, not an indication of increasing insanity or breakdown.

It seems a paradox, but divorce often occurs because the individuals are hoping for a better marriage, not because they have given up on marriage. Likewise, people go into therapy because they hope for a better life, not because they have retreated to a state of despair. One unexpected consequence of this state of affairs is that by and large those in therapy are often better off emotionally than those who are not.

THE ANALYTIC IDEAL

It is clear that a revolution in our thinking has come about. But the terminology used still reflects the age-old concepts, or more precisely, misconceptions. People are "sick"; they need "doctors"; their "illnesses" are curable or incurable. The medical analogy dominates the scene all along the line.

A more relevant and informative way of talking about emotional problems starts with Freud's discovery that what is wrong with the psychiatric patient is not some odd brain disturbance, but deficiencies, more or less serious, in his whole way of living. The particular symptoms that emerge cannot be separated from the total life style.

This can be expressed in the concept of the analytic ideal. Man can achieve his greatest happiness if he can love, experience sexual gratification, allow himself pleasure, feel deeply yet be guided by reason, have a place in a family, occupy a role in society, have a sense of meaningful identity, work, communicate, be creative, and be free from gross psychiatric symptomatology.

Such an analytic ideal has been given various names: mental health, the ideal image of normality, genital primacy, maturity, and so on. It is simplest to maintain the term "analytic ideal" to stress that it is an ideal which must be actively sought, rather than a special solution or a special state of mind.

Whatever name is given to it, it is the analytic ideal that has, and justifiably, captured the popular imagination. Here, virtually for the first time in history, is a way of living, buttressed by a sound psychology, that makes good sense, fits in with the historic traditions of humanism and democracy, and is within the reach of the ordinary man. It offers an unprecendented opportunity for a real revolution in human relationships. It is this image that has made psychology the most popular subject on the campus, and vaulted the psychoanalyst, in spite of his small numbers, to a position of enormous prestige and power.

THE PROCESS OF THERAPY

To convince people that the analytic ideal represents a desirable goal for mankind has been difficult, yet the number of persons who agree is constantly increasing. What is more difficult is the translation of this ideal into reality in actual cases. In order to orient the reader to what follows, a brief clarification of the process of therapy* will be given.

* No distinction is drawn in this book between psychoanalysis and psychotherapy, although they often differ in practice. In theory, however, all therapy is a derivative of psychoanalysis. This point has been clarified more fully in some of my more technical books, such as *The Healing of the Mind*.

THE INITIAL STEP
GETTING THE PATIENT INTO THERAPY

The first step is, of course, to get the patient to accept therapy. This is more easily said than done. It depends heavily on the general cultural climate much more than on the severity of the individual's symptoms. At the present time we must rely mainly on the general educational process which convinces an increasing number of persons that their lives can be altered for the better by analysis. In any individual instance, however, it seems to be more or less a matter of chance when or how or why an individual enters therapy. Obviously, however, a great many do.

CLARIFYING THE ANALYTIC IDEAL: FROM SYMPTOMS TO WAY OF LIVING (CHARACTER STRUCTURE)

Traditionally, and today as well, people start with some symptoms that bother them. The first step in therapy is to help them see that the symptom is only a surface manifestation, the tip of an iceberg, as some have put it. Underneath, and far more important, is the person's whole way of living. Technically, this way of living is called the character structure (or ego structure). The word "character" here, however, does not carry any of the moral connotations that it does in ordinary language; it is merely a way of describing how the individual functions. For example, the "compulsive" character is a person who has a compulsive need to see that everything is in its right place, that there are never any unexpected breaks from routine, that nothing is ever disordered, and so on. Any variation from the usual routine makes such a person extremely anxious. If this anxiety brings him to therapy, it is first necessary to help him to see that the real problem is in the way he follows certain preordained routines, even though these routines may be doing him serious harm.

The shift from the focus on symptoms to the focus on character is carried out through a discussion of the various components of the analytic ideal. Is his love life in order? Does he enjoy sex? Is the family life conflicted or harmonious? Is his work enjoyable or a horrible chore? As the patient relates his life story to the analyst, these and similar questions come to the fore, either directly or indirectly. In this way the patient comes to see, sooner or later, that the real problem lies in his distance from the analytic ideal. The therapy is now oriented to moving toward that ideal.

ON HOW PERSONALITY IS FORMED

Psychoanalysis does not offer the patient a course in psychological theory. Nevertheless, it is an essential part of every analysis to help the patient understand how he came to be the way he is.

Fortunately, the theory of personality formation is a relatively simple one. People are the products of their early family environments. They come to be the way they are because of the way their parents treated them. While "constitutional" and "genetic" factors certainly play some role in personality formation, we are still virtually in the dark about what this role is. We are not at all in the dark about the decisive effects of early experiences.

As a result of these early experiences, the child, who is at the mercy of the parents, builds up an inner image of what the parents want from him. While in the early years he obeys the actual parents for fear of punishment, later, after five years of age or so, the inner image takes over more and more. This inner image is known technically as the "superego." Since there is no good equivalent for this term in ordinary language, the word will be used throughout the book.*

The superego is experienced by the individual as a kind of inner voice which utters commands and prohibitions, and decides whether something is right or wrong. Any violation of these superego dictates makes the person extremely anxious. At the same time this whole process goes on at an unconscious

* Readers who wish to check on the meaning of a word may do so by consulting the glossary at the end of the book.

level, so that the person cannot really explain the true motives for his actions.

THE UNCONSCIOUS: MAKING THE UNCONSCIOUS CONSCIOUS

What is most striking about a piece of neurotic behavior is its "bizarre" quality, i.e., its apparent incomprehensibility. Paradoxically, psychoanalysis has taught us that all of human behavior is essentially rational, i.e., comprehensible, but that the rationality often exists at an unconscious rather than conscious level. Thus, the proper unraveling of the unconscious becomes one of the cornerstones of every therapeutic process.

What is it that is pushed back ("repressed") into the unconscious? Anything the parents did not find praiseworthy — primarily the impulses that every child has and which he has to learn to handle in a socially acceptable way: soiling, sexuality, (in childhood, especially, masturbation), behaving in a group, eating properly, sleeping, and the like. The analytic ideal seeks to teach the individual to gratify these impulses in a manner which leads to love and happiness; by contrast the superego in neurotic behavior continually punishes the person for his forbidden wishes. While these may be pushed out of consciousness, they nevertheless continue to exist, i.e., they become unconscious. Thus, what is found in the unconscious is a whole mass of pressing, pushing, driving impulses which, whether the person knows it or not, prod to find expression in some overt way. Since these expressions are forbidden by the surperego, conflict results and the person suffers.

To make the unconscious conscious is a formidable task. In one sense in fact it still represents the core of the whole therapeutic process. The wishes, originally pushed back into the unconscious because they aroused the disapproval of the parents, can no longer be brought to the fore because they make the person too frightened. It is almost literally true that the neurotic remains a child who is terrified of what his parents will do to him if he is "bad."

Two devices are relied upon to help the person bring his forbidden wishes to consciousness. One is the warmth and sympathy of the analyst, who must be a permissive, accepting figure, different from the terrifying, forbidding parents. But it is only gradually that the patient accepts the authority of the analyst, and reassures himself that he is not the awful person he always thought himself to be.

DREAMS: THE ROYAL ROAD TO THE UNCONSCIOUS

The other device is the dream, which can still justifiably be called the royal road to the unconscious. For this reason Freud's book *The Interpretation of Dreams*, first published in 1900, remains the cornerstone of all of modern psychology. The major value of the dream in analysis lies in the fact that its significance cannot be sidestepped, as is the case with virtually everything else.

The structure of the dream is fairly simple; it embodies the forbidden wish and the punishment for it. However, people do not express their wishes so directly. What comes out instead is a variety of disguises. The analyst is trained to break through these disguises and support the patient in expressing his forbidden wishes. Once they come out into the open, they are seen not to be so awful, which implies that the patient can now learn to live with himself more easily.

THE PARADOXES OF ANALYSIS:
RESISTANCE AND TRANSFERENCE

While this process of bringing forbidden wishes to consciousness can be described easily enough in theory, in practice it faces powerful obstacles. Primary among these are resistances and transference. Analysis cannot be made intelligible without clarifying these two concepts.

Resistance refers to the fact that the patient will fight the treatment process. He may refuse to come, or may not come on time, or not listen to what the analyst is saying, or may refuse to produce relevant material by keeping all kinds of things secret out of a sense of shame, or may fight in a hundred other ways. How the patient will fight cannot be predicted in advance; of only one thing can we be sure; that he will fight the analyst at some time or another.

In one sense this resistance can be understood as similar to the reaction of any person to an authority figure. Pupils do not obey teachers, soldiers do not obey their officers, workers do not obey their bosses, patients do not obey their doctors, etc. In any kind of situation where one human being is in a position to give orders to another, the subordinate person is highly likely to feel resentful of his position and to express this resentment in a variety of different ways.

In the analytic situation this resentment is made considerably stronger by the fact that the analyst exerts only moral authority over the patient. If things get too bad, the patient can always leave, and many patients do. What is particularly annoying to the patient is that he must recognize many unpleasant truths about himself. Furthermore, he has to pay a fee, has to keep hours set up by the analyst, and has to talk about matters that are otherwise often kept private or secret. All of this adds to the resentment and the resultant resistances.

A second universal phenomenon in treatment is the development of a *transference*. By "transference" we mean the emotional relationship between the patient and the analyst. After shorter or longer periods this transference moves into the center of the stage, and together with the resistances comes to make up the heart of the treatment.

One example can be cited here, though many others are given throughout the book. Frank, the man who had made a pact with God that he would not have sex with a girl before marriage, remained extremely anxious. Instead of dealing with his anxiety, which obviously came from childhood taboos about sex instilled in him by his parents, especially his mother, he became convinced that some miracle drug would be discovered that would "cure" him in some magical way, much as penicillin had cured a whole series of formerly difficult or intractable diseases. He spent many evenings going to the library to read up on drugs. He filled the analytic hours with discussions of drugs.

He was in treatment in the early 1950's, when drugs were less readily available. Had he been in treatment later, he would undoubtedly have experimented with a great many.

In the transference he was particularly annoyed because I bore a physical resemblance to his older brother, whom he hated. No doubt there was such a physical resemblance; also the brother and I were nearly of the same age. But equally clearly such similarity was completely irrelevant to his problems. No so to the patient. Hour after hour was filled with reproaches against me for being too much like his brother, both physically and intellectually. Hence, for a number of years a large part of Frank's analysis was taken up with his preoccupation with drugs and with his annoyance with his analyst.

In other cases the resistances and transferences take different forms, but they always remain at the center of the analysis. It is not surprising that 90 percent of all treatises on techniques are devoted to the management of transference and resistance.

THE BEHAVIOR OF THE ANALYST: "DYNAMIC INACTIVITY"

The behavior of the analyst has been the subject of considerable discussion. In general, he is forced by the circumstances of the situation into what many look upon as a passive position. He must wait for the patient to reveal the necessary material, he must not get angry at the resistances, he must sit back while the patient goes through the ups and downs of his tranference reactions.

Many have urged that the analyst should be more active than he is in the Freudian tradition. Without going into the technical details of this controversy, it is above all important to note that what the analyst engages in should best be called "dynamic inactivity," rather than passivity. It is inactivity in that he cannot force the turn of events, but must react to the various initiatives of the patient. But it is dynamic in that his waiting serves a crucial purpose, that of allowing the patient to grow and develop at his own rate.

At first the patient as a rule demands some quick solution

from the analyst, again along the lines of a medical miracle. This demand is one of the roots of the early resistances. It may be so strong that the patient leaves for one of the many magical nostrums available on the current scene, such as "psychocalisthenics" or scientology (which started out as a form of therapy and then turned into a religion), or behavior modification (which includes every conceivable device in the world, from hypnotism to drugs to muscle relaxation).

But once the patient stays, or returns from the land of magical make-believe, which is usually the case, he comes to appreciate the inactivity of the analyst. Sometimes for the first time in his life, he is not harassed or pushed into premature moves, or hurried in any other way. No time limit is set for the analysis, and none can be set. Eventually the patient comes to value the hours, months, and years which the analyst consecrates to him. It can truly be said that there is scarcely any other professional relationship in this world where a person receives such extended interest and care over such a long period of time.

There is no such thing as a short analysis. All claims to the contrary are either sensation mongering or quack salesmanship. All of the cases in this book went on for a number of years, some shorter, some longer. Again, while at first the patient resents the seemingly inordinate time required to make fundamental changes in his life, after a while, eventually he feels pleased that no one is hurrying him to do the things he is reluctant to do. Freud's experience is often duplicated today: at first patients do not want to stay; toward the end they do not want to leave.

THE DIFFICULTIES OF ANALYSIS

No attempt is made in this book, nor should one be made, to conceal or underestimate the difficulties involved in the analytic process. The analyst himself undergoes a training far more thorough than that of any other mental health practioner, often going on for a period of ten years. People form tenacious resistances, which again may defy any resolution for many years; some are never resolved.

The cases presented in this book offer typical examples of the problems involved in analytic work. But they also show that when the problems are tackled seriously, and both analyst and patient work at them, significant and lasting changes for the better occur.

It is not possible, nor would it be desirable even if it could be done, to present a verbatim account of several hundred hours of analysis. Such a presentation would be tedious at best, unintelligible without extensive explanation at worst.

Instead, what I have done is to try to extract the highlights of each case, and present them in reasonably narrative form. Patients do come, they do go through analysis, and they do get better. The outline of the process is frequently more illuminating than the technical description of the process itself. There is, however, no intention of concealing or dissimulating the many obstacles that lie in the path of good analytic work.

TOWARD THE ANALYTIC IDEAL

In order to best understand the lives of the persons described here, the reader should keep the analytic ideal in mind. The whole terminology of contemporary psychiatry is hopelessly confused at best, often grossly misleading. Instead, the patient should be seen as a human being in a human situation, even as you and I. Many women have been abandoned, like Holly, many men have drifted through life aimlessly, like Jim, many have abstained from sex because of fear of religious sanctions, like Frank.

Technical terminology has been reduced to a minimum. Instead, the emphasis has consistently been on the various aspects of the analytic ideal. The reader can best appreciate the growth of each patient by trying to see how the analysis helped him to move closer to this ideal.

PART II

The Case Histories

Sally,
The Promiscuous Woman

The patient, Sally, a tall, attractive woman, came to analysis because of the distress caused by an unhappy love affair. Originally she stated that she was thirty-six years old; later it appeared that she was thirty-eight.

LIFE HISTORY

Sally was the oldest of three children. She and her eighteen months younger brother came from her mother's first marriage. The sister, ten years younger, was a half sister, the issue of mother's second marriage.

Mother's life had emphasized excitement all the way through. Sally said that she had been married three and a half times. Sally saw her as a cold, bossy, flirtatious, self-centered woman who had never really taken any interest in anybody except herself.

The first marriage, to Sally's father, ended in divorce after about seven or eight years. While it lasted there were terrible fights, with constant screaming and yelling. There was much acrimonious court action. Sally remembered being coached about what to say to the judge. Alimony was awarded, but its collection provoked more quarrels.

Mother waited a number of years before remarrying. As she told Sally once, men should support a woman nicely. Sex

23

was of no importance to the woman; its main purpose was to please the man. Still, a woman should make every effort to excite men.

Mother finally found a man, much older than herself, who was well off financially. Sally had hoped that he would be a second father to her, but he turned out to be cold and distant. One child was born, but the marriage did not last very long. Mother remarried a third time after Sally had married. This too broke up.

At the time of the analysis, Sally's mother spent much of her time flirting with men. She would dress up in a tight skirt and halter (at sixty!) to go for a walk. She liked to go to dance halls in the afternoons, where she went through one man after another.

In spite of this background, mother took a high moral tone towards her daughter. When Sally in one desperate moment confessed her affair to her, mother told her that it was totally immoral; she should either give up her husband and go off with the lover or give up the lover and stick to her husband. She once commented that Sally was using her diaphragm too much; a woman should not enjoy sex.

About her father Sally remembered almost nothing. He had left when she was four or five. Vaguely she recalled him as a tall dark man, and it was in this guise that he appeared in her fantasies and dreams. When the parents broke up, mother evidently refused to let father see the children. He followed them around, screaming, shouting, and creating public scenes. Once right after a parade, he kidnapped her brother, returning him a few days later. Sally was always jealous because father had not taken her instead.

Although she had been born in Baltimore, father's family lived in New York. She knew their name, but never made any attempt to contact them. Once during the analysis her interest in her past was aroused to the point where she called them up and made an appointment to visit, but this was called off at the last minute.

Of her early life Sally remembered almost nothing. She recalled almost nothing that had happened before twelve, and very little from twelve to sixteen. From her relatives she learned that after the break-up she had gone to live with her grandparents, while brother went to stay with an aunt, mother's sister. How long this lasted she did not know.

Apart from the kidnapping incident, the only other early childhood memory was one of finding a condom in the parent's bedroom when she was about five; all she knew was that it was a dirty thing. At about ten she overheard her mother having intercourse with her second husband; this perturbed her greatly.

At mother's insistence she began to work at twelve. Although she was a good student, she flunked her last term in high school. In any case her mother would not have let her go to college. She began to work full time at a fairly early age.

In spite of her lack of formal education, she was gifted in many ways. She had developed skills in various artistic media, particularly ceramics, in which she once won a prize, and sculpture. But no sooner had she won the prize than she gave up ceramics. In music she played the mandolin well enough to be part of an orchestra. One day, without rhyme or reason, she just walked out of the orchestra, and never played the mandolin again.

These sudden outbursts were characteristic of her. She described herself as a cold woman, indifferent to everybody in her life. "I have friends for years, then when they disappear, I forget them and never think of them again." This coldness alternated with the most violent rages, even in public places.

At sixteen she began to date. Her first beau was a boy, John, whom she saw every day over the summer. She was madly in love with him. But towards the end of the summer he abruptly said goodbye, and never saw her again. She was heartbroken. This pattern of the first love affair she regarded as typical for her life. Obviously, it was closely connected with the underlying coldness, which covered up the fear that she would again be deserted.

Once her dating life had started, Sally's mother became extremely intrusive in her love life. Every month she would cross-examine her about her period. Typical of Sally was the split feeling that part of her was good, while another part was horrible. For example, Sally referred to the period as the "menses"; here as in many aspects of her sex life she maintained an extraordinary prudery. Once mother discovered her necking on the beach with John; in a rage she called her a whore, which left an indelible impression.

After other brief relationships she met her husband, Harry, when she was seventeen. Since Harry was going to be a professional man, this relationship was encouraged. But Sally held on to her virginity. In order to have a sex life she married at twenty-one. When she married she was a virgin. However, the marriage had to be kept secret for a year and a half.

The marriage was not based on any intensive love feeling; it was in many ways similar to her mother's second marriage, one of convenience. As a result it proved to be a deep disappointment. About six months after they began to live together Sally went off on a cruise alone. It was on this cruise that she began her pattern of promiscuity, which persisted for about ten years.

On the surface at least she was filled with self-loathing for what she had done. Once when I asked her why she hadn't had any children sooner she replied, "Because I was whoring around." Typically she tried to confess her guilt to me, and ask for penance. She seemed quite surprised when I remarked at one point that if she had screwed around so much she must have enjoyed it.

Her sexual pattern in these ten years involved a large number of casual sex experiences, mostly in the Catskills, where she spent the summers, and in Florida, where she spent the winters. She always insisted that she had orgasms, even before analysis. With a number of men she entered into longer-lasting affairs, sometimes for as long as a year. With others they would be one-night stands. Or rather, to be more precise, one-hour stands. For, as appeared during the analysis, she had never slept the night with any of her lovers. This was all the more remarkable because she frequently had sex with a man half an hour after she met him, anywhere, out in the open if asked to do so. The refusal to sleep with a man was but one of the many curious contradictions in her personality.

There were other contradictions connected with her attitudes towards sex. It was essential to be well groomed all the time. Although her physician had specifically advised her to shower less often, she washed with extraordinary frequency. At one point during the analysis she revealed that she never came to a session without taking a shower beforehand. She never allowed herself to be seen in the nude by any of her lovers, nor, for that matter, even by her husband. Her choice of language was always extremely proper. At one point she was telling me about a neighbor who used the "vilest" language, with liberal sprinklings of words like "fuck," but she could not allow herself to utter the word. Much of this virgin-prostitute combination arose out of an identification with mother.

The husband, Harry, seems to have been aware of what she was doing in those ten years, but looked the other way because he apparently was doing the same thing. One time in fact the husband of one of Harry's girl friends called Sally up to tell her about what was going on between Harry and his wife. She did not dare mention it to her husband. However, it later came out that this incident triggered off the violently unhappy affair with Bob which had brought her to analysis.

Some time during this period the husband developed such excruciating headaches with consequent depression that he was unable to work for about a year. Since no organic cause could be found for his headaches, he was referred to a psychoanalysist. He stayed in analysis for about four years. Although he subsequently maintained that it had done him no good whatsoever, he was able to return to work. Because of his own experience, he served as a constant source of encouragement to his wife to continue her analysis on the many occasions when she wanted to quit.

About four years before the analysis began Sally became pregnant. The child, she and her husband both said, was unplanned but wanted. It was a boy, Paul. Sally proved to be a very uninterested mother. By hiring a variety of baby sitters, and joining in a nursery association, of which she became president, in her building complex, she arranged enough free time to do whatever she wanted.

But the boy reacted by developing a far greater attachment to his father. Whenever he was in trouble he called for Daddy, who apparently spent a great deal of time with him. This preference for the father was a source of great irritation to Sally, who frequently lost her temper with the boy and punished him, including beatings, a good deal. Still, having some guilt feelings about what she was doing to her son was one of the factors that kept her in analysis.

Throughout the years the relationship with her husband was full of quarrels and misery. He shouted and yelled at her, even beat her a few times; she did the same to him. Yet there was never any serious question of divorce.

There were few girl friends in her life; her constant search was for men. One constant friend, whom she spoke to almost every day during the analysis, was a woman in a similar predicament, also in analysis because of an unhappy love affair. Sally would dramatize her experiences to this friend, yet even with her withheld or distorted certain essentials of her life situation.

There was no history of any overt homosexuality. At one point in the analysis she recalled an incident in Florida where another woman had approached her sexually; she declined. She wondered what Lesbians did to one another. "Oral, I suppose," was her comment, and then she dropped the subject.

The lover who precipitated her into analysis was a man by the name of Bob, a fairly well-to-do businessman. Money played a considerable role in her amours; she generally picked lovers who had money, although she did not benefit by it in any way. To some extent it was a protest against her husband, who was going through a difficult struggle in his profession.

She had met Bob about seven years before, on one of her trips to Florida. The first night they had sex by the side of a lake. Thereafter she saw him on and off for a number of years, indifferent to whether he would ever call again. He was one of many. Sex for an hour or two was all that mattered.

As later reconstructed in the analysis, it was only after she had been informed by another man that her husband was carrying on an affair with his wife that she began to take Bob more seriously. It was then that they began to have regular dates in the apartment of a friend of his, because he lived with his mother and would not bring her to his place. As will be seen, tremendous emotional storms developed about Bob, but she never said that she loved him. She always said that she envied his wealth, his social position, and his large family. His greatest asset was his expertise in bed, although for a while she complained that he was impotent. Yet she daydreamed about him a lot, and often fantasized being married to him.

At the time the analysis began, one interesting artistic hobby remained. She would shop extensively for cheap antique tables which could be bought for $5 or less. When one was found, she would polish it diligently for days or weeks on end, refurbish it, and then sell it for about $75.

There were two significant repetitive dreams that she had been having for years. In one she was in an elevator, endlessly going up and down, unable to get off. In the other she was on her way to a party, but always interrupted before she could get there. We used to refer to these as her "elevator dream" and her "party dream." After a while we formulated the goal of the analysis in terms of stopping the elevator and getting to the party.

This is an example of how easily symbolism fits into ordinary language and discourse. Her two dreams were much more graphic than a dry statement of dizziness (elevator dream) or isolation (party dream). The psychoanalytic theory of symbolism rests upon the finding that the symbols are extensions of the ordinary meanings of the words.

COURSE OF ANALYSIS

Sally was the kind of woman with whom there is never a dull moment. As in real life, although she pretended to be submissive to me, in reality she dominated the analysis all the way through. While this pattern was consistently analyzed she never gave it up entirely. One consequence was that the analysis readily lends itself to subdivision into varying stages, depending on her major concerns at that point. Seven such stages can be distinguished. Since she returned eleven years later for more help, and stayed for six months, a postscript is also available.

Although I tried to get her to come more often, especially after the suicide attempt which occurred in the sixth month of analysis, on one excuse or another she never would come more than twice a week. Except for the last two months, when she cut down to once a week because of her pregnancy, this was the frequency with which the analysis was conducted. The analysis lasted about two and a half years.

Preliminary Skirmish: Attempted Seduction of Analyst

As might have been anticipated, in the first part of the analysis, she behaved very seductively towards me, attempting to please me in many ways. In the very first session, before she told me anything, she sat down on the couch and deliberated about whether to take her shoes off or not. "Once you take them off you can't get them back on," she said. Still, it took her several months before she would relax her controls sufficiently to lie on the couch.

Her opening statements in this initial session revealed her ambivalence further. "My problem is lovers — I've had one lover after the other. I don't want them, but I can't break away from them. That's my problem too — I never know what I want; I want one thing and then the opposite. I want them and I don't want them.

"I've been going with Bob now for seven years. I've broken off with him several times but I can't stay away. I'm involved in a horribly messy affair with him. I hate him, I'd like to stick a knife in his back and turn it, yet I seem terribly attracted to him. Can you change an attitude like that?"

It was this constant ambivalence and her thinly veiled attempts to seduce me that set the tone for the first part of the analysis. Every session she appeared smartly groomed, wearing a different outfit. Often she would ask whether I liked her hair up or down, whether I liked the outfit she had on, whether she looked good or not. Generally I handled these approaches with a noncommital "What comes to mind?" which made her laugh, although she sometimes said that she felt annoyed by the "rules of the game." Occasionally I would point out to her that she wanted me as a lover rather than an analyst, which she would vehemently deny.

One hot summer's day when I came into the waiting room she was taking off her stockings; one was already off.* I must have looked rather startled, since she laughed and said, "Don't

---

* Times change women's clothing. In 1950, when Sally was in treatment, panty hose had not yet been invented, and a woman could still take off her stockings without removing her panties.

worry, I'm just taking them off because it's so hot." She then proceeded to go through the hour with one stocking on and one off. But again the interpretation that she was out to seduce me was rejected. On another occasion she was wearing a blouse held together by a brooch at the center. Playfully she took off the brooch, exposing a considerable portion of her bosom. This too was tossed off as "meaningless."

When asked from time to time point blank what feelings she had about me she would say, "I regard you as a professional man for whom I have the highest respect. I have no personal feelings about you." She insisted on calling me "Dr. Fine," although it would have been more natural to address me by my first name, since we were about the same age.

Then again she would also reveal many positive feelings about me and the analysis. She pitied her lover because he did not have a Dr. Fine to talk to. Other people in analysis made much less progress than she did. The analysis was so important to her that she would not miss a session for all the world.

Yet the transference was markedly ambivalent. On the one hand she progressed rapidly; on the other she was getting nowhere. In one session she felt liberated; in another she saw no way out of her dilemma. Therapy was great, but it was so painful that she developed a headache every time she came; it disappeared as soon as she left.

Although I had the impression that the positive feelings aroused by her contacts with me were genuine, I also felt that they had a strong element of pretense. She was buttering me up, trying to show me how good I was, so that I would find her more desirable. When this was pointed out to her, she flatly rejected the idea, even though it was obviously something she had done with many men. It was part of the seduction which she still had to deny. Still in a way it was known to her, for she once commented that I was the only man in the world she could trust, and "that would come to an end right away if I held your hand."

As her seductive ploy was brought out into the open more and more, her defenses weakened to the point where she could display more anxiety and guilt. To some extent the guilt portrayed seemed to be part of the wish to impress me. She would insist that she was bad, that decent women didn't behave like that, that she was a horrible creature, etc., then go out and do the same thing all over again. Still, part of the guilt, especially in relation to her son, was quite real.

The anxiety mounted as she came closer to me in the analysis. Characteristically she would hold back a lot of significant material, then come in and say, "There is a lot I haven't told you;" whereupon she would reveal more of the story. The deep split in her life began to perturb her more and more because she could no longer cover up the anxiety that led to it, rather than because her sense of shame was now exposed to the light. However, shame rather than guilt remained more typical of her to the very end.

No sooner had the analysis started than the relationship with her lover Bob became increasingly stormy. Once before she had broken up with him, when she was pregnant. He had offered to take her to Europe instead, but she would not go.

It became clear that as a result of the support of an analyst, and the growth thereby made possible, she could now evaluate her situation more objectively and make more demands for herself. Bob's favorite motto was "Look, ma, no hands," a phrase which crystallized his attitude to life. There were to be no emotional involvements. Once she began to feel he was caring for her, she became frightened. He dated other women as well as Sally, and occasionally went on orgies with his friend the Professor, who was later to play a significant role in her suicide attempt. As she began to look at him more coolly, she saw him as insecure, self-centered, and immature. Yet he had money, was good in bed, and did not shout at her, unlike her husband. She wanted to marry him, and had he asked her at this point she might well have accepted.

But marriage, of course, was the furthest thing from his mind. He did become perturbed by her analysis, which he designated as a battle between him and me. As far as he was concerned there was no need for analysis. He did offer to pay half of her analytic bill, an unusually generous offer for him, but this was apparently intended to tie her closer to him.

It was obvious that she would offer to give up her lover in order to please or impress me, and it was important to forestall such a maneuver. Accordingly, whenever she asked me point blank whether she should give him up I tried to help her to clarify what she was getting and what she was missing in the relationship. If she gave him up, it would have to be for her own sake, not for mine.

The ambivalence continued. At one point she dreamt that he married his sister-in-law's sister. This was a girl who was having a long-standing affair with her boss, a married man with two children, which made her very unhappy. Her first reaction was, good, if Bob gets married I'll be rid of him. But then the idea made her so anxious that she woke up in a cold sweat.

The inception of the analysis also brought some pressure to bear on her husband. They had been talking about a house for many years, but had postponed any decision, obviously since both were so uncertain of the marriage. Now that she had gone into analysis, he decided to take the plunge. About two months after she had started they bought a house in the suburbs.

As the owner of a house she felt a new pride. "I am a woman with a refrigerator," she would say. Now it was more important than ever to give up Bob.

Her first attempt to break off was typically histrionic. They had spent the evening at their place of assignation. Around 11 o'clock she said, "Well, shall I take my clothes off now and get it over with? I have to get home. I realize what role you've cast me in, a prostitute." Bob was terribly shocked; a quarrel ensued. Why couldn't Sally be like other women he knew, sleeping with one man one night, and another another night. She replied that she was not that kind of a woman, she had only one lover, and didn't go in for them wholesale. He said he was beginning to care, but didn't want to get to the point where he'd get involved — he was not ready for it, physically, mentally, morally, or financially. Finally they went to bed. When she left he chatted with her in the car for a while, saying this was the best part of the evening. When she got home at three o'clock, her husband was furious. She said she had run out of gas; he exploded: nonsense.

Shortly thereafter another old lover called her for a date. She refused. It was going to be worked out with her husband; she was through with lovers.

After the incident described above she stayed away from Bob for about two weeks. He called her repeatedly, but she would not see him. At the same time she left the door open. One session she reported, "I really gave it to him good. You'd have been proud of me. I told him he was irresponsible, egocentric, that he never thought of anything but himself. What did he have to say when I asked him what he'd do if Harry walked in on us? He said, 'Well, your Dr. Fine has won out.' I said he had nothing to do with it, it's my own decision. I really feel now he's past. But at the end I couldn't keep it up all the way. He said, 'I'll call you again and we'll talk it over,' and I said, 'when?' Oh, why didn't I keep it up all the way?"

To stay away from Bob too long proved to be too difficult. First she began to fight with her mother, who was staying with her at the time. Mother had just made out a will, leaving everything to the younger daughter, which infuriated Sally. Mother ran around with too many men, was too critical of her, too cold and unloving, the source of her misfortune.

Then there were the fights with her husband. What annoyed her most was that he would bawl her out in a loud tone of voice in front of the boy. Her own tantrums she preferred to ignore.

Towards her son a curious change came about. She became very attached to him, so much so that incestuous feelings were not far from consciousness. "I made love to him physically," she said one day, meaning that she had been kissing and caressing him (the boy was then about four years old).

Without Bob she felt liberated. Yet she could not tolerate all the tensions in her life without this safety valve. After several weeks' abstinence she was seeing him again and expressing terrible guilt about her actions.

At this point in the process of asking more from Bob she began to demand more of him sexually. For the first time she asked him to perform cunnilingus on her (oral contact she called it — she could not use any ordinary words to describe it). Harry had done it to her, Bob never. He did it several times, then she made him stop, because it was making him her master. At this point she revealed that even in the analysis she wore a shoulder watch so that she would not have to be dependent on me for the signal to stop. Otherwise I too would be her master. Around this period she also recovered a dim memory of a tall dark man, her father. Most of her lovers, including Bob, seemed to fit this description. She sensed rather vaguely that the search for love was a search for her father.

In the meantime sharp mood swings were prominent. Mostly these were connected with Bob. One week she saw him four nights out of six, coming in to tell me how horrible she felt, yet unable to tear herself away from him.

Underneath the constant ambivalence about the lover there was a deep sense of despair about her life. She was full of self-reproaches. She felt she was always resisting. Nothing seemed to work out in her life. All her talents were gone. What could she look forward to? At times she felt like killing herself, but I need not worry because she would not do it as long as she had a child.

The dream life was of a nightmarish quality, culminating later in a period of outright nightmares. Here are some representative examples.

"I'm in an elevator, running up and down, up and down continuously. I'm driving. The elevator is full of people. It comes to a sudden stop with a crash. My child is off in one corner, and I can't reach it."

This was the first of many elevator dreams, as already mentioned. It produced many associations. The elevator symbolized her feelings, and the way they go up and down. The crash was like the parade at the end of World War I, when her father kidnapped her bother; it symbolized the break-up of the family. Her great fear was that she could not bring the constant mood swings to a stop without someting awful happening. Her driving symbolized her need to control, and her furious wish to destroy people. She was disturbed by the idea that one of the people to be destroyed was her own son.

"I'm in an accident, bloody, crushed, only this time I'm not in an elevator."

To this dream she brought out her terrible feelings of panic. She was awfully scared, fearful that she would go off the deep end.

"Bob was married off to my sister-in-law's sister."

She awoke in a cold sweat. This dream brought the first inkling that the compulsive drive for the lover was tied up with the search for her father — the tall dark man. It was also involved with her brother, who resembled her father.

"I stole a small object from the room next to Belle S.'s grandfather's room in her apartment."

Woke up feeling terribly frightened. Belle S. was a friend from adolescence with whom she had had no contact for years. In the absence of further associations I offered a symbolic interpretation of stealing father's penis, but it made no impression.

"My mother has died. I think I've done something about it, but Harry assures me she's committed suicide. They put her in the ground. I knock my head against the ground in grief."

This dream brings out the hatred of mother and the attendant guilt. Harry is the father who takes her away from the cruel mother, thus gratifying the childhood Oedipal wish.

"Paul [son] is dying or dead."

Woke up frightened. This dream, the first of many, horrified her more than anything else.

"I go to call on Bob in his apartment. He opens the door, one with a frosted window pane and a shade on it. I see that there is another woman in the apartment, so I go away.

She described this dream as "laughingly obvious." At the same time the obsessional preoccupation with Bob had become stronger, his telephone number buzzed in her mind all the time, she daydreamed about him constantly — he loves me, he doesn't love me, I love him, etc. To block the fantasies she had to keep herself busy all the time. The dream is again an Oedipal disappointment.

"Paul was dead and they brought him to me."

She had started to scream in her sleep. Husband woke her up. The death wishes toward her son were tied up with death wishes towards father; she freely admitted that at this point she hated all men, except perhaps the analyst.

"The house is on fire. A man, a strange, shadowy man comes in and tells me the fire is approaching. I go to get my baby but before I get out of bed I have to put my bathrobe on."

This dream, which preceded the suicide attempt by a few days, is markedly similar to the first dream in Freud's famous Dora case. Both are Oedipal dreams, although in Dora's case the father appeared clearly, while here he is a shadowy man. The associations to putting her bathrobe on brought out for the first time her extraordinarily prudish attitude towards nudity; she never even allowed herself to be completely nude in front of her husband. "A decent woman doesn't do that."

The seesaw reactions to her lover, the seductive attitude to the analyst, and the frightful anxieties about her son dominated the first section of the analysis. Suddenly she made a suicide attmpt, which set the analysis in an entirely different direction.

Reaction to Disappointment: Suicide Attempt

The turmoil reached a climax in a suicide attempt. Friday night there was a terrible fight with Bob. The next day, Saturday, she was feeling very depressed. She was all alone in the house. Thinking she would put an end to it all, she took about twenty thyroid pills her physician had given her. She expected to die, and would have been glad to get it over with. But the main result was that her heart began to beat very rapidly.

When her husband came home a little while later, she immediately told him what she had done. He called the doctor, who prescribed ipecac, but did not feel it necessary to see her. In spite of her husband's urging her to call me on Sunday, she would not do so. Through it all it was necessary to maintain control. She kept the regular appointment the following Tuesday. At that time she showed little emotion, reporting the entire weekend's experience without tears or signs of depression. She did begin by saying, "Dr. Fine, I have a lot of things to tell you. What I have to tell you probably won't shock you but it will startle you."

Whether the suicide attempt was genuine or not is hard to

say. There had been no real warning, and it was never repeated again. From her behavior and description one would surmise that she was more intent on shocking everybody around her into paying her more attention than on actually killing herself.

The next few sessions were spent analyzing the events of the weekend. On Friday she had gone to see Bob at their place of assignation, his friend's apartment. Henry, the Professor, Bob, and his friend were there, sitting around talking. Henry, she said, is a real degenerate, a man of no principle.

"Suddenly Bob said to me, 'Let's go into the next room.' " She said no, not that. He urged her to be an adult. So she went.

The next day there was a violent reaction. She felt horrible; how could she do such a thing? There is such a thing as morals, she said, and you can't go around doing things like that. This led to the suicide attempt.

On the surface it was the shame attached to having sex while the "degenerate" professor was in the next room that drove her to try suicide. From the loathing with which she spoke of the professor it can be surmised that she was tempted to try out some of his "degeneracies." One that she had herself mentioned was to go to bed with two men at one time.

At the deepest level, however, the suicidal gesture was a profound protest against the split life that she had been leading. She had to come to some resolution, but did not know how. By having everybody be more solicitous of her, which was the immediate consequence of the pill taking, something might happen. It was an exhibitionistic act, to break down the lonely wall she felt between her and other people, a wall which went back to the earliest relationships with mother. At the same time it was a deep cry for some genuine contact with other human beings.

A Period of Nightmares

For several months afterwards Sally went through a period of continuous anxiety, marked most notably by afternoon nightmares. Around three or four o'clock she would lie down for a nap. Shortly after she fell asleep she would wake up screaming "No, No!" All these nightmares involved the death of her son, in a variety of ways. One that she particularly remembered was:

"Paul is sick, and vomits. He falls down somewhere and disappears."

The suggestion that she wanted to get rid of her son and lead a carefree life again met with incredulous disbelief. But when an aunt told her that she was really a cold person who should never have had children she paid more attention. The death wishes towards her son proved to be the most powerful motive for remaining in analysis to effect a real inner change.

Battles with the Husband

The affair with Bob came to an end with the suicide attempt. At that point I suggested that she stop it, since it was doing such terrible things to her. Her reply was, "That's the first time you've told me that." The combination of my suggestion, the growing understanding of Bob, and the general analytic maturing made her strong enough to look more carefully at what she was doing with her life.

Naturally, the lover was not given up without a struggle. Session after session she came in saying that he was hurt. He kept on calling her, but she would not see him.

Finally, about five weeks after the suicide attempt she met him "by accident" at a dance. He took her out to dinner, they went to his friend's place, and had sex. "It was awful." she complained. Actually, the worst nightmare period went on for about two months after the suicide attempt, then the dreams took on a radically different cast. After a dream of seeing a little girl dead in her coffin there were almost no anxiety dreams for the remainder of the analysis. It was clear that anxiety and the lover were closely connected.

A few weeks after she met him "accidentally" she discovered that she had forgotten her coat at the apartment. Unannounced, she went back to get it one day. He came downstairs, would not let her in; obviously, he had another woman there, which he freely admitted. She took her coat and left.

Shortly thereafter she took revenge on him in characteristic fashion. She called him up to tell him that she was pregnant, intimating that he was the father. Disturbed by this news, he wanted to see her. She hung up. A few days later when he called she screamed at him that he was a heel, and hung up again. That was their last contact.

Fantasies about him remained for quite a while. Mostly they took the form of saying, "He hurts." Occasionally she would daydream about reestablishing the relationship. In about three months these fantasies disappeared too.

Once the lover was out of the way the fights with the husband became more intense. Before whenever she quarreled with her husband, she ran to her lover; now this was no longer feasible. The marital battle now had to be settled in its own right.

Thus, complaints about Harry were repeated over and over again. First of all he shouted at her too much, abusing her in all kinds of ways. He called her a neurotic bitch, an ugly long face. At the slightest provocation he called her a stupid idiot. Several times he had beaten her.

The second complaint was that he spoiled the boy. As a result the boy did not obey her, but looked to his father. This in turn irritated her to the point where she would scream and yell at the child, often hitting him as well. The husband would then come to the defense of the boy, when a new fight would break out all over again.

Both of these complaints were handled by trying to get her to see what role she played in the total picture. This came out most directly in the relationship with the son. Because of her preoccupation with her lover, and, at a deeper level her identification with the mother who had rejected her, she paid very little attention to the boy. Consequently he was thrown back to his father, who also sought in his son the emotional gratification that he was not getting from his wife. Then too when she did turn to the boy, she would bawl him out, or spank him, or on rare occasions overexcite him sexually, all of which made him shy away from her.

All this was so obvious that a fairly immediate result of the analysis was a marked improvement in the relationship with the boy. She also calmed down to the point where she could tolerate mother-child dates with other mothers, which also helped him to get over his fear of her. By the time the analysis ended the relationship with the boy was better than it had ever been.

The conflict with the husband was more complex, because he also had a large residue of unresolved resentment towards her carried over from his childhood feelings about his mother. Sally once said that his family and hers were two peas in a pod: — cold, rejecting, self-centered, argumentative.

Still, his actual rejections were combined with kind and loving actions, so that it was worth her while to look more carefully at what she was doing. Gradually the sex pattern began to emerge. In the beginning of the marriage they had experimented a lot with one another. It was fun, but came to an end pretty soon. They both drifted away to a succession of lovers. In this period sex was infrequent and unsatisfactory.

Now, under the impact of the analysis, she was eager to get back to him. But unconsciously she had to play the role of a virginal queen, who could not reveal her sexual longings. Once he saw a very sexy bathrobe which he offered to buy her; a married woman, she stated haughtily, does not wear such robes. Many times as they lay in bed she wanted him, but remained cold and aloof, as was fitting for her self-image. "Inside hysterics, outside an iceberg," she would say. As this self-image was consistently analyzed she began to move closer to him. Significantly, the first step came with the management of her anxiety. After a while, whenever she felt anxious the impulse came to her to move closer to him, to let him comfort her. He had been rebuffed by her so many times that he approached her infrequently. Once she began making herself more available, he was pleased and responded accordingly. As she increasingly divested herself of her guilt and shame about her body, under the impact of analysis, the relationship steadily improved.

Needless to say, their relationship had many ups and downs, and stormy scenes persisted until a late date. One night she ran out at one in the morning, wearing nothing but a nightgown and bathrobe; the cold brought her to, and she went right back. Another time she was in such a fury at him that she could think only of shoveling the dirt on his grave. However, these and similar outbursts tended to pass very quickly, leaving no hard feelings. Both spouses were stubborn, determined, self-willed people; it was not to be expected that they would get together without violent battles.

In the meantime, the fights with the husband came to be seen as part of her general struggle with men, going back to her father. More and more the fantasy became conscious that this tall dark man would come to get her some day, thus altering her life in some magical manner. No man lived up to this image, so she hated them all. The hatred mixed with the longing accounted for her constant ambivalence. As her anger was analyzed, it diminished and made way for the positive feelings.

She Attempts to Take Revenge on Men

From the first it was clear that Sally was a most vindictive woman, but it took a good deal of time to tie up this vindictiveness with her total pattern with men. In the struggles with lover, husband, and son she was quick to take revenge, but always there was some pretext which served to rationalize her actions. It never came out directly in the transference, so that it could not be interpreted there.

Around this time an old lover, Sam, called. Sam was a physician with whom she had had an affair about eight years previously; he had evidently tired of her and dropped her. On the surface it was a matter of indifference to her; another lover followed immediately.

Now when Sam called, he was in distress. He put the request rather bluntly; unhappily married, with two children, his wife was now pregnant for the third time, and would not have sex with him. So he was calling Sally, remembering the good times they had had together, to see if she would. At first she was horrified by his request; then she decided to play a subtle game with him.

Pretending that she remembered him with great pleasure, she invited him out to her house when her husband was on a trip out of town. They had sex in her own nuptial bed. She used every bit of sexual expertise she had ever acquired to make it a memorable evening for him. When he left, she assured him she was wild about him, and would be available whenever he wanted her. Inwardly she was already gloating about what she was going to do to him.

Naturally, Sam called the next day. She put him off on one pretext or another. He called again; she put him off again. In the analytic sessions she went on and on about how miserable he must be feeling, and how delighted she was that she could do this to him. If it had not been for the analysis she might have let him call indefinitely.

We used the incident to help her to clarify her wish to get even with father-husband-lover, who had always misused, exploited, and then abandoned her. She was able to see that in the long run she was hurting herself more than she was hurting him.

But the revenge wish was brought home to her most sharply by two transference dreams, in both of which she identified me with her lover.

"I want to go out with Bob but can't. Instead I go out with someone else whom I'm not particularly interested in; he reminds me of you. We go to a cleaning store; I lie down on the counter on my side seductively and kiss him.

Next thing I know I'm in the subway all alone, without my bag. I get off and go to the ladies' room (I've never in my life been there). There are a lot of people there; it's more like a powder room, and they're talking of going to a party.

I want to go to the party too but to do so I need money. I don't have money. I see rolls of coins, as in the bank, quarters, dimes, and nickels. I steal a roll of dimes and rush to the door. There's a lady cop at the door, who accuses me of stealing. I deny that I've stolen and frantically rush to the toilet, throw the roll in, and pull the chain."

The first part stands for the analyst. Since she cannot have her lover Bob she goes to an analyst. Her anal view of the analyst also comes out here (cleaning store). That she is not particularly interested in me is part of the tease. The seduction on the counter was related to her constant ambivalence about the couch.

The next part is related to the repetitive dream about getting to a party (see also below). There was a virtual subway phobia, so strong that she would almost never ride in the subway.* First there is a move back from genital to anal (she loses her bag and ends up in the toilet of the dirty subway). This also must have some homosexual meaning. The party means father, whom she has just run away from.

The money is tied up with her constant dreams of wealth. If she had enough money, she could find father. She steals the money, but mother (lady cop) catches her. After throwing the money back into the toilet, she has to conceal her body (phobia about appearing in the nude, even in front of her husband).

In this dream she is still fearful of mother, and convinced that Bob will reject her. Several months later she had another transference dream in which her own wish to reject vindictively came out in undisguised form.

"I'm in J.'s [Bob's friend] apartment with you, only you look like Bob too. You try to open the windows and can only get them open a little way. I say I can do it much better, and open them wide. While I'm opening them up, you come up behind me and put your arms around me, as if to kiss me. I turn around and say, "Well, I guess that's all of that [meaning the end of our relationship]."

The windows symbolize the vagina. She opens them up for me, then when I accept she walks off — the classical seduce-and-reject pattern of the adolescent girl.

Much later, towards the end of the analysis, another seduce-reject dream brought out the deep depression which this pattern left in its wake.

"You call me to ask if I can change the hour from 9:30 to 9. Haughtily I say no. Half an hour later you walk away from me."

This was accompanied by two other dreams:

"Bob asks me to go to some hotel. I say no, haughtily. He walks away."

"There are a lot of open graves."

To the change of hour she associated her pregnancy, which

---

* Again a comment is in order about how times have changed. In those days the subways were perfectly safe.

had just begun. She wanted me to ask to be the father of the baby, which she refuses, whereupon I reject her. In the next dream Bob asks her for sex; when she says no he leaves. The open graves in the last dream symbolize her depression. The whole trio is again part of the central pathological sequence seduce-reject-feel abandoned. Through the identification of lover and analyst she could see that it was her own inner dynamics, not the external reality.

Finally, about six weeks before she stopped, a dream about her father brought out her anger at him directly, as well as the identification of so many other men in her life with him.

"I am in a courtroom. My father is there, a tall man with gray hair, curly like Harry's, a combination of Sam and Bob. I ask if I can speak to him; we go out in the hall. There's a boy of thirteen or fourteen there. I berate him bitterly for having neglected the boy completely."

To the courtroom she associated the legal action her parents had been involved in; she had been told about it, though she remembered nothing directly. The dream brings father back, and also gives her a chance to vent her spleen on him.

Calming Down: Off the Elevator and To the Party

We have often referred to Sally's repetitive elevator and party dreams, and noted that these terms were used symbolically throughout the analysis. Now it is possible to trace through her dreams how she was finally able to get off the elevator and reach the party.

The first elevator dream, reported early, has been described above. Among other things the elevator stood for the incessant ups and downs of her love life, remorselessly pushing her from one lover to another. Some four months after she had broken up with Bob, a dream helped her to see the Oedipal character of her longing and some of the deeper meanings of her symbols. It should be mentioned by way of introduction that she brought this dream in triumphantly, announcing that the elevator had stopped:

"The elevator has stopped, and is pushed over. We're

on the side where the shaft is showing. I step out with the elevator operator, a vague sort of person.

The scene shifts and there is a big apartment house with glass windows. I tell somebody downstairs they shouldn't allow such houses. I'm sitting in the apartment of the third floor, naked, the only person in the house. Downstairs there is a group of men talking. They can see me. My aunt A. comes along and gives them an object, a baby rattle on one side and a religious scroll on the other.

The scene shifts again and I'm in a house with very long windows, such as they have in Baltimore. Mrs. H. [a neighbor] is on the roof, looking down on me. Suddenly I become furious at her and shout, "You God-damned yente!" Then I take to washing one of the windowpanes."

The first part of this dream she has succeeded in stopping the elevator, and in finding an operator (in contrast to the previous elevator dream where she was driving). The elevator operator is analyst; she wishes to submit to the analyst to get over her constant inner turmoil, particularly the rages.

Once she is off the elevator she can exhibit herself in the nude to a group of men, i.e., she has my permission to be sexual. This is in marked contrast to the suicidal experience, when she felt so horribly humiliated by the fact that there were two men in the room next to the one where she was having sex. Her aunt A. is mother's sister, a rather kindly figure who disliked her mother too. The baby rattle stands for her motherhood, the religious scroll for her supermorality (superego). The aunt, while not so permissive as the analyst, still does not punish her. The windows stand for her constant preoccupation with being discovered, the split between the demure housewife and the rousing love-wench.

In the third part of the dream the neighbor is one who is in reality similar to her mother. Now she feels spied on, and screams at the mother-superego. Then she restores appearances (washes the windows).

This dream may be regarded as a transitional dream, part of the process of getting away from the harsh superego. She could not get off the elevator because the superego-mother would not allow her any libidinal gratification ("You're a whore" was the constant cry). Now she can face the superego,

and can even show herself to men nude; the superego is no longer so punitive. At the same time it is still there.

Six months later came the last significant elevator dream:

"The elevator is back. There's a purse in it. Sylvia D. is
leaning over to pick it up, and I'm holding on to her. She
leans over too far and I let go. I go down and pick her up
from the bottom.

Somebody comes and tells me my mother has died. I'm
horrified, wake up frightened."

Sylvia D. is an older woman, a neighbor similar to mother.
The wish to kill mother is thinly disguised in the first dream,
quite open in the second. The purse is the money, the where-
withal to get to the party and father. The dream represents an
Oedipal triumph.

Thus the elevator symbolized first of all the turmoil of the
battle with mother, the heart of her Oedipal problem. It also
stood for the constant hysterical rush of feelings, for sexual excitement, masturbation, ambivalence, rage, and even the busy
work in which she so often engaged to cover up her inner conflicts. Truly an overburdened symbol!

The elevator had to stop before she could get to the party,
which soon became another central theme. At one point she
dreamt:

"I'm in an amusement park with Bob. There's a merry-
go-round. We want to jump on a horse; one comes by but
is occupied. We have to wait for a ride. Then he jumps on a
horse without me.

Then the scene shifts, to his friend's apartment. Bob is
getting married. There's a drawer with linen or shorts with
the initial R. There's a big crowd of people. On the dresser
there's 50¢ in two quarters. When I hear that Bob is getting
married I faint dead away.

After I come to I learn that he will divorce his wife. But
I take the 50¢ and leave."

The party here is her lover's marriage to another woman. It
symbolizes both her mother's sexual escapades and her image of
a happy family. Throughout she is rejected by the lover. Her
only consolation is the two quarters; probably this stands for
two testicles, referring on the one hand to her wish to be a man

and on the other to her deep-seated feeling of rejection when
father kidnapped brother instead of her. Since R. was my initial,
the dream also had a transference meaning. In addition, taking
the 50¢ (two quarters) stood for a wish to castrate him.

Another dream:

> "There is a hayride — people in a car, riding away. One
> is a girl I know, happily married, two children. The car is
> green (my favorite color). I run after it but never manage
> to catch up."

The hayride reminded her of her adolescence, and an incident with some girl friends. She was friendly with a group of
three, when one day they advised her they didn't ever want to
see her again. She was deeply hurt. In her present situation, in
the suburbs, she is afraid of making friends because something
of the sort might happen again. The analysis of these feelings
led her to break down much of her reserve about her neighbors.

> "Mrs. Alben Barkley invites me to a party. I want to go
> but first have to fix my hair. No matter which way I fix
> it it's not quite right, and I never get to go to the party. In
> the meantime some women in the powder room are taking
> care of Paul [son]."

Barkley was then vice-president to Truman, so to be invited
to such a party made one an important person. Hair reminded
her of her constant efforts to keep herself immaculately groomed.
The dream brings out her lifelong feeling of not looking quite
right. She described herself as tall and angular (an inaccurate
description) rather than petite and feminine. Here she is still
getting rid of her child.

Finally several months later she came in triumphant: she
got to the party.

> "Mrs. Truman invites me to a party. I am sitting next to
> her. Suddenly a girl, a plain-looking girl, is attacked by a
> man and thrown out. She asks for help but does not get it."

Since Mrs. Truman was then the wife of the President, this
dream brought out both Sally's grandiosity and her wish for a
warmer mother. To the girl she associated her sister.

Thus, at the deepest level the party symbolized reunion
with the good mother. On the one hand she wanted to get to

father, on the other to remain with mother; this was also part of the ambivalence and the elevator moving endlessly up and down. In any case, the dream imbued her with a sense of liberation.

VICISSITUDES OF THE TRANSFERENCE: THE RELATIONSHIP

A number of comments have already been made about the transference to the analyst; they can be brought together here and reviewed in more detail.

On the surface at least, it is hard to know whether to classify this as a positive or a negative transference. Both feelings were expressed, directly and indirectly, at various times. Mostly, though, there was a need to keep me at a distance, a need which diminished only gradually.

In the beginning, as mentioned, a seductive attitude was displayed, only to be immediatley denied whenever it was called to her attention. Slowly the seduce-reject pattern crystallized out in the transference as well. She had always hoped for men to fall in love with her, then it would end. Finally, she brought the dreams described above, in which I try to seduce her and she then breaks off with me.

On a few occasions some more usual fantasies about me came through. Once she asked point blank if I was married. When I moved to a new apartment, she lost her way in the house, thereby allowing her to explore my apartment "by accident." Once when I went off on a vacation trip, and she discovered by accident where I had been, she was angry at me for not telling her.

But except for these few minor incidents she maintained a reserve with me which was similar to that with other men. Time and again she would say to me that there were certain things she had not been able to tell me, and now would. The consistent analysis of this attitude served to break down the deep feeling of distrust of all people which had plagued her all her life.

Essentially, she was able in the analysis to revive the major features of her Oedipal trauma, overcome many of them, and move on to a new way of living. In this process I represented more of a compensatory fantasy for what she had never had in childhood than a resurrection of some good relationship which had been lost.

PREGNANCY AND TERMINATION

After she had been in analysis for about two years and three months, her menses suddenly became irregular. The physician whom she consulted made a diagnosis of an early menopause (she was then forty-one, though, since she had misstated her age at the beginning, I thought she was thirty-nine) and advised her to have another child. Since the first had been born by Caesarian section, she felt it would be wise to take his advice now. Psychologically she felt she was ready for it, although there were still some fights with the husband. I agreed that to devote herself to husband and children would be a good resolution to her difficulties.

A repetition of a battery of psychological tests which had originally been given at the beginning of the analysis showed improvement along a number of lines. The report said (in part):

> The first Rorschach* was full of bewilderment, symbolism, and a grandiose compensation for feeling of inadequacy. She is now much more reality bound, shows no sign of confusion, and is beginning to realize the nature of her fears and inadequacies.

Thus the testing confirmed the clinical impression. She has found much more inner peace, the elevator has stopped, she has gotten to the party. Her anxieties seemed manageable within the framework of her new or rather revised life. The door was left open for further analysis whenever she felt the need for it. It was anticipated that she might require more help when the children demanded less of her time.

POSTSCRIPT

About eleven years later Sally did return for more help.

*The most commonly used psychological test.

Things had been fine for ten years or so. She enjoyed her chilren, the marital relationship had straightened itself out, she felt much happier.

Then she became restless. Tired of housework, she started a small free-lance sales business in which she made many personal contacts. A few months ago she had started an affair, this time with a neurotic musician who made fabulous amounts of money from recordings. Again she felt terribly depressed, at times even suicidal. To relieve the tension, she had gone off on a trip, ended up going to bed with a number of men. She was ready for more analysis.

The second period of analysis lasted about six months. There was none of the terrible depression and anxiety that had been manifest the first time. Sex and the search for a very rich man were a compulsive drive she could not understand.

It soon became clear that she was overidentifying with mother, who, according to Sally's earlier description, had married for money and had gone through three and a half husbands. The interpersonal conflicts were of a similar kind, but less intense. In about six months she was ready to go off on her own again.

There have been no further direct contacts. Indirect reports from people sho have met her indicate that she seems to be doing well.

DISCUSSION

The surface problem, which provides the title for this paper, was Sally's promiscuity. Yet this was truly merely a surface problem; there was far more involved underneath.

The deeper problems which have been discussed were her terrible anxieties, including frequent nightmares, terrible rages and desire for revenge, especially on men, conflict about really letting herself go in sex, bad self-image, and overidentification with the destructive mother. It was to these deeper problems that the analytic work was directed, while the sex pattern was merely a surface manifestation.

Much has been written about the dynamics of promiscuity. Particularly prominent in Sally's case were the search for father, the pattern of revenge against men, the identification with mother, and the repressed homosexuality. The search for father gradually became conscious, even with regard to some of his physical characteristics. The revenge pattern was verbalized in so many different ways that its close connection with her style of life could scarcely fail to impress her. While the homosexuality was close to the surface, appropriate material related to it was rarely offered, so that it almost had to be ignored. This is another example of how in practice analysis is guided more by the kinds of material that the patient produces than by our theoretical prejudices.

Promiscuity is a problem gauged differently by different cultural groups. With such culturally determined conflicts the first step analytically is to convert them into an inner problem. Because of the crippling anxieties present this could be done easily enough with Sally; in other cases it is far more difficult.

Actually, she had given up the extreme promiscuity before she came to analysis. What precipitated her search for help was the disappointed hope that she could find some real love with Bob, rather than the meaningless flings she had had with many other men and the constant battles with her husband. Basically, she was a love-starved girl, who was baffled everywhere that she turned to look for love.

In addition she could be described as more of a shame than a guilt person. A shame person is one who is dominated by what others might think or say; a guilt person is more concerned with his or her own inner convictions. Guilt persons lend themselves more readily to analysis than shame. This is why Sally came to analysis only when she was really desperate, i.e., when she could no longer maintain the facade of her life.

The first year of analysis centered on her overwhelming fears. The elevator had to be stopped, in her pictureque symbolism. While promiscuity can be altered in a variety of ways, the reconstruction of her fear-ridden outlook upon life could only be accomplished by analysis. Thus, while the external change in this case looks small, since she maintained the essentials of her life unaltered, the inner change was enormous. This inner change can be summarized under seven headings:

LESS ANXIETY: This was one of the major changes. Her search for love was a defense against the inner fears. When these diminished, she could look for love more realistically.

ABANDONMENT OF THE COMPULSIVE SEARCH FOR FATHER: The unconscious hope that some day Daddy would come back had been with her since childhood. All the men in her life represented father in one form or another. When she no longer needed father, she could see them more realistically.

LESS NEED FOR REVENGE ON MEN: Once she could give up father, she no longer needed the revenge pattern which had been such a marked feature of her love life.

MORE SELF-ACCEPTANCE: By working through the early family traumas she was able to give up the self-image of an ugly abandoned child, continued in later life as a self-image of an unattractive angular woman.

MORE SEXUAL PLEASURE: It is a well-known paradox of the promiscuous individual that sexuality gives little pleasure. Although she described herself as orgastic even before analysis, the meaning of these "orgasms" had to be carefully explored. As is so often the case, when this was done an increased sense of pleasure in her sex life was reported. One notable point was that she was for the first time in her life free to enjoy oral sex.

GREATER FREEDOM TO ENJOY LIFE: The fear and rage blocked her capacity to enjoy what she had. Since she had a natural zest for living, one of the positive results of her identification with mother, once the fear and rage diminished, life became a much more pleasurable experience.

PERMISSION TO COME OUT INTO THE OPEN: One of her greatest conflicts centered around her shame. She was literally a woman with two separate lives whose major pleasures had to be concealed. Once she could be more self-accepting, this concealment no longer had to be maintained. To some extent, however, she remained excessively dominated by shame.

Harvey,
The Transformation of a
Shlemiel

The patient, a twenty-six-year-old man whom we shall call Harvey, acquired the title "schlemiel" as a kind of birthright, since his mother alternately referred to him as "schlemiel" or "schmendrick." At other times she would endearingly call him her "thirteenth abortion."

Originally he came to treatment because of a general dissatisfaction with life. He was considering going to California just for a change of scene, but when a friend suggested that he try analysis he accepted willingly.

LIFE HISTORY

Harvey was the youngest of six children, most of whom had experienced much emotional conflict in their lives.

Father, who died when the patient was twenty, was one of a family of twelve, eleven boys and one girl. Born in Russia, he came to the United States at nineteen. At first he studied architecture at Cooper Union. But upon graduating he switched to music, which he found more lucrative. Although financially successful as a theatre musician, there were periods when he refused or did not care to work, especially when he was older. In one of these periods his wife had him jailed for nonsupport. After a few months in jail, he got out and went back to work.

Mostly father was remembered as a meek, shadowy figure

who, like the rest of the family, was frightened by the domineering mother. Few memories of him persisted, even though he had died so recently. Once he took Harvey fishing early in the morning. Another time when one of the girls came home late from a date, mother called her a whore; father intervened on her behalf, with little success. Generally Harvey felt sorry for him.

Mother, about a year older than father, was the daughter of a rabbi who brought her up very strictly. Unable to get along with her parents, she ran away from home at fourteen to go to live with her sister. She married at the early age of seventeen. It was widely rumored that she was pregnant by another man when she married; the other man was said to have been a musician.

At the time of the analysis mother was living with one of her sons, who, like the rest of the children, resented her bitterly. Occasionally she worked as a practical nurse. She was hypertensive, demanding, quarrelsome, and depressed, almost a textbook caricature of the Jewish mother. There was little in her life other than the self-defeating battles with her children.

Harvey, as the youngest, seemed to be the particular object of her venom. As mentioned, she alternately referred to him as a schlemiel, a schmendrick, or the thirteenth abortion. By this she referred to her oft-told story that she had had twelve abortions before he was born, in a desperate effort to avoid a sixth child. Evidently, the family was very badly off at the time, and an additional mouth was felt as too much of a burden.

As far back as he could remember Harvey was a timid, frightened little boy. Mother kept on bawling him out — he was a no-good bum, just like his father. His earliest memory, from about the age of three, was a picture of himself hiding behind her skirts. Many times in infancy he had been put in a basket under the table and totally ignored. Once when he was a little older he was hospitalized because of a crushed finger; his recollection of the incident was that it was frightening to be away from his mother.

When he was about five or six the family bought a candy store near the beach, which provided them with a meager living. They also lived nearby. Weekends and summers they used to rent out space by the hour or day for people to change to go to the beach. It was Harvey's job to steer potential customers to the house; he resented this chore bitterly, but could not say anything about it.

His oldest sister, sixteen years his senior, began to take a strong interest in him when he was about seven. She had a convertible car and would drive him places. Her friends were all fascinating people. This sister remained a glamorous figure in his eyes. In her youth she had been an actress, and had traveled a great deal. She had made three stormy marriages. In one she lost custody of her child, apparently because her husband had caught her with another man. The present marriage seemed to be fairly happy. At the time of the analysis she was living in Europe, so that Harvey rarely saw her.

Around this time, when he was seven, Harvey was put into one bed with the next older brother, Nathan, another of the dominant forces in his life. Nathan had little schooling. He played the saxophone well enough to work at it, but also had a variety of other jobs. At one time or another he had been an electrician, handyman, TV repairman, watch repairman, window cleaner, and waiter. This last had been his main source of income for a number of years at the time of the anlaysis. It was particularly important because he had been able to get Harvey a job as a waiter a number of times.

Beginning around the age of seven, there had been a lot of homosexual play between Harvey and Nathan, with Harvey always in the passive role. Nathan would generally wind his body around Harvey, and they would often sleep that way. Harvey liked the warm feel of it, and never protested. Once, however, Nathan had anal intercourse with Harvey. This bothered him, and he told one sister about it; she laughed. The anal intercourse was not repeated, but the body embraces persisted for years.

Nathan used to boast and brag about his conquests of women. Physically he was very big, even taller than Harvey, who was six feet two, and much heavier. Since he was four years older, throughout childhood he had always looked like a giant to his kid brother. Since he also used to beat Harvey up occasionally, this stamped him clearly as a successor to the sadistic mother. Harvey feared and loved him, just as he had done with mother, well into adulthood.

In school Harvey was an indifferent student. He was timid, and did not do well in the academic subjects. He did show promise in both art and music, drawing and playing the piano. But he was too busy to exploit these talents. Shortly after beginning in academic high school, he was forced to quit for economic reasons, whereupon he began to work during the day and go to school at night.

Because of his poor scholastic record, when he returned from the service he went to a school where he would major in art. In spite of his abilities he was flunked out after a few years. Then he went on to one of the city colleges, where he was still a student at the time the analysis began. Inability to graduate and find a suitable career for himself was one of the symptoms which brought him to analysis.

His sex life began shortly after puberty, again in a passive way when he allowed a male cousin to masturbate him. There was no more overt homosexuality; instead there was a compulsive drive for women which seemed to get him nowhere.

About a year before coming to analysis he met a girl, Mimi, with whom he fell violently in love. Mimi was everything he was not. Angered by her "establishment" parents in another city, she had fled to New York, where she more or less lived by her wits. She was a gay, carefree girl with no thought for the morrow. There was naturally a whole string of men in her life, of whom Harvey was probably the least important. But he was dependable, especially when she was in financial trouble, which was quite frequent.

They lived together for about six months. In that time he was deliriously happy, despite the fact that she treated him very shabbily, even boasting openly about her conquests of other men when she would go out without him. Then one day she literally threw him out, telling him that he was too dull for her, and that she had found a more exciting guy.

This, however, did not deter her from asking Harvey for money when she found herself pregnant by the other man. Her relationship with the new lover was quite similar to Harvey's relationship to her. To tell him that she was pregnant would have invited an immediate rejection, so she turned to Harvey instead. He was prepared to give her his entire life's savings because she "just could not tell either the other fellow or her father" and refrained from doing so only when I pointed to the severe masochism involved in such an action. When he finally refused her, she told him that no matter what he would have done she never would have seen him again.

COURSE OF ANALYSIS

For financial reasons Harvey could only afford to come twice a week. The analysis was a long one, extending over a period of nine years. Although he moved slowly much of the time, the eventual outcome could be considered satisfactory.

The analysis followed a rather typical course. At first there was an analytic honeymoon, in which he released all kinds of new feelings, with consequent jubilation. Then came the inevitable setback, when he realized that it was not all going to be peaches and cream. In this period he was helped to clarify a dynamic picture of his life, with all the repressed rage, homosexuality, anality, distrust, and blocking of feeling. To break away from this crushing self-image he ran to a long series of girls, only to find eventually that no one could help him from the outside. With this realization came a deep resentment of the analysis, which became the major topic of discussion in the last few years.

It must not be supposed, however, that these stages followed one another in strict chronological order. Rather, these are themes which weave in and out of the whole analysis, at times one stressed more than the others. In order to organize what would otherwise be merely a bewildering conglomeration of material, the analysis can be divided into these thematic discussions.

The Analytic Honeymoon: Harvey's Need for Love

For the first two years of the analysis he went through an analytic honeymoon. Much of the obvious masochistic behavior was dissipated by the consistent interpretation of its unconscious roots in his childhood.

The immediate results of this honeymoon period were noticeable and substantial. First of all, he succeeded in moving away from mother to an apartment of his own; really the first time in his life he felt free enough to be on his own. For this his mother cursed him out roundly, as might have been expected, but now her reproaches fell on deaf ears. He could easily see that he was not responsible for her suffering and bitterness.

Second, he stabilized his employment pattern, and began to function in architecture, the career which ultimately became his life's work. A number of masochistic thrusts had to be analyzed before this could happen. To begin with he felt, as a result of the positive transference, that the analysis was the most important experience of his life, and that he would have to work regularly to support it. The identification with Mimi's scatter-brained rebellion was dissipated. Then he discovered that he was color blind, which put his initial commitment to teaching art out of the question. Yet he persisted in his attempt to become an art teacher, even after his color blindness had been brought out into the open. Third, a job, originally temporary, as a draftsman, convinced him that he was quite competent at it. Now he was well enough psychologically to build on an activity in which he was competent, rather than search for one at which he was bound to fail. And finally, with the help of the analysis, he had completed the last few credits required for his degree, which again gave him some sense of pride in his accomplishments.

A third change was a shift in his pattern with girls, from the masochistic suffering he had experienced with Mimi to a more consciously assertive and aggressive masculine position. This shift did not resolve the problem, but led him into the two-woman dilemma, to be described below. Yet it was a significant step in the right direction.

Fourth, he was able for the first time in his life to place his trust in another human being, the analyst, without feeling deeply disappointed. At times it reminded him of his sister driving him around in her convertible when he was a little boy. But it was also different, a really novel experience. More will be said about the transference later. Here it suffices to note that the analyst was providing compensation for the wrongs Harvey had suffered as a child.

Finally, there was the vital gain of learning a new mode of communication, through dreams, associations, and memories which had been completely closed before. He was a highly cooperative patient, verbal, able to report many dreams, skillful at free association. This opened the door to a whole new world which had been completely closed before.

Dynamically, this first period of analysis was devoted largely to a discussion of his fears, their infantile roots, and their unconscious meaning. He produced copious material, listened eagerly to the interpretations, and was able to grasp much of the interplay between his fears and his other impulses.

Very early he broght in the first dream of the analysis:

"There are some actors standing in front of a house. I want to look at them, but if I do they will throw a spear at me."

To the actors he associated his family, especially his oldest sister (she had been an actress in her youth). The house meant the peace and security of childhood, which he had never known but nonetheless longed for so intensely. This was the first indication of the central significance of a house in his unconscious thinking; later the symbolism of a house became a topic for extended discussion. The dream brings out his helpless rage at the family, and his longing to return to them.

Another dream highlighted the masochism as a defense against overpowering bodily anxieties:

"I see an X-ray section of my body. There is a blood clot in the brain, which is traveling towards my heart. If it gets to the heart I die. To stop it I open three holes in my chest to let the blood out. Blood doesn't come out right away, so I squeeze it and it does."

The X-ray of the brain stands for the analysis. He is terrified that some fatal defect will be uncovered (the blood clot). Opening the holes in the chest symbolizes both the masochistic submission and the homosexuality.

What is particularly striking in this dream, as in numerous others, is the way in which horrible punishment is warded off at the very end. Here it is still warded off by a sacrificial maneuver (squeezing the blood out). Soon this was replaced by escaping, a mechanism which he had adopted many times in his life. The next dream was typical:

> "I'm in a house. There are gangsters and thieves after me, so I want to escape. I try but see no way out. Finally I think if I'm nonchalant I can just walk out calmly; I do that and succeed."

The immediate precipitant of this dream was an unhappy sexual experience with a new girl. As usual his first approach to her was sexual, and she responded with a mixture of rejection and teasing. He had found her too passive, even though she had "submitted" to sex right away. She enjoyed it, he didn't. A few nights later when they went to bed again she refused to have sex. Angry at the refusal, he went to sleep. At three in the morning he woke up and left.

In the dream the house is again a symbol for the restored happy family, the great yearning of his life. To the gangsters and thieves he associated mother and brother Nathan, who were always picking on him. Leaving is the only solution he can see to the danger; at any rate it is better than being hurt. Another important association to the sex is that his next older sister was frequently punished because she stayed out too late with the boys.

A few sessions later a dream brought the homosexuality into the open clearly.

> "I'm in a house with five other people, men and women. There are three rooms. I wander into one room where there are two women."

To the two women he associated Lesbian actions. The house with six people is his own house. He feels rejected by the women, and projects his homosexual wishes to them. Then he had a simple wish-fulfillment dream which pleased him very much:

> "I'm in a house with wood on stone. Buckminster Fuller is there. Then I go into the next room and lie down with a woman. I sit up and she strokes my brow."

Buckminster Fuller was one of his heroes in architecture.

The house with wood on stone stood for a kind of construction that he liked very much. In the sex with the woman he still sees himself in a passive role, being stroked and caressed by her.

Soon, however, the wishes are rejoined by the punishment; the superego cannot be thrown off so easily. He dreamt:

"I'm up in an airplane; the others are going to jump out but it's dangerous and I don't want to. Finally the plane gets close to the ground and I see that I can just walk out."

To the airplane he associates dangerous, risky activities which he always avoided. It also symbolizes the break-up of the house which he had always dreaded so much as a child. It is significant, though, that here too he can simply walk out of the danger spot.

In the thirty-fourth session a dream brought out the family conflict even more directly:

"I am sitting at a long table with my mother and father; Nathan is between them. Nathan is talking angrily to my mother. I become frightened, leave, and go out to the ocean. There are sharks which frighten me; they turn into whales with blunt noses."

Noteworthy here is bringing the dead father back to life, thus restoring the family. Still he is left out; Nathan is between them. Nathan then expresses the anger to mother which Harvey feels but cannot bring out. Once it does come out, he has to run away. In other words, the greatest fear is the fear of mother's retaliation if he should talk back to her. The ocean was one of his favorite places; it also symbolizes the good mother. To the shark he associated mother's biting tongue; the whales stood for the good mother. The longing to have father back is important.

In the very next session a striking dream brought out the yearning for mother, and her connection with the frustrating love affair with Mimi:

"I go out west with my mother, where we expect to meet Mimi. I walk out in the street. An atomic explosion comes, and then two rockets. I get burned and go to the drugstore, where they give me four oils, castor oil and three others."

Again the house theme comes up here; this time it stands

for himself and mother, whom he had obviously identified with Mimi. To go west was his original intention when he came to me to speak about analysis. The dream was set off by angry feelings about me — he complained that I was inhuman, did not sympathize with him enough, and did not struggle enough with him emotionally as other friends do. The wish for mother is thus set off by the feeling of rejection by father.

The atomic explosion stands for destruction because his sexual wishes for mother have come out into the open; it also symbolizes her anger. The drugstore is the analysis. Castor oil brought up many anal associations. Father was a dirty man; he used to take his snot and smear it on the wall. Harvey himself was never very clean; he did not bathe very often, or groom himself with any amount of care. Occasional stomach complaints, including constipation, had plagued him all his life.

This dream may be contrasted with another one, about father, which came up about a year later:

"I am in Moscow. Stalin is being carried into his tomb by a group of officials, on a canvas [like firemen use]. I go in and find myself in a huge department store in Paris with many rooms. In one place there is a terraced balcony with three levels. The store is empty. I go out of the store and find myself on the streets. I take a trolley, but have no money and do not know where I am going."

To Stalin he associated a hero, or a great man. He was not a communist, but admired Stalin for his achievements. Physically Stalin bore a marked resemblance to his father.

To Paris he associated enjoyment, especially women. To the department store he associated a design he had once drawn in school, which had received much praise.

The dream occurred shortly after he had broken up one of his usual ambivalent amatory relationships. It symbolized his wish to follow father (Stalin) to the grave and be reborn in a house of his own design (Parisian department store). But then the house is empty (as in the previous dream) and he wanders around lost.

Towards the end of this period of analysis a dream brought out his feeling of greater inner security, coupled with the ability to be on his own.

"I'm walking along Coney Island Avenue, between Ocean Avenue and Ocean Parkway. A man comes at me with a gun. He fires at me, but I don't get hurt. I think I can go home to West End Avenue and be free of this danger."

To the man shooting at him he associated James Cagney and the gangster roles that he portrayed; Harvey had often wished he could live like that. The area described is an area in Brooklyn where he had been brought up; West End Avenue was the area in Manhattan where he was now living. James Cagney also stood for the bullying brother. The dream brings out the wish to be free of the bullying once and for all.

A few months later came another graphic dream, in which he brought out the wish to be free of mother.

"I am two people: a little boy about to marry a little girl and a grown man married to my mother. I go out on the street, and lie down, feeling helpless but able to know what is going on. I know that my mother will have to kill herself; I hear her blow her brains out."

This dream followed an incident with a new girl which brought out his recurrent dilemma. He saw this girl that day not because he wanted to but because of a sense of obligation, which was similar to that with mother and with people in general.

The division into two people is striking: he is both boy and man. Clearly, to be a man he must marry his mother, a denouement both wished for and feared. The helpless feeling is a dynamic factor in his masochism: by being helpless he forces mother to kill herself. Also there is the feeling that he is trying to work through, that no matter what he does eventual liberation can come only through his mother's death. Additionally, the dream brings out the tremendous rage at his mother, which carries over to other women and spoils his relationships with them.

Which Girl to Choose? The Two-Women Dilemma

Once he had overcome the fantasy that some day Mimi would return to him, Harvey began a long series of affairs. In these a stereoptyped, repetitious kind of behavior soon became noticeable. On meeting a girl his initial ploy was always to try to seduce her. Most of the time he succeeded. But once the girl had been seduced he felt an enormous sense of obligation to her. He *had* to see her at regular times, to be good to her, never get angry at her, take her places, and the like. All these obligations naturally aroused tremendous resentment. This resentment was hard to handle. It was useless to express it directly to the girl, since she would not understand. To swallow it and turn it against himself was the lifelong defensive maneuver that he was trying to overcome. There was a third alternative: to let things slide with the girl and take up with another at the same time. This led to his two-women dilemma, the analysis of which continued from the very beginning to the very end.

This dilemma was naturally multidetermined. At the deepest level it represented the two sides of his mother, the good and bad, which he had never been able to reconcile or escape. At a later stage it stood for mother (bad) and sister (good), especially the oldest sister who had been so nice to him in childhood and whom he looked up to with so much warmth and affection. Still later it became the clash between the incestuously forbidden mother and the sexually acceptable girl friend. To feel free with girls he had to have mother's permission, which was hard to get or utterly impossible. Unconsciously, the two women also allowed him to get his rage out at his mother, since he knew very well that they would both be hurt when the affair broke off.

Another meaning of the two women was a manifestation of his unconscious homosexuality; he could imagine two women engaging in sex, while he could not visualize himself doing it with another man. Finally, the two women stood for an identification with brother Nathan, and his numerous conquests. Later this notion that to be a real he-man you had to conquer lots of women was projected to me.

The most graphic depiction of his dilemma came out in a dream towards the end of the analysis.

"I go into an art store. Two women are there. One takes me to the back; I figure she is going to offer herself to me. She shows me two figurines. One has three figures. If you take out the middle you see a hairy vagina or bottom. In another, if you screw off the top you see birds kissing a a penis. Some cops come in; we realize they know there is pornography going on, and we run. They chase us, finally catch up. One policeman starts telling me his troubles. It looks as though they're not going to punish us."

At the time of this dream he was going with the girl he later married, and occasionally dating others. To the art store he associated pornographic books that he liked to read; it also clarified the pleasure in looking, one motive for his lifelong interest in art.

The confusion between the anus and the vagina* is obvious in the image of the hairy vagina or bottom. It had taken him a long time to get to the acceptance of the vagina as a warm, accepting organ rather than a hole left after the penis had been removed. The second image brings out the wish for oral sex most directly. He had always wanted girls to suck his penis, but had been too shy to ask for it until he was well along in his analysis. Lately he had been attracted more by oral sex than by intercourse. The cops stand for the analyst, who is nonpunitive. Thus the superego now gives him permission to indulge his sexual fantasies. A subsidiary wish in the dream is to have the analyst (cop) tell him more about himself; this was a constant source of complaint, which led to the release of much negative feeling all the way through.

There were numerous explicit dreams about getting permission from mother to go with another girl. One, towards the end of the analysis, was:

"I'm in bed with Gloria, kissing her. My mother and father are in the next room. My mother is having one of her hysterical fits. My father comes in, walks around, and walks out again."

Gloria was a casual friend whom he was seeing alternately with the more important girl, Helen, whom he eventually married. Father is restored to life, and gives him permission to be sexual. Mother, however, is having a fit. Evidently one reason for having two women was to annoy mother; Helen was also a mother symbol.

At an earlier stage, he had met a girl, Susan, who was

---

*Compare the slang expressions for sex: a "piece of ass" or "tail."

typical of the domineering women in his life. She had been through five years of a Reichian "analysis," which left her with the ability to vomit at will. At first she tried to induce Harvey to go to a Reichian analyst; he refused and got her instead to try more systematic therapy.

As usual, however, his defense against his anger at Susan was to go out with other women. In one dream he brought out the wish and the punishment most explicitly:

"I'm with Susan and another girl. Susan takes the laundry out. I kiss the other girl. When Susan comes back she gets angry and both walk out on me."

The loss of both girls symbolized a total rejection by mother. This rejection was obviously a castration, a punishment for his sexual desires. In this dream he is punished; in a later one, however, he feels free enough to release his anger at the girls.

"I'm in a room with three friends [girls]. One says, "Why don't we stay at Harvey's?" I'm solving a crossword puzzle with the help of the dictionary . . . I'm skating; there is no ice. I skate into a new modern bus terminal. It turns into an old antiquated one."

Here he first gratifies his wish to have three girls, then turns them into old antiquated bitches (the bus terminal). After this dream he became increasingly aware of his hostilities towards women. In another dream later on he became more aware of his wish to frustrate them:

"I go to two parties. When I come back, I discover I don't have enough food."

Part of the two-women dilemma was the hostile denigration of any woman that he came close to. Conscious complaints were infrequent. Instead, he would begin to feel obligated, see the woman as either too demanding or too undemanding, too active or too passive. Nothing could ever satisfy him. A number of dreams brought out this hostility in graphic form:

"I'm out with two fellows from the office, the chief draftsman and chief engineer. They each have a girl; the chief draftsman has a new car. I have a dog."

His "dog" here symbolizes both how he feels in relation to

the other men and his view of women. ("Dog" or "bitch" is a commonly used derogatory term for women.) In another dream later on he saw a woman with four nipples. With such a fantasy of the all-giving mother, any ordinary woman would fall short. Further, since mother did not have four nipples he hated her and, by extension, all women. The keen sense of disappointment when he discovers the woman is not all he wants is also brought out in the following dream:

"I am in an apartment with Barbara, another girl, and a Cuban without a beard. He tells us about the more genuine anti-Castro movement. Then we pair off. I am kissing this new girl, fondling her breasts, while she reveals her body to me. I feel very aroused sexually. It is next morning. We are taking leave of one another. Now I seem to see her face, it is not as pretty as the night before, wine wasted, almost a weird and ugly face. She tells me she works for —————, and that her best friend is —————. I feel threatened with imminent exposure of our affair to Helen. This woman tries to invite me to dinner on June 1, but I tell her I don't make arrangements so far in advance."

Here too Helen (his steady girl) becomes a mother figure who prevents him from relating to other women.

Naturally, in the process of working out the woman dilemma his mother was a topic of constant conversation. Abandoned by all six children, she was a bitter, resentful old woman who derived almost no pleasure from life, not even from her grandchildren. Yet it was still difficult for him to break the ties with her emotionally. In several dreams she committed suicide (see above). This was his passive-aggressive wish to get rid of her.

Towards the end of the analysis he had an open incest dream:

"I'm in bed with my mother. She had big folds of fat around her vagina and I wonder how my penis can get through. Finally it does."

The dream aroused more amusement than shock. Yet he was keenly aware of his overattachment to mother if he was still having such dreams about her.

After many vicissitudes he finally settled on a girl, Helen, with whom he was very much in love. She was warm, affectionate, cuddly, and interested in him. On the negative side there was the fact that she was not Jewish, that she had a variety of somatic ailments, and that she could not have children. But as the dynamics of his relationship to mother were analyzed, together with the homosexuality, and the fantasies about other girls, he found himself more and more in love with her. Shortly after the analysis ended they were married. A letter a few years later indicated that they were very happy together.

The Homosexual Conflict

It was clear that there was a strong latent homosexual component in him. Yet, despite the extensive childhood sex play with his brother, it never developed into overt homosexuality. Its chief manifestations were his passivity and his prolonged difficulty in settling on a woman; unconsciously in the back of his mind there was always the hope that he might never have to make a choice. Both disguised and overt variations came out in his dreams.

One vivid dream brought out the conflict between his heterosexual wishes and the wish to be a woman to Nathan.

"I'm riding along in a new car with my brother Nathan, Mimi, Henry, and another fellow. We are out in the country looking for a place to stay overnight. We come to one place, and they have no room. I look back and see a lot of beautiful girls in there but can't go in because of Mimi. She has a baby. The baby is in the car. Two old women point it out to me. I get in and drive off. Before I know it my brother Nathan has taken over; I can only manage the auxiliary brake. As we drive along there are logs and bumps in the road; I tell him how to avoid them."

Mimi was the girl whom he had loved so unhappily; Henry was the man who had replaced him. It will be recalled that he had wanted to give Mimi all of his life savings to abort Henry's child. Now he takes over the child, thus symbolically giving birth. Nathan then takes over and becomes the man to him. He shows Nathan how to make love to him (avoid the logs and bumps in the road). In a dream much later a similar theme came up, in which he was Nathan's woman, preparing the food for him.

The most vivid dream about homosexuality was the following:

> "There are a lot of men in my place screwing. Tom is screwing Walter, George somebody else, and John beckons to me; I won't go."

His first association was to another dream, in which he was in bed with a boy. Next he thought of dogs screwing in the street; he had heard that they fasten themselves together in such a way that it is hard to tear them apart. The dream followed a paradoxically unsatisfactory sex experience with a new girl, Sylvia. Paradoxical because Sylvia was almost the ideally available girl that he had always fantasized. She accepted him whenever he called, with or without notice. Her sex was very passionate, and she was particularly fond of sucking his penis, which he had rarely been able to get girls to do.

Yet after an evening with her he still felt empty and dissatisfied. The sucking was something that men did with one another as well, so the frustration with her was due to a measure of repressed homosexuality. He began to bring out more fantasies of forbidden sexual actitivies.

Several months later he had another orgy dream, in which a number of repressed wishes came to light.

> "I'm in a restaurant-bar. Couples pair off and go to rooms. I'm in a room with two girls, Sally and Linda. We all take our clothes off. We all masturbate. Then we masturbate one another. Then Sally sucks me off. I think Sally and Linda can satisfy one another . . . I'm out in California on a fishing boat."

Sally was the girl that he was seeing regularly; Linda was a friend of hers. The dream brings out a variety of what he considered "perverse" wishes — masturbation, homosexuality, fellatio, orgy. California was his original goal when he came to inquire about analysis. So the main desire is to gratify every wish, then run away and do nothing.

Somewhat later another dream brought out a similar dynamic picture.

> "A man is inviting me to a party [implication: homosex-

ual]. There will be liquor and food, and it will be very convivial. It's Friday night. I go. On the way I meet two homosexuals, who approach me. I protest, and go to the police to complain."

The key here is to the reference to Friday night. His girl friend used to go out to their summer place early Friday, while he would work late; this often left him free on Friday evening. Usually he would be tempted to see another girl; sometimes he did that, sometimes not. The dream brings out the forbidden homosexual wish which bothered him every week.

Finally, a dream near the end of the analysis brought out the strength of the wish to be a carefree little boy again.

"There is a pussy on the third rail. It gets electrocuted, then limps back to life. . .Jack is on a train, leaving. He has no baggage. I say, "How can you go away without baggage?""

To "pussy" he associated a recent comment by Helen about being electrocuted on the third rail. Jack is her brother-in-law, who had made a compromise in life. In the dream he first kills off the girl then wishes to take off like Jack. At the same time these wishes are restrained. The dream is part of the working through of his wish to remain a child.

Anger and Suffering

With his childhood background, it was to be expected that it would take a long time for Harvey to get over his suffering attitude of life. He had never been able to fight well, and always had to seek out protectors. Now that he was an adult he had no one to turn to.

In a sense it was to be anticipated that the service (World War II) would offer him many gratifications. It was a kind of family, in many ways more secure than any he had ever known. And the aggressive actions were not only permitted but encouraged by his superiors. He had fought through the European theater of war, and it left him with many pleasant memories.

But in civilian life he felt lost. In one sense the unhappy affair with Mimi was a search for a protector, similar to mother and brother in childhood. Only now the reality frustrations were too great.

In the first part of the analysis, the main problem was to throw off the yoke, real or fancied, of the aggressors of his childhood. This meant freeing himself first from mother, second from domineering women, and third from exploitative bosses. All three of these involved struggles which persisted throughout the entire analysis, but in all three he was ultimately successful.

With his mother the initial step was to leave her home with its protective-crushing influence. Since he had already been away several times, he could face up to his mother's wrath about being rejected. Within a few months he was out of the house, but naturally it took much longer to work out the inner image of the bad mother.

The pattern with women has already been discussed above.

With bosses there were a number of obstacles to overcome. For his first job as an architect-draftsman he found a man running a small office who was extremely tyrannical. He demanded an inordinate amount of work from Harvey, and was never satisfied with the results. Harvey became the scapegoat, bearing the brunt of all of his boss's frustrations and resentments. Still, Harvey wanted to learn the business, so he stuck it out.

Once he had acquired some experience, he was able to leave this first job for much better opportunities. Here, since he did not have a degree, he was given mainly routine work. So long as he was just learning this did not bother him too much.

Eventually, however, he began to yearn for a chance to build a whole house. On the one hand this represented his old childhood fantasy, to have a secure happy home; on the other hand it stood as well for the more adult wish to be master in his own house.

Realistically, it was premature for him to expect more advanced assignments on his job; as yet he was still untrained for them. Nor was he so shabbily treated, as on the first job, that he had to rebel. His background as the youngest child was useful here because it helped him derive pleasure from the work situation that he was in.

Instead, he hit upon an ingenious compromise: he would build his own house. Together with two other friends, one a lawyer, the other likewise an architect, he bought some property in a summer resort near New York. Except for some highly technical pieces of equipment such as the electrical system, the three built the house from scratch.

For several years Harvey spent almost every weekend between April and October working on this house. Unfortunately, just when it was almost done one of the men insisted on leaving the team. Although it was never brought to fruition, the project was a great achievement for him.

With all the analysis of his aggression, Harvey never became a violent man. Towards women especially he was rarely able to experience any strong feeling of anger. Nevertheless, he did find a satisfactory solution to the problem. Here once more theoretical predilections have to bow before empirical evidence.

"I'm out in a field with a man and two women. An airplane flies overhead; the man traps it and brings it to the ground. Then six airplanes fly overhead; we set out to trap them. I go into a hut and see a piece of driftwood. I think I can use it as a weapon, but it is too big. I get a stick and go off to battle. The four of us are up against about a hundred, all with sticks, but in this battle they can't hurt us and we can't hurt them. We retreat outside the iron gates and the battle ends."

Most significant here is the last part, where four people battle a hundred to a standstill. He strove for a situation in which he could neither hurt nor be hurt, a compromise solution from his childhood. But in the very next dream he became frightened about this stance.

"I'm sitting in a theater, in the first row. People in the audience start throwing rocks; I run away."

To the rocks he associated childhood fights in which a boy once hit him in the back with a rock. Thus, he alternates between a standstill and flight. Several sessions later another dream brought out some real aggression, which was followed by beating up his brother Nathan. These two dreams were:

"There are about twenty or thirty people fighting with knives. They're killing one another. I'm off on the sidelines watching. There is a man sitting down with a knife in him. I throw another knife at him."

"My brother Nathan is driving a car, with my sister Elaine and myself. I tell him he is a poor driver, get angry, and punch him; then I feel good."

In these dreams he is obviously eager to enter the fray. Nevertheless, it is necessary to recall here that dreams after all are wishes: his wish was to be more violent, but it did not come out that way in real life. What did come out was that since he could now tolerate the violent wishes sufficiently to let them come out in dreams, he could be more forceful in his everyday dealings with people.

The seesaw of aggression and punishment persisted for a long time. In most of the material the antagonist was his brother Nathan, who had been his tormentor all through childhood. Evidently, the resentment was so deep that it took a long time to unravel. A dream towards the end of the analysis tied up the resentment with sexual prohibitions.

"I'm in an apartment masturbating. A fellow is looking in. I jump up, say, "You can't do that." Then I sweep people out of all the rooms — fifty or sixty of them. Then over to Nathan's, who is in a beach chair — I start jumping on him and kicking him. He turns into Helen, who is kicking me."

The novel elements here are first the masturbation and second the transformation of his brother into Helen, his future wife. He needs the woman (good mother, older sister) to calm down his rage at his brother, especially when his brother tries to prevent him from enjoying sex. Part of his attraction to Helen was that she never became angry at him. In one sense this was a neurotic compromise, since he picked a woman who was the exact opposite of his mother. But in another sense it was realistic, since who wants a woman who is angry all the time?

VICISSITUDES OF THE TRANSFERENCE

Finally, some comments are in order about the unfolding transference manifestations throughout the analysis. As mentioned, it began with the analytic honeymoon which lasted several years. Then, as Harvey came to see that he would have to make a considerable effort to resolve his problems, there were increasing instances of negativism and resentment. Towards the end of his long analysis (nine years) he was consistently annoyed about the amount of time that he had devoted to it. In spite of this resentment, however, the underlying feeling remained essentially positive throughout.

The vicissitudes of the transference can be traced best through the series of dreams that he had about me. In the first he dreamt:

> "Four of us, two men and two women, are at an analyst's office. One analyst is admonishing the women. You are there. You turn into a beautiful woman, and I have sex with you."

This is a typical dream in men, in which the male analyst becomes a woman, thus offering sexual gratification together with everything else. (See case of Jim below, in which the same fantasy appeared.) Another wish here is for an alliance with the analyst in which he can feel free to bawl out (or hurt) women.

As could have been anticipated, such a dream, with its impossible demand, sooner or later boomerangs into feelings of anger. This came out several months later.

> "You are too poor to have an apartment with so many rooms, so you have to move to a smaller one. In the meantime you have no place to see patients and you ask me to stop analysis for a while."

To begin with the dream expresses his annoyance about the fee (too poor). At another level this relates to potency (many rooms, many women); it thus represents a wish to castrate me. Striking here is the reversal of the anger: I send him away, when really his wish is to quit.

The immediate impetus for this dream was a conversation with a fellow student who was getting his doctorate in psychology. This fellow assured him that psychoanalysis was old hat, and that physiological changes accounted for all emotional disturbances. But, of course, this remark would have no effect if there had been no underlying fear of getting too close to me.

The next dream expressed a combination of homosexual and filial wishes.

> "I am in your office on the couch; you are on a couch

on the other side of the room. We can see one another as
we talk. I fall asleep. You come over and shine a bright
light in my eyes. I shield my eyes. You go away and go
snooping around the room."

To the snooping he associated that he was once snooping
around my office when I was out. The light symbolized the
analysis. Shining the light in his eyes is analyzing him, also playing with his testicles (eyes), a homosexual act. The two of us lying on couches together also symbolizes homosexuality. Here
too he wishes to get closer and is afraid to do so.

In the next dream he expresses his anger at not having me
all to himself.

"I go to see you in a school. You are seated at a desk at
the end of a long corridor. You begin to talk to me in front
of a large crowd of fifteen or sixteen people. I don't like
that and ask to have them leave. After they leave, I become
more aggressive, raise my voice, pound the table, and chase
out an old man and woman who are at your side. Outside
the trees are green, the sun is shining. Joey comes along
and throws me an apple."

To the school he associated my "formalistic" approach
which he frequently complained about. The crowd conceals the
wish to be alone with me, which then comes out directly. The
green trees had a special meaning for him because he was red-
green color blind. By being alone with me he gets food and love
(the apple) together with improved vision (potency). He is also
able to assert his wish to be the only child, which he had not
been able to do when he was a child.

In the next dream he wants me to encourage him to become a father.

"You suggest to me that I adopt a daughter. I get one,
one foot tall, dressed in blue; she wraps herself around my
neck. Then I want to adopt a son, six inches long, but
can't make up my mind."

Children were far from his mind, so the dream puzzled
him. The little girl who wraps herself around his neck symbolizes his own incestuous wish for his mother. The six-inch son
refers to the usual image of the size of the erected penis; he is
ambivalent about the incest. The main wish is to be a father,

i.e., a mature man, but he must adopt rather than beget; he wants me to castrate him, under the surface a wish for fatherhood. From another point of view the dream also brings out a homosexual wish, since he "gets" a daughter from me.

No further clear-cut transference images appeared until much later.

"I'm in your office, on a shelf, about eight feet above the floor."

This represents the simple wish to be my baby, perched high and dry on a shelf in my house.

Again several years elapsed before he had another dream about me. This was:

"You and I are together on the street. You have a hypodermic and give me a shot in the arm."

Here he brings out the wish to have me be with him all the time. If that could be arranged, he would have constant reassurances (shot in the arm). The very next session he had another dream along similar lines:

"I'm walking back to your office. First I'm going to take the tunnel, then I realize I have half an hour so I can take the bridge. On the way I meet Keith, who says, "Hello, Harry, my friend."

The evening before he had had nothing to do. He thought of going to a bar, finally wound up just walking around. To the tunnel he associated the hustle and bustle of work. To the bridge he associated a frequent fantasy of childhood; walking over the bridge was a great thrill for him. Half an hour is the amount of time it took him to get to my office. Keith is a former roommate who took a lot of interest in him; he never knew why. This he also associates to me; quite often he wonders why I take so much interest in him.

The dream represents a wish to meet me on the street, during his walking.

Some time later he dreamt:

"You and I are in a car."

The car is a convertible, like the one his oldest sister used to ride him around in when he was a little boy. The dream is thus a direct transference wish to have me be as nice to him as his sister was.

Finally, shortly before the end of the analysis he dreamt:

"You are a Roman emperor, and have your face imprinted on a coin. You have a harem and have orgies. It all comes easy to you."

At this time he was struggling with the conflict between marrying Helen (which he later did) and chasing many girls. He projects to me his wish to have a harem. Once he had worked through this wish and all its childhood connotations he was ready to enter into marriage.

The sequence of transference dreams, with some exceptions, reveals a transition from the wish to fuse with me at the oral level to the wish to be my child to the wish to identify with me. By working out this series of fantasies he was able to achieve a stable, gratifying self-image for himself.

DISCUSSION

The changes brought about in the transformation of the "schlemiel" into a mature functioning man can perhaps best be described by a systematic consideration of the various components of the analytic ideal.

LOVE: Before analysis Harvey experienced love as a masochistic submission to some strong figure who could do with him as the other person wished. The original of this cruel authority was his mother, liberation from whose clutches was one of the central goals of the treatment. After that came the older sister, who was consistently kind to him, but disappeared after a few years. Then came his brother Nathan, who in most respects was a repetition of mother, though he did help Harvey out in various ways which mother did not, and he was not clinging, as she was. After him came Mimi, another kind of cruel mother figure, who was his main "love" when he began analysis. Mimi was replaced by the analyst, as a result of the analytic work. Here for the first time he was able to release a great deal of resentment over a long period of time. As the childhood roots of this resentment were methodically worked out, he became more and more secure in his love for Helen. Eventually this led to a happy marriage.

Concomitant with the developments in his love life came a change in his social relationships. He was able to handle friends, employers, and casual acquaintances on a much more mature basis.

SEXUALITY: When he came to analysis sexual gratification was still hampered by unresolved homosexual, anal, and incestuous strivings. As the analysis progressed, these were replaced by a compulsive drive for women, particularly for women who would perform fellatio on him, an experience which he had previously been too guilt-laden to accept. This led to the two-woman dilemma, in which he always had to have two women because he could not trust himself with one. Eventually this was resolved by the acceptance of a satisfying sexual relationship with his wife Helen.

PLEASURE: Before analysis there were relatively few areas in which he could allow himself any pleasure. Life was a burden in which you had to do your duty, much like his henpecked father. Gradually he began to accept more pleasure. At first it was largely in the sexual field. Later this was expanded to include music, art, and a more general enjoyment of life. It must be admitted, however, that here further analysis would most likely have led to a further expansion of the libido, and consequently to more *joie de vivre*.

FEELING: Before analysis the main feelings experienced were fear, timidity, and resentment. Gradually the fear and timidity were replaced by an increasing sense of self-confidence. The resentment diminished, but a certain amount remained, especially since the block against expressing anger to other people was never adequately resolved.

REASON: Where before analysis there was a constant masochistic desire to please other people, which blocked his capacity to think clearly, this was slowly replaced by a firmer grasp of the reins of his life. In both love and work, at the end he functioned at a mature level, rather than in compliance with unconscious compulsive, ultimately self-defeating strivings.

SENSE OF IDENTITY: The term "schlemiel" aptly describes his sense of himself before analysis; his image of himself as a little three-year-old boy hiding behind his mother's skirts is a good graphic description. When he began he had not yet finished college, and had only vague ideas about what to do with his life. After several years of analysis he was able to move forward towards the profession of architecture, which brought together many different strands of his life, including the identification with father. In addition to clarification of his life's work he was also able to find himself as a man and father. The identity transformation is in a sense the most striking of all the changes brought about by analysis.

FAMILY ROLE: When he first came he was still the little boy living with mother; in fact for a while he did literally live with her. This slowly gave way to an increasing sense of security in himself as a grown-up man. He was eventually able to assume the role of husband and father with feelings of accomplishment and gratification.

SOCIAL ROLE: His social life was not unusually different from other men of his circle. He was not an isolate, but had little interest in social reform. This aspect of his life was least affected by the analysis.

CREATIVITY: Although some creative outlets were present even before analysis, he was not a particularly creative person. Eventually he accepted a job with the government because he felt that he did not have enough creativity to make a go of it in private as an architect.

WORK: When he began, work was a meaningless chore. Education was stymied by his failure to finish. All of this changed in the course of analysis. He was able to find an area of work which gave him much gratification.

COMMUNICATION: The analysis opened for him a whole new area of communication in dreams, fantasies, childhood experiences, and observation of himself and the world. In all these he proved to be quite adept. It can truly be said that the analysis opened a new inner world for him, which he was able to put to good use.

PSYCHIATRIC SYMPTOMATOLOGY: His symptoms did not really fall within the purview of classical psychiatry. If he is called a "masochistic personality," this only means that a new psychiatric category has been created to fit analytic discoveries. At best one could say that he suffered from too much anxiety before analysis, and that this was brought under much better control. However, this belies the fact that the whole diagnostic armamentarium of psychiarty had no real relevance for an understanding of his problems. He was a human caught up in an unhappy life situation. I have discussed this point at greater length in my books *The Healing of the Mind* and *A History of Psychoanalysis*. It is most meaningful to say that as a result of the analytic work he was able to find much more happiness in life.

Alice, The Analysis of a Normal Woman

Alice, a twenty-seven-year-old teacher, was a self-referral to a low-cost psychoanalytic service. Since her mother paid for the analysis, this mode of referral served her need to keep things anonymous more than her financial problem. She was accepted for treatment immediately at a rate of three sessions a week, which was maintained throughout the analysis. The analysis went on for a period of three and a half years.

The presenting complaints were marital dissatisfaction and painful intercourse. She stated to the interviewing psychiatrist that she feels inept and retiring both socially and professionally. She is anxious, overcritical, and though she desires warmth and feels warmly, she is unable to express these feelings towards men.

LIFE HISTORY

Alice was the older of two siblings; the other was a boy four years younger. All through her life she had had the strong conviction that her brother was favored by both parents; there was, however, nothing objective that she could point to to support this conviction.

Father was a successful doctor, a self-made man. Besides being a doctor, he was active in politics, and had even run for office a number of times. Since he was a member of a small unpopular leftist group, he had never been elected. Mother was initially described as an artistically inclined housewife.

Both parents were highly overintellectualized. They did the "right thing" by their children; Alice said she had been taken to every museum and art gallery in the city before she was ten. But there was little sign of any personal warmth, or any capacity to communicate feeling. Anger and hostility were especially frowned upon. In sexual matters the parents were more lenient verbally, but basically intolerant and repressed as well. In spite of this unconscious prohibition of the display of any strong feeling, the family would have been considered a model environment for any child by conventional social standards. The father made a comfortable living. Both children were brought up with care and devotion. There was never any overt sign of marital or familial discord.

Her earliest memories went back to a boat trip the whole family took to California, to visit with the maternal grandmother. From this trip a number of pleasant and unpleasant memories remained. One time she was putting figs and nuts in a box with mother; this was very nice. But on the boat to California she was separated from them and anxious. And in California the maid once hit her because she was naughty; she was afraid to tell mother. Of grandmother she retained many pleasant memories. One that she came back to a number of times was watching grandmother put clothes on the line.

Another anxious separation memory dated from about the age of three. The family was driving along in their car, when something broke down. They left her asleep in the car while it was being fixed. Suddenly she woke up, frightened because her parents were not there.

There was no indication of any meaningful problem in the first four years of life. Apparently, the first serious conflicts arose in the Oedipal period. In later life her fears were primarily sexual.

Up to the time she was around four, father was in the habit of drying her after her bath. This she remembered with much gratification; she could even recall the nice sensations in her genitals when her father dried her there.

Then one day this suddenly stopped. She was told nothing, other than a vague remark that she was too old for that sort of thing. It was a terrible trauma. She remembered many temper tantrums from this period, but had never before tied them up with the Oedipal disappointment.

At about this time her brother was born. There were only vague memories of him as an infant. Primarily, as mentioned, the strong feeling persisted that he was somehow the favored child. This was accentuated by a brief trip the parents took with the new baby, leaving her alone with the maid because she was in school and anyhow she was "big enough" to be alone, a feeling she did not share, since she felt terribly abandoned by them.

Towards the close of the Oedipal stage, when she was about six years old, a marked change of personality took place. The temper tantrums stopped and were replaced by a turn to a masochistic character structure, resulting from the internalization of the hostility. One vivid memory from this period was that once when she hurt herself, she went to bed but would not tell mother how bad it was for fear she would call the doctor. "I'll sleep and it will go away," she told herself. This was the first clear indication of her distance from mother, and reluctance or inability to share feelings with her. A book she read around this time described a boy who loses his mother in the forest; she read it many times, even though it was horribly frightening.

A rebellious negativistic streak set in at this time. School annoyed her because everything was prescribed. She longed for freedom, but could see no way to find it. One solution was to run away, which she tried on occasion all through the school period. Once at seven she ran away from the maid and her brother. Another time she began to run away to New Jersey, where some relatives lived. However, these rebellions soon came to an end.

But the basic defense was a severe repression of feeling. On the surface she was the good little girl, obediently doing all the right things. This facade was maintained by blocking off any threatening feelings. For example, whenever there was a violent scene in her memories she would close her eyes, a defense she maintained until it was worked out in analysis. When mother's father died, she played the piano, seemingly indifferent to the loss. When father's father died, she argued against providing his grave with a stone, since he was dead and the money would be wasted on him.

One of the few later acts of open rebellion she recalled was putting some fish in the counselor's water at camp when she was ten. The counselor did not notice, and drank the water, which amused the girls immensely.

With the onset of puberty another significant change took place. She began to engage in open, violent quarrels with mother on the slightest pretext. It began with an incident when mother slapped her when she was thirteen; she could not recall the provocation. What she did complain about all through the analysis was the degree to which mother tried to dominate her. For example, when she was a little girl mother liked to dress her in white clothes, which interfered with her fun with the other children. Later mother wanted to pick her clothes for her. This domineering attitude was coupled with verbal protests that Alice was free to live her life as she chose. Through all this period father seemed, in her words, to be only a "shadowy figure," busy with his medical practice.

Both school and love life began to be sources of disappointment, and her masochism became steadily more entrenched. The college of her choice turned her down, which made her feel ashamed for many years. The fact that she was accepted by an equally good college where she did quite well was, of course, no consolation.

Dating began late, at around eighteen. She felt insecure and in conflict about her sexual feelings. Since the parents were permissive on the surface, she could date, and have sex occasionally. But she did not respond, which baffled her. There was no one with whom she could discuss her sexual conflicts.

Her first serious involvement came during the summer she was nineteen. She was then a counselor at camp. The boy said he loved her, she loved him. But at the end of the summer he suddenly broke off the whole relationship, without explanation. That winter the same thing happened with another boy.

While she was able to have sex from her nineteenth year on, she described her sex life as highly unsatisfactory except for rare occasions, usually following a few drinks. Casual sex encounters were accepted because it was the "liberated" thing to do, but she did not really know why she was doing it.

When she was twenty-one she met her future husband, Jim, on a hiking trip. She described him as a rather surly fellow of somewhat lower intellectual and economic background. He needed help to get through graduate school. This seemed an opportunity and she married him to provide the help. His need for her came out as protestations of love; she had never had any strong feelings of love for him. Because he wanted her so much, and because the outlook as a single girl seemed so bleak to her, she married him the next year, when she was twenty-two.

The marriage was soon marked by discontent and rapid loss of affection for her husband. About a year before coming to analysis she had started an affair with a fellow teacher. Both in the marriage and in the affair sexual intercourse was painful, which she handled by keeping sex to a minimum. Altogether there had been very little sex during marriage; neither she nor her husband had much drive.

In spite of her problem she entered analysis with a fair amount of resistance. There was one family member who was a prominent analyst, but she was ashamed to ask him for help, and anyhow she felt that he would recommend classical analysis five times a week, which she was reluctant to undertake because "her case was not so serious."

COURSE OF ANALYSIS

The analysis lends itself in broad strokes to a division into five stages: (1) freeing herself from her husband, (2) sexual release, (3) discharge of anger and resentment at many people, (4) development of wish to become a mother, (5) termination.

Freeing Herself from Husband

The immediate reason for coming to analysis was that although she felt herself to be in an impossible marital situation, she was unable to leave her husband. He for his part did not want a divorce, but would not oppose her; his only request was that since he was a graduate student it should be deferred until he had passed his final examination, since otherwise it would interfere with his work. But she needed the support of a permissive parent to try it on her own.

About two months before beginning analysis she had a transference dream:

> "I'm walking along Central Park West with my analyst. He's too young and I'm afraid it won't work out. I go back to his office and see the girl transcribing notes there; I'm bothered by that."

This dream brought out a number of themes which were repeated many times in the analysis. First, there was the wish for social contact with the analyst — to go for a walk on Central Park West, where she had often walked with her father when she was a little girl. The anticipated frustration of this wish was a deeper reason for her initial resistance. Second, the analyst was too young for her. This was a variation of the wish for father — she wanted a more mature man. Actually, her husband was slightly younger in years, but he was considerably less mature in other ways, both emotionally and financially. And, finally there is the triangle situation, the third person this time being the analyst's secretary. The Oedipal-triangle conflict proved to be the deepest conflict in the analysis; much of our work was devoted to unraveling its various ramifications.

Relating this dream brought some immediate transference material in which she was trying to cast me in the role of a forbidding parent. She had expected that I would order her not to discuss her analysis with her lover, or to leave her husband. At the same time she fought these "prohibitions"; for example she would check her watch many times during the hour to make sure that the announcement of the end of the hour would not come as a surprise.

As she came to see that the analysis would not produce a repetition of the fights against authority of her childhood, she began to look at the marriage more dispassionately. It was part of her general feeling that life held little pleasure in store for her, so she had to rescue others. The love for her husband had never been as intense as that for her lover, or for the first boy friend who had jilted her after one summer. Since her husband refused to do anything about his own problems, and the marriage offered fewer and fewer gratifications, once the support of an analyst was available, it was not hard for her to break up the marriage. After about six weeks of analysis she felt strong enough to leave him. As mentioned, he put up very little opposition.

Sexual Release

Once Alice's marriage had broken up, she became more involved with the lover. But he was married, and did not want more than a casual affair. She saw this as part of her pattern of being second best all her life. A dream revealed how she was repeating her childhood fear of being abandoned.

"I move in to the city. . . A lot of people come in. I drive out to find Jerry, but can't find him."

Moving into the city meant coming closer to the analyst. She now began to experience a conflict between the analyst and the lover. As the positive transference grew, the attachment to the lover diminished.

The analyst at this point represented a permissive father. With him she began to relive her adolescence, making up for the sexual frustrations of that period.

Once she realized that nothing of a permanent nature could emerge from the relationship with her lover, she began to date other men as well. It was at this time that she revealed that the sex relationship with her husband had been much worse than originally depicted. Over the five years of marriage they had had sex only a few times, and then only when they had been drinking.

One day she brought in a cartoon from *The New Yorker*, showing a girl coming to a party with five men on a dog's leash; this was one of her favorite fantasies. For the next year or so she acted out her fantasies with a number of different men.

At one point she had two lovers whom she was seeing regularly, one on one night, the other the second night. When neither of these was around there were other men.

With so much sexual activity, the sexual problem, painful intercourse, cleared up entirely. Primarily it had been the result of superego tension, rather than severely blocked libidinal desires. With one lover she became regularly orgastic.

After several months, she produced the first significant transference dream:

"I'm in your office. I'm sitting up on the couch with you, talking face to face."

This dream had occurred while she was on a brief vacation trip out of town. It was not reported immediately, but came out only when her lover urged her to be more emotional and less intellectual in the analysis.

To sitting up she associated improvement. When the sexual implications of the dream were pointed out to her, she accepted them readily.

In this period the transference remained markedly positive. She did not know on what basis the referral to me had been made, but she felt the choice had been a wise one. She saw herself as a good analysand who was making continual progress.

Aware of her impersonal family, she began to wonder about the other patients. One amusing fantasy was that she would stuff notes in the coats in the clothes closet, eventually getting to know a number of them in that way. She also began to urge friends and relatives to go into analysis; again this was related to her wish to break down the emotional coldness of her early family environment.

Much time was spent on her resentment of the principal in her school, a disciplinarian who had little use for psychologists. Further, he used his position to feed a private law practice, which was theoretically forbidden, though commonly done. For a while she and some of the others built up a dossier on him, with the thought that eventually it might be presented to the state or the Board of Trustees. To some extent, this was a reflection of the positive transference to me, but to some extent it was realistic. Her anger at him persisted until she left the school.

Through this stage the triangle dreams continued, showing how the sexual release was helping her to work out the Oedipal conflicts. Here are some typical ones.

"I'm out ice skating with Sam and his wife."

Sam was her husband. To ice skating she associated an activity that she had abandoned during her marriage, and that she now planned to take up again. To Sam's wife she had an odd association: Sam had a strong wish to see the women fighting, and she was going to gratify his wish. The dream also reminded her of how left out she had felt when she was out with her parents the day before.

> "There is a fight on about Dusty. Sam's family takes him."

Dusty was the dog she wanted. In a perverse mood Sam had refused to let her have him. Associations brought out that it had been much easier to give affection to the dog than to her husband.

> "I'm in a room with two twin brothers. One says, "Why don't you divorce me and marry him so you can have children? I can't."

To begin with this dream was another variation of her wish to have two men. The novel element was the desire for a child. A subsidiary factor was the castration of the brother whom she makes unable to have children. One associaton was to the anger of her own brother, and the wish to emasculate him.

> "John, Harry, and I are having dinner. Harry leaves. John says, "I am glad."

Harry was one of the many lovers at that time; John was a casual acquaintance whom she wanted. In the dream one man again bows out, leaving the field free for her. This was part of her penis envy, the wish to beat out the man.

Discharge of Anger and Resentment

Although some resentment had always been present, it now began to come to a head, displacing in emphasis the sexual release which had predominated up to that time. A turning point came with a dream which was in marked contrast to the previous triangles.

> "Ethel K. and I and some other people are driving along in her new car, which is the color she originally wanted. A truck comes up and makes a left turn. She runs right into it and smashes the front. I say, "Oh, what a shame," and something about the insurance."

Ethel K. was a friend who had recently bought a new car, which made Alice envious. Most striking was the indifference to the crash. This indifference served to conceal her own wish to smash into the truck, which symbolized father and men in general. In other associations to the dream she stated that one of her lovers had asked her to go away with him in the summer; but she was tired of him and wanted new blood. When her husband called, she could hardly recognize his voice. She saw me as a shadowy figure. It was clear that she was now out to release her anger at men.

From here on for a long time the hours were filled with a seemingly interminable series of complaints about all the men in her life. One night she woke up at 2 in the morning, furious. She began to shout at the man who was sleeping with her (she knew him quite well): "What are you doing here? Who am I? What am I doing here? Where are we going?" In her rage she finally kicked him out of bed and out of the house.

With her lover there were now constant quarrels. He was too immature, too inconsiderate, too attached to his wife. Alternately she would wish that the wife would die or that the lover should just disappear.

Almost every new date had something wrong with him. Yet even with all this her fury remained at a rather intellectual level for the most part. Incidents such as the one where she kicked the man out of bed were quite rare. It was hard for her to give up the lifelong controls; at the same time she recognized that the men were not really doing her any harm.

For quite a while she gave way to her wish to "let me have it." On Fridays (her hours were on Monday, Wednesday, and Friday) she would have a few drinks before the session. Then she would come and tell me I didn't understand her or that I was just as cold as her father, or that this kind of analysis didn't work. Yet here too the anger never reached any marked intensity or emotional excitement.

The greatest resistance shown was in one session where she revealed that she had made a date at the same time as the next session and would have to cancel. She had been afraid to tell me earlier because it would make me angry. This led to a discussion of her fear of making people angry, which was tied up with many childhood memories. At the same time the anger was related to the wish to have me as a date rather than as an analyst.

Together with the anger at men came first a revival of good feelings about mother. After shopping with mother one Saturday, she dreamt:

> "Helen and I go shopping. We come to a flower store run by a kind of Ladies' Auxiliary. We each get a flower, gray, white, and green. She unwinds hers. I turn mine the wrong way, but I merely unwind it and start all over again. This is different from what I used to do before. They [Helen and the salesgirl] go out for a cup of coffee. I say I'll mind the store, and don't mind being left. This reminds me of the Red Cross and of how I'm different now."

Helen was a close friend whom she had recently sent to an analyst. The identification of Helen and mother was quite clear. The Red Cross incident occurred when she volunteered her services as a teenager during World War II; she was very awkward and embarrassed about the whole experience. The flower store symbolized good feelings about mother. The whole dream brought out the wish to recapture the good times with mother and grandmother. Homosexual feelings could not be reached directly, but she did bring out that her mother was constantly trying to kiss her and hug her, which she had never done when she was a child. The dream made her very happy because she saw it as a sign of strength that she could be grown-up (mind the store) while her parents went out. The working through of this material did help her to reduce the conflicts with girl friends, which in turn made it easier to share an apartment with two other girls.

But together with the good feelings about mother went a great deal of anger. Even now mother would not let her alone. Mother insisted that she come to visit every weekend; if not, she would not get a birthday present. Mother wanted to pick her clothes, fill up her time, tell her what to do and where to go. Mother could not really understand why she needed analysis.

Through all this Alice began to reevaluate what had happened with mother. Objectively she could see that mother now had relatively little effect on her life, yet the deep resentments remained. One time she bought a present for father which he could not possibly share with mother. This helped to crystallize the Oedipal conflict for her. Many memories began to fall into place. It became increasingly clear that all her triangle situations were repetitions of childhood, and that the root of her conflict with mother lay in the Oedipal rivalry.

In the transference for quite a while she wanted me to be the ally in her fight with mother. As this was consistently analyzed, the Oedipal struggle also came out more and more clearly; with the help of certain accidental circumstances in the transference, she was able to see that the deeepest root of her antagonism to mother was simply the fact that mother had father, while she did not.

Shortly before the vacation that ended the first year of analysis she had another transference dream:

> "We're at a picnic outdoors. A girl comes up to you, who knows about me. You motion to her that I'm in analysis with you; she is quiet."

This was another triangle dream, but with the important difference that now there were two women and a man, instead of two men and a woman. Thus, it is closer to her earliest childhood, before brother was born. The main wish presented is the same as that in the dream reported earlier shortly before she entered analysis: to see me socially rather than analytically. Unlike the other dream, though, this time she is preferred in the competition with the other girl. The picnic was part of her image of what I would do over the summer.

By an odd coincidence she did meet me on the subway once during the summer vacation. As so often happens with patients, the meeting left her uncomfortable and angry.

Together with the positive feelings about me went some castration wishes against her lover. In one session she dreamt:

> "Sam and I are driving along. We pass a wrecked car just like his, but it is not his."

This dream is similar to the previous one with Ethel K. It brings out her hostility in thinly disguised form: Sam's car is wrecked, but it is not done by her, and it is not really his; Sam is destroyed, then the hostility is immediately denied.

As mentioned, when she returned after the summer her

associations centered chiefly about deep resentments — of her boss, her lover, her mother, and of me. She was accepted for graduate school, which cheered her up some. This was also seen as a victory over mother, since father now took over the major part of her support, a move which, rightly or wrongly, she thought was opposed by mother. Her hatred of mother was so strong at this point that she began to contemplate switching from teaching to some other field because teaching was a sublimation of her wish to be like mother, and she wanted no part of that. One manifestation which was discussed extensively at this point was her manner of avoiding any kind of violence. It had even interfered with her professional work: she became acutely uncomfortable when she was given a class of emotionally disturbed children, and eventually had to be transferred out of there.

After much resentment had been discharged, there came another triangle dream with two women and a man.

"I'm in bed; across the room is Helen. In a window in the middle comes a man; I wave him away but he won't go, so I let him look."

Helen was the girl friend to whom she had previously associated mother. An additional element of competition with Helen centered around the latter's analyst, who never seemed to give his patients a chance to talk; Alice was particularly angry at him.

To the man she associated me. The dream was thus both a direct sexual wish to have me see her in bed, and an Oedipal wish to have me prefer her to mother (Helen). It may be noted that the window is a classical symbol for sibling rivalry.

Shortly thereafter she had a more direct transference dream:

"I'm in your office. I'm sitting up. On your desk is a tray with papers. I turn it over. You say you bought some books; I tell you you shouldn't have."

Associations to this dream were to my "intellectual" character and approach, which she saw as very similar to her father's sober medical attitude to life. The wish was to upset my intellectualizations and make everything more emotional. A number of memories came out pointing to the desire for closer emotional and physical contact with father. The negativistic attack on my papers and books was also a disguised sexual advance.

Following this came an elaborate dream which made a deeper impression on her than any before:

"I go back to the school two weeks before I'm supposed to have left. I call up sick. Then I go in the evening to pick up my car. Sam is there and Gloria [the secretary]. It is on a place near a river bank. Dr. J. has committed suicide in my car and turned it over. I call four times for help from Jerry before he finally comes."

Dr. J. was the principal at the school, whom she had hated so much. Yet even though she had left there several months before she was still dreaming about him.

The dream related otherwise to her wish to have a child. That morning she and two other students were discussing the psychology of the unmarried mother; they were fantasizing that it might be more fun to have a baby out of wedlock than to be teachers dealing with girls who did. Part of the wish to have a baby was to anger mother. To the four times she called for him she associated four children. Two weeks was the middle of her menstrual period; she was then menstruating.

The incident with Dr. J., the principal, continues the series of images about using a car to kill someone. This time he commits suicide in her car. The murderous wish against father-man comes to the fore more than ever before.

Briefly, the dream says: Rather than be a student, I would like to kill father and have a baby.

Emergence of Wish to Have a Baby

The above dream ushered in a new period in Alice's analysis, in which her dominant fantasies centered around the wish to have a baby. No doubt this might have happened anyhow, but it was stimulated by my wife's pregnancy, which sooner or later became obvious to all patients because my office and home were in one apartment. Naturally, the fantasies revolved about having my baby more than might otherwise have been the case.

At one point she dreamt:

"I'm in your office. You give me a number of cards, indicating my progress and giving me assignments. On the last one there is a note of my resistances."

Here the sexual fantasies come out in highly intellectualized form, just as had been the case with father in early childhood. In fact, for quite a while she had thought of becoming a doctor like father, and somehow she related much more easily to doctors than to other men.

In associations to cards and assignments she spoke of flowers especially. That night she woke up from her sleep to go to the bathroom, a rare event for her — her association was that Daddy often took her to the bathroom when she was a little girl.

Shortly thereafter she dreamt:

"I have to hand in an exam to Miss C. When I come to class, I realize I have the wrong one and decide to hand it in the next day."

Miss C. was her favorite instructor. A few days before Miss C. had shown great tact and delicacy in stopping the girls from talking about unmarried mothers. To the wrong exam she associated the low-cut gown she had worn to a party that weekend. The dream was a wish to return to the good mother with whom she would not have to be concerned about her sexuality.

About a week later, my daughter was born. Alice's session was scheduled for Wednesday evening. That Wednesday at about 5:30 I had to take my wife to the hospital without having time to notify my patients. Instead, I posted a sign on the door advising them that I had been called away unexpectedly, and asking them to keep their next appointment.*

* It is interesting to note that there happened to be three patients scheduled for that evening, all young unmarried girls. One married shortly thereafter, left analysis, and promptly had three children. A second maintained, incorrectly, that the baby had been born during her hour. Some years later, when she was still in analysis, she came to the sessions throughout her pregnancy, refusing to discontinue even in the ninth month. Shortly before one session her water broke; the obstetrician advised her to wait until the morning, so she came to the session anyhow. This allowed her to act out the fantasy that the baby was being born during her hour, just like mine. When her baby was born, it developed jaundice, which required a hospital stay of two weeks. As a result the patient never missed a session! The third patient was Alice; her subsequent reactions to the birth of the baby will be discussed later.

When Alice saw the note on the door, her first thought was that I was ill. On her way home she bought some cake, something which she ordinarily never did. It was like the experience in childhood when she was sick and thought that she would sleep instead of calling the doctor; sleep would drive everything away.

When she was told on Friday that my baby had been born, her rather characteristic reply was: that is a great challenge. Evidently, she was the child, waiting to see what kind of a father I would be, compared to her own.

Immediately after the birth of the baby her jealousy of the other patients became much more intense. She needed insurance in the form of being the only patient. Naturally, this was tied up with her feelings about the new baby, and about the birth of her brother. Several months later she revealed that she had been nursing a great deal of resentment because I had never shown her the baby.

The first dream after the birth was:

"We are having a dinner — Judith and boy friend, Mary and boy friend, and I. They take my liquor. I am very angry but say nothing."

Judith and Mary were fellow students, rather casual acquaintances. So far as she knew neither had a steady boy friend. The liquor stands for both milk and her drinking to loosen up her sexuality and hostilities; without this food she had to fall back on the old defense of sulky withdrawal. This dream presents a double triangle situation in which she is cut out entirely.

An even more graphic presentation of her dilemma about having a baby came out in the following dream (two weeks after the birth of my daughter):

"I am in a room where a woman is delivering. I carry empty bottles from a bookcase which is about waist high."

With this dream she introduced several symbols which persisted in one form or another to the end of the analysis. There was first of all the body image of a girl who is unable to gratify her wish to be a mother and, to a lesser extent, to feel completely feminine. The image is that of a body with empty bottles on top and a bookcase on the bottom. The empty bottles symbolize the nonfunctioning breasts. The bookcase stands for the intellectualization of her genitals. The dream represents a wish to assist my wife in the delivery, together with the self-depreciating fear that she is not up to it. Undoubtedly, this recapitulated the trauma of her brother's birth, although no conscious relevant memories appeared.

With the breakthrough of her wish to have a baby, her desires turned back to positive longings for men (father) again. By this time the transference had become so strong that it occupied the center of the stage for the remainder of the analysis. In a transference dream months later she brought out the switch and the fantasies connected with it very clearly.

"I tell Judith off. . .I'm on an island. A little way from me, across the water, is another island with a bunch of men. One jumps off the diving board but can't reach me... I am with you. The analyst has turned into two people — two hours he listens, one hour I sit up and he interprets."

Judith was her fellow student with whom she was in considerable competition. The men on the other island symbolize both her wish to have a group of men at her beck and call and her desire to keep them all at a distance. The man who dives also stands for her wish to have a man perform cunnilingus (go down) on her, which she was then in the process of working out.

After chasing away both the girl friend and the men she has me (father) all to herself. Here the symbol of two men reappears, this time one to listen and one to interpret. At a sexual level this represents the passive (listen) and aggressive (interpret) components. At this point she is reliving the stage when she wanted her father all to herself, to gratify all her desires. At the same time father is already splitting up in two: one to take care of her, the other to make love to her. This is the conflict that succeeds the Oedipal stage, and also the one that reappears in adolescence. The discrepancy in time (two hours to listen, one to interpret) indicates that to keep the man passive (supportive father) was still more important than to have him make love to her.

The working through of the transference neurosis had rather dramatic effects on Alice's life. For the first time she was able to live without a boy friend immediately available. As a result she was able to break up with several lovers she had been holding on to for fear that nobody else would come along. From now on if she went with a man for any length of time it was because there was a real spark between the two of them, and not because she needed reassurance or revenge. Further, she now felt sexually mature enough to relate to a man on a basis entirely different from what had occurred before.

In spite of, or perhaps even because of, the predominantly positive transference, in the latter part of the analysis she still had to work out a great deal of resentment. Finally she was able to reveal that she had been going around for months angry at me for not showing her my baby; it was easy enough to see that this was a scarcely veiled request to have me give her a baby.

For quite a while she began to demand group analysis instead of, or in addition to, the individual sessions. Actually, we had established long before that one of her major defenses was the ability to present a facade of perfect adjustment in a group; it was only in intimate individual situations that her anxieties appeared. This was a reflection of her early family environment, where the parents put up a front of a perfect or model family to the world, while they were at a total loss about how to handle their children's deeper feelings. In view of her ability to present such a front, it was considered technically inadvisable to put her in a group. It seemed highly probable that the transference would be worked out without introducing extraneous factors, and that did indeed turn out to be the case.

The fantasies about a group centered largely about a chance to get out all her anger; she was simply unable to bring everything out in the individual sessions. Here a kind of intellectual misunderstanding came to light; on the basis of her reading she was convinced that only if she could break out in screaming frenzies of rage at me would the analysis be able to reach a successful conclusion. I urged her to deal with her own experiences and not with any textbook preconceptions about what was supposed to happen.

Together with the emergence of her wish to be a mother went a greater awareness of her attitudes towards women; this led to a working through of many homosexual feelings. In one session she dreamt:

> "I'm talking to Miss C. She says I'm right about the consultant and that I can switch to another school if I want to. I decide to stay."

Miss C. was an instructor who had become an important figure in her life. The consultant was a man she could not tolerate. He did seem especially inept from what she reported about him, but her anger was all out of proportion, much as had been the case a few years earlier with the principal at her school. Alice-instructor (mother)-consultant (father) is another variation of the Oedipal triangle. At a deeper level she wanted mother to support her in her anger at father. The consultant also stood for me, even though she denied most of the obvious connections. Shortly thereafter she dreamt:

> "I go diving for bottle caps."

This dream uses several of the symbols described earlier: diving (going down) and bottles (breasts). The dream represents a wish to let herself go more in sex.

A few sessions later:

> "I'm with Linda in a dam. We swim in the upper part, unwilling to go down."

This is a thinly disguised homosexual dream. Linda is a casual girl friend. "Top" and "bottom" also stand for the intellectual and the emotional, the head and the body. This conflict comes out in somewhat different form in another dream:

> "I'm on the upper story of a building with no walls. They start shooting at me from the bottom."

The new elements in this dream are first the exposure (a building with no walls) of her upper part and second the dangers involved in letting go with her body.

A year after my baby was born a startling experience in the transference made her more acutely aware than ever before of the power of her unconscious drives ("shooting from the bottom"). Her hours had remained unchanged, Monday, Wednesday, and Friday. On the Wednesday closest to the baby's first birthday, i.e., almost exactly one year after the earliest session, she came in to tell me that her period was late. Since there was a realistic possibility that she might be pregnant, I offered no interpretation at that point. Friday she called to tell me that the menstrual flow had started. It was then that I pointed out the anniversary character of her response.* Typically, after discussing her feelings she said, "You should write a paper about that."

Working through the negative aspects of the transference persisted almost until the very end. At one point she dreamt:

"I go to the gypsies for a reading. It's in a dirty room. very primitive. They charge me $1 for the session, $1 for the waiting room, and $4 for a sandwich. I think it is outrageous."

No adequate associations were obtained to the money figures, but they were obviously way out of line. It was one final protest against the analyst for not giving her a child, and not gratifying her as a woman in other ways.

A few months before the end of the analysis she had an incestuous dream which surprised her:

"I'm out with Henry. He turns into my brother."

Henry was a recent date, who bore no resemblance to her brother.

After three and a half years of anlaysis she felt sufficiently changed to propose termination. Her personal relationships were much happier, even though no husband was in the offing. The sexual problem had disappeared entirely. She could feel deeply, and express her feelings without fear of criticism. Most of the resentments had been worked out. Her last dreams were interesting:

"There is another girl waiting to take my place. I let her."

Again the Oedipal situation, but the wish involved is to let the parents have their pleasure; she is content to go off on her own.

"I'm in your office and talking to you. The bookcase is where the couch is."

* Along related lines, Dr. Max Deutscher has collected data about girls' reactions to their abortions. He finds that the anniversaries of the abortions are "celebrated" by the girls in quite remarkable ways.

The "bookcase" was a recurrent symbol, as mentioned earlier; it stood for the intellect, the part of her father which she had both loved and hated. The dream is a wish to substitute an intellectual relationship for the analytic.

A few weeks after termination she sent me an exquisitely sculptured pussy cat, with a note: "I know I shouldn't, but I want to." From other sources I learned that she remarried, had a child, and felt very happy in her new life.

DISCUSSION

The first point that merits discussion is whether the case should have been terminated when it was. I did actually urge her to continue, but she was adamant. A review of what had been accomplished and what remained undone led only to some empty intellectual formulas — empty bottles, to use her symbol.

The dreams indicated a fair amount of material that had not been worked through, but then again dreams generally do. It is necessary in these cases to rely on clinical judgment rather than any artificial methods of evaluation.

In fact, the decision to terminate was more hers than mine, although I was not vigorously opposed. She had made up her mind to give herself a trip to Europe, and to terminate, and she did both.

Yet in retrospect the decision worked out well. A postanalytic integration also seems to have taken place, not as extensive as in the case of Peter (see below) but of considerable value. In order to evaluate it better some attention must be paid to the psychodynamic changes effected.

The title for this case has been deliberatley chosen: the normal woman in analysis. By all accepted cultural standards Alice represented in fact the acme of normality — that is, statistical normality. She was married, successful both scholastically and vocationally, not subject to any violently disturbing emotions.

Here is the kind of case that has been created by the advance of psychoanalytic psychology. It was primarily the sexual maladjustment that brought her to treatment, secondarily the excessive repression of all her feelings. There was no identity crisis, no sense of alienation from herself or from others. Actually, as she progressed in analysis a sense of alienation developed because she became aware of how much the people around her were hiding.

As so many others have done, she tried to overcome the parental sexual taboos by deliberate experimentation: she was "liberated." The resulting sexual experiences led to no corresponding qualitative change. Instead they produced a new dilemma: she could have sex, but could not confess to anyone that she was not enjoying it. True to her upbringing, she fell back on keeping up appearances. This broke down only when she realized how much more real emotionally the experience with the lover was than with the husband; the sex was of secondary importance. The guilt attendant upon an extramarital affair could also not be easily assuaged.

The childhood background was outwardly perfect, inwardly full of flaws. I have elsewhere suggested the formula: with an intact family look for sexual problems, with a broken family look for a security problem. That certainly applies here. The family, it could be said, was kept intact by the sexual repressions of the parents, which were passed on to the children as internalized defense mechanisms. Had she been content to make a marriage like her parents', which could well have been done with her first husband, she would never have entered analysis. But the psychological impact of the analytic doctrine that life should be an enjoyable experience was too strong for her.

The question of the advisability of termination can now be taken up again. The goals of the analysis were to free her emotionally along sexual and other lines. There can be no doubt that these goals had to a considerable extent been realized. But such a "freeing" admits of no easy quantification. Even if some attempt had been made to measure it, as with projective tests, the results would necessarily have been equivocal. Projective tests would certainly have indicated much improvement, but the question would have remained: how much?

In this situation the patient is faced by a philosophical problem: at what point should the process of internal growth be drawn into the background to make room for external reorganization of her real-life situation? This is a question which only the patient can answer; at best the analyst serves in an advisory capacity.

Ideally, a case of this kind should follow the recommedation made by Freud for analysts: to return to analysis every five years or so, in order to work out the conflicts created by new life situations. But analysts themselves have been reluctant to follow Freud's advice, unless they encounter serious problems.

When there is little suffering, the philosophical or educational impetus is rarely enough to push the person to analysis. Evidently, this is one of those cases where the patient experienced little suffering in her subsequent life struggles.

Jim,
The Drifter

Even before the first interview Jim manifested considerable anxiety. He had had no direct referral, but had merely heard
a general comment about me from one of his school instructors.
His first call had come while I was on vacation, and he was so
informed by the answering service. In spite of this, he called
several more times, and was obviously quite impatient and eager
for contact when telephone communication was finally established. His behavior in the first interview was, however, in
marked contrast to the great anxiety previously displayed; as
later appeared, he had been going through a near panic state
that was halted by the onset of therapy. Yet in the beginning he
could show none of the anxiety. In fact, as is so often the case,
the reverse occurred. The reason for coming, he said, was to
gain clarification in his vocational problems. He was at that moment unemployed, and undecided as to what to do. For the
past year he had been living on savings and taking some odd
jobs in painting. There was no pressing financial necessity for
working at that moment, but he had to find out.

After listening to more details of the history, including a
psychological examination done some three years previously, I
suggested to him that his problem was not vocational but emotional and that he should try analysis. At this he balked rather
strongly, objecting pointedly that he did not feel his problem
to be a deep-seated one. He wanted me to tell him what could

be gained by such a procedure. To this I replied that an intellectual discussion would be of little avail, but that in such cases it was customary to have a trial period of two months, at the end of which time he would have a better idea of what the analytic experience was. This he accepted. He could not come more than twice a week, ostensibly for financial reasons.

LIFE HISTORY

A review of his life history revealed that it had been pervaded by a sense of aimlessness for a period of many years. He was the second of three children; both the elder and the younger were girls. Soon after reaching adolescence a severe withdrawal pattern made itself apparent. He went to college in another city, but he dropped out before getting his degree. There was no purpose in college for him. During this period there was still some contact with his family. Then he left his home area entirely and moved to the Pacific coast, where he went to a theological school for a while and supported himself by odd jobs as cook, dishwasher, etc. Before leaving home he had had almost no dates with girls, and no sexual experience of any kind. In the Pacific city he went steady with a girl for some time, but was too frightened to have any physical contact. In this period he had one brief homosexual experience, when he was masturbated by an older man.

The theological studies were abandoned and soon thereafter he was inducted into the Army. Almost from the first day he showed tremendous resentment. He would not march, he would not drill, he would not obey. Because of a hearing deficiency he was assigned to limited service; here too he rebelled at the work assigned to him. His resentment mounted, and he finally had a severe anxiety reaction for which he was hospitalized. For months he remained in the military hospital, crying all the time. There was no pyschotic ideation; it was a breakthrough of so much of the feeling stored up over a lifetime. No treatment was given during his hospital stay. After several months he was discharged from the service, with no disability pension because it was decided that his hearing deficiency antedated the Army. Typically, he was indifferent to this decision and made no attempt to appeal it.

After discharge, he did not return home, but remained in the city in Texas where he had been stationed. The Army doctors had advised him to seek out Army psychiatric treatment; he could see no necessity for it. He spent his time drinking, gambling, and with women. One Wac he remembered from this period was very sweet on him, but as usual he was indifferent. At this time he had his first heterosexual experiences, with a prostitute, and, curiously, he reported no difficulties. When his money ran out, he left Texas and returned home. Significantly, although he was now living in the same city, he shunned his family, particularly his mother.

Vocationally, his situation improved. He took some business training and succeeded in clerical-administrative work. But it did not take him long to feel dissatisfied, and he drifted through several jobs. He finished college, though still with no idea of what he wanted to do.

Emotionally, the outstanding change in the postwar period was an active homosexual life. He went to live with a gifted artist whom he admired very much, who he said opened up a whole new world for him. The sexual contact was confined largely to mutual masturbation. After breaking up with this friend, he repeated a similar relationship with another strong personality, also a creative individual. This too ended in an unsatisfactory way. During all this time he avoided any close contact with girls.

There followed another trip away from his native city to a university some distance away. His goals were so vague that he was not encouraged to continue, and he returned to New York. It was at that point that he sought out help.

Some years prior to consulting me, he had gone for vocational guidance, at which time he had been given some tests. He was advised to return to college, which he did, but, of course, no personality change occurred. The psychological examination proved in the course of therapy to be remarkably accurate. It made the following points about the patient:

"1. High intelligence potential. 2. Very unrealistic. 3. Had no long-view goals. 4. Considerable evidence of posttraumatic emotional experience. 5. Full of guilt feelings and fluctuates

between anxiety or depression or both. 6. Rebellious and negativistic. 7. Feels exposed and vulnerable. 8. Compulsively defensive. 9. Feels rejected and has a great need for being accepted.
10. Affective relations extremely amateurish. 11. Pronounced
difficulty in sex identification with possible marked homosexual
involvement. 12. Jumps into situations impetuously — imprac-
tically. 13. Seems to be suffering from organic or physiologic
problems or subject to psychosomatic complaints; may be fear
of results of masturbation."

COURSE OF THERAPY

With such a history the first point that had to be understood was the resistance to therapy. He was after all a highly
intelligent person with some knowledge of modern psychology.
He had had a nervous breakdown in the Army, for which treatment had been recommended and refused. His lifelong experiences had been ones of inadequancy, blocking, and frustration
in all major areas of living. Most of his life he had felt subjectively quite miserable. Objectively he knew that many people
with such conflicts were helped by psychotherapy; in fact at
one time he had even thought of becoming a social worker.
Why, then, had he fought therapy so strongly? Even in this
analytic situation he had begun, so to speak, on the sidelines.
He had come for "vocational guidance." Initially he had not
known that I was an analyst; he thought of me only as a clinical psychologist. In fact, had he known it, he might not have
come. He did not see the need for more intensive treatment or
more frequent visits. Actually, he said, he was just coming to
see what this was all about, and did not know how long he
would stay.

As the analyst repeatedly called attention to the discrepancy between the severity of his problems and the reluctance to
do anything about them, it gradually dawned on the patient
that his life up to that time had been pretty aimless, and that he
really had no idea of how he could go about changing this sense
of aimlessness on his own. It also became clear to him that this
aimlessness had been with him for a long time. The unnecessar-
ily long trip to go to college he could now see as a needless de-

tour. When he left college without a degree, it was because there
was no purpose in anything. Various enthusiasms had temporarily covered up the feeling of aimlessness. For a while it was a
famous professor in college. Later it was Zionism. In the Army
he had really let himself go emotionally — particularly in drinking and gambling. After the Army it was homosexuality. That
too passed. At the time the analysis was beginning, it was masturbation and movies. Outside of these two pastimes everything
was frustrating and disappointing, and all the passions of the
past had been forgotten.

To trace the meaning of this aimlessness then became the
central topic for him in therapy. It did not take long for him to
see that his conflicts derived from the lifelong battle with his
mother. The patient, who at the time of beginning treatment
was thirty-seven years old, had very vivid memories of his mother and her domineering ways. For quite a while the complaints
poured out in an almost never-ending stream; in milder form
they continued until the end of therapy. For the first six years of
the patient's life the family had lived on a farm in Pennsylvania,
but the father had no talent for farming and they had to return
to New York. The father then went to work for the mother's
brother, who, according to the patient, was a modern Simon
Legree. After many years of this drudgery, the parents bought a
small candy store which they still had at the time he came to
see me. This prospered because, it was said, the mother took
over. She had sole charge of the cash register because the father
had once paid a bill which turned out to be not due. Ever since
the mother had redoubled her vigilance, because if left in the
father's hands the business would go to rack and ruin. The father was deprived of the right to handle money.

In the household the mother also bossed the father completely. She even prepared his food down to the last slice of
bread and butter, and he was obligated to eat it. Several times
once even during the time the patient was in therapy — the fa
ther had simply thrown his plate out in toto, in protest against
being spoon-fed. The protest did not last.

Extreme vigilance was practiced by the mother to see to it
that the daughters did not stray from the righteous path. Her
suspiciousness was so great that when they went swimming, the

father was ordered to go along secretly and make sure that no wrong was done. It was no wonder that the older sister was reported to be dull or feeble-minded, and had dropped out of school at an early age. The younger sister seemed to have escaped relatively unscathed.

The patient felt very bitter towards his mother. When he was a child she used to beat him severely; against this he built up a "hard-shell" defense. His greatest victory came when his mother beat him with a strap and he could hold back his crying. He was force-fed. No interest was shown in his schooling; his mother could see no point in buying a book for him. He had no close friends, because he could not bring them home. The household, as he remembered, was one with no cohesiveness; everybody lived in an isolated world. His mother, he felt, had great contempt for him; she compared him unfavorably with his cousins, many of whom became successful professional men, and predicted that he would come to no good end. The mother permitted herself no enjoyment of any kind. She lived near the store and never left the neighborhood. By the time he was grown up, the parents had amassed a considerable sum of money, which he contemptuously referred to as "mattress money"; it was merely saved, never spent.

Outside of an occasional outburst, such as the one described above when he threw out his food, the father had only one defense against the mother — increasing religiosity. He chose a synagogue where it was forbidden for women to be in the same section as the men. The mother, incensed at this segregation over which she had no control, refused to go at all, and the father thus acquired a sanctuary where he could be away from his wife.

It was easy for the patient to see that with his rebellion (throwing out food, leaving mother, rejecting women, rejecting love) and pursuit of learning, he was imitating his father, for whom he felt considerable sympathy. It was also quite obvious that many of his character traits had developed as ways of handling his mother. The inability to feel served to stifle the resentment he felt towards her. He could not get close to other people (including the therapist) becuase they might repeat what his mother had done. Women were taboo because of the ever watchful maternal eye; and in fact he had to be thousands of miles away from her in order to be able to go out with women at all. He had to lie about himself to others (he would tell them that he had been married at one time) for fear that they would otherwise scold him unduly as his mother had done. The aimlessness derived from many causes: it was at one and the same time a rebellion against the mother, who had of course always urged him to be successful, an opportunity to release some gratification, and superego punishment for the rebellion and the gratification.

While these initial insights allowed him to make more sense of his life then ever before, they were still highly intellectual and in theory would produce no deep or lasting effect. During the two-month exploratory period, which ended quite successfully in that he could see his need for analysis and determined to finish it, a number of transference resistances came out and were analyzed. First of all, he experienced deep resentment toward the analyst, especially when any interpretation was given not to his liking. At other times, he recognized, such resentment would have led him to break off the relationship. Here he could see that the resentment toward his mother was being carried over inappropriately, and he changed his reaction accordingly. Bringing this resentment to consciousness helped him for the first time in his life to see the dynamics of his repetitious withdrawal; frustration led to anger which led to withdrawal, since the aggression towards his mother always had to be inhibited.

At the same time he showed great ambivalence about the manner in which he paid the fee. Sometimes it was by the session, sometimes by the week, sometimes every two weeks, but almost every week it was different. Analysis of this ceaseless variation brought out several significant points. He was not short of money. In fact, he had a sizable amount saved up, again something he did not want people to know; it was his own "mattress money." Yet he never kept much with him. He liked to go to the bank and make withdrawals of small sums. For a period he did this several times a day until things came to such a pass that the bank asked him to transfer his account. This made him very angry with the bank; they made enough money on him, paid him only 2½%, and ought to serve him. It thus became apparent that the bank was like a mother who should always have the food ready for him whenever he came to eat, and should make no demands on him. Underneath the hatred of the bad mother lay the yearning for the good mother, and it was only when this hidden yearning was brought to light in the transference situation that any real change could be effected. By switching the manner of payment of the fee all the time, he was testing the analyst out to see what kind of a mother he would be.

After the withdrawal, resentment, and testing, the next transference manifestation that came to light was the transfer of omnipotence. The analyst became a magical figure who could by a wave of his finger solve all the patient's problems. This first came to light in a dream shortly after analysis began: "I go to a dentist, a woman; she drills my teeth." In associations to this dream, the dentist was described as a woman of about thirty. To the drilling he associated the analyst. The dentist is made into a woman to facilitate sexual contact. Often we find that the first dream in analysis combines the core of the patient's neurotic problem, together with its attempted solution. Here too this would seem to be the case. He wants to be drilled by a woman; the sore tooth is symbolic of his inadequate self and body image; the drilling makes him a passive recipient of sex (in contrast to the male role). Dentist-analyst-lover are all one, who again makes no demands on him and gratifies his passivity.

The uncovering of his omnipotent wishes brought forth much new material. When he was about ten, he conceived the idea of reading through the entire library and getting to know everything, just as father's only weapon against mother was the holy books of religion which led to the all-powerful Deity. It did not take long to shatter this illusion of omniscience, and it was then that he began to transfer the omnipotence. When the sexual problem of puberty was reached, he fantasized a powerful oriental man who would take him aboard a ship and use him to satisfy his desires. (This fantasy came close to realization in his first homosexual experience.) At college he worshiped a very famous professor, yet felt inadequate to approach him or to study with him. In theology school again a famous man was his idol, and again he could not approach him. His homosexual experiences were all with stronger, more powerful male figures who could introduce him to many unexplored intellectual fields. He had some interest in literature; at one time he had done a little writing, then stopped. Typically he fancied that he would be a critic, and he picked for critical study several famous American women novelists whose entire background stood in marked contrast to his mother's.

The search for the omnipotent figure and the feeling of frustration consequent upon this search also provided a most significant clue to his all-pervading sense of aimlessness. To have a meaningful life one must regain the all-powerful analyst-mother; variations on this theme were numerous and took much time to work through. In one dream the analyst introduced him to some famous chess players, and then put him to bed. In another dream when he came to the session the analyst opened the door and ushered out a beautiful young girl for his benefit.

From time to time the flow of free associations would be impeded by the persistent question: "What do you think?" he would ask me. Gradually it became clear that the patient felt he had no right to say independent opinions or feelings. For a while the analyst became the only thing in life that mattered. Everything was aimless. When I went on vacation Jim counted the days until my return. And he fantasized that I would spend my vacation time writing papers — a transfer of his own incapacity for enjoyment combined with a wish that the analyst should be thinking of him all the time (the ever-vigilant mother). Only gradually did he come to see that greater participation by himself would bring more fruitful results, that the analysis was a cooperative enterprise, not a dictatorial one.

The last, and most enduring, manifestation of the wish to make the analyst God was excessive gratitude. At the end of every hour Jim would say, "Thank you." Even when this had been analyzed time and time again he continued to repeat it. Analysis revealed three components of this excessive gratitude: self-depreciation, transfer of omnipotence, and attempted cover-up of any anger he might feel toward the analyst.

In varying measure, and in one form or another, these continued to come up throughout the course of treatment.

The self-depreciation was seen to be another important source of his withdrawal. He felt sure he would be defeated, and therefore developed the formula "If I don't play, I can't lose." Although compulsive masturbation was one of his main complaints in the early part of analysis, he completely denied any connection between the masturbation and sexual frustration. The masturbation was free of fantasy, it was a purely mechanical stimulation. The absolute denial of any sexual desire naturally required analysis. No insight dawned upon him, however, until he had relived an experience from earlier days. Several years before, in another city, he had been friendly with a group of people in analysis, for whose attachment to their analyst he had nothing but contempt. One of these people was a girl who had a great need to "make" every man she came across. Inevitably the patient, who acted indifferent to her, became a great object of desire. She did everything she could to get him to have sex, even to appearing before him in the nude, and going to bed with another man while he was in the next room and could readily surmise what was going on. Consciously the patient felt great contempt for this girl, yet continued to visit her rather regularly. He could now see that his behavior in this situation had a double root. On the one hand he derived gratification from rejecting the eager woman (revenge on mother). On the other hand he could now admit that he had some sexual desire for her, and that this desire could come out only when he was physically thousands of miles away from his mother. Consequently he could see that his vehement denial of sexual desire to the analyst was again a transference of feelings which were called out by his mother.

With this memory and transference insight the sexual feelings began to break through. One dream was:

"I am at a party with Sally, Henry, and others. I leave with Sally. I get an erection. She says, "I'll go to your room." Then I bring up the moral problem."

Sally was a woman who had been interested in him for a number of years; he had, however, never reciprocated. Henry was an old homosexual partner; he was still friendly with him, but there was no longer any physical contact betweeen the two.

The similarity between this dream and his behavior some years before did not escape him. He wants the girl to approach him; when she does he rejects her on "moral" grounds. At the same time here the sexual desire breaks through ("I get an erection.") With this dream the general defensive pattern of the denial of feeling became a matter of concern to the patient. For some time he could make little headway with the problem. Then he suddenly had another dream which proved to be quite a shock:

> "I'm out in the country with my family. I'm walking up on a ledge; they're down below. I'm in a square. My father is driving a car; he has my mother and sister in it. He drives clumsily and crashes into a house. But they're safe."

He awoke frightened. While there were a number of familiar elements in this dream, the new feature was the violence of his emotion; he had not believed it possible. One of his associations to the dream was the wish that his parents would die, which again brought home to him the repression of his feeling life, and the psychic dangers involved in releasing it. At the same time he could also see that when he would allow no feelings to break through, life indeed could be a meaningless and aimless affair.

After these dreams and the concomitant transference material, the severity of the superego was sufficiently mitigated to permit him to seek out contacts with women. Characteristically he became interested in Sally, who had been a great admirer of his for many years. He had to be certain there would be no rejection before he could allow himself to feel more deeply.

Not long after, in the second year of analysis, he had his first heterosexual experience. Typically, when he reported it he showed no emotion. When this was pointed out, he revealed particularly his fear of his former homosexual partner and of his mother's biting tongue. By this time, however, he had considerable insight into his superego formation and these anxieties could be disposed of. A most surprising development was the absence of any lasting sexual problems with Sally. Here was a man who established his first lasting relationship with a woman at the age of thirty-eight, after a lifetime of inadequacy, compulsive masturbation, and homosexuality. Yet apart from some prematurity in the beginning he had fully satisfactory orgasms and his partner did too. Whether this is to be ascribed to the analysis or not is certainly hard to say.

A general loosening of the personality set in. He became much more relaxed. His job, which had hitherto been an impossible chore, became much more acceptable. The deep dissatisfaction with everything in his life disappeared. He would come in beaming, and often remark at the beginning of the hour that the world was a wonderful place. His hostility toward his family became manageable. The central problem for some time then became the working out of his relationship with Sally. As was to be anticipated, certain resentments cropped up, especially once when she was sick. Dreams for a while pointed to some protest. For example, in one:

"I'm in an Army barracks. A sergeant is ordering us to do calisthenics. I can do it, but choose not to."

The day residue and associations pointed particularly to the job, where he was acting in a rather provocative manner, such as making snide remarks about his superior, and narrowly avoiding trouble. These conflicts were also worked through.

After some twenty months of analysis he felt that he had come far enough to marry, and also to think of termination. Dreams and conscious material again showed a transfer of omnipotence to the women. For example:

"I'm in a synagogue. Sally is off to one side of the Torah, where the men usually are, leading the service. The others try to shout her down. I protest."

From the associations it appeared that Sally had succeeded where his mother had failed. He had reconciled himself with the good mother. Although there certainly was a strong element of dependency in his feelings about Sally, it was not the kind of dependency which seemed to lead to any conflict. In the year or so in which he could be observed with her it seemed to be in every respect an ideal relationship. Sally was past the child-bearing age, but she had a nine-year old son, to whom he became very devoted.

Towards the end of the treatment the psychological tests were repeated. The two Rorschachs, administered by the same examiner at an interval of about five years, furnished an excellent basis for evaluation. Forgoing changes for the better became evident from the comparison.

With his marriage the analysis was terminated. It had lasted about two years. The termination left the road open for further treatment if he at any time felt the wish for it, although it was not anticipated that under ordinary circumstances any great need would arise.

DISCUSSION

Clinically, a dramatic change had occurred in the patient. When he came for treatment he was emotionally inadequate, vocationally crippled, given to overt homosexuality, perhaps a borderline psychotic (some would classify his Army breakdown as a psychotic episode). When he left, his emotional life was highly positive, full of love and constructive activities. He was better off vocationally than ever before; he had achieved orgastic potency and established a satisfactory heterosexual love relationship.

In view of the excellent result achieved, which is often enough much harder to duplicate in similar cases, we are led to inquire what the therapeutically effective factors were here. I would stress three: First of all, the vicissitudes of the transference relationship were consistently analyzed. Second, the patient had already gone through such excesses of hostility in the course of his life that he sedulously and consciously avoided too much of them in the analysis. Third, the patient came in a state of acute anxiety. He had already had one breakdown in his life and was most eager to avoid another. Hence, the analysis moved for him in a kind of life-or-death atmosphere. He listened with the greatest of intentness to every sentence and every word I uttered. Whatever insights were gained were worked out with dispatch. On looking back one can say that he was so eager to learn that few sessions were felt by him to be unfruitful.

Holly,
The Abandoned Woman

Holly had come to analysis on a New Year's Day, panicky because she had just been abandoned by the man to whom she had been betrothed for a year. Her anxiety in the beginning was so great that she had asked for the first session on an emergency basis.

LIFE HISTORY

As is so often the case, the rejection was highly traumatic because of the unhappy life history that preceded it. Holly was the older of two siblings, the other being a girl seven years younger. Presently her parents were divorced and the mother remarried, but this had been preceded by years of bitterness and quarreling.

Father was a small businessman from eastern Europe. In his native country he had prospered, but the war clouds of the Hitler era forced him to emigrate in the 1930's. Eventually he found his way to Cuba, where Holly and her sister were both born.

On his arrival in Cuba father was married to another woman, by whom he had two children. This first marriage was evidently quite unhappy. Not long after his arrival father fell in love with Holly's mother. In order to marry her he divorced his first wife, who then went off to Israel with the two children, both boys, where they had been ever since. Holly knew the names of her half brothers, but nothing else about them.

Businesswise, father prospered in Cuba, but both his health and his marriage deteriorated badly. In his early forties he developed a peptic ulcer, perhaps as a result of the continual friction with his wife, who refused to cook the foods prescribed by the physician. For a long time Holly did most of the cooking, and cared for him in other ways. In his fifties he had a heart attack, which incapacitated him further. He regarded it as right and proper that Holly should take care of him in his illnesses, especially since his wife openly rejected him.

When Holly was about eighteen, mother finally left father entirely, and came to this country. Shortly thereafter, partly as a result of the unstable conditons, the rest of the family followed.

It was never entirely clear how father managed to make a living in this country. He worked only occasionally. He did have a wealthy brother, who may have supported him. Because of his health father moved to California. Once there he made constant demands that Holly come and take care of him. When things went badly with her, she was sorely tempted to accede to his request.

Father acted towards her like a stern parent of the old school. She was to obey him, and if she did not obey, he had the right to beat her. Physical punishment was meted out all through her childhood, once even when she was in her twenties. Although rebellious, Holly remained attached to him. In spite of her own constant financial distress, she even sent him money from time to time. In the family structure she was definitely "Daddy's girl," and no matter what happened, she derived considerable emotional sustenance from that image.

Mother, who was considerably younger than father, was a source of constant shame and humiliation to Holly. Throughout her childhood it was widely rumored that mother had a number of lovers. Mother neither denied this nor admitted it. She did constantly scream at father that he was not a real man, which Holly interpreted to mean that he was impotent.

Perhaps because she was Daddy's girl, mother definitely favored the younger sister, Clara, and had little use for Holly. She did not even like to cook for Holly, usually considering rice and eggs to be good enough for her. Not infrequently the fights between mother and daughter became quite violent, and sometimes the two actually came to blows. Since Holly was the first born, the mother may have blamed her for having to stay in the marriage.

Mother openly conveyed to Holly a hard, cynical attitude towards men. "Use them for what you can get, then get rid of them" was her consciously espoused philosophy. Men are good for only one thing, to support women.

With such a philosophy, it is not surprising that mother deserted father entirely when his illnesses became too severe. She did not want to be tied down to a sick old man.

Once in this country, mother dated a number of men. When Holly came here and discovered what her mother was doing, she felt ashamed and humiliated. Eventually the mother remarried, making no bones of the fact, even to her husband, that her major motive for marriage was that she did not want to work. Her second husband, Philip, proved acquiescent up to a point. When she demanded that he name her as beneficiary in his life insurance, he agreed, but when she demanded a cash settlement of $5,000 to make her feel comfortable he refused. Nevertheless, mother remained in the marriage. She continually complained to Holly about how stingy her new husband was, and constantly urged her daughter to squeeze whatever she could out of men.

Holly remembered her childhood as an unmitigated horror. One of her earliest memories was of going to the roof all alone, where she would daydream of a nice quiet house in the country, away from all the fighting and screaming. In reality her major outlet became school, where she did well. As will be seen, this later became the source of constant conflict, but eventually of brilliant success.

Apparently mother's bark was worse than her bite, since Holly was permitted to hit her in the course of their fights. In fact, it seemed as if there was more physical punishment from her father than from mother.

Feeling herself ugly and skinny, Holly cried a lot about her fate when she was a child. In fact, the crying continued throughout the entire analysis; tears came easily to her.

One of the few pleasant memories of childhood represented a typical combination of gratification and punishment. Sunday mornings, when there was no work, she would manage to steal 50¢ from her father and sneak out to go horseback riding. The parents did not know where she was and would send out panicky alarms. When she came back after a few hours she was invariably beaten for her disobedience. Father did not want her to ride a horse because she might "hurt herself."

There were boys throughout childhood, in spite of the severe restrictions father placed upon her. Her earliest experience was at the age of seven, when a boy had anal intercourse with her. In the analysis at first she thought of this as traumatic, later she recognized the pleasure she got out of it.

When she was twelve the fights with mother reached such a fever pitch that she was sent away to New York, where father's brother lived (the same brother who later supported him). Here she enjoyed school, but felt herself to be somewhat of an outsider in her aunt's house.

When she returned to Cuba, the situation was no better. But since she was now an adolescent, the fights were no longer so terrifying. Further, since father's business was carried out at home, she began to help him with some of the minor manufacturing operations. Much of her free time away from school was spent in father's shop assisting him. It was at this time that she also learned to cook for father, which her mother refused to do, so that for several years she was taking mother's place in many respects.

Dating in this period was quite sporadic. There was one boy she was quite interested in when she was about fifteen, but he dropped her after a brief romance, thereby setting a pattern for future relationships. Mostly, however, she was too preoccupied with father to think very much of boys of her own age.

When mother finally left Holly was alone with father for about a year, finishing school and taking care of him. In this period she was completely devoted to him, scarcely paying attention to her life outside. One incident from this time came up repeatedly in the analysis. One night she was tired and lay down on father's bed to take a nap. He too came to rest; since this happened frequently she paid no attention to it. Several hours later she awoke, horrified, to find father's arm around her. Again she wished to attach "traumatic" significance to this experience until she became aware of her own wishes.

Her life in New York was quite stormy. First of all, she did not know where to live. Successively she tried uncle and mother, but neither was satisfactory. Finally she took an apartment that she shared with several other girls whom she had never known before. This kind of arrangement produced other conflicts, which were not really resolved until near the end of the analysis.

Since she had done well in school, she wanted to continue, though without any clear idea of what she wanted. She was admitted to the city university, but without any credit for the additional work that she had done in her home country. In school here she did badly. At some point during the term she would generally get very depressed and drop out entirely, not only losing all credit but getting a series of F's which hampered her in her further schooling. In all she passed only a few courses. By the time she came to analysis she could be readmitted to a free university only under many conditions, compliance with which seemed virtually impossible. Nevertheless, she dreamt constantly of getting back to school to get her degree.

Work likewise showed a history of ins and outs. She found that she had various skills, particularly secretarial and accounting, but that she could not hold a job for long. Depression would set in fairly soon, and she would quit. Fortunately, times were good and she could get a new job almost as quickly as she had lost the old one.

The drifting caused by the recurrent depressions affected her in many ways. A car seemed to be all-important in her life. She would buy one, take on a huge debt, then have to sacrifice it; this too went on a number of times.

Naturally, her prime drive remained the romantic one, and her life, before and during analysis, centered successively on a series of different men. About a year after coming here, when she was nineteen, she met Herman, an unemployed actor, with whom she promptly fell in love. With Herman she had her first extended sexual relationship.

But Herman turned out to have a refractory sexual problem — most of the time he was unable to ejaculate. Holly, of course, thought this was her fault, an opinion which he reinforced. This was the first of many relationships in which the man made her feel guilty about what was happening, and she masochistically acquiesced. Clearly this was a continuation of her Oedipal conflict with father.

Because of her guilt, as well as her need to be different from mother, Holly did everything she could to help Herman with his problem. In the beginning he did ejaculate occasionally. She became pregnant, and had an abortion without his knowledge. She supported him by working as a waitress since he wanted to leave himself open for a call from the theater. But nothing ever clicked for him.

Sexually likewise she tried to handle everything. She would play with his penis for hours, sucking him, and doing anything else that he liked. But nothing helped; he could not ejaculate.

After several months he began to hit her, blaming her more and more for his difficulties. This was the final straw. The relationship had begun in July, marriage shortly thereafter. In November she left him, and in January the marriage was annulled. The whole episode, which later filled her with a deep sense of shame, was concealed from everybody, including her own family.

The restaurant where she had been working as a waitress was owned by an older man, Arnold, in his forties, who was separated from a wife and two children living in another city. It offered her a perfect Oedipal gratification, and after the breakup with Herman an affair soon started. In this affair for the first time in her life she experienced continual sexual gratification, since Arnold proved to be a very good lover. It was in this period, when she felt herself loved and wanted, that she finished some of her college courses.

But Arnold tired of her after a few months. He was willing to keep her on as a waitress, at which she was very competent, but such a situation would have been too painful for her, so she left. There followed a long series of jobs, in each of which she would do well, suddenly get depressed, and quit. As an ace in the hole she could always work for her uncle, which she did several times.

After Arnold came a fleeting series of dates with a young student by the name of Stewart. However, Stewart was evidently too timid to approach her sexually, so the relationship remained platonic. She found him too passive in other ways as well, but at least he was a date when nobody else was around.

After Stewart came Juan, a Mexican physician who had a residency in surgery in this country. With Juan there was an intense love feeling on both sides, stimulated among other things by the fact that they had the same native language.

Juan too turned out to be a good lover, and they found one another agreeable in many other ways. Thoughts of marriage began to arise in her. But now her deep sense of shame came to the fore. If he knew about Herman, what would he think? This could be concealed, since not even her close family knew anything about it. Her mother, however, could not be hidden. Sooner or later he would find out about her, and then the marriage would be canceled. In the meantime Juan treated her in the typical manner in which a Spaniard treats his *novia*. He called her every day, saw her as much as he could. Her happiness was diluted only by the constant torment that he would find out about her mother. Since her mother now lived far out of town, there was no real occasion to introduce them. Someday, though, she knew, they would have to meet, and that would be the end.

Sure enough, the day arrived. It had no effect whatsoever on Juan. But in Holly the fears were redoubled.

Actually a much more difficult stumbling block was Juan's mother, who made frequent trips to New York to visit her beloved son. This woman was determined that her physician offspring should marry a girl of excellent family who could offer him many financial and social advantages. The Oedipal drama was repeated; Holly found an enemy in Juan's mother.

All this may have had some effect on Juan, or, more likely, his own overattachment to his mother may have come into play here. He began to find less and less time for Holly. Since he was a surgical resident he had an excellent alibi: either he had to be at the hospital because he was on call or he was suddenly called upon to operate. Once in the operating room he could no longer be reached by telephone.

While all this was true, she suspected that he was tiring of her and switching to other girls, which turned out to be true.

Finally matters came to a head when he refused to invite her to spend New Year's Eve with him, using surgery again as a convenient excuse. When she protested, he decided that they might as well break up. It was this break-up which precipitated her into analysis.

COURSE OF ANALYSIS

The analysis was conducted at a frequency of two sessions per week, because of her financial situation. Later it was increased to three per week. It lasted four years.

Since Holly's main concern was with her view of herself as an abandoned woman, the treatment necessarily centered on a series of love affairs which went on during the analysis. Almost inevitably, this concentrated the analytical material on everyday events, rather than fantasies or childhood memories. Recollections from childhood were brought up mainly to illuminate what was currently going on, in spite of the analyst's persistent attempts to get her to understand her childhood better. As so often happens, in spite of the haphazard production of material she did acquire a good understanding of how her life had gone. With the exception of her relationship to mother and contacts with girl friends, the analysis can most readily be handled by reference to the various men who dominated her even in these years.

Aftermath of the Abandonment by Juan

In the beginning her associations were dominated by her affair with Juan. Why had he abandoned her? They could have had such a wonderful life together. Now everything was hopeless.

His main reason must have been the mother; his mother would never let him marry into a family in which there was a woman like her mother. Although she had been careful to keep him away from her mother, that had not been entirely possible. The few encounters must have soured him on her. No trace of conscious resentment against him was to be found at this point (that did come out later); it was all her fault, and above all her mother's.

With such a mother she would never be able to marry. Here she recalled especially mother shouting at the top of her lungs that father was impotent, and her deep sense of shame all through childhood about having such a mother. Alternately she would decide to cut herself from mother entirely or, out of guilt and longing, to pay her a visit which usually ended in more fighting and mutual recriminations.

At first mother had agreed to pay for her therapy, even though she had no real idea of what it was about. After a few months she stopped, alleging that she did not have the money. Since she always boasted of how well off her new husband was, Holly did not believe her plea of poverty; she ascribed it, probably with justice, to mother's hostility to her.

The relationship with mother was also kept up because she felt much affection for her younger sister Clara. Typically she put herself in mother's shoes, complaining that Clara was in a bad way because of neglect by mother. It did indeed seem to be true that mother was doing as poorly with her younger daughter as with her older. Nevertheless, Clara saw herself as mother's child, and behaved ambivalently about Holly's efforts to help. Clara would ask her older sister for advice, then refuse to follow it. For example, at one point Holly arranged an appointment with a therapist which Clara simply refused to keep. Eventually Clara tended to side increasingly with her mother's resentment of Holly.

Mother even in this period continued to behave in an ambivalent manner towards her older daughter. At times she would warmly invite her out for a visit, and give her a little money. Then again she would refuse to let her visit a party given by some close relative by telling the relative that Holly was too busy to go. Eventually this would get back to Holly, who would be furious.

A fair amount of material here and throughout related to her varied roommates. In order to save money Holly would take an apartment larger than she needed and rent out part of it to other girls, whom she solicited by newspaper advertisements. No roommate managed to last very long. Very quickly arguments would develop, often set off by some peculiarity on the part of the other girl. For instance, one girl insisted on keeping all the food bought by the two separate, which was manifestly impossible in a small three-room apartment. This led to incessant quarrels about whose egg was whose.

No unconscious homosexuality came to the fore directly, either in fantasies or in dreams. It could only be offered as a general interpretation on occasion, which naturally carried little weight. Nothing came out in the history pointing to any strong homosexual trends. The only evidence in fact was the constant need to battle with one woman after another. Once even after a roommate had moved out, Holly deliberated for quite a while whether or not she should demand part of the security to compensate for wear and tear on her dishes and linen. The girl understandably refused, which led to much acrimony. Later the quarrel was patched up and the two remained friends.

The closest that she came to any homosexual impulses was with one roommate, Helen, of whom she was particularly fond. When Helen married and moved out, Holly was genuinely sorry. One night she had a nightmare:

"I spent the night in the dream killing people with a knife, but they would not die and whatever organ I attacked regenerated before my eyes. The feeling of terror that finally woke me up was either seeing the knife fly through the air coming to cut me in half or the feeling that I was being cut in half."

The dream woke her up in a panic. She called Helen in the middle of the night, asking if she could come over. Helen permitted her to come and stay there for the rest of the night.

The nightmare represented the rage at father and Helen's new husband, whom she wished to castrate. However, the castrating knife was turned against herself, which induced panic. Among other things this dream and its attendant circumstances showed the repressed hatred of father which still affected her relationships with men.

Towards the analyst her feelings initially were quite ambivalent. Wary of all men by now, she did not know what to make of him. Little material appeared in the beginning. She kept her hours punctually, talked freely, and paid her fees regularly, as agreed upon. For the sympathetic interest shown her by the analyst she seemed grateful, yet she kept her distance.

Since she had begun on a New Year's Day, the duration of her analysis could readily be timed. The next New Year she quipped: "This is our first anniversary." Then unexpectedly she began to come late, fifteen minutes, twenty minutes. Life was depressing, and she could see little point to the analysis. One day she did not show up at all; a few hours later she called to say that she had forgotten the hour entirely.

When she came in the next session, she had no idea why she had forgotten the session. Only a vague dream appeared:

"I'm angry at the mechanic fixing my car."

It was easy enough to interpret this as a transference dream. This interpretation brought forth a surprising bit of information. Shortly after the first session she had begun a sexual affair with a fellow by the name of Clyde. With Clyde, who worked as a lathe operator, she felt nothing in common except sex. She had picked him up in a singles bar, and gone to bed with him immediately. Thereafter they met regularly to have sex; occasionally they would go to the movies, but nothing else. This went on for several months, then she had suddenly dropped him because a sexual relationship alone was not enough for her.

The question naturally arose, What was her need to conceal the whole Clyde affair from me? She wanted me to think well of her, and if I knew how loose she was sexually, I would condemn her. Further inquiry along these lines revealed that she had, since coming to this country, on occasion picked men up whom she did not know and had sex with them. Sometimes she would see them again, sometimes not. At this point she was really panicky, certain that I would stop the analysis.

It was clear that there was more. The request for more associations brought out two repetitive significant fantasies which she had never been able to tell me before. In one she is sitting in the subway, spots a handsome man, gives him a sign that she is willing, and they go off to have sex together. In the other she is sitting in the movies, a man comes and sits down next to her. He begins to feel her up. She offers no resistance. Gradually he reaches her clitoris and fingers her to orgasm. She is ecstatic, but says nothing. Then they go off somewhere and have intercourse.

Revelation of these two fantasies led to other material. In sex she could only reach orgasm through the stimulation of her clitoris; intercourse that did not involve the clitoris did not satisfy her. Memories of some childhood sexual experiences came up here which have been mentioned before, particularly the intercourse in her behind when she was seven and the incident with her father, when he put his arm around her while they were asleep in the same bed.

Another new memory came up here. When she reached puberty, she became friendly with another girl, Sylvia, who was quite promiscuous. For hours she would listen to Sylvia's stories, fascinated. Sometimes she would fantasize doing the same thing, but as long as she remained in Cuba she never did. Sylvia had also emigrated to the United States and the two saw one another occasionally.

All these revelations were used first to clarify the transference distortion and second to help her alter her image of herself as an abandoned woman. What was bothering her underneath the rejection was her own sexually promiscuous wishes; the battle was really between her desires and her superego. She saw me as a superego, similar to the Puritanical father. Her jealousy of Juan derived in part from her own wish to have a lot of men, which she projected to him.

The discussion of this first major transference distortion led to a new sense of freedom on her part. If I was not going to be the bad father, I must be the good father who would let her have anything she wanted. No longer did she need reassurance that I would not raise the fee to a point where she would have to leave therapy, as she had heard other analysts had done. The idea that I disapproved of her sexual activities she could see was obviously preposterous. However, the notion that she could have orgasms even without the participation of the clitoris was one that she could not accept. It was clear that there was much guilt feeling to be worked out about childhood masturbation, even though as yet there were no direct memories of conflict in this area.

Shortly after these disclosures she began another purely sexual relationship, again with a manual laborer, Joe, whom she regarded as her intellectual inferior. Again she had little use for him outside of bed, but there she said he was excellent. And once more after a few months she discontinued the relationship, determined to find a more satisfying love.

Affair with Milton

The first man after this period who aroused any romantic feeling in her was a physician from another city, Milton. He was quite interested in her in the beginning, coming in to the city on a Friday afternoon and leaving Sunday evening. Unlike the others, he was a gentle man who treated her very kindly, taking her to concerts and plays which she could not have gotten to otherwise, and wining and dining her in first-class restaurants.

There was only one fly in the ointment: Milton was a poor sex partner. Either he ejaculated prematurely or he abstained from sex altogether. One way or the other she was left unsatisfied. Fearful that the experience with her husband Herman would be repeated, she did not try to help him out sexually, but left it up to him. Since he was a physician, she did suggest, after discussing it with me, that some psychiatric help would be useful. But he attributed his sexual difficulties to a sense of rejection by his wife, from whom he had been separated for about a year. It was not so serious that it "required" psychiatry; it would pass in time.

Rather than pass in time, it began to make Milton more and more discouraged about the relationship. Soon he was finding reasons why he could not get away one weekend or another. When he finally gave her number to a friend of his who lived in New York, she knew the end was in sight. After a few more frustrating dates, they broke up.

This break-up did not affect her unduly. It did help to clarify the pattern which now became a focus for analysis. Either she had a sexually gratifying experience with someone she did not love, like Clyde or Arnold, or she had some feeling for a man she could not enjoy sexually, like Herman, Milton, and really, as she now confessed, Juan. For all the time that she was with Juan she was so tense and jealous that she could not let herself go in bed. It was easy enough to help her to see that this split was an inevitable outcome of her Oedipal situation, and she now began to explore the role of her father in her love life.

Further Affairs

Shortly after the "first anniversary" she started another affair, with a lawyer by the name of Marvin. Here too she concealed it for a few weeks, fearful that I would reprimand her. This kind of transference reaction, to me as the bad or angry father, came up continually and took a long time to work out.

Marvin was giving her the rush act, seeing her four to five times a week. Still, although she liked him, she was very cautious. He was quite antianalytic, saying among other things that he knew one girl who had become promiscuous as a result of psychoanalysis. He couldn't see why she needed it; for himself he would never go. Her second reservation related to sex. Even though he saw her almost every night, Marvin had as yet not asked for sex. She was beginning to worry that there was something wrong with him.

In the meantime she reviewed the many ways in which she might be inadequate for him. Her deep sense of shame again came under scrutiny here. One new fact that emerged here is that prior to and during her marriage she had never used any contraceptives; this was why she had become pregnant. Contraceptives were avoided because she simply did not believe that she could become pregnant, i.e., that she could function as a grown-up woman.

Although the shameful feelings predominated, she was also eager to have sex. She began to think of other men, and wondered whether it was right for her to date anybody else as long as she was seeing Marvin. This was interpreted as part of her masochistic need to give up everything for father, really a feminine version of the rescue fantasy. This masochistic rescue fantasy was what had made her pursue the devastating relationship with Herman.

After knowing Marvin for about three weeks she could no longer stand the tension and seduced him. As she had feared, he was quite inept sexually. At first he could not manage to enter her; then when he did he could not ejaculate. She was terrified

that he was another Herman, although unlike him Marvin functioned very well professionally.

The new relationship created a number of dilemmas for
her. The sexual situation was unsatisfactory, yet she could not
bring herself to discuss it with him. On the one hand she wanted
to be with him all the time, to love and be loved; on the other
hand she wanted to be with other men as well.

At the same time she also wanted to get back to school, especially since her present job was temporary and unsatisfactory.
As a compromise measure she decided to take one course.

The discouragement brought about by the new affair was
reflected in a slackening of interest in the analysis. She began to
come late regularly, sometimes missing almost half the session.
Her productivity during the sessions fell off. Much anger was released towards the therapist and towards men in general. This,
however, was not carried very far because it began to sound too
much like her hated mother.

Another complication arose when Marvin invited her to go
skiing with him. The invitation pleased her, but she was reluctant to spend the money required for the skiing equipment.
Equally, she was reluctant to ask him for the money for the
weekend, especially since he did not seem to be very well off.
This brought up for analysis her self-image as an all-giving
woman-mother rather than a receptive female. Eventually he
paid for part of the trip, while she paid for most of it, which
left her angry because her financial situation then, as so often,
was precarious.

Mostly, however, the complaints centered around sex. She
would jealously count up the number of days between intercourse, experiencing each further day as a deep deprivation.

Interspersed with the conflict with Marvin were occasional
episodes with mother, concern about her sister, fights with
roommates, and continuing depression. Once mother called her
up in great alarm, saying that she had broken up with her husband and was going to call the police if he tried to get back into
the house. This reevoked many similar episodes from her childhood. Mother calmed down after a day, because her husband,
unlike Holly's father, threatened to take action against her.

At this point the sexual problem with Marvin was brought

out into the open. As might have been anticipated, he maintained first of all that there was no problem and second that if there was a problem it was all her fault. He was too "refined" to tolerate the condom well as a contraceptive, while she in turn balked at getting a diaphragm. She didn't want to be one of those girls who run around with diaphragms in their purses — obviously a reference to her fear of promiscuity. But Marvin insisted that if he could not ejaculate, it was only because of the use of the condom.

Although she earned extra money by doing tax returns in the spring, she once again found herself in money troubles. Courses, clothes, a traffic fine, payments on a new Porsche car, all mounted up. Even the analytic fee had to be postponed for several weeks.

Over one weekend, when she was just over her menstrual period, they had sex without any precautions. Marvin ejaculated normally. "You see," he said, "the so-called problem is all in your mind." Finally she blurted out, "I don't love him; I've never loved anybody." This feeling was tied up with sex and a feeling of dirtiness about herself; she didn't really have the right to love anybody.

Her associations then turned to father and Herman, how she had slaved for the two of them. It became clear that she had subordinated her own needs to theirs because of the deep conviction that she didn't deserve anything better.

The situation with Marvin deteriorated further. A big fight when she was in a bad mood led him to call off one evening; she immediately suspected that he was out with another woman. Again they drifted along without sex for several weeks, Holly counting every missed day. One evening when they were out together they stopped off at a drug store. He asked her whether he should buy anything, obviously referring to condoms; She angrily replied, "Don't ask." That night she had one of her rare dreams:

> "There is a man on top of a building, throwing things into the patio. I'm looking on."

To the man she associated the analyst. Throwing things was an expression of anger. The patio reminded her of the architecture of her childhood. Since throwing things into an opening is a fairly obvious sexual symbol, the dream brought out the wish to make me angry, which in turn meant sexual. At the same time she was wondering what kind of a sexual partner I would make (she is looking on).

Above all the dream offered an additional clue to the affair with Marvin: the angry man whom she had to rescue in an ambivalent manner represented father; her attachment to angry, impotent (in the wider sense) men was a way of working out her attachment to her father.

More manifestations of the positive transference came to the fore. One session I was inadvertently fifteen minutes late. When I apologized, she said, "That's all right, you have a right to be late." On another occasion she revealed that in admiration of the many pictures on my walls she had recently begun to buy paintings for her own apartment. Clearly I was moving from the dubious, often bad, father to the good father.

Marvin continued to be a disappointment to her. Recently he had been sick for three weeks, so again there was a long period without sex. Once when they were out on a date with his sister and brother-in-law they told him to go home because he looked so sick. At the office she was also having a hard time. Again depression became the dominant feeling.

Several weeks later she came in, again in bad humor. She didn't know where to start. My silence reminded her of the silence of her parents, who used to punish her in that way. Sometimes they would go on for days at a time; it drove her crazy. The same roller coaster came up with her courses: she had not done her homework, so she'd have to drop out. Everything looked black; she felt discouraged.

Casually she mentioned that she and Marvin had broken up. Again something of such vital significance had been concealed from the analyst, who was thus still the bad father. But the break-up with Marvin was followed by an improvement in her spirits. Then she had another angry dream:

"A man is coming at me with a knife. I feel terribly frightened, as though something is hurting me."

This time there were no specific associations to either the

man or the knife. The dream was given a symbolic interpretation: she wants to be hurt (attacked sexually) by an angry father. This was one of the deepest sexual roots of her masochism.

Once she was through with Marvin her feelings about herself and her life improved markedly. For this she gave the analysis full credit. She realized that she had been pursuing a self-defeating course with men, could recognize in broad outlines how her childhood had led her to it, and was determined to be different in the future.

With no current boy friend, her associations turned back to her family, especially father. Just around this time father wanted to come to New York for a vacation. It was she who loaned him the money, although her total annual income at the time was only $3,800. She could have asked her uncle (father's brother), but she did not want to; it was her obligation. Still rescuing father. In one session, as she talked of the amount of money she had given father over the years, occasionally at the expense of vital necessities for herself, she wept unrestrainedly. Shortly thereafter she dreamt:

"I'm back in Cuba. There are about five girls coming towards me; I don't like them and pass them by. I also see an old friend and say hello to her. Then I go home to where father and mother are.

To the five girls she associated the various roommates with whom she had so little in common, who in turn reminded her of her classmates in school with whom she felt little kinship. The friend whom she says hello to is Sylvia. The dream is a wish to restore the family, with more sexual permissiveness (Sylvia) than it ever had. It was this fantasy of mending the numerous schisms in the family that came back to her over and over again; she was the family healer. Now she was beginning to see that no matter what she did she was not going to bring the family together again. It was an idle fantasy, reminiscent of her childhood daydreaming about a pleasant cottage where everybody would be happy again.

For a few sessions the desire to rescue father became extremely strong. Why shouldn't she make father happy by going to live with him in California? She could take care of him, much as she had done in adolescence. Maybe this is what a daughter should do for her father.

This was followed by an inevitable reaction. Why didn't father find a woman of his own? Why did he demand comfort, money, emotional support from her which could more appropriately be supplied by a wife? There was no point to reenacting the tragedy of her adolescence. Increasingly she became aware of her desire to recapture her childhood, and the emotional turmoil that this created in her.

As might have been expected, men soon reentered her life, and concern with the family inevitably receded into the background. A number of men casually flitted into and out of her life in this period. Only two assumed even minor importance.

Both were sexual affairs, on the pattern of Arnold and Clyde. One presented quite a paradoxical picture. Leon was a gynecologist who seemed to have chosen his specialty because he loved the vagina so much. When not at work he was pursuing women amorously. He never pretended to Holly that she was the only one, nor even that she was especially important to him.

They met one evening at a small party given by one of Juan's friends; most of the men there were physicians. That night he took her home with him and they had sex. That weekend they went away together. Then for two weeks he did not call. When he came back he offered neither excuse nor explanation. Their relationship was a sexual one; that was part of what life was all about.

Unlike Marvin, Leon was a magnificent lover. He knew because of his professional and personal background, every nuance of how to please a woman sexually. She had one orgasm after another with him. But, curiously, she complained that he was *too* perfect. A man should have some weaknesses; he was just a fucking machine. After a month she refused to see him any longer.

With another lover in this period, Jim, a free-lance airline pilot, she felt no anxiety because there was a definite time limit to the relationship. They met in March, and Jim was scheduled to leave on a long assignment in June and he was not going to come back. He was not as good a lover as Leon, but she could let herself go with him because she knew that nothing would come of it.

Finally, another serious affair developed, this time with Bill.

Affair with Bill

Again a physician. Bill was a thirty-one-year-old surgeon; she was twenty-five when they met. He was a quiet, unassuming little man, somewhat shorter than she in height, who had great difficulty expressing his feelings. At his work he was superb; in fact, his friends were strongly convinced that some day he would be at the top of his specialty. But in private life he was extremely shy. At first this attracted Holly, especially as a contrast to the aggressive narcissism of men like Leon; later it became a source of continual conflict, especially when his reticence took the form of deep ambivalence about marrying her.

When she met him, he was still working at a hospital, with some private practice, and about to take his boards. The boards kept him busy almost every night. Holly could see a place for herself in his life by taking care of his everyday affairs, keeping the books for his practice, and generally being a companion to him. He went along with this arrangement, and a warm relationship blossomed.

Sex was good. He had a technique for involving her clitoris in intercourse which was original and effective. That he was not too vigorous a lover did not bother her unduly; she had had enough casual affairs and now wanted some permanence, which he seemed to be in a position to offer her.

After a while he began to tell her more about his life. The son of a physician (general practitioner), he had always felt destined for medicine. He had one older sister. When he was in his teens, father suddenly died. The family was well off, so there was no financial problem. But he felt that the emotional burden of the family fell on him, and it was more than he could handle. Gradually he withdrew from both mother and sister, first into his school work, then into his profession.

Relationships with girls had always been difficult for him. He never married. Before Holly there was only one girl who had any meaning for him. They went together for a year, when she left him for another man who was more at home with his feelings.

When this girl left him, he went into therapy, for about nine months. Subjectively he felt that nothing was accomplished, since he spent all his time picking the psychiatrist to pieces. He swore he would never go back to treatment again. Yet objectively he seemed to have improved, since his relationships with girls became much freer.

As long as Bill was immersed in studying for his boards, Holly was satisfied with him. She too used this period to get back to her own eternal quest, for college credits. For a while they were very happy together.

Once he had passed his boards, the question of marriage entered both their minds. He was very hesitant about committing himself, not critical of her, but just not sure that he was ready to get married, or even that he wanted to get married. His first concern was to expand his private practice so that he could make an adequate living, and that took time. But even apart from that he just could not make up his mind.

In spite of his indecision, he did everything to make her believe that he was going to marry her. The most important was to introduce her to his mother and sister. Mother became her most ardent champion, assuring him repeatedly that Holly was the ideal girl for him. His sister was more lukewarm, but he was not very close to her. Mother even became friendly with Holly, regardless of what Bill was going to do.

The two continued to spend a good deal of time together. Now that his exams were out of the way, she became increasingly impatient with his affectlessness. Her love for him, never overwhelming, began to diminish. She began to tell herself that she'd be just as pleased to break up with him as to marry him.

For quite a while she was torn between giving him an ultimatum (marry or break up) and hoping that he would leave her. He on his part gave no clear indication of what he wanted — merely continual wavering.

Then two events occurred almost simultaneously. First he was recalled into the Army, to be sent to Vietnam. As she was about to say goodbye, he said, "No, not goodbye; you and I belong together forever." In this roundabout way he proposed to her.

Because of the way in which the proposal came, as well as

her previous doubts, she was not deliriously happy about the idea of marrying Bill. He seemed to have proposed almost as an afterthought, and almost as though he wanted to have somebody to come back to. Still, he had popped the question, regardless of the manner in which it was done. Perhaps marriage with him could work out.

Some six months before Bill had proposed, there was a brief fling lasting two weekends which had made a deep impression on her. In the waiting room of the analyst's office she met a young man, Richy, whose hour followed hers. After some post-session flirtations, the two eventually got together. They spent two tumultuous weekends together, mostly in bed. Richy was a man who had made of sex a fine art, and this, coupled with the aura of the transference, sent her head spinning. She was madly in love, when he dropped her as suddenly as he had taken up with her.

Almost till the end of analysis Holly would bring up this fling with Richy, blaming me for its disagreeable termination. At first she even accused me of ordering Richy not to see her, or of revealing some of her shameful "secrets" to him. This did not last long. Mostly she rebuked me for not analyzing Richy properly, since she was certain the two of them could have been quite happy together. Naturally, the transference element was interpreted here, but she vigorously denied it. For a long time, whenever she was angry at me, she would bring up the "Richy affair."

Even though she would much have preferred Richy to Bill, it was Bill who had agreed to marry her. For the next year the pros and cons of such a marriage were thoroughly aired in the analysis. As might have been anticipated Bill was a poor correspondent. Months would go by without any word from him. It did not take her long to realize that this was not her fault, since his mother began to call her from time to time to find out whether there was any word from her son. She even invited Holly to visit a number of times, assuring her over and over again that she was very eager to see the marriage take place.

Once away from this country, Bill resumed his characteristic hesitancy. More and more it appeared that he had proposed only because he was frightened by the prospect of going to

Vietman.

After about six months of waiting, he was given a leave to the United States. They met for a hectic weekend in San Francisco. But Bill showed neither passion nor enthusiasm. It was finally clear to her that even though he might be a good husband on paper she would never be happy with him. When he left to go back to the war zone, they both knew it was over, though nothing was said.

The pretence was kept up until he was actually reassigned home. At that point she asked him whether he wanted her to come to the base and marry him. When he hesitated once more, she knew it was hopeless. The engagement was officially broken.

In the meantime her life had stabilized in a number of ways. She held on to a job for several years, earning continual promotions and increased responsibility because of the high quality of her accounts. For the first time in her life she was free of debt and even had a little money in the bank. After many ups and downs with roommates she finally found a small apartment at a reasonable rental in which she could live alone.

Spurred on by all these successes, she returned again to her old dream of finishing college. But to do that she had to go full time. By this time she was strong enough to ask for help. She confronted father with her desire. He said that he had set a sum aside for her marriage. Instead she wanted it for school; he agreed to give it to her. Mother contributed a small amount, a student loan did the rest.

At the same time she felt too wobbly to try to get through college without analysis. She asked if she could pay half the fee and have credit for the other half. Not too surprisingly I agreed. The bill that she ran up she paid in full less than a year after she had finished.

School, Marriage, and Family

Apart from marriage, school was the great dream of her life. The opportunity to finish college on a full-time basis rather than piecemeal courses crammed in after a wearisome day at the office was almost beyond her wildest fantasies. She was given advanced standing and permitted to carry heavy loads, twenty to twenty-two credits per semester. Well motivated, she was near the top of her class, carrying off a number of honors.

Shortly before she was due to graduate, one of her advisers asked if he could see her at home to discuss her program. This seemed an odd request, but since he was an attractive young professor she readily assented. Thus began the affair with Ethan which eventually culminated in a most happy love marriage.

Ethan was a handsome, romantic, young professor. He was separated from his wife, but not yet divorced. At first she had many misgivings about this, but when the analyst pointed out that it really made no difference she could see that she was using his marriage as an excuse to avoid intimacy. He had also been through some analysis, though he wanted more.

The two were ideally suited for one another. Sexually they functioned together perfectly. He was as anxious to find love as she. Shortly after they met they decided to get married. He received an appointment in another state, which meant leaving the analysis. Marriage had to be postponed until his divorce was final, but as mentioned this created no real hardship.

With her departure from New York, the analysis was terminated. Less than a year later, she wrote:

> "Regardless of ...pettiness, I've never been happier.... Our relationship has deepened and blossomed to degrees previously unimagined, for both Ethan and myself."

DISCUSSION

The case has been presented from the point of view of the various love affairs that Holly had had in her life and that emerged as the analysis progressed. This may seem superficial, especially since it corresponds so closely to the patient's immediate concerns. Yet love is the central experience of every human being's life, and the detailed examination of the love life represents the most profound penetration possible into any human being's psyche.

Naturally, the analysis of her love affairs was accompanied by a concomitant recapitulation of her childhood. Without the working through of her childhood conflicts, especially the Oedipal, the love affairs would never have become comprehen-

sible. Such "current" analysis, as recommended by some theoreticians, is indeed superficial, amounting to little more than
moralistic exhortation. Yet without the clear beacon light of a
healthy romantic love, the analysis of her childhood would have
left too much untouched. She had to grasp her Oedipal complex,
the fantasy of rescuing an impotent father, her masochistic
image of love, the repression of her sexuality because it was too
incestuous, the projection of her anger and sexuality to the
man, and much else.

Noteworthy, especially in contrast to many of the other
cases presented in this book, is the almost complete absence of
dreams. There was mainly the recurrent dream of a man lunging
at her or her lunging at the man, a typical female expression of
her sexual-aggressive wish for father. Once there was some in-
timation of mother twisting her body, thus reviving the fears of
the bad mother, but this did not quite reach consciousness. Perhaps there was less fantasy about the mother because the surface battle was still so strong, whereas she felt mainly strong
affection for father. In any case it did not appear, again showing
that the analyst has to deal with the material available, and not
be disappointed because some preformed scheme in his mind is
not acceded to by the patient. This case also shows once more
that people can be quite adequately analyzed whether they
dream or not.

In transference, there was a gradual growth from an image
of a bad or at best lukewarm father to that of a good father
who would stand by her in every emergency. Her request for
permission to postpone payment of half the analytic fee was
part of testing to see whether the analyst would really be a good
father, and help her to realize her lifelong ambition of finishing
college. I agreed to her request because I felt that it could help
her the more effectively to get over her projection of the bad
father to other men.

At the end Ethan appeared almost as a *deus ex machina*.
And yet in one sense it was bound to happen, if not with him,
then some other man. In reality the analysis had helped Holly
to progress to where she was ready for such a man. There is a
kind of self-fulfilling prophecy in love: the masochistic woman
attracts the sadistic man who confirms her bitter complaint that

all men are no good, while the sexual romantic woman finds a sexual romantic and builds a relationship where both find happiness. Some French *philosophe* has penned an aphorism that every woman gets the husband she deserves. Analytically this could be rephrased to the effect that every woman gets the husband for whom she is emotionally ready.

Above all Holly's self-image had to change in the course of analysis. Her view of herself after the rejection by Juan as an abandoned woman was in the deepest sense a paranoid distortion; it was she who wished to sleep with a variety of men and then abandon them. As she grew, she was able to give up the emphasis on abandonment and shift to seeing herself as a healthy woman ready for love. When that happened, it was inevitable that she should find a man who reciprocated.

Sheldon,
The Frightened Boy Genius

Sheldon, a seven-and-a-half-year-old, was referred to me for therapy because he had many fears and an especially acute phobic reaction to movies showing accidents. One time he vomited; another time he ran out of the room shouting, "No, no."

LIFE HISTORY

Sheldon was the elder of two siblings, the younger being a girl two years his junior, Heidi. The parents had been married seven years before Sheldon was born. Both parents in the course of their lives manifested rather marked personality difficulties.

The father, a machinist, was, like Sheldon, the elder of two siblings. He came of a poverty-stricken immigrant family, as a result of which he blamed all his troubles on the economic system. Although for the most part politically inactive, especially since the children came, he did belong to a small left-wing splinter group.

One odd incident which occurred several years after Sheldon started treatment illustrates the kind of man his father was. The family was then living in a middle-class housing development in the Bronx, where many of the residents had cars but he did not. Outwardly he did not express any resentment of this, but he discovered that because of the shortage of parking space one crosswalk which was supposed to be reserved for pedestrians was always blocked by some car that had parked there illegally. Thereupon he appointed himself a committee of one to correct this situation (it probably would have been easier to correct it if he had notified the authorities directly). He had gummed stickers printed at his own expense saying "Parked illegally; move your car." Stealthily, at night, he would go out and paste a sticker on the unsuspecting cars. Since he chose stickers which could not easily be removed, the cars were all damaged, with consequent trouble and expense to the owners. No one knew what he was doing, not even his wife.

The car owners pooled their resources to trap the man who was damaging their cars. He was caught and brought to court. The judge let him off on two conditions, first that he reimburse all the owners for the damage inflicted, second that he undergo psychiatric treatment.

In treatment nothing of any great consequence came out. His relationship with his wife had deteriorated to a point where they communicated little beyond the bare necessities and rarely had sex. He revealed that he had never taken his son's difficulties seriously because he had had similar problems as a child and had "outgrown" them. One of his most vivid memories was that when he was about eleven, his parents had a quarrel as a result of which his father wanted to leave the house forever. "Go," he cried, "I will take care of mother better than you." He said he meant it too. Therapy was discontinued because there was really nothing to talk about. As he saw it, pasting the stickers on the cars was unwise, but at least he had struck a blow against an unjust social order.

The father had no special interests or hobbies; the family did not even have much of a social life. Both parents devoted themselves to their children. The father was impatient with Sheldon and frequently angry at him, but he never hurt him physically.

The courtship between the father and the mother was rather odd. He was then living in New York, she in Boston. They saw one another only weekends ostensibly because of the expense of traveling. Finally after a number of years they married. But even then they continued to live in separate cities, still meeting only on weekends. Apparently the marriage did legitimize their sexual relationship in their minds. Only about a year before Sheldon was born did they manage to find an apartment together in New York. Even then their life together was interrupted by his wife's illness, as will be seen.

The mother was similar in many ways to the father — withdrawn, depressed, without interests, blaming everything on the economic situation, and finding her only outlet in taking care of the children. Her situation was made worse by several recurring illnesses, and her reaction to the children's growing up and leaving home was much more pathological.

Before her marriage she had been a librarian, but once married she never went back to her old occupation. She was the eldest of three children. For quite a while she was the only one in the family working, a fact in which she took much pride. This was her main conscious reason for not moving to New York any earlier to stay with her husband.

Even before marriage she showed many signs of depression. At times she felt the world was so unpleasant that she did not want to bring children into it. When she did start to try to get pregnant, it was a year and a half before she conceived.

Then illness set in. While she was pregnant with Sheldon, it was discovered that she had a uterine tumor. Surgery was postponed until he was about six months old, but because of the illness she went back to live with her parents shortly after he was born. The removal of the tumor was followed by the discovery of a thyroid disturbance, which also called for surgery. While Sheldon was still an infant, she had a thyroidectomy, which kept her in the hospital for two weeks. Then because of the tumor she was advised to have another baby as quickly as possible. The new baby was colicky and ill and required a lot of attention. In the meantime Sheldon was taken care of by his maternal grandmother. His father was still working in New York and he had little time for his son, even under the best of circumstances. Not until Samuel was almost three was the family reunited in New York and the mother able to give her son more attention.

As Sheldon grew older, his mother showed increasing signs of nervousness and irritability. Unfortunately, she applied for medical help to an acquaintance who was a quack, full of bizarre theories (he had been "psychoanalyzed" by Henry Miller in the heyday of three-week analyses right after World War I). One of his theories was that nervousness was due to a "midbrain allergy," a diagnosis which he gave to Sheldon's mother. Since he was a licensed medical man and a friend, she placed implicit faith in him, his "diagnosis," and his treatment, which consisted of frequent injections of a mysterious substance called "omnidin." This omnidin was supposed to be a composite of all known hormones, with some unknown ones added.

Under this treatment she began to pull her hair out, to a point where she became quite bald. She filled in the bald spots with lead pencil, but she was still too ashamed of herself to venture out in the street. Accordingly, she oscillated between the doctor's office and her home, becoming more depressed each day. Since her friend's "treatment" was free (at least he did not overcharge), it was all the more difficult for her to break away from him. By this time both children were out of the house and leading independent lives, so that her depression had little effect on them. When last heard from, she was confined to her home in deep melancholy, her doctor-friend having died. It was most fortunate that at least she resisted her friend's efforts to pull Sheldon out of psychotherapy and give him the "omnidin" treatment too!

Into this gloomy, affect-deprived environment the children certainly cast the only ray of light. It was only natural that soon both parents began to orient their entire lives around the children, especially since both Sheldon and his sister turned out to be extraordinarily bright. As long as Sheldon and Heidi were at home, the parents seemed to be ordinary, self-sacrificing people whose major gratifications in life came from their children. But once the children had left home, the deep pathology inherent in the parents, particularly the mother, came to the fore.

The developmental history obtained from the mother was quite revealing. Pregnancy and birth were normal, even though the tumor was discovered while she was pregnant. Sheldon was bottle-fed because she did not have enough milk, to which she added, "The doctors didn't encourage me very much."

Sheldon had a nurse for a month after he was born. Either she or his mother would always pick him up at night when he

cried. Significantly, after three to four months he stopped crying. He never woke up at night. His mother insisted that his sleep
was always very relaxed. Sheldon "showed no reaction," she
said, to the surgery she had when he was six months old.

He gave up the bottle without difficulty when he was
about a year old. He was a very good eater; in fact she described
him as a "two-spooned baby" — one who eats with both hands.
He had no allergies.

As was typical of her almost affectless attitude, she stated
that he was never toilet trained. He needed a little urging to
urinate at ten or eleven months when he got up from his nap.
He didn't ask on his own until past his second summer. Bowel
training was never made into a battle. When he was past two, he
would just ask. She stated that he was very regular in his functioning, going about once a day, usually in the evening. To him,
as to the whole family, going to move his bowels was a big
period of relaxation — he would take a book to the bathroom
and stay there, as did both parents.

On the birth of his sister the mother as usual reported
that Sheldon had no reaction, even though the new infant cried
day and night. She stressed that "he has always been a very
reasonable child." The only comment he ever made about the
sibling relationship was recently, when he said to her, "I'll always be two years older."

Her first awareness of any difficulties in him came with his
speech when he was about three years old. His speech development, which presented a serious problem when he came to treatment, had been slow. He had begun to speak in words at about
eighteen months, in sentences at about twenty-one months. His
voice was very thick and guttural, and it was very difficult to
understand him because his thoughts seemed to come faster
than his vocal apparatus would permit him to express them. (He
was almost unintelligible to me in his first year of treatment.)

When he was three, his mother thought he had an orderli-
ness which was unusual for a child of his age. The unexpected
seemed to upset him. If he played with a toy, he would check it
to see if all the pieces were there when he finished.

When Sheldon was a little less than three, his mother had a
second thyroidectomy; this meant another long stay with her

parents in Boston. He sucked his thumb at night until then, but abruptly discontinued it while his mother was in the hospital. On her return home he clung to her excessively, asking twenty or twenty five times a day: "Are my hands clean?" She assured him, in a "reasonable way," that he could be dirty if he wished, but he continued to cling.

Simultaneously he developed a fear that the cleaning woman might fall and hurt herself. He also became frightened of the noise of fire engines and of other loud noises. From that time she remarked on a variety of fears, culminating in the episodes which brought him to therapy.

Masturbation, she said, was never a problem because she would disregard it. In the summer after he was three he did quite a bit, then he stopped. He had no problem about nudity. She stated that she never deliberately undressed in front of him, then added that she had had very little sex since moving to New York.

He was always shy of other children. At around four he invented an imaginary playmate, Bob, who could fix anything and do anything, and an imaginary city, Okinbacki (he later elaborated both these in other forms, as will be seen). Many times he would rather go with his mother to the park than play with other children at home. She said that he made a very good host but was never invited home by the other children.

For several years they lived in a crowded three-room apartment in New York. The parents slept in the living room, the children in the bedroom. When he began treatment, they were about to move to a four-room apartment where there would be one bedroom for the children and one for the parents.

Asked about his sexual interests, she denied seeing any. Then she said he did like to watch his sister in her bath. And lately he had been taking more interest in his mother's body, leaning up against her breasts and playing with her hair. When he did that, she liked it. But it was not really sex, nor was it when he came into her bed in the morning to "roughhouse."

His health had been good. He had contracted chicken pox, measles, and mumps and recovered from each uneventfully.

From about the age of five he had become concerned about death. Often when the subject was mentioned he would show apprehension. His mother did not know what it came from, but thought perhaps it was connected with the death of his paternal grandmother when he was four. Sheldon did not talk about the death, but his mother recognized that it had made a deep impression on him.

Since he was born in June, he entered school shortly after he was six. He loved it, and thrived. But his speech was so bad that it interfered with everything, so in November, several months after he started school, his teacher recommended that he be sent to a clinic for speech therapy.

After a year of speech therapy, the speech clinic recommended that he be put either into a public school for gifted children or into a private school because of his high intelligence, that the family find a larger apartment, and that he receive psychotherapy. The only recommendation that the parents acted on was the psychotherapy.

Several other facts came out at the beginning of his therapy. His IQ was indeed astronomically high; he was a true genius (in a second Binet about a year later he obtained an IQ of 197). His reading ability seemed to be at the 14th year level, or almost twice his age, not 5.0, as the first test noted. One of his main preoccupations was maps, and he had memorized the map of the subway system of the borough where he lived.

At an emotional level he was even worse off than the descriptions indicated. His nervousness was so extreme that he habitually chewed through the collars of all his shirts, creating among other things an excessive laundry bill for the parents. This nervousness was not, as his mother implied, precipitated by frightening movies, but was generally observable; she described him as "intense." He had no friends. One of his pet activities was to "take his father to court." This involved bringing up his father on charges, usually unspecified, before the court, which was himself. Acting as prosecutor, judge, and jury all rolled into one, he would find his father guilty and sentence him accordingly. The family looked on at this game with amused tolerance, totally oblivious to the deep-seated rage toward his father that his game was revealing.

COURSE OF THERAPY

The therapy, conducted at a frequency of two sessions a week, lasted five and a half years. In the course of it the mother and the father were each seen regularly for periods of several months. They showed neither response nor interest and soon discontinued, but they came in after that for occasional consultations until the end of Sheldon's therapy.

His therapy lends itself to certain natural divisions. For the first eight months he communicated little with me, except to express occasional grandiose fantasies, and when he did communicate he was often unintelligible, as mentioned. Then he began to talk more about his sleep problem and his dreams. This was followed by direct game play with me, where his great need was to defeat me.

Once he found that he could not achieve a real-life victory, he returned to fantasy, where his aggression came out more directly. This in turn was followed by a search for physical contact with me, then by fantasies of opening the lines of communication to me. After that he incorporated me into his fantasy world, and finally he became able to tell me directly about what was going on in his life.

The whole process may be viewed as one of increasing communication with other people, through the analyst as intermediary. As Sheldon found that he was able to communicate, his symptoms subsided and his social relationships improved markedly.

Grandiose Fantasies and Space Communication

The first period was characterized by a release of various grandiose fantasies. He hardly talked to me at all. If I offered an interpretation, he ignored it; if I asked a question, he would not answer.

In the very first session he gave a clear indication of how he was going to behave. Without looking at me, he dashed off into the playroom, where he quickly grasped what was available. He went to the doll house and made a schoolroom; the mother was the teacher. He moved the children about, then he said,

"There is a big hurricane coming," and put everybody in one room. "The little boy sets out to save the room, from either the hurricane or a hydrogen bomb. He succeeds. And that is how an eight-year old boy by his scientific and mechanical genius saved the world." He left little doubt that his idea of saving the world was conscious and serious.

Communications Via Dreams

Then came a dramatic shift. When he came in, he said, "I want to talk to you; I can't sleep lately." He told me a number of things about school and his family, but mostly he was concerned with his "bad dreams." He related several of these, one of which went as follows:

"The giants take a special weapon away from me. It can make anything smaller or bigger. I go after it. I follow them to the cave, where there are lots of dead bodies around. With the help of the FBI I get away from them."

The dream was easy enough to interpret as a fear of castration, but that made no impression on him, nor did it elicit any new material. In fact, the dream was quite similar to the games in therapy. What was new was that for the first time he was now asking my help with a problem.

For quite a while after that the sleep disturbance and the dreams came up in almost every session. Intermingled with this were old themes of war, ruling, and rebellion, as well as new themes: he would hint at what was happening in his life or occasionally tell me something.

For a few sessions he reported no dreams but said he had good dreams that he did not remember. He began to be concerned with good and bad dreams. Each night he asked his mother to promise him that he would not have any bad dreams; she, as usual excessively rational, asked me how she could promise any such thing; after all, she had no control over his dreams.

Then he devised a game about a big bomb which had to be set off by a smaller bomb after they were joined by a hundred feet of radio cable. The cable was part of the symbolism of communication and probably also represented the large penis he needed to be ruler.

Next he told me a good dream:

"A millionaire has the atomic bomb. He gives it to me."

Thus he dreamed of getting all the power. Still, he could not fall asleep and asked me why. I said that things were bothering him that came out in the dreams and games; if he told me more about them he would learn to sleep better. He said, "But I talk a little more now." Thereupon he laid the cable and set off the big bomb with a loud crash.

Next time he again began by saying that he was afraid to sleep. He said that lots of bad things happened to him in the course of the day, but when I asked what he went back to the games. This time the good men wiped out all the bad men and peace was declared. In the very next session war broke out all over again: "If I don't have war I don't get ideas," he said. He bombed out a rebellious area.

War continued for a few more sessions. The main new element was that he built himself a barricade; inside he was safe, outside he was not. Then he went on to blow up prisoners and bury them; this generally presaged a temporary end to hostilities.

Acceptance of Normal Competitive Games

The lull in the war was followed by a sudden switch to the normal competitive games which were all over the playroom, and which he had hitherto ignored. In these his grandiosity came out in his fanatical desire to win, and the variety of tricks that he resorted to if he was in any danger of losing.

Naturally, the shift to realistic competition took place with much caution and occasional backsliding. First he ventured on a domino-building game. At this he proved to be much the more adept, so he continued all hour. But in the next sessions robbers came with all kinds of stolen supplies, and they had to be taken care of.

His mother reported a recent dream of his:

"A witch comes along and takes Heidi away, leaves me alone."

Since Sheldon had not reported the dream, it could not be discussed; it was clear that his grandiosity involved getting rid of his sister, as well as fear of the bad mother.

During this period he switched to rummy, and since the cards favored him, he began to win. As long as he was winning, he was satisfied, except that sometimes he would press up against me, apparently seeking direct physical contact. But after showing me a new game of cards he regressed to fantasized aggression again. Most likely the games had roused in him a desire to hit me, and, fearful of this wish, he went back to his fantasies.

Falling Back to Aggressive Fantasies

Apparently frightened by the combination of reality and physical closeness, he fell back to his aggressive fantasies. This time he used the toy soldiers. For quite a while he exhibited a repetitive pattern of behavior whereby he looked for a traitor who would be tortured and then put to death, sometimes by being blown up alive. The interpretation that he was angry at somebody had no effect. After a number of traitors had been put to death, rebellion broke out in various parts of his territory, He put these down in short order. Finally he was named commander-in-chief of all the forces and brought all the rebellions to an end.

During this period his mother reported one dream of his:

"The Indians are going to shoot an informer."

Evidently, he had been working out the fear that his secret language would be discovered and that his "evil" thoughts would be punished.

Search for Physical Contact

Once he had announced that he was the commander-in-chief, another sudden switch took place. He went back to a variety of reality activities and games, but with this major difference, that he sought out physical contact with me over and over again. The most common form was to read a comic book while leaning up against me. As usual, interpretations or not, he persisted in his pattern until he had tired of it, and went on to some new phase.

In one session he read the comics and played a card game. Here he won heavily and told his mother about it. During the game he began to masturbate for the first time. In the next session when he lost at cards he became very excited. He started a "very big game," with twenty-five scores, embracing virtually everything we had done before. As usual, he still tried to alter the rules in the middle to give himself a higher score. His mother reported that he was no longer chewing his clothes, and that for the first time in his life he had invited another boy to come home with him.

He reported a dream:

"I'm in the woods. A woman is staring at me."

He dreamed this twice, and it frightened him, but he could discuss it as reflecting a fear of being separated from his mother. Around this time she reported that even though he was still afraid of "those things" (pictures of accidents) on television, he had recently asked his parents to force him to stay and watch the pictures so that he would get over his fear.

Shortly thereafter he brought in another dream, quite interested in what I would say:

"I'm waiting for a bus with a lot of boys. It doesn't come. We use devices to get it. We see something which is like the wallpaper in my room; when we see that I know it is time to go home. I go downtown with my father; there we see the wallpaper design and go home."

In association he spoke of the other boys in his class and in the Cub Scouts, which he had recently joined. The dream represented his conflict between being with the boys and staying home with father.

As mentioned, this period in the therapy was marked primarily by his yearning for physical contact and the various efforts he made to get it from me. Behaviorally it was characterized by a more realistic approach to games and by a willingness to talk about dreams and everyday activities.

Communication with the Analyst in Fantasy

The physical period came to an end as abruptly as all the

other periods. One day he came in and started talking about fantasy games connected with parkways, bridges, tunnels, planes, and the like. These all symbolized means of increasing his communication with me. These fantasies went on for well over six months before their attraction for him became exhausted and he could talk directly about whatever was bothering him.

In one typical fantasy there was a parkway breakdown and a tunnel breakdown. To compensate for these he built a bridge with the pillow from the chair where he had been sitting to my chair.

In the next session came planes. There were rocket planes in groups of seven. After these came single-piston planes. These could fly all over, hit anybody anywhere (thus his grandiosity was still coming out here). They could shoot from Mexico City to Buenos Aires. Next time he reported a vague dream about building a plane of his own.

A few sessions later he brought out a fantasy about low-flying planes, each with two rods which moved the plane at low altitudes when sunlight shined on them; they required no fuel. Thus perpetual sunlight gave perpetual motion. This was a beautiful symbolic expression of his wish for a good mother (perpetual sunlight) who would give him permission to have any pleasure he wanted (perpetual motion).

From planes he switched to highways. There were many highways in Europe, six-lane highways. New York to Brussels needed more highways opened. When I commented that he was trying to break down his inability to talk to me he merely made a motion with one finger on his left hand pointing to himself and with a finger of his right hand pointing to me.

For quite a while the bridge-tunnel-parkway theme dominated. There would be four-lane highways between Los Angeles and San Francisco, two-lane parkways from New York to Washington, and tunnels between Chicago and Milwaukee. Any interpretations made virtually no impression.

Incorporation of the Analyst into the Fantasy World

Soon another significant change occurred: I became a more direct part of his fantasy world. He had long had a distant country which he ruled, calling it Smithland. Here he appointed courts, ministers, judges, and juries; he called people to account; in short, he was the undisputed master. Now he began to appoint me to various posts in this kingdom.

First he offered to make me a councilman and representative from various areas. He even gave me a choice of the area that I could represent.

In the next session he was back at his communications, making a bridge to my chair. Then he fell silent. When I commented that there must be something bothering him, he replied that he was bothered only by the fact that I did not believe he was not bothered. This was but one of many instances which showed that the unfolding of his fantasies virtually had a rhythm of its own, immune to outside pressures.

Next time he again began by building a bridge to my chair with pillows and then appointing me to high office. This time I was appointed to the court, but I had my choice of positions, the higher the court the better. He told about some trouble he had with a gym teacher in school, but when I commented that maybe he would rather have me as a gym teacher than the other fellow he fell silent. He continued to call the tune.

For quite a while this pattern continued. After building a bridge to me, he would appoint me to high office, then give me a choice of a precise spot I would like to be in. Through all this the reports from his family were that he continued to show behavioral improvement.

He commented that he had been resting quite a bit here (at times he would take brief naps during the sessions). Now he began some guessing games. What is it that is found only in big cities, but was originally out in the country? Subway markers at the edge of the platform. He even gave me a bag to fill up for Goodwill Industries, in which he was now involved; I accepted. At the same time he began to talk more about reality events.

The social progress made him more aware of his speech problems because he was afraid that his fast speech would make the other boys walk away from him. By now his speech was quite intelligible. Once he verbalized the problem, he was able to bring it under control fairly quickly.

Direct Communication with the Analyst

After about five years of analysis, when he was almost thirteen, his fantasy world virtually disappeared and he was able to talk to me quite directly about all the major concerns of his life, including masturbation. At first he spoke mainly of school and the scouts.

But one day his mother called me in great alarm. She had noticed some "strange" sex play of his. When he hinted at this in the sessions and I asked him about it, he promptly explained that it was his way of masturbating.

Since the parents reported that his major problems had been resolved, and suggested termination, it was decided that a break in the therapy could be ventured. Sheldon, when queried, also felt that he was ready. After a five-and-half-year period, the treatment was satisfactorily terminated.

POSTANALYTIC DEVELOPMENTS

Occasional contact was maintained after the conclusion of the analysis. Outwardly Sheldon continued to be a brilliant student and a seemingly happy boy; inwardly, however, certain conflicts remained.

Several years later, during his second year in college, Sheldon ran into some serious trouble with the authorities. Because of his defiance of college regulations, which he insisted were quite absurd, he was suspended and threatened with expulsion. Fortunately, he was permitted to resign "for medical reasons," which did not prejudice him in his future career. He transferred to another college, where he completed a bachelor's degree and eventually a doctorate without mishap.

At the time of his run-in with the authorities in college he had some more therapy, which resulted in greater inner composure that has evidently stood up well over the years.

When last heard from a few years ago, he was a typically intense, brilliant, young intellectual, struggling with the problems characteristic of his group, but coping reasonably well. Intellectually, sexually, and socially he functioned at a high level, though certain deeper problems remained.

DISCUSSION

The most striking feature in this case is the continual growth in Sheldon's ability to communicate. In the beginning the inability to communicate left him terribly isolated, thrown back on his own inner life. It may well be that his extraordinarily high IQ was due in part to the extreme elaboration of his own thoughts, forced on him by the fact that he had to keep so much to himself. Some researchers have tried to show that the IQ is a reflection of the personality structure. Although as yet too little is known about it, the thesis seems highly plausible. Certainly, it holds up here. Unable to relate adequately either to his family or to his peers, he concentrated on intellectual tasks to the exclusion of almost everything else.

It is noteworthy that his communication problem was the first one for which help was sought. But it was attacked peripherally, via speech therapy. Only when speech therapy did not succeed was psychotherapy undertaken.

But what if the speech therapy had been "successful"? The word must be put in quotes, since the criteria for success in such a case are so nebulous and subjective. Obviously, in spite of all his difficulty in speech he was functioning at a high level in school. Had it been decided that his speech had become "normal," the deeper problems would have been entirely overlooked, no doubt only to burst out in a more devastating form at a later age.

As a matter of fact in one sense this was exactly what did happen. Although his speech unintelligibility was of long duration — it had first become quite noticeable when he was three, but was then attributed to "nervousness" or "excitement" and disregarded — it was not seen as a cause for referral until he entered the first grade. There can be no doubt that the problems present at the time psychotherapy was begun had already been there a year earlier, yet no attention was paid to them. The practice, followed in this case during that year, of tackling only the peripheral problems and ignoring the deeper ones unless the peripheral ones did not respond, is certainly the usual one on the contemporary scene. Yet as this case and numerous others show, it is a serious error.

In line with his urge to communciate, his panic at the sight of an accident on the screen should be seen as an anguished cry for help. It was fortunate that this at least did meet with a positive response.

Exacerbating his communication problem was the persistent inability of his parents to understand what was going on in him. Accordingly, it became progressively worse as he grew older. Had he never entered psychotherapy, he might very well have developed into a full-blown schizophrenic later in life or at best become a "mad genius."

Much of the intricate interplay between the personality of the child and that of the parents can be traced. It will be recalled that his mother always emphasized how "reasonable" he was, just as she stressed her own "rational," unemotional attitude to the world. In other words, he quickly had to learn that any sign of affect was taboo, just as the parents had repressed almost their entire emotional life. The anxiety and anger, deeply repressed, had continued further deleterious effects on his ego. Menawhile, the parents would deny their own problems and concentrate on the children. In one sense Sheldon's disturbance was exactly what his parents wanted: it gave them a cause for concern outside themselves and postponed the day of reckoning when they would have to reflect on what was happening in their own lives.

The genesis of his anxiety and anger could also be traced easily enough. Originally overattached to his mother, he deeply resented the intrusion of his father into the picture. The sharp Oedipal struggle apparent at the time of therapy followed an oral phase in which his mother almost literally wanted him to be her entire life. It will be recalled that during the first three years the mother had spent most of her time with her family in Boston, while the father maintained his job in New York. Sheldon experienced his first separation trauma when his sister was born and the second when the family was reunited. He could not express his reactions to these two separations, so he shifted them into his fantasy life, where they flourished and grew into the world that he later revealed in therapy. At various points he must have tried to share his feelings with his parents, but they remained insensitive to his needs. In this sense his parents consistently made him worse in spite of their good intentions. It will be remembered that he said hardly one word for the first eight months of the analysis; it took that time for him to realize that some stranger could be more understanding than his own family.

Therapy with the parents yielded no result; both were too distant as human beings to benefit in any reasonable way. Family therapy, had it been tried, probably would have led to just as little. This was clearly a case for intensive analytic therapy. In spite of the parents' inability to change, the boy benefited enormously.

As with other cases, the question must again be raised here whether termination should have been undertaken when it was. Would further therapy have avoided the unfortunate conflict that he got into in college? Probably, but the practical circumstances at that time made continuation virtually impossible.

A more important question is whether the analysis of a child will per se offer adequate safeguards against the outbreak of some deep neurotic conflict in adulthood, many years after the childhood analysis has been terminated. This has never been systematically considered in the literature. The present case would indicate that later conflicts can be made more tolerable but not avoided in their entirety. In any successful analysis, the ego, which guards the individual against serious emotional trouble, is strengthened. But life circumstances frequently create situations that are hard to handle. Here too it is more prudent to look for improved strength rather than an absolute cure.

Gloria,
The Reformed "Easy Lay"

LIFE HISTORY

Gloria, a married woman in her late forties, was the fifth of six children. Of the siblings five were girls, one a boy. The family lived on New York's East Side in the Yorkville sector all of the patient's life. Father was a small businessman, a dealer in surgical supplies. His business was located in this general area, and he preferred to have his home nearby. Most of the time he made a modest but adequate living; however, there were periods when the family was in bad straits. At such times the children were expected to work and contribute to the household.

In the patient's family, father was the dominant figure. He was born in Germany, and came here when he was grown; German was always easier for him than English. The patient remembered him as a handsome, aggressive man, with a big moustache. He had a violent temper and would frequently get drunk. At such times he would sit in the living room throwing knives on the table and cursing loudly. This would scare all the children out of their wits. He was always threatening to leave home, though he never actually carried out the threat.

Somehow everybody knew that father had lots of women. It was even rumored that he had had incest with his own daughters. Patient remembered once overhearing a conversation in which mention was made of sex between father and Mary, the oldest child. Mary was later said to have become a prostitute for a while. Father died when the patient was nineteen.

Mother suffered passively through all of father's antics. She devoted herself to the traditional Kinder, Kirche, and Küche (children, church, and kitchen) and was the main stabilizing influence in the children's lives, though it was father who provided all the oomph. Mother was Hungarian technically, but German was also her mother tongue. The parents were married here. She was still alive, age seventy-nine, at the end of the patient's analysis.

The patient recovered only a few memories of her childhood. She always thought of herself as "dirty Tessie" because Mother would not change her pants often and feces stuck to them. The wild scenes with father drunk, throwing knives, screaming, and threatening to leave, go back all through childhood.

Her first clear memory was from the age of five. She was all dressed up in her best clothes and went for a ride in a horse-and-buggy with Daddy. A picture was taken of them, which she kept for a long time.

This and the next memory set a pattern for her life. She was taking violin lessons from a Mr. C., who induced her to open his fly and fondle his penis. She remembers quite well how much she enjoyed it. One day she said to a neighbor boy, "Let's play like Mr. C. and I play." Her mother overheard her and asked her what she meant; "innocently" she told her the whole truth. Mr. C. was instantly dismissed and another teacher was hired, but no action was taken against him.

When Gloria was nine her brother-in-law, husband of the second oldest sister, began to have sex play with her. He would place her on a table, take off her panties, and perform cunnilingus on her. At first she enjoyed it, later she said she was revolted by it. He also took pictures of her, including a picture of her exposed vagina; this picture played a role later on in her life, as will be seen. This sex play was continued for about four years before it was discovered by her father, who threatened to beat the brother-in-law up if he ever came near the girl again. Several times afterwards he approached her anyhow, but she refused him.

For several years in early adolescence (until she was fifteen) there were no heterosexual experiences. She did have some sex play with a girl friend; the two put their breasts into one another's vaginas and smelled around the genitals. This happened only a few times, she said.

During these years she remained a studious girl, concentrating on her music, especially the violin, though she was also quite proficient at the piano. Later in her adolescence she and two of her sisters had their own radio program.

Shortly after her fifteenth birthday she embarked on an inordinate amount of sexual activity. She and her two sisters would march up and down from Lexington to Third Avenue and from 82nd to 86th Streets picking up men.

As she later put it, she allowed the men to do anything they wanted to with her. Usually they would take her somewhere and have intercourse with her; it did not matter where. Sometimes it was a room, at other times it was some dark spot in the street or a hallway.

Sex became a total obsession for a number of years. At school she could think of nothing else but whether or not she was pregnant, and would resolve never to do these things again. After school she went right back to the street and any boy who wanted her. Sometimes she would go with her sisters, very often she would be alone.

During this period she gave almost no thought to the consequences of her behavior. Twice she contracted gonorrhea, three times she had abortions. Her main fear, however, which terrified her, was that her father might discover what she was doing. Apparently, he never did.

As she described herself in this period, she was the proverbial "easy lay," the girl who couldn't say no. Once a boy she was going with brought up several other fellows who had sex with her for money, and she realized that she had been a prostitute. This was too much for her, however, and she called a halt to it.

She fell madly in love with one boy whom she knew at this time; he was the only love of her life. He showed some interest in her, but his family would not permit marriage. She never forgot him. Twenty-five years later, when she accidentally heard something about him, it still aroused a warm feeling in her.

Subjectively she was completely miserable in her adolescence. Her schoolwork went steadily downhill and there was serious danger that she would flunk out. Her wish to become a concert violinist went by the wayside. For a while she did leave school, but came back to it later.

At about the age of twenty she met her present husband. Typically he was the brother of a dentist with whom she had had sexual relations and who then wished to get rid of her. The brother likewise began to have sex with her, but he also took a more abiding interest in her, and became the great stabilizing influence of her life.

For a number of years she saw other men as well as her future husband, though he, with a few exceptions, remained faithful to her. He helped her to get back to school and to get a job. She finished college and became a music teacher in the New York high schools. She did this until her retirement.

At one point before marriage they had a fight and temporarily broke off. Her fiance, piqued by rejection, started an affair with a prostitute by the name of Sally. From Sally he acquired syphilis, which he later transmitted to the patient after they got together again.

When the syphilis was discovered, some time afterwards, both were treated and completely cured. Treatment of that day, however, involved a long series of injections in the buttocks, which left scars the patient called "bumps." These "bumps" and the history of syphilis were a source of tremendous shame to the patient, far worse in fact than her previous sexual activity. Much time was spent in the analysis in uncovering what all this meant to her, and the fear that someone would discover her history of syphilis remained with her almost to the end of analysis.

The two were finally married when she was about twenty-five. Her husband became a social worker, employed by the city; he held this job until retirement.

The husband was an extremely anxiety-ridden individual. At the age of twenty, he had attempted suicide. Shortly after she became pregnant, he had a nervous breakdown, which evidently meant severe anxiety and incapacity to work. He recovered sufficiently, and went into psychotherapy with a prominent

psychoanalyst. Some minimal change occurred. His later therapeutic history will be discussed below.

In the marriage, the patient assumed the dominant role,
which fitted into the husband's passive-dependent character,
though consciously he protested a good deal. The husband was
never permitted to leave her alone; up to the first year of analysis he had never had an evening out without her in some seventeen years of married life. She was extremely erratic and moody;
again he was compelled to put up with it. Somehow she had
developed the ability to cry at will producing real tears, and
used these hysterical outbursts to force compliance with her demands. She drank rather heavily, though never to the point
where it interfered with her work. Although both had regular
civil service jobs, they could never save money because as soon
as some accumulated she would spend it all on new furniture
and redecorating the house.

After some years of marriage the couple had one child, a
boy. Children had been postponed because of the depression;
actually, as noted above, the husband had a severe anxiety reaction when his wife became pregnant, so that deeper reasons
must have been at play as well.

Naturally enough the child soon became the center of the
universe for both parents. The patient was possessive and eventually quite openly sexually interested in the boy. A physician
told her once that the boy had a small penis, which provided
the excuse to focus constant attention on it. She continued to
dress and undress in front of him and to share the toilet with
him to a very late age; when he was fourteen, she still wanted
to have him fasten and unfasten her brassiere, because "it was
so hard to get at."

It is not entirely clear why but the boy was taken for professional consultation about his psychological problems. He
went to a nursery school and was first given some psychological
tests at the age of four-and-a-half. His IQ (Stanford-Binet) was
138, but the examiner noted overindulgence and confused
handling by the parents. The nursery school teacher, after a
home visit, stated that he was treated as an adult by the parents.

At about seven-and-a-half, the parents took him to a psychologist for examination because of frequent urination, some-

times twenty times during the school day, and constant sniffling (not further clarified). Both the psychologist and a consulting psychiatrist to whom he was sent called him "schizophrenic" and told the parents the diagnosis. What they meant is, as usual, most obscure but the diagnosis at any rate had the effect of frightening them all into therapy, and helped to keep them going at times when strong resistances appeared.

The entire family was accepted by a clinic, and each was given a separate therapist. The patient was seen by a social worker once or twice a week for a year and a half. As she remembered it, this therapy was mainly inspirational and centered on a lot of sound advice on how to live and bring up children. Patient reported that she was annoyed because the therapist would frequently doze off during the sessions.

Treatment was terminated that spring, although no one felt that any problems had been solved by any of the patients. The agency felt that they could do no more.

It was the husband who took the initiative for further treatment. He felt anxious a good deal of the time, depressed, suffered from premature ejaculation, and felt browbeaten by his wife.

Initially he went to another analyst, and it is of interest to record this story of why he did not continue with him. In his first interview the patient, in telling about his life, related how he had had sexual intercourse with his sister-in-law when he was seventeen. The analyst asked, "Do you feel that that was an ethical thing to do?" This question annoyed and puzzled him so much that he decided not to return, using money as a pretext.

I accepted him for treatment and he began in a state of great elation. As soon as he started, his wife requested an interview with me and asked if I would accept her for analysis. Motivated partly by the previous history and partly by their ages (both were in their middle forties) I agreed to treat both at the same time. Characteristically the patient said that if I did not accept her she would not go to anybody else.

The husband stopped after about eight months, again ostensibly because he had no money. Symptomatically he made some surprising changes in this short period: his anxiety lessened, and his premature ejaculation problem cleared up. However, he still felt very unhappy with both his wife and his work and returned for more therapy several years later. This will be described more fully below.

The wife continued her analysis religiously for five and a half years. She was determined to be completely comfortable and happy in all life's endeavors and left only when that goal was reached in her subjective estimate. Her main resistance was a lessening of the frequency of sessions from time to time.

When she came to treatment, patient had a variety of complaints. She suffered from a number of fairly acute anxieties, which up to that time had been handled by phobic withdrawal mechanisms. She became anxious in ordinary social gatherings, and had therefore almost entirely withdrawn from social contacts with persons other than her immediate family. Two particularly prominent fears were that her history of syphilis would be discovered and that her brother-in-law would vindictively send the picture of her vagina to the Board of Education, which would lead to her dismissal. An especially acute reaction that plagued her at the beginning of treatment was dizziness when on a podium. In her school she coached and directed a children's orchestra, which played at many assemblies and performed at other times of the year. This dizziness was becoming so strong that she was considering taking sick leave from her job for a while.

Besides these fears, there were many other areas of disturbance, although most caused no subjective discomfort. She was frigid, but said that she could take or leave sex. She was overweight, and drank too much. From her human relationships she derived no real satisfaction. The idea that she had produced a "schizophrenic" son caused her real anguish, and, as mentioned, was one of the stimuli that led her to continue therapy during some of the rough periods.

COURSE OF ANALYSIS

The patient developed an immediate, strong, positive transference. This transference took on specific sexual coloring; it rarely extended to thoughts of marriage or nonsexual activities.

In this initial period, the dreams were of two types: (1) she was a fallen woman; (2) she was having sex with me in many different places, which generally brought back scenes from her adolescence. The first dreams were usually interpreted in a sexual sense, and tied up with fear of punishment. The sexual dreams were used to get her to talk about her past, but while she was willing to give associations up to a point, she would generally balk at giving too much detail. While the falling dreams disappeared after a few months, the sexual ones continued all through the analysis.

Realistically, a prime source of concern in the beginning of treatment was her son. This was only natural, since she had been told only a short time before that he was schizophrenic, and he was behaving in a strange way. Every day after school he would come home, take off his clothes, get into pajamas, and look at television. The family lived in a three-room apartment, which meant that they were always together in the living room, except when the boy went to sleep in the bedroom. The parents slept on a couch in the living room, which was opened up into a bed at night.

The patient taught at a school a few blocks from her home and came home at 3:00 o'clock. The boy's school was also nearby, and he likewise came home at 3:00 o'clock. The husband worked later, and was home in the evenings. Nobody ever went out alone, so that mother and child were together all the time except when they went to school.

Although the boy was then ten years old, the mother acted in an openly seductive way. She walked around in her underwear, and asked his help to get dressed or undressed, particularly with her brassiere. She preferred the boy's help to her husband's. As mentioned, she was intensely interested in the boy's penis, which, she had been told by a physician, was undersized.

The seductive attitude towards the boy, which was totally unconscious, naturally tied in with the rest of her personality and life history. In addition to analyzing her needs, however, I made the direct suggestion that she stop seducing him and discontinue immediately the mutual exposure which was going on. Although she could not really see why, I was the doctor and she would do what I said.

Deprived of the pleasures of nudity, the boy rapidly

changed (he was not in treatment with anyone at this time). He got dressed and went out to play with other boys. No trace of his so-called "schizophrenia" remained. Some remarks about his later development will be made below.

Two other concerns dominated Gloria's everyday associations in this early period. One was her complete dissatisfaction with her husband. He was dull and incompetent. A woman's place is in the home, and he should make enough money to allow her to retire and take care of the house. He was always reading stupid books. He was not a good father to the boy. He didn't appreciate her need to redecorate the house.

These complaints were either uninterpreted at this stage or used to get her to release more feeling about other men in her life. Much of the material related above about her adolescence and her father came out in this way. The resentment towards her husband, however, continued for a number of years. Interestingly, it took some time before she said anything about his premature ejaculation, although after a few months of treatment with me, this symptom demonstrated some remarkable improvement.

The second source of reality concern was the assembly performances and the annual concert. In addition to her regular teaching duties, she trained another group of students to give a concert once a year, in May. This was likewise under the auspices of the Board of Education. This concert worried her particularly because she became dizzy during the performance and was always afraid that she would faint. It had, however, been going on for seven years and she had always handled it.

One important association to the podium fear was that since she was up higher than the audience, and with her back to them, they could look up her skirts. This led to the revelation that for years she had not worn underpants; instead she wore what she called "chafies," cotton padding extending around the body. The refusal to wear pants certainly suggested an intense repressed exhibitionistic wish, which also came out in many other ways. Unraveling the various devices that she used to disguise her exhibitionism was a goodly part of this woman's analysis.

As we approached the end of the first year in analysis, I

notified her in June that I would as usual go on vacation in about a month. This brought forth a flood of protest and a desire to terminate, the working through of which proved very fruitful.

In one session she began by saying that she had been quite angry with me last time because of a remark I had made — that where there is no affection, there's no marriage. She had gone home and asked her husband if there was affection in their home and he had said "sure." After that she had a dream:

"I'm in the dinette, which is in reversed position. A painter is painting the wall. He paints it white but there are blue streaks in it and dots. I say it is such a lousy job I won't pay. I'll report him to the landlord and the office of rent control."

To the reversed position she associated the analytic situation and her desire to reverse the positions. The painter she saw as the analyst. To blue she associated depression. Dots meant the bumps on her behind. The dream was interpreted as a wish to take revenge on me. This anger had three roots: (1) I had not restored her behind to what it was, which in turn led to the childhood memory of "dirty Tessie"; (2) I was going away on vacation and leaving her; (3) I did not gratify her sexual wishes.

Several days later she had another dream:

"I'm lying in one bed, Paul [husband] in another. I'm afraid he will disappear."

To this she associated a fight with her husband, which made her afraid that he would leave, and this led to the childhood fear that her father would leave home.

In spite of all interpretation, she insisted on cutting down to one session per week over the summer; analysis was somehow connected with school. The sexual material now annoyed her and she just wanted to get rid of it.

One night during this time she woke up screaming "Did my father penetrate me?" This nightmare brought back another frightening experience. Once she had had a tooth removed, and had gas administered. Under the anesthetic she had a dream that God dug his finger deeper and deeper into her abdomen. The dentist, who was her brother-in-law, reported that while she was anesthetized she went through motions that looked like coitus. She was dreadfully afraid that the nightmare about God would be repeated if she ever took an anesthetic again, and tried to avoid anesthesia at all costs from then on.

Another revealing dream:

"...I'm lying on a couch. Sarah [sister] wants to marry the man she is with, he doesn't want to marry her. A one-legged man comes over to me and starts hugging and kissing me."

The situation with the sister existed in real life. She had been kept for many years by a married man who refused to marry her. On the one hand she wanted to get married, on the other she enjoyed the easy life in which she was taken care of in exchange for sex. To the one-legged man she associated Toulouse-Lautrec, which made her a whore. The dream is a wish to be a whore or a kept woman; this she readily accepted. The allied wish to castrate the man (Toulouse-Lautrec) she denied.

Another dream:

"I'm wiping my behind in the living room, putting the tissues on the table."

The anal exhibitionism here is obvious. In this connection she also discussed the pleasure she had in having her anus played with by her husband. In this she saw nothing problematic, even though she derived more pleasure from her anus than from her vagina; it was just part of her nature.

In the next session she stated that she had decided to continue analysis and would resume at two sessions per week in the fall. She also reported a dream:

"I am up on the roof. Paul, Sam, and Al [son] are near a place which is low; I'm afraid they will fall off."

Sam was a friend of her husband's whom she did not like; he had been over the night before. She could absorb the connection of her symptoms with the lifelong fear of desertion, but said nothing about the wish to push all the men off the roof.

Two sessions later she reported that her husband, who had recently left his own treatment, was urging her to leave analysis. He now wanted her to save money and buy a house. She was reluctant to go into a house, and wanted to stay in analysis. She was now able to see the futility of constantly throwing out old furniture and refurnishing the house; its symbolic meanings, in terms of herself and her vagina as the house could likewise be discussed. This was the last session before the vacation.

When she returned in the fall she felt all cured — all her problems were gone. While I was inquiring into the meaning of this, her husband called and wanted to take over one of her hours. When I refused, she felt quite pleased, and said that she would keep coming even if she had no problems.

The events of the first year of analysis can now be briefly reviewed. She established a strong transference, primarily positive and full of sexual fantasies. She unburdened much of the anxiety of her past and corrected a troublesome situation with her son, which yielded some significant relief. She released a great deal of resentment towards her husband, which she began to see as connected with her feelings about men and her father all through her life. She was beginning to see some connection between her recurrent anxieties and her vivid sexual fantasies.

As we have mentioned, the analysis was a long one, five and a half years in all. In the succeeding periods, certain well-defined themes appear and persist for a while, then disappear. Later they may recur again in weakened form, until they finally vanish altogether. The subsequent material will be organized around these themes which mark the course of her psychic development. My thesis is that by and large the analysis did take the course of a progressive liberation, even though the chronological sequence used here is not as strict as might be thought from the presentation.

Working Through the Sexual Feelings for the Analyst

After the return from vacation, the positive feelings for the analyst again had the upper hand. In one dream:

"Louie asks me to marry him. I think what will happen to Paul and the boy. My brother says, "Will you do something for me?" I think he wants me to lay for him; I say, "Sure." He says, "Lend me some money; I'm disappointed."

To Louie she associated the analyst. The incestuous meaning of sexuality is obvious here.

A few sessions later came a jealousy dream:

"You take me by the hand to a party. There you ask another woman to escort you to your office."

Somewhat later she dreamt:

"I'm lying on a couch. You [the analyst] come and lie down next to me. I think this is not allowed, but maybe he'll make an exception in my case."

Many associations to the idea of being an "exception" came up. She was different from the other children in her family, different from other girls, now is different from other teachers. "Being an exception" and "being different" were linked to her exhibitionistic wishes.

Then she brought in two dreams:

"I am on the couch. Mr. W. gets on top of me fully dressed, and comes in his pants."

"I am on the couch. A man gets on top of me. I say I love him very much. He says I make $160 a week for evenings. I think now I don't have to work. Also $85 for the daytime. This is a disappointment."

In both these dreams I was the man. The $160 was her mental calculation of my income, which, of course, she compared with her husband's.

Getting Rid of Other Men

In the midst of these fantasies about me, she "got rid" of the other men in her life — her son and husband. She dreamt:

"Al falls down a sewer. I go down and pick him out."

The fantasy of birth through the anus, a common one in little girls, could easily be reflected here. Quite clear is the identification of the child with feces.

A few weeks later came an even more outright rejection dream:

"I am with Al in an open field. I put him off to one side in a room; I go off the other way to an outhouse. A girl comes up and bawls me out for making so much noise."

To the girl she associated an Indian girl in school whose boy friend was killed.

Shortly after this dream, the fights with her husband reached such a pitch that she notified him that she wanted to separate. (This sort of thing had been going on for years.) He took it passively. Then she was horrified by what she had done and they made up again. That night she dreamt:

"Paul is dead. A man with thick lips approaches me to have sex. I say, "All right, provided that you marry me the next day." He agrees. Then I remember with horror that you have to wait three days for the Wasserman."

Thus she wants to get rid of husband (bad father), but is afraid that the syphilis will prevent her from getting another man (good father).

Sexual Release

After all this material had been worked through, a noticeable change came about in her feelings about sexuality. She secured a diaphragm. She obtained more pleasure vaginally, although she held on to the rectal pleasure as well. She began to have occasional orgasms if her husband would play with her clitoris during intercourse; she preferred coitus *a tergo*. Somewhat later she developed a pattern of giving herself an orgasm by masturbation after intercourse was over. One day she came in and said that during the week a sudden revelation came to her: Everybody fucks. After that, her guilt about her sexual activities lessened.

Oedipal Victory

The release was accompanied by feelings of victory, identification with her mother, and pregnancy fantasies. She dreamt:

"Miss C. is walking down a flight of stairs. When she has only two to go, she falls and breaks her neck. Mr. N. comes in, puts his hands on my breasts and starts making love to me. I can feel he has an erection. I say, "Can't you see that there is a woman with a broken neck there...""

Miss C. is a fellow teacher. Mr. N. is her supervisor.

Earlier came a dream which brought the first mention of the mother after the initial life history.

"I walk along a dirt road."

To the dirt road she associated the country place where her mother had been living for a number of years. In the relationship with her mother she had always been a good girl; in the entire analysis, no feelings of antagonism towards her were released.

Around this period, as came out much later, there occurred a rather remarkable bit of behavior. Although she visited her mother quite frequently, she now began to write her daily postcards and continued this for a period of years. The content of the cards was quite trivial: a cake she had baked, or some remark about her husband or son. All this only came to light years afterwards when she casually revealed that she had skipped a day.

A most unusual dream:

"I am out in the open field. Helen [sister] is at one breast, sucking. I'm pregnant. I say to her, "Don't do it out in the open; it's so embarrassing."

Helen is her sister. The dream contains a variety of Oedipal gratifications: she is mother feeding a baby, is pregnant with another, and can show it to all the world (open field). Of course, there is still punishment (it is so embarrassing), but it is mild.

Acceptance of Narcissistic Gratification

The overcoming of masochistic trends paralleled the release of her sexual feelings. Around this time, with the release of sexual feeling, she also became more outgoing. She was able to allow her husband to go out without her, and she in turn could have some social engagements without him. Very important, and dating from this time, was the resumption of piano playing and study. (Eventually she resumed all her former interests and became a member of a quartet.)

The superego, of course, did not give up so lightly. Throughout the above development there was a recurring theme of punishment.

Punishment by the Father

"I am outside Carnegie Hall with two tickets. A man approaches me, offers me $50. I hesitate, then sell them. The police arrest me."

$50 was for her the price of an abortion. Sex leads to abortion and punishment.

Refusal to Accept Father's Punishment

Two dreams turn out in retrospect to have marked a turning point in the analysis.

"I'm lying on the bed. Al lies next to me, and has sex from the side."

"I'm in my living room. My father's coffin is there. I say, "No, that can't be possible because it is off in the funeral parlor."

The combination of sex with her son and the refusal to admit the father back into her house meant that she was defying him really for the first time in her life, and accepting her sexual feelings.

Restoring the Inner Image of the Good Father

She had some dreams about her sisters, especially Charlotte, whom she promptly killed off. Many memories about Charlotte came back: she always felt ignored in relation to her and felt that father preferred Charlotte.

"I am looking in a pool. The water disappears and I see straw."

To the pool she associated admiring herself; to the straw, horse manure such as she remembered on her father's farm. Here another childhood memory came back; for many years her father had a farm in an outlying area and she loved to go there. It was there that she rode in a horse-and-buggy with him (her earliest memory), and there she enjoyed herself in many other ways with him. While the dream has an ambivalent meaning,

since she turns into horseshit, the associations particularly
brought her back to the happy times with him.

After three years of analysis as outlined above, an entirely
new phase was entered. Upon her return from a two-month
summer vacation, the patient insisted on cutting down to one
session per week. No amount or kind of interpretation would
prevail upon her to come more often. Faced with the alternative
of accepting her manipulation or discontinuing the analysis, I
chose to continue and try to understand her resistance.

At the same time, the nature of the material produced in
the analytic hours underwent a profound change. Where before
it had been a dream analysis, in which the stress was on her in-
stinctual drives, particularly the sexual, now it turned into an
analysis of everyday events, in which the emphasis came to be
placed on character defenses, anxieties, and deep-seated resentments. Here, too, certain trends dominated the analysis for a
while and then gave way to others.

Ambivalence Towards Nephew

This started earlier, but came to a head around this time.
Her nephew had entered a nearby college. Since he lived in the
country, while she was nearby, she had generously offered to
let him come and live in her house for a while. No sooner done
than regretted. The apartment was already too small for the
three of them, especially since analysis had led to more re-
striction of movement for them. With a fourth person, the situation became unbearable. With this experience, the broader question of her relations to people came to the fore. I offered her a
general interpretation that she tended to cling to and manipulate other people. She resisted this for a long time, but eventually came to agree with me.

Clinging and Manipulation

This came out in so many different ways that only the
highlights can be given here. A broader view of her personality
was now brought to the fore. When she became anxious, instead
of handling it realistically, she tried to manipulate another per-

son or situation to protect her or to afford her relief. In this process she naturally came to cling to people rather than to accept them as people and relate to them at an adult level.

Relationship With Son

Again the character complex of clinging and manipulation to cover up sexual desire was noted with respect to her son. She was afraid to let him travel very far around the city. She conjured up fantasies that he would become a juvenile delinquent. She began tirades against war, which amounted to annoyance at the fact that he was approaching draft age. It was evident that basically her attitude to him, as to all men, was that he should stick around, take care of her, and protect her from her loneliness and fears. Her incestuous wish for the boy came to the fore more and more. It could be seen how this was a continuation of her incestuous wish for her father. However, although she showed much improvement in this respect, for a long time she could not accept her wish for her son as a natural one. All agreed, however, that the analysis of the total situation brought about a considerable improvement in the mother-son relationship.

Relationship With Analyst

The insistence on cutting down to once a week, coupled with the conscious desire to prolong the analysis, and a passive wish to have me cure her husband and son while I left her alone, were all clearly a part of the character complex of cling and manipulate. Although little direct sexual material was forthcoming in this second phase of the analysis, it was easy enough to tie it up with the profuse and lush fantasies of the earlier period.

Continuous analysis helped her to accept her sexual desire for the analyst as a realistic one, which eventually enabled her to give up the cling-manipulate pattern.

After a while she acquired the ability to analyze some of her own transference reactions. Once she came in while I was playing the piano. Although she could not see me she fantasized that I was the one who was playing, and that after the analysis was over she would give me piano lessons. The wish to prolong the relationship and to turn it into a social one was readily apparent to her.

Relationship With Women

Most of her fellow teachers were women, and she did not get along very well with them. She had few friends among them, and her social contacts with them were extremely limited.

Three people in school came up repeatedly in the course of the analysis. One was Ann, who was the wife of a dermatologist; she herself was a teacher (of home economics). Ann was her ideal; her marriage was perfect, she had an extensive social life and no fears. She wanted to get closer to Ann but was prevented from doing so by her fear that Ann's husband, with his expert medical knowledge, would immediately discover her history (the syphilis again!). Some anal-homosexual material also came out, in that at times she was afraid to be in the toilet with other teachers, especially Ann. Analytically, Ann stood for the "perfect mother" whom she could never aspire to be.

A second person who became important for a while was the school nurse. She was a full-blown paranoid, according to Gloria's description. She believed that invisible electric rays penetrated through to her from the apartment below, and had other delusions. In spite of her pathology, she continued to function in her job.

Evidently the woman had been in this condition for many years. Somehow, perhaps as a result of the therapeutic changes, the patient became friendly with her and discovered what was going on. As usual, she immediatley wanted to send her to me for treatment (I refused).

The realization that the nurse was psychotic brought up her own fears about herself, which had been buttressed by inept psychiatric diagnosis. We analyzed the meaning of schizophrenia to her and saw that it related to the passive wish to be taken care of. It also explained her withdrawal from female companionship. Analytically, the nurse was her own bad image of herself.

A third person who became a subject of analytic discussion was the principal, an unmarried woman in her fifties. This principal was almost a textbook caricature of principals: arbitrary, overdemanding, unresponsive to children and to human needs, a true disciplinarian. Many fights occurred between them. Eventually the patient came to see that the principal stood for the "bad mother," and she handled her more realistically.

In the course of time, the various identifications and projections involved in her relationships with women were worked out to the point where her social life improved considerably. However, she always preferred the company of men.

A Religious Conversion

After the battles with the husband had been analyzed over and over again, the patient conceived the idea that if she converted to Judaism it would please him and cement the marriage. The patient had been born a Christian, but her family was freethinking and there were no meaningful religious ties. The husband had been brought up as an orthodox Jew, then broke away from it. He remembered Judaism as a religion where the chief rule was "Man tur nicht," (You must not) and later returned to a reform version because he wanted to express his feelings of belonging to the Jews. He went to the temple on Fridays and weekends and engaged in some of the social activities there. Both parents also thought in a general way that religion was good for the boy.

The conversion spread over a period of almost a year. Although she had to profess belief in the doctrines of the Jewish faith, it cannot be said that her theological convictions were strong. Primarily, she spoke of how handsome the rabbi was, and of the pleasure she derived from going to the temple on Fridays and weekends.

Termination Stage

Some four and a half years after the analysis had started, the patient began to talk about termination. Most of her anxieties had either disappeared or considerably diminished and she was handling her life much more realistically and effectively. I agreed that she could terminate, but explained that termination

was a process, not a specific point. Tentatively, we set the end
of the year as the termination date, with the understanding that
if she wished to come after that she could do so.

The most noteworthy new material that came up in this
termination stage, which lasted about a year, was a number of
dreams about her parents dying. It will be recalled that her
father died when she was nineteen, while her mother was still
alive. These dreams were interpreted mainly as an expression of
hostility towards the parents, and a wish that she could get rid
of them and finally be a grown-up person in her own right. At
the same time the dreams brought out some of her own feelings
about death, which were worked through surprisingly quickly.

Although she matured considerably in that respect, to the
end she maintained a rather bashful-bride attitude towards sex.
She told a joke in class about a boy who was always urged to
practice (as she was always urging her pupils to practice). When
he got married his friends asked him, "Did you practice?" The
other teachers kidded her about the joke, but it took her some
time to see it.

Still, basically her attitude towards sexual pleasure had
become much healthier. One of her last dreams was:

"I'm kissing a man; I keep on pressing my lips up against
his."

A word may be said about her final sexual adjustment. She
did not usually have orgasms in intercourse, but often pretended
that she did to make her husband feel better. She liked the
position a tergo, and in that position, when he played with her
clitoris, she had clitoral orgasm. A favored mode of gratification,
however, remained masturbation to a clitoral orgasm after intercourse was finished, when her husband was not in the room.

At Christmas she decided she wanted to stay in analysis a
little longer, until she felt completely comfortable. She remained
another ten weeks. When she left she felt very happy.

There were several contacts with the patient after termination. A few months later she called to tell me that she had read
that people get better just as quickly without psychiatry, but
she didn't believe she could have made the changes she had
without my help. About eight months after she left, her husband

sent me a note saying that she was very depressed, had stayed out of school for a couple of weeks, and should see me. Shortly thereafter she herself called, sounding quite cheerful, said that her husband was all wet, there had been an impossible situation at school with her principal which she could handle only by pretending to be sick and staying out for a few weeks. She assured me that she was feeling fine and that if anything ever did happen to her she would call me. Some fifteen months after termination she called to tell me that she had finally been able to join a quartet at a professional level, and was very happy about it.

A year and a half after termination her husband called to tell me that her sister Susan was in the hospital in a coma after an overdose of sleeping tablets. He had just been given the news and did not know how to break it to his wife. He was sure she would become hysterical, although this hadn't happened for years, and wanted to know whether she could reach me this weekend. I assured him that she could, and talked to him about his fears. She never called. In the period since she had stopped, he told me, things had been going very well.

THEORETICAL COMMENTS

The following questions can be raised: (1) What changes were brought about by analysis? (2) To what extent would these changes have occurred in any case? (3) How does the structure of the personality appear in the light of the therapeutic experience? (4) How did the therapeutic changes occur? (5) What were the therapeutically effective factors?

Changes Brought About by Analysis

An evaluation of the total history allows one to subsume the changes under four headings:

REDUCTION IN ANXIETY: Overall, this is the most striking feature. Where before Gloria was always worried, unhappy, and fearful, after analysis she was relatively free from anxiety much of the time. Realistic anxieties, when they came up , were handled more effectively.

INCREASE IN SEXUAL PLEASURE: Although she did not achieve full vaginal orgasm, the pleasure she did experience was considerably greater than before. It can be said that she advanced from an oral view of sex to a phallic one. Before she would, for example, allow the man to have sex with her while she lay there passively, or would allow him to ejaculate into her mouth and ask nothing further for herself. Now she enjoys the sex act, participates in it, but her maximum pleasure is derived from clitoral masturbation. It could, of course, be argued that she should have continued analysis until she did achieve vaginal orgasm. This raises many questions, particularly the role that vaginal orgasm plays in the total psychic economy of the woman. In any case, the fact remains that she refused to continue in order to achieve that goal.

INCREASE IN SENSE OF WELL-BEING: Most of the time she felt happy. In this sense Freud's rule-of-thumb goal for analysis, to work and to love, was reached. It is to be noted that much of her sense of well-being came from narcissistic gratification (e.g., piano playing). She is not imbued with much of a love for other people, although she gets along with them well enough. This goes with her unwillingness to pursue analysis further in order to get over her preferred narcissistic mode of gratification.

GROWTH IN INTERPERSONAL RELATIONS: To a considerable extent she overcame the clinging-submissive-manipulative attitude towards other people which was so typical of her all through her life.

Role of Analysis in Change

The problem involved in ascertaining how much of the change is to be attributed to analysis and how much to other factors is a formidable one. Nevertheless, it is a crucial one, and must be approached in spite of all the difficulties involved.

For our patient, only one significant change in her real

life occurred in the course of the analysis; the change in her husband. Though what he achieved in his own therapy was to my way of thinking minimal, changes did occur. Mainly, he became much less anxious, got over his premature ejaculation, and became much more interested in her sexually. However, his basic attitude towards her did not change, as witness the call he made to me because he was afraid she was going to have a hysterical fit over her sister's attempted suicide, when actually it was his own fear that was involved.

The changes that did take place in him certainly made life more pleasant for the two of them. But the content of the analytic sessions shows that her antagonism to him was a deep-rooted one, based on her own Oedipal situation and anxieties. Hence, we can reasonably say that it was only the inner reorganization which made her more accessible to him.

In the course of her own life, two situations are available for comparison with the analysis. One is the time when she and husband began to go steady and she gave up the promiscuous pattern with other men. This led to more outer stability in the form of marriage, and at least neutralized some inner energy and made it available for a job she liked. However, the main features of the illness remained.

The second situation is that of the nonanalytic therapy which preceded the analytic. So far as I could see, this had no effect whatsoever. As is to be expected, she wanted the therapist to function as a guide and mentor, which the therapist did, possibly because of the diagnosis of "schizophrenia" and the emphasis on the social work attitude. But the results of all this were, as mentioned, nil.

Some basis for comparison is also afforded by the other sisters. The oldest, whom the father had reputedly had sex with, became a prostitute for a while and lived a fringe existence all her life, as our patient had in adolescence. Another was for many years a kept woman, and eventually attempted suicide.

Thus, all these girls were dominated by the drunken, sexually excited father, and incorporated him as a main feature of their superego. The struggle took different forms but led to many unhappy experiences for all of them.

Although the patient received a lift from one superego pro-

jection (her husband), this proved to be both highly inadequate
and temporary. The detailed study of her life history shows that
the changes could not have been achieved without analysis.

Structure of Personality

A review of our patient's life shows that as far back as she
can remember she was dominated by a strong superego, mainly
an internal image of her father, which set the course of her life.
The childhood seductions were obviously enjoyable sex with
the father. In adolescence she always hoped to find the good
father in each pick-up; the girl who couldn't say no, couldn't
say no to her father, and in her dental chair hysteria said yes to
him. By this constant attempt to project the superego, she became extraordinarily amenable to outside male influence and
what direction her life took depended on the accidental circumstances of what men she ran into. That she met her present husband was, in this sense, a fortunate turn; if another kind of man
had persisted she might have become in reality a prostitute,
kept woman, drunkard, or even homosexual.

Characteristic for this patient is that the sexual, constructive aspects of the superego outweighed the nonsexual, destructive ones. The awareness of her father's sexuality served as a
spur to find substitute father figures who could give her what
she was denied by her own father. The guilt aroused by sexuality, though strong, was never as intense as the shame derived
from an earlier stage. In the seesaw of these various emotional
currents we can see her dynamics at play.

As to the role of the mother in the patient's development,
the history offers little enlightenment. She was a European
woman, and evidently brought up her six children with the traditional European emphasis on the home. She was apparently
neglectful of her children (as a child the patient was always running around in dirty pants). The first clear memory of her
mother comes up in connection with the loss of the sexual
pleasure derived from the violin teacher. Later, however, the
mother plays no role at all. We could say that for the little girl
the mother's lack of feeling made the boisterous father all the
more attractive.

In the analysis, the patient was able to separate the good father from the bad one; I was good, her husband was bad. Gradually her husband assumed the more human proportions of being both good and bad but except for brief intervals I never lost my halo. Why she never developed a negative transference requires some explanation.

Evidently the mother's resentment against the father was mixed with a strong longing. The father's anger, in his drunken moods, was so tinged with sexuality (even to the knives being thrown on the table) that the sexual father became a stronger part of the internal image than the angry one. As long as the patient was unmarried, sexuality maintained the upper hand. Once she had a husband, she identified with the mother and intensified the resentment. In the analysis she repeated this pattern: I was the father, so sexuality predominated; her husband was the mother's husband, she the mother, so resentment was stronger. (We can see here one reason why many women develop a strong hatred for their husbands after marriage.)

What is it that determines the relative weights of sexuality and hostility? To this question two answers are currently available: constitution and the bad experiences with mother. About constitution we are as much in the dark as ever. The oral trauma here was apparently not as severe as often seen in other patients; the mother at any rate was not overtly psychotic or given to uncontrollable emotion. Yet the patient came to the verge of a psychosis, and her sisters fared quite badly in life. It would appear that, in ways most difficult to formulate, quantitative factors are decisive.

What is more significant and most decisive here is the nature of the superego into which all these elements are poured in varying degrees. In this superego, of course, the character of the parents themselves must be given due weight, a point which is too often omitted. In attempts to further differentiate her from other people, the superego must be compared and contrasted in the greatest of detail.

How Did the Therapeutic Changes Occur?

Here three factors particularly can be singled out: the analysis of transference, the release of unconscious material, and a combination of analysis of desire and grasp of reality.

The analysis of the transference occupied roughly the first three years of the analysis. It was predominantly sexual, predominantly positive, and could readily be connected with the feelings about her father.

In the release of unconscious material, dreams played the major role. Free association played a lesser role, while there were only a few childhood memories.

The analysis involved a combination of id and ego approaches. It is my feeling that either one alone would have been insufficient. In the ego structure, the primary focus was on the superego.

Factors Making for Therapeutic Effectiveness

It could be said that the prime factor was that the neurosis fitted snugly into the transference. Her major mechanism in life, the projection of the superego to a man, was once more carried out here. This accounted for the primarily positive feeling about me all through the analysis. She accepted the daughter-father role with me, and still maintains it, though in considerably diminished form.

Comparison with other cases indicates that technique must be described in a flexible manner. The transference neurosis appeared almost as soon as she started, in contrast to others in whom it comes much later, or never. No strong resistances or negative transference, such as we so often encounter, appeared. The analysis was conducted on the basis of two sessions weekly, later one, yet the result was still strikingly good. Both her husband and her son were seen by me, yet this did not interfere with her progress.

What, then, is essential to the psychoanalytic process? In this case only the release of unconscious material, the approach to the total personality, and the systematic analysis of transference. Frequency of sessions and contacts with family turned out to be of secondary importance.

Peter,
The Addicted Physician

The patient, a thirty-three-year-old physician, whom we shall call Peter, was first referred to me about a year before he started. His wife, who, as will be seen, dominated his life, objected to the idea that a physician should go to a lay analyst. In deference to her, he went to a man who, she discovered, was considered the most promising young analyst in New York, even though he had not yet reached the status of institute membership.

In this first analysis, the analyst adopted a vigorous attitude toward the drug to which the patient was addicted. He interpreted the drug as milk, and insisted that Peter take the drug every four hours, as though he were an infant on a rigid feeding schedule. Further, he informed the patient that he would be seen in psychoanalytic therapy three times a week and would sit up, switching to psychoanalysis and the couch when it seemed appropriate. Peter did not understand these reservations, in spite of his medical training.

In three months of this treatment Peter made considerable progress. When he first went into treatment he had been too depressed to work. His therapy was subsidized by his family. One source of resentment for Peter was that the analyst would not reduce his fee as a professional courtesy; another was his feeling that the psychiatrist was jealous of his (Peter's) greater medical knowledge.

Nevertheless, the immediate result seemed to be excellent. Peter recovered sufficiently to get back to work. At this point the analyst announced that the sessions would be increased to five per week, that they would switch to analysis conducted on the couch, and that henceforth the patient would have to pay the fee out of his salary. Peter deeply resented this last demand because the increased analytic fee exceeded his entire salary.

Accordingly, he discontinued treatment. The analyst then called him up, offering to take him back for psychoanalytic therapy at three sessions per week and agreeing to let him go on accepting financial assistance from his family. But Peter, angry, would not return.

Instead, he went to another analyst, a Horneyite. This shift in theoretical orientation (the first was a Freudian) was significant, since all through the analysis with me he wavered between a Freudian and a Horneyite approach, using this as an intellectual resistance which was very hard to handle. In any case, he distrusted the first analyst's interpretations about the need for mother's milk, preferring to feel that he had resorted to the drug because he could not handle his present-day conflicts. Further, he tended to regard it as a "bad habit," later using this as a rationalization for going to a psychologist.

Unfortunately, the second analyst tried to "technique" him too. First he told Peter that he would not accept him for treatment unless he gave up the drug. To this Peter reluctantly agreed. The net result was that he would take the drug in the doctor's toilet (the connection between the drug and the toilet was quite significant, as appeared later), denying that he was still addicted. The analyst would then spend a major portion of the hour telling Peter about other severe cases whom he had helped, particularly alcoholics. Apparently here there was no attempt at interpretation at all. After about three months of this, Peter left, shortly before the summer vacation. In the fall, desperate, he called the doctor to resume treatment, but the doctor would not take him back.

In the meantime his addiction became steadily more disturbing. One psychiatrist whom he tried to consult for "medical help," as he put it, wanted him to wait a week for an appointment. This angered him so much that he would not go.

It is understandable that when he finally did come to see me he was quite desperate. He called on a Saturday at 5:00 P.M. and was given an appointment at 7:00, two hours later. The fee was reduced to a level where he could afford to come three times per week, with the suggestion that it might be best to make it more often, but this was left optional, especially in the light of the experience with the first analyst. During the first session, I commented that he seemed to place great importance on being liked by everybody; to this he responded with great enthusiasm, asserting that it clarified a lot in his life. When he left he said that it was the best session he had ever had.

The analysis was conducted on a three times a week basis at first; later it was increased to four sessions per week, and for the last few months five per week. The analysis was interrupted by a brief hospitalization for an appendectomy and two hospitalizations for withdrawal. Eventually he was able to withdraw from the drug. Sporadic contact was maintained for a period of ten years, in which time he did not relapse into addiction. While it is clear that he did succeed in giving up the drug, the degree to which a basic change in his character structure was effected is less clear.

LIFE HISTORY

Inasmuch as a good part of the analytic work, especially after the beginning, centered on Peter's addiction, I could piece together his life history only from occasional comments made in various sessions. To the pressure of the drug must be added his intellectual resistance (Horney) that his childhood really had nothing to do with his troubles. Only the major outlines of his life history came through.

Peter was the youngest of four boys. His father was a tailor who made an adequate living, but his mother was a chronic invalid. His father reacted to her invalidism by going out with other women, virtually deserting his wife entirely. "He never gave a damn about anything," Peter once said, "so he lived hale and hearty to a ripe old age."

As far back as he could remember, Peter was a frightened, insecure little boy. He had been told that as an infant he had

had night terrors, but he retained no conscious memory of them. He showed the characteristic pattern of the rejected infant, which would fit in with his mother's chronic invalidism. Then came a period of anal obstinacy, which resulted in lifelong constipation. Even after he had been practicing medicine for many years, he persisted in giving himself enemas.

As a rationalization for his addiction, he held on to the conviction that he suffered from pneumonia and colitis, which were masked by the drug. Were he to give up the drug, they would break out in full force and quite likely kill him. When I questioned these diagnoses, he refused to discuss the matter on the grounds that his medical knowledge was so far superior to mine. (This incidentally, was one reason he had given for choosing a lay analyst. He had felt that the previous two analysts were jealous of his greater medical expertise, but when they disagreed with his judgment, he found it difficult to prove it to them.) The pneumonia-colitis diagnosis, although couched in scientific terms, had a delusional quality about it; in ordinary language he was terrified that his body was falling apart.

Prior to the virtually complete incapacitation of his mother, which took place when he was about eight and ended with her death about four years later, he was terribly frightened of punishment by everybody else in the house. His brothers regularly tormented him, while his mother often beat him with a rubber hose. He grew into a masochistic, dependent boy who was constantly concerned with gaining other people's approval. This eventually led to a front of superficial excitability, which was one of his most obvious traits in later life.

During the first period of his illness, when he was unable to work, his brothers united to support him and finance his analysis. Nevertheless, he was so estranged from them that he never spoke of them during the analysis. The only incident that he did mention with pride was that he had saved the next older brother from abdominal surgery by submitting a questionable x-ray evaluation to a prominent specialist, who had concurred with his opinion that there was no carcinoma so that surgery was contraindicated.

The marked clinging-homosexual component had been present in him from earliest childhood. This was brought out, among other ways, by his two nicknames in childhood: Pesty Peter and passionate Sarah. The role of his homosexuality (it always remained latent) in the later personality formation was quite noticeable.

When his mother's illness became acute, Peter was called upon to nurse her. Since she was completely bedridden and he was alone with her, the nursing was a highly seductive-destructive affair. She was careless about her dress, asking only for relief from her symptoms.

It was obvious that he was highly stimulated by the situation, although he remembered little of what he went through. He did recall dreaming of different parts of her body, both before and after she died. Often he would crawl into bed with her, deriving comfort from the warmth of her body. Once he got an erection, which made him feel very guilty. Another time he gave her codeine instead of digitalis, whereupon she accused him of trying to murder her. This incident tormented him for quite a while.

After his mother's death he entered a new phase, in which the major conscious purpose of his life was to control all of his desires. His life goal was to rest, relax, and work. He himself saw this as identical with what he was now trying to do with the drug. Although he had several early sexual episodes with a girl cousin when he was thirteen and had been approached homosexually by an older man when he was twelve, his determination to control all his desires persisted until he was nineteen. He concentrated on his schoolwork and apparently was a model boy for a number of years. He even frowned upon masturbation.

Unable to get into any of the local colleges because of poor grades, he went off to a college out of state when he was nineteen. There he went through undergraduate college and medical school. Although he was not a brilliant student and did not even have books when he was in medical school, he got through with satisfactory grades.

But once out of town all his controls vanished. While in college and medical school his sexuality was let loose. Since he was an outgoing, handsome young man, he found no shortage of girls. As he remembered this period, it was one of indiscriminate sexuality. Once when he was short of rent money he even had sex with his landlady, some thirty years his senior.

Although he was having a great deal of sex, he remained utterly insatiable. He began to have insomnia at this time, and it never really left him until after the analysis. When he could not sleep, he would go out and find a girl, which would at least give him some relief. His ability to get through school under these circumstances he ascribed to the fact that its standards were much lower than those that he had been accustomed to in New York.

Nevertheless, his struggle for control continued. Two fantasies dominated his thinking in his teens. In one he was a whore, receiving men all the time. The emphasis in this fantasy was that as a woman he would never have to stop feeling the man; there would literally be an endless line of men ready and willing to service her (him). The other fantasy represented the opposite pole. In this he was an English lord, austere, sedate, and completely devoid of any emotion. Obviously, this represented the extreme of the control that he had been searching for since he was thirteen.

Although he was having sex all the time, analysis brought out the usual conventional guilt feelings and castration anxiety. The vagina was a "smelly place"; he could never bring himself to kiss it. Fellatio he also avoided. Even as late as the analysis, after he had been practicing medicine for many years, he could not remember the words "fellatio" and "cunnilingus." It was not until he was in France during the war as an Army officer that he allowed a woman to swallow his semen. One effect of the drug, incidentally, was to deaden his sexual desire, at times for weeks on end. He had the usual fear that his penis was too small. However, once he had had a chance to examine many penises in the course of his military duties, he convinced himself by actual measurement that his penis was of about average size. At the time of the analysis the main manifestations of his castration were a certain disinterest in sex and an inability to love women.

When he was twenty-three, his father remarried. Outwardly, of course, he showed no reaction, but the impact of the marriage was revealed by his reaction to liquor. Before the wedding alcohol had never meant much to him. As a result of the drinks at the wedding, however, he became deathly ill. There-after he never touched alcohol again.

Shortly after graduation from medical school, he married the librarian of the hospital where he was interning. He described her as a warm, motherly person who had taken good care of him. They had two children, a boy and a girl.

After the birth of the children and completion of his residency in internal medicine, he decided to enter private practice. With the help of his family and friends, he opened an office for general practice in a small suburban town. It was then that his surface veneer of happy-go-lucky adjustment collapsed.

In order to build up his practice, he undertook regular social contacts in the community. Since he had always been inept at social gatherings, this public relations campaign proved to be a complete fizzle. His private practice never reached a point where he was self-supporting.

Faced by economic problems, he reacted with a number of somatic symptoms, chiefly persistent headaches. At first he controlled these with codeine. Then, when they persisted, he switched to dolophine,* which he continued to use to excess except for the last few weeks of his addiction, when he turned to morphine. On rare occasions he took dilaudid or nembutal. As usual, he denied the reality of his addiction for a long time. He had long since forgotten the original reason for it, the headaches. After a while he began to take dolophine for any situation that made him anxious — when his wife was angry at him, when some relatives whom he could not stand came to visit, when he felt a pain anywhere. All the while he kept on assuring himself that he could give it up whenever he wanted to.

But whenever he did abstain, even for a day, his anxieties became overwhelming and he experienced the withdrawal symptoms of abdominal cramps and rapid heart beat. His medical knowledge was useless. Several times he experienced such agony that he called a fellow physician in the middle of the night.

After several months of this, on the advice of relatives and friends, he hospitalized himself for withdrawal. Here, without any real medical or psychiatric supervision, he experienced

* The generic name for methadone, now the usual term.

intolerable agony which he would afterward refer to as "that time in Jersey." In less than a week he had signed himself out against medical advice and returned to the drug.

By this time his practice had virtually disappeared. As mentioned above, with the assistance of his family he then went into analysis. The first experience at least got him to the point where he could take a hospital job. This he maintained in one form or another for a number of years. It was not until long after the analysis with me that he was able to reestablish (or more correctly, establish) himself in private practice.

COURSE OF ANALYSIS

Although the analysis was a stormy one, as might have been anticipated, it was possible to maintain an intensive analytic situation with him for almost two years. In this period Peter was able to acquire some insight into his personality and his addiction. He was anything but an ideal analytic patient, attempting to rely much more on manipulation than on insight. But he was able to accept the interpretations of his manipulations. Even though his capacity for grasping analytic ideas was quite limited, especially with regard to his deeper, more forbidden wishes, he persisted until he had given up the drug.

In view of what had happened previously, I put no pressure on him to withdraw. At one point he asked me point blank: "Should I give up the drug now?" I replied that it was entirely up to him. This made a deep impression on him, since, he said, nobody had ever allowed him so much freedom before.

It was clearly necessary to let him acquire much more insight before withdrawal could be attempted. Accordingly, as mentioned, I tried to sidestep the topic as long as possible. This could be done for about two months, and it seems in retrospect that this two-month period was decisive for the ultimate favorable resolution.

The transference was strongly positive from the very beginning. As will be seen he soon conceived of the analysis as a struggle between his wife and myself, a struggle in which he was much more tempted to play the role of a child going through a liberation process with me than of an adult male playing the father role with her. Typical of the almost magical quality of the positive transference was his remark when I first suggested that he lie down on the couch. "You must be telepathic. I was just going to suggest that myself." At another point, after a particularly bad fight with his wife, he said, "Now you're the only person I have left in the world."

Nevertheless, almost from the beginning the analysis was characterized by his wish to get more from me, for which he brought into play a variety of manipulative devices. The hours were never satisfactory for him. Hardly a week passed without his trying to shift one or more hours, often on some trivial pretext. As a rule I rejected that request, and he would accept without protest. All along, however, he continued to express the feeling that there simply were too many demands made on his time, and that the analysis was just another demand. "Everybody was exploiting him" was the underlying complaint.

At the same time on a number of occasions he showed up at my office several hours before the appointment. He hoped that he could be seen earlier, although he knew that my schedule was so full that this would rarely be possible. Again, reality or no reality, this could be used to reinforce his feelings of rejection.

Except for the fee, which he paid religiously and without complaint, every aspect of the transference, though specifically positive, sooner or later became a source of resistance. When he did finally lie down on the couch, he was unable to produce any associations. When something good occurred to him, he would sit up, saying, "I have something important to tell you."

As has been mentioned before, the fact that I was a psychologist served as an odd form of resistance. He persistently refused to discuss his physical symptoms, since as a physician he could understand them better than I did. But when I suggested that he discuss his physical symptoms with another physician he objected that there was really nobody in the world he could trust except me. I usually interpreted this as a reflection of his childhood, when he could not rely on anybody, but the interpretation made very little impression on him.

Early Period

For the first two months it was possible to stay away from

the addiction question entirely. Thereafter it was always in the forefront of the analysis, especially in the later stages, when the law enforcement authorities were after him. Nevertheless, I made every effort to conduct the treatment analytically, even until the very end.

In the early period, he brought up a number of childhood memories that were of considerable use in unraveling his dynamics. Most of what I described earlier came out in this period. Later the immediate problems were so pressing that it was rarely possible for him to turn the clock back to see how he had come to be what he was.

After about two months came the first significant break in his pattern, an intensification of the transference drama. Without any urging on my part, he announced that he was going to withdraw. A week or so later he announced that he had succeeded. A few days afterward he told me that he had made up the whole story.

This led to a discussion of his need to please, which was tied up with the powerful rescue fantasies of his childhood. The first time he had sex with a girl, when he was in his teens, he had bought her a pair of shoes afterward. He was always trying to rescue people in one way or another.

Yet, as is so often the case, the rescue fantasy was strongly ambivalent. At one point he took on a free psychiatric patient who was obviously being neglected by the hospital, but the true purpose clearly was to show what an unfeeling therapist I was. One patient whom he had preserved from his private practice was an elderly, virtually bedridden woman in her seventies. He visited her twice a week to give her "shots," which he frankly admitted had no value. On the surface this was a repetition of his experience with his mother, but at a deeper level there was also hostility involved in his pleasure at the substantial fees he received for the house calls, which he thought of as totally undeserved. Actually, he was probably keeping this woman alive, but the whole experience covered up numerous inner conflicts.

His fabrication also brought his withdrawal problem into sharper focus. He could go without the drug for two nights, but the third night filled him with overwhelming terror. It was so horrifying that he could not even verbalize what frightened him so. At best he would refer to "that time in New Jersey," when he had withdrawn in the hospital without adequate supervision. Most often, he would say it was just "too awful," and he could not face it. Henceforth we would refer to this as his "third-night anxiety"; as time went on, it and its dynamic elucidation moved more and more into the center of the analysis.

A third outcome of the withdrawal fib was that it brought into focus the struggle with his wife. As will be recalled, she had objected to the choice of me as an analyst, resulting in his going to two other analysts first. Once he had started, she evidently became jealous of his strong attachment. She began to badger him for "results"; what difference did it make how good his analyst was, she argued quite rightly, if he did not get better? Even without this, she had reacted to the whole breakdown-drug episode by becoming the carping mother figure. He, in turn, began to treat her as a superego figure rather than a human being, and the battle was firmly launched, to be terminated only by their ultimate divorce.

At this point, however, there was still no talk of divorce. He merely wanted to be freed from her persistent pressure. An interview with the wife was arranged around this time, but it changed nothing.

In the midst of all this a phone call suddenly came in from his girl friend. It turned out that he had never told me of this girl, a social worker whom he saw on occasion. She was very much in love with him, a feeling that he did not reciprocate. However, she too began to question my capacity as an analyst, and he had to defend me all over again. The relationship with this girl ended fairly soon. No strong sexual or romantic desire appeared in him until toward the end of the analysis.

DREAMS: The patient dreamt infrequently, and his dreams were extremely simple, primarily anxiety and masochistic dreams punctuated occasionally by a rescue fantasy. At the beginning he reported two dreams from his previous analysis:

"Some kids are beating me up..."

"I go fishing and am trying to get a kid out of the water who is drowning, but I can't get him out."

In the first few months of analysis he reported the following dreams:

"I reach for the drug and can't find it..."

"Breaking glasses..."

"I'm in Paris, going from place to place. I didn't seem to fit in with any of the people — I was deficient somehow, uninteresting. I didn't know whether they knew about the medication or not. [This went on all night.]"

To the last dream he associated his present situation at the hospital, where he felt so different from the other physicians. He often wondered, angrily, why his colleagues never noticed anything strange about him. particularly the pupillary changes caused by the drug. It was clear from this and other material that the drug merely accentuated feelings of strangeness, inadequacy, and separation that had been with him all his life.

"I'm in a big house like [the one in New Jersey*]. I run all over looking for the drug. There is a small bottle; it breaks, and the contents run out."

To the theme of the bottle he had no special associations. I suggested that this might symbolize his anger at his mother, which currently carried over to his wife and authority figures, but this interpretation aroused no response.

Dynamic Trends

It is impossible to divide this analysis into any clearly demarcated periods after the first few months. Instead I will trace the manifestations of various basic drives as well as possible.

SEXUALITY: Although he had led a very active sex life during his years in college, graduate school, and the Army, not long after the children were born he lost most of his interest in sex. During the time of the analysis he had occasional sex with his wife and other women. These other women were so insignificant emotionally that at times he would not even mention

* The house where he made his most recent withdrawal attempt. See above.

them; what happened would come out inadvertently at a later time.

In intercourse with his wife, the drug apparently had the effect of postponing his ejaculation. Sometimes he would go on for hours without ejaculating; sometimes he would even fall asleep during sex. On occasion he would simulate orgasms in order to have an excuse to discontinue. His wife had relatively little desire at this time, and they had sex only on his initiative. He could go for weeks without any manifestation of sexual desire.

During the earlier withdrawal attempt, he experienced what he called a "continual penile itch" accompanied by a constant desire to urinate. He felt this as excruciatingly uncomfortable, apparently becuse he refused to recognize its sexual character and the accompanying wish to masturbate. Once his withdrawal attempt had ended and he had returned to the drug, his "penile itch" ended.

It was clear that a major function of the drug was to kill his sexual appetite. This could be traced back to an identification with the suffering asexual mother rather than the pleasure-seeking sexual father. The drug allowed him to combine the two major fantasies of his adolescence, the whore who received men all the time (through the drug and the paranoid feeling of being looked at constantly) and the English lord devoid of all feeling. But his absence of sexual desire was not felt as a problem.

HOMOSEXUALITY: A strong latent homosexual component was obviously present, but it broke through in disguised form only a few times. When we actively discussed withdrawal, he dreamed:

> "I am screwing a woman. Just as I am about to come, I reach down, although it is very uncomfortable, and suck her penis."

In association to the dream he brought out the squeamishness about oral sex which has been mentioned earlier. His search for his mother's penis was obviously one determinant of the inhibition of ejaculation which was such a marked feature of his sex life.

Later on, when he was discussing what the drug was doing

to him, he suddenly pulled his pants down to show me the innumerable needle marks in his buttocks. Again my interpretation of the homosexual fantasy fell on deaf ears. It is possible that a good deal of his homosexuality was sublimated through his medical practice, as in his overcoming his fear of having a small penis by examining the penises of many men, especially in the service. Obviously this involved a degree of attention to the size of his patients' penises that was quite irrelevant to their complaints. Still another aspect of his homosexuality was the small amount of insight he verbalized, even though his transference was so positive. He was deriving so much unconscious homosexual gratification from the analysis that insight was secondary. In fact, it might have spoiled his transference pleasure.

DEPRESSION, AGGRESSION, and MASOCHISM: It scarcely came as a surprise to find that a severe depressive-masochistic complex formed the core of Peter's personality. He had clearly identified with his dying mother. It was perhaps pure coincidence that his addiction lasted for exactly four years, the same duration as her terminal illness. Or perhaps this also was part of the identification. The point cannot be pushed too far.

It took some time for the depression-masochistic features to become apparent to him, but he did eventually build up a good deal of insight into them, in contrast to the sexual elements, my interpretations of which he dismissed as "too Freudian."

For quite a while he was able to cover up his depression by a magical and wishful thinking. He would give up the drug next week — no problem. Or he had already given it up — just a few loose ends to pull together. Once he decided that the drug was really a psychiatric problem, meaning that up to then he had thought of it as purely organic. One day he would just give it up — why all the fuss? Why didn't the authorities just leave him alone — he would get over it soon. Why didn't his wife leave him alone? Why did I insist he come to sessions so often (we had just increased to four sessions per week)?

Whatever overt aggression he expressed he directed mainly at his wife. Apparently she had no other complaints about him than the drug, but this she continually nagged him about. He in turn objected that she failed to grasp what he was going through. In one fight he literally twisted her breast, again showing that he was transferring his rage at his mother to her.

As the analysis progressed, his veneer of cheerfulness began to give way to an increasing display of anxiety and depression. In one session he asked point blank "Am I psychotic?" When I asked him what he understood by psychotic, he could only verbalize vague feelings of unreality. Then he would say from time to time that he was forgetting things more and more, attributing this to the drug.

The dependency and masochism of his way of life also became increasingly clear to him. Once he exclaimed about his marriage "I married her to suffer — do you realize that?" At times his suffering became so acute that I offered him the interpretation that his masochism was so severe that he had to hit rock bottom before he could start up again. Later, as will be seen this became quite meaningful to him.

Gradually the depth of his underlying anxiety crystallized out of the analytic material, even though the material produced centered so strongly on the drug and on his wife. Underneath he was truly panicky. He had pneumonia and colitis, the symptoms of which were masked by the drug. He was psychotic. He had cancer. He could not function. Sometimes suicidal thoughts broke through, though he was never actively suicidal.

The few dreams he produced in the second six months of analysis were a mixture of fear and magical thinking. Several were typical examination dreams. In another he was competing with one brother. The most significant came when he was recuperating from an appendectomy.

"I'm in a war theater. It's very bloody. We go down a hill, pick a soldier up, and come back; we do this over and over again.... I'm a wealthy man and move to another place."

The "war theater" referred more to the childhood memories of the battles with his brothers than to any combat experience. The dream brings out the underlying wish to beat out father and brothers which had been so deeply repressed.

When the analysis was in its tenth month, three developments combined to force me to attempt a more active role in the withdrawal process. First, he had by now written out so many prescriptions for the drug, with such a meager private practice, that the federal authorities became alerted to his goings-on. It became more difficult for him to get the drug, and he had to resort to a variety of fabrications, such as stories of terminally ill cancer patients with intractable pain, to get a supply from pharmacists. Even at that he had to go to pharmacists outside his area, making up stories about why he was so far away from home.

Second, a mounting sense of futility was becoming apparent in him. For the first time he could even see no point to analysis; why not go out and live? This was similar to the feelings of futility that had come up with the previous analysts. Yet he remembered how, after he had left them, his anxieties had accumulated to a point where he could not handle them.

Third, he had found a physician who had opened a free clinic for addicts. This man's system was to withdraw the addict "cold turkey," merely providing him with companionship and coffee for the night. Here, however, the patient turned physician again, showing more interest in helping the other addicts than in getting any help for himself. However, association with this group exposed him to theft and even one blackmail attempt, when it became known that he was a physician. The self-degradation involved in the addiction became all the more obvious to him.

Since his withdrawal was blocked by his third-night anxiety, which did not yield to ordinary analytic interpretations, I offered to see him through the third night at my apartment, on the assumption that the material that came out in this way would be helpful in the analysis. Up to this point he had never been able to verbalize anything about this third-night anxiety, except that it was too horrible to face.

At first he eagerly assented to my suggestion. We made arrangements for a physician of his choice to be on call and for a night nurse to be present, and I told him he would be free to see me any time during the night that he felt the need. With everything all set to begin at midnight, he called at 10:30 P.M. to cancel the plan. He just could not find the strength to face it; nor could he verbalize what frightened him so.

Accordingly, the analysis continued along the lines hitherto followed. Several times we made arrangements again for him to spend the third night at my apartment, and each time he would call it off at the last minute. Once he asked whether he could spend a week at my apartment, but this seemed inadvisable. Hospitalization did effect a withdrawal without consequences, but he would revert to the drug as soon as he was released; he had tried this twice. His efforts to confront his third-night anxiety outside a hospital had failed. Manipulative efforts appeared futile.

However, the continuation of the analysis now came to be increasingly affected by concern about the legal authorities. He never knew whether they had caught up with him or not, so he was perpetually apprehensive. Here for the first time he made bitter complaints about the system, about persecution of addicts, and the like. Though he still hated his wife, whom he was now planning to leave, the "enemy" had now shifted to the government. At an unconscious level this naturally played into his self-punitive trends. Just as he had said at one time that he was taking the drug to spite his wife, now he said he was taking it to spite the government.

After several warnings, which did not lead him to reduce his consumption of the drug, his narcotics license was taken away. This led him to even more illegal activity, such as the forging of prescriptions. Evidence was collected. Finally the government offered him a choice: either he went to Lexington, Kentucky,* for rehabilitation or he would be sent to prison for violation of the medical practices act. In either case his medical license was to be revoked. By then the analysis had been under way for about twenty months. It seemed more sensible for him to go to Lexington and resume the analysis when he was released.

The stay in Lexington apparently had some shock effect on him. There he met a number of men to whom addiction and incarceration had become a way of life. One man had been there twenty-seven times; many others had repeatedly come and gone. In spite of the tight security, some managed to smuggle drugs in. One method was to swallow the drug in a condom and then pick it out of the feces.

Withdrawal at Lexington was "cold turkey." He reacted

* The national center for treatment of drug addiction.

with agonizing abdominal pains. As he was lying on the table in terrible suffering, many of my interpretations came back to him. One that he kept on repeating to himself was "You've got to hit rock bottom." He saw more plainly than ever before his terrible impulse to degrade himself.

But the third-night anxiety was still there; hospital withdrawal did not affect it . Upon his release from Lexington he came back to New York and to the drug. Still, there was a difference. Instead of dolophine he turned to morphine. And he made an immediate attempt to face the third night.

He looked up an old classmate for assistance, Dr. L. This man had been going through an ordeal of his own. After a promising start in psychiatry, he had begun to act out in the wildest sexual manner. He demanded sex with all his patients, both male and female, justifying the request with the rationalization that since the incest taboo lay at the base of all neurosis, it was only by confronting this taboo directly that the patient could be truly liberated. Most of his patients left. One who remained was Sally, an extremely inhibited, attractive young nurse. She had been through eighteen months of classical analysis on the couch, literally unable to say a word. Finally she left, switching to Dr. L.

When Peter came to Dr. L. for help, he met Sally and promptly fell in love with her. Once he had sex with her in the presence of Dr. L., which made him more aware of his homosexual wishes. It was not repeated.

About two weeks after his release from Lexington, Peter tried withdrawal in Dr. L.'s office. He stayed there day and night, with Sally present all the time. I visited him there four times a day. Finally he lived through the third night uneventfully. None of the dire consequences that he had so long feared came true. He felt liberated.

At this point he was faced with the need for total rehabilitation. He had left his wife, lost his job, and been deprived of his medical license. His first step was to go away for a long rest. He traveled for about two months. Free from the pressures of making a living or taking care of other people, and reflecting on the insights that the analysis had given him, he was able to stay away from the drug.

POSTANALYTIC DEVELOPMENTS

The analysis was never resumed systematically. Occasionally he would write or call if he was in New York. Several times he tried to see me again, but the practical difficulties were too great. However, he maintained some contact for about ten years after the end of the analysis.

Although the termination of the analysis was so abrupt that many questions were left unanswered, he seemed to make steady progress with himself, even integrating many of the interpretations that he had fought so vigorously during the analysis. Externally, the changes were striking: he divorced his wife and married Sally, by whom he had three children, one of whom died. This second marriage and family provided much more happiness than the first.

In spite of demands that he would previously have found humiliating, he persisted in the effort to regain his medical license, eventually succeeding several years after it had been revoked. He was put on parole and required to report once a month to a physician and a judge to review his status. With all of this he complied faithfully.

As a result of his own experience, he became interested in psychiatry, which he then practiced together with internal medicine. For a long time he remained in hospital settings, where he felt more comfortable, but eventually he was able to build up a private practice.

Although he constantly expressed the hope that he could make arrangements for more analysis, this never materialized. The changes that he consolidated after the analysis was concluded can be gauged from the correspondence. Here are some relevant excerpts from a letter he wrote me several years after he had stopped treatment with me.

> We arrived here Monday, October 12th, in time to see a beautiful sunrise. Despite the exotic atmosphere and beautiful surroundings, the beginning of this new life held much insecurity for me. Would I make good? Be accepted? Get along? Was I running away and kidding myself? Was psychiatric training a way of avoiding analysis? Seeking answers by myself? There are many ramifications of these

questions and answers and only time will help solve them....
I started work the same day and pitched in at a rapid
pace. I soon had to slow down. I found I couldn't get out
of bed in the morning — didn't want to go to work — didn't
want to do anything — did only that which was essential.
I would leave things up to the time they were due, and
then feverishly run through the work. I was bogging down.
Sally was her usual permissive and supportive self, but it
didn't seem to help. I couldn't blame the drug, because I
hadn't taken any for several months. On December 23rd
we had a baby girl. . . . When I went to take Sally home
from the hospital five days later I took my first dose of
Dolophine. I proceeded to take it on and off until I went to
a physician and got a prescription for fifty tablets. Until
then I had gotten it from the hospital two tablets at a
time. The first day I took eight tablets — then got scared
of becoming addicted and went to the medical director,
turned over the drug to him, told him the story, and asked
that he take me on as a patient. He was reluctant at first
because of our relationship at the hospital, but because
there were no good analysts [available] he agreed. I have
been seeing him twice a week since the first of the year
and have felt better and have been able to work better. It
is interesting too that I have been able for the past two
months to take on a few patients in intensive therapy,
whereas heretofore I felt too threatened. . . .

I have become more aware of my relationships with
people. I try to understand what goes on in me and those
with me. I don't always get it right off, but then I'm not
thrown. I go over it later on when I am distant and try to
tie things up. I don't always succeed, but it is less threatening when you can try to be objective. I am more able to
understand my repressed and suppressed hostility. I can
even let go now without fear of punishment. This lets me
feel hostile without acting out and at the same time not
being overwhelmed by it.

Later that year he wrote:

It's been a good year. I'm in better shape than I've been
for years. No drug for over a year. Better relationships. . . .
Still too passive and not liking it. Less impulsive. Better
endurance and greater tolerance to frustration. Better

acceptance and handling of reality. Less masochistic but it is a tough fight because the passive component with fear that aggression means hostility is too frightening, and I'm not too good at sublimating the aggression as yet. But I have succeeded in accepting myself more . . . .

The next six months are critical ones . . . At least I shall not be running headlong into a decision which my distorted conscience (superego) usually forced upon me. I'm going to try to play it slow and safe, realizing that circumstances and environment may not be so kind and therefore trying to make the most of the situation and not allow myself to be thrown by disappointment of desire. I am quite anxious to get the necessary training to do analysis, but will forego it if it is either 1. inadvisable, 2. too difficult, 3. sacrifices are too great. . . . I shall be thirty-seven years old this month and have been insecure too long. It is about time I stopped gambling and seeking Nirvana and settled down to living and building a few buttresses.

Somewhat later he came in for a few sessions, but since he was living out of town the practical difficulties were too great. Then he wrote:

I know I felt mighty sick while seeing you — how sick you probably know better. As far as the drug is concerned, I have not taken any [for years]. A good example of my resistance to it was a recent attack of renal colic, which I lived through, although there was a legitimate reason to ask for opiates for relief. I still have the stone, which is passing slowly down the ureter. I am better able to live with pain, discomfort, and anxiety. I make less demands upon myself, pratically in difficult situations. I relate to people on a much healthier basis. I don't make unreasonable demands in a relationship, but then I am no longer desperate. . . . I might also tell you that there is less "acting-out" on my part so that the loss of addiction has not resulted in any other serious or evident symptom or syndrome.

About ten years after the analysis was finished, he again came in for a few sessions and again found the practical difficulties too great. His situation then was pretty much the same as that depicted in the last letter: no drug, fairly happy with his wife and children, working, but still dissatisfied with the passive-dependent-masochistic aspects of his personality, of which he had become acutely aware.

I have had no contact with him since.

DISCUSSION

There is general agreement on the psychodynamics of the drug addict. The literature stresses (1) the basic depressive character, early wounded narcissism (defects in ego development); (2) intolerance of frustration and pain (lack of satisfying early object relations); (3) lack of affectionate and meaningful object relations, which adolescent addicts attempt to overcome through the pseudocloseness and fusion with other drug-takers during their common experience; (4) the artificial technique used to maintain self-regard and satisfaction; and (5) the change from a "realistic" to a "pharmacothymic" regime, which may lead to severely disturbed ego functions and to conflict with reality. The addict is a borderline individual who hovers on the brink of a serious break with reality. Only rare exceptions have been noted.

Still, one aspect of addiction is unclear: why do some patients with this personality constellation resort to drugs, while others do not? Some have hypothesized that the pharmacological effect sets off a specific psychodynamic reaction, which is different with different drugs. This has yet to be confirmed. It is generally believed that the more serious the pharmacological effects (of heroin, morphine, and LSD), the more regressed the individual. The whole question belongs to the still unresolved problem of the choice of neurosis.

Just as there has been widespread agreement about the dynamics of addiction, there has been widespread pessimism about the rehabilitation of the addict. Few problems have attracted more concentrated professional interest, more governmental funds, and more disappointing results. Of recent years, two radically new approaches have captured the professional imagination: the methadone treatment for heroin addiction and the group-living approach. While both of these are certainly superior to anything tried previously, their ultimate value is still in dispute. With the methadone treatment the question of withdrawal from methadone remains open. It is of interest that the patient in the present case was addicted to methadone, then still referred to as dolophine. The main difference was that he had to take it by injection, while now it is administered orally. Nevertheless, his successful withdrawal was a heroic task. What happens in others remains to be seen.

Both the methadone treatment and the group-living approach, such as Daytop and Synanon, suffer from serious drawbacks. Whether these patients can ever get back to a less artificial way of life remains to be seen.

Psychoanalysts have devoted relatively little attention to the problem. It has been called the "stepchild" of psychoanalysis. Studies of drug-taking adolescents are quite pessimistic about the results. In the entire psychoanalytic literature there are only a few successful case histories.

Since the difficulties involved in treating drug addiction are so formidable, the details of any case history should prove interesting with regard to both the dynamics and the technical problems. As in other cases, the dynamic structure of this patient was not particularly different from that of other severely disturbed individuals. His deep-seated oral anxieties were overwhelming: he feared disintegration, both physical and psychological. Consequently he lived in a constant state of terror. In such a state relief is the only solution possible — immediate drastic relief. But the relief is not so much a pleasure as an alteration in the state of consciousness. Nothing is pleasurable to him as long as his present state of consciousness persists; conversely, if his state of consciousness is altered, everything looks good to him. The psychic situation is one in which the only solution is to escape the crushing archaic superego. This could be done either by the drug or by literal flight. If neither of these works, flight can be effected by suicide, a wish which came up occasionally. This is why the addiction can be considered a suicide equivalent and why so many addicts literally kill themselves.*

* In another case which came to my attention, an addict, a young man of twenty-three, took large doses of heroin. Many times after an injection he would lie motionless, pretending to be dead. His girl friend, alarmed, would then wake him up, whereupon he would say it was all a game. Even to her the suicidal wish involved in this "game" was quite clear.

The mother-son symbiosis was accentuated here by the accidental factor of her illness and his role as child-nurse-physician to her. The incestuous stimulation was so great that injections came to have an unconscious meaning of incest to him. Hence the drug killed his sexual desire, for he had mother again. The injection came to symbolize incestuous intercourse, treatment of mother, and even possible death (he was a "mainliner") leading to reunion with her.

The symbiotic attachment to mother was repeated in the transference. To be with me became much more important than the insights I offered him. Yet at the same time the relationship was enormously stimulating, especially along homosexual lines. The drug served to keep all these feelings out of consciousness.

While the dynamic picture is familiar, the technical problem requires more extended discussion. Fairly early we were able to crystallize out the "third-night anxiety," and for the major portion of the analysis our efforts were devoted to unraveling the meaning of this fear. Then the analytic work fairly quickly was threatened not by any regressive danger or ego weakness but by external reality: he was in imminent danger of being arrested for obtaining the drug illegally, and in fact the formal analysis was forced into a premature termination by his hospitalization, which he chose as an alternative to prison.

Ideally it would certainly have been best to continue the analysis *lege artis*. Quite possibly then the third-night anxiety would have yielded to patient though necessarily slow analytic exploration. And it is highly probable that if such a slower, more careful unfolding of dynamic resistances had been permitted, the overall personality change might have been much greater.

The technical problem encountered in this analysis, the pressure of external reality, is encountered in varying degrees in every analysis. Often when such cases are reported in the literature, a remark is made to the effect that the patient terminated "for external reasons." Since analysts have no control over these "external reasons" and prefer to work under virtual laboratory conditions, it is understandable that this factor generally receives scant attention, if any at all, in treatises on technique. Yet, as every analyst knows, it is quite important.

Fortunately, in the present case, we had almost a year of

pure analytic work before the external situation forced us to depart from systematic technique. His experiences with the previous two analysts clearly demonstrated the futility of a frontal attack, both of which showed that the forced confrontation came too soon.

At the same time the kind of analytic crisis created here, while unusual in content, is not so unusual in structure. In a great many analyses after a variable period of pure analytic work some basic anxiety crystallizes out in such a manner that it inevitably becomes the central focus of the analytic work for a long time. It may even be that this is true of the majority of analyses. In many cases the preoccupation with this focal anxiety eludes attention because it is so pressing for the patient, while the analyst, who feels unable to resolve it by a head-on approach, seeks to sidestep it. Nevertheless, the patient comes back to it again and again.

What is characteristic of many cases of acting-out disorder, perversions, and schizophrenias is that the reality consequences of the central anxiety cannot be ignored, either because the patient's ego is too weak to handle them, as in schizophrenia, or because there is some really overwhelming outside force, as in the present case. By contrast, in a patient with obsessional preoccupations or some mild phobias, the reality consequences of the central anxiety can be ignored indefinitely. The latter type of case we are apt to think of as pure analysis, while the former is seen as "manipulation" or "supportive therapy," but these terms merely mask the true state of affairs.

The decision as to whether or not to ignore reality is often a difficult one for the analyst, yet a most necessary one, on which the outcome of the analysis may very well hang. It always rests upon clinical judgment, as it did in the following case, rather than upon any technical diagnosis:

A homosexual man had developed an odd method of seducing other men. He would move close to another man in a fairly crowded subway, cover them both with a newspaper, and then proceed to give the other man an erection. As soon as the man had an erection, the patient would get up and leave the train.

His first analyst, alarmed by the possibilities of his being caught, repeatedly stressed the reality danger of being arrested, which the patient pooh-poohed, since he "knew how to approach." When the analyst persisted in the discussion of arrest, the patient left treatment.

When he came to see me after a lapse of many years, I decided to ignore the problem for the time being, on the grounds that since he had been doing this for so many years without being caught, he must have developed some special skill for selecting suitable partners. Eventually this practice disappeared in the context of the general analysis of his homosexuality.

In the present case, after the first year the possibility of a sudden interruption of the analysis by an arrest became increasingly imminent. Accordingly, I made the third-night anxiety the focus of analysis far more than hitherto, and far more than I would have otherwise. While he reached no resolution of this anxiety before his arrest, the analytic work did leave strong impressions that proved to be of invaluable service in the postanalytic integration.

POSTANALYTIC INTEGRATION

At the time that the analysis was interrupted by Peter's arrest (after some twenty months), it was by no means clear what the ultimate outcome would be. It was quite possible at that point to regard the whole analysis as a failure.

Yet the subsequent history shows conclusively that the analytic work left a deep imprint that had a marked effect on the course of his life. It seems highly unlikely that he would have been able to withdraw, leave his unhappy marriage for a new and happy one, and go through a whole host of other traumatic experiences without the intensive analysis. It is therefore legitimate in this case to speak of a "postanalytic integration."

The psychology of such a postanalytic integration may be conceived of in this way. In his analysis he was living through a symbiotic, homosexual transference which was largely a repetition of his good experiences with his mother. His oral gratification in the symbiosis was so important that words left little impression; he was basking in preverbal bliss. Yet part of his ego retained enough control to remember the gist of the interpretations, especially those that were less "Freudian" and fairly close common sense.

Once out of the analysis, he retained the analyst as a fantasy good mother to whom he was some day going to return. This helped him through many trying times and allowed him to avoid the deep regression that he had been through before. On the whole his life situation remained favorable. His ego was then strong enough to accept the new experiences in a pleasure-seeking rather than masochistic manner, because the fantasy-analyst was the core of a new superego, which was gradually replacing the old harsh superego derived from childhood. Return to analysis might very well have led to a regressive breakthrough of more self-destructive oral wishes, so there was probably some unconscious calculation in his repeated efforts to come back to analysis, followed by quick discontinuation of the attempt. The therapist he saw for a while during the year after he left, when he suffered a mild relapse into addiction, evidently approached him in a supportive manner. A magical transference of the kind that he had developed to me was avoided, probably because his ego had been strengthened to the point where he no longer needed one, and this too helped to integrate some of the previously learned material. But this therapy lasted only a short time. He accomplished the bulk of his postanalytic integration without outside help.

The follow-up period of ten years is sufficiently long to warrant the conclusion that a significant character change was effected by the analysis.

Beverly,
The "Evil Incarnate"

Beverly, a forty-four-year-old woman who looked much older than her age, was referred to me by the psychiatrist who had been treating her for several years. He had to leave town, and the referral was made on a few days notice. The patient had no opportunity to work through the separation.

The patient appeared somewhat agitated but in adequate control of herself. She called for an appointment (arranged for the next day). An hour later she called again and asked to see me the same day. I agreed. When she came, she explained that she was frightened by the change and wanted to "nail her fear" down as soon as possible. Initially I saw her three times a week.

LIFE HISTORY

Beverly's history had been most traumatic. Her mother died when the patient was a year-and-a-half old. The father took her to live with his parents. When she was three he went to Puerto Rico for five years and she lived with her maternal grandparents. There were no other children present. The grand-father was deaf and used an ear trumpet.

When she was six, she developed some sickness of unclear origin and was kept out of school for a year.

When she was eight her father returned home, but did not take her to live with him. Just before her tenth birthday, he remarried and brought the girl to his home. By his second marriage he had four children, all of whom were then alive and well.

When Beverly was about fourteen, the father again left. He took along his wife and the other four children but not the patient. Consciously, she had never experienced any resentment toward her father for this continued rejection; nor did she ever really grasp how serious it had been. Beverly was left with an aunt for a while, then sent to boarding school.

In adolescence Beverly became an active homosexual, and had a number of violent affairs with other girls. In these she was usually the passive partner who admired and looked up to the other girl. After a while, whipping fantasies became prominent, which culminated in inducing another girl to whip her with a tree twig when she was about eighteen. She was unable to finish high school.

When she was twenty she made up her mind to give up homosexuality, and carried out her resolution.

When she was twenty-six she was married to a man with similar interests, and for a number of years the marriage seemed to be a very happy one.

Shortly after the birth of her children, Beverly began to go to psychiatrists. The first symptom was the fear that she was a homosexual. No one, however, seemed to be able to help her, and she grew steadily worse. For reasons which she could not fully clarify, she switched therapists some eight or ten times.

During this period her husband came back from an assignment in Europe and told her he had fallen in love with a European woman. He said nothing would come of it, and he never expected to see her again. Not long after, the patient's symptoms worsened. She was in poor contact with people and developed the strong conviction that nobody wanted her. When she was hospitalized she was sure that the hospital would not accept her because harm would befall them. She had delusions that people were after her. At one point she did attempt suicide with sleeping tablets. She presented a typical picture of paranoid schizophrenia.

Before coming to see me, she had been hospitalized three times. She had been given electric shock the first time and insulin the last.

During the last hospitalization, she was treated by Dr. A.; the psychiatrist who referred her to me. He was a dashing, young handsome man to whom the patient, for the first time, made a strong transference. After some nine months in the hospital, she was discharged, considerably improved. The psychotic symptoms had disappeared, although she was still extremely frightened and dependent. Dr. A. continued to see her three times a week.

Unfortunately, Dr. A. also managed the patient's affaris *in toto*. While she was in the hospital, recovering from insulin shock, he approached her with the advice to divorce her husband. Since he recommended it, she went along. This had made the dependency on the psychiatrist much stronger, so that his sudden departure was even more of a blow than it would otherwise have been.

The husband agreed to support her, so that she could get along on a very modest scale without working, and could still manage to pay for the therapy.

COURSE OF ANALYSIS

Because of the way in which she had been handled by Dr. A., the treatment with me began on a completely supportive level. She would bring me letters she had written to her husband, or the children, or part of a manuscript she was writing about the hospital experience, and ask for my opinion. Naturally, the weaning away from her dependency had to be gradual, and in the initial period I referred her to a lawyer and a doctor, and made various other decisions for her.

About five weeks after the therapy with me began, she received a note from her husband telling her of his marriage; the note came before she had been officially notified that the divorce decree was final.

This incident naturally caused some regression, but the full effects were not immediately apparent. She denied any feeling about the remarriage: it was one of those things, and she fully accepted it.

The whipping fantasies became stronger. Her homosexual wishes also increased. Her attitude towards therapy became markedly ambivalent. One week she would not even think of work, but would concentrate entirely on treatment; the next week she did not feel the treatment was really so essential, she was all right, and it would be better to spend the money for a home with the children.

Around this time she had a dream:

"I'm talking to D.E. [a cousin]. He's laughing and full of high spirits. I touch him; he shrivels up."

The dream was used only to try to help her to see how angry she was, but she completely denied any such feelings.

A few days later she came out with the idea that she was doing people harm. This was the beginning of the recurrence of the psychosis.

At the next appointment she was quite disturbed and could not talk too clearly. She had to move that very day. She had arranged to take another room which was far beyond her means. I forbade any change, and took a much more active role. I explained to her that the sickness was breaking out again, and that she would have to come in every day for treatment. From this point on, for the next two months, I saw her seven days a week, and encouraged her to come twice a day if she felt the need for it; this did happen several times.

From here on, more and more of the psychotic material came out. This can be grouped under several headings:

AUDITORY HALLUCINATIONS: Voices said a number of things. One said, "That B.— woman," referring to Dr. B., a female physician who had treated her over a period of years. Voices shouted the names of other people whom she had known in the past. The radio talked about her, mentioning names of people she knew.

At other times she heard "You're a bathroom woman." "You're a bedroom woman." "You're a Commie."

DELUSIONS OF HARM: She became convinced that she was doing harm. She felt marked out and peculiar. "I riffle people," she said. She felt that she could do me no harm only because I was an analyst.

After a few weeks she began to visit Fountain House, a

rehabilitation center for discharged psychotics. She soon came
to believe that she caused "consternation" there, and stopped
going.

BIZARRE IDEAS: For a while she told of police cars driving up to her and the policeman saying, "Clink you." Once she
reported that when a hotel clerk gave her the *New York Times*
a razor blade was hidden in the paper. An especially persistant
conviction was that someone came into her room and disarranged her things. Particularly, the marking up of library books
by this unknown stranger was awfully frightening to her, and
for a long time she was advised to stay away from libraries.

She thought that she was "dripping information," and that
she was a "public woman." One night she was "boiling" and
everybody outside in the hall where she lived was "boiling."

The intensity of the psychotic material varied from day to
day. At times the voices would be almost continuous. At other
times they would come over her in what she called "flurries"
and then disappear for a while.

THE THERAPEUTIC APPROACH: She was encouraged to
call on the telephone whenever she felt the need to do so. I
adopted an air of absolute certainty, and repeatedly assured her
that I knew exactly what she was going through. I would also
comment that she acted better or worse on certain days. I made
direct suggestions about handling environmental problems, and
kept myself fully informed about every aspect of her life. These
suggestions were usually followed, though they did not always
work out.

Within this framework, the material produced was treated
analytically. Hallucinations were explained as inability to distinguish between what was going on inside her and what was
going on outside, and related to her wishes. The difference
between a wish and an action was emphasized. Peculiar words
were traced to their sources via associations, in exactly the
same way that dream-language is analyzed in the ordinary analysand. Her confusion of some words, and their double usage, was
worked out. The transference was handled as an oral regression,
which she talked about but did not really grasp; she once said,

"You're a very strange-looking mother to me." Wherever feasible, her present symptoms were linked up with the past.

Some examples of the therapeutic approach may be cited from the daily notes written at the end of each day.

She's still worried; begins every session this way. She must move from the hotel because she is hurting the people there. I explained that she was not hurting anybody; it was a fear inside her, and a fear differs from an act.

She repeated almost incessantly that she must move to another apartment before she could continue treatment. She is "wide open," "dripping" information. The radio is talking about her, mentioning the names of people she knew. I explained these as her thoughts and again told her not to move.

She was feeling much better, though the radio was still talking about her. Her need to attach herself to me, and make me the only person in the world, was interpreted to her. Would I know if she did anybody any harm, she wanted to know? I assured her that I would.

When my telephone rang she heard a voice say "That B. woman." I explained to her how she develops hateful feelings when I stop paying attention to her, just like a child, and turns these against herself. This was tied up with her early deprivations.

She can't read the New York Times because if she does she will hurt the people on the Times. She can't get over the feeling that in the past few months she had made some horrible mistake. She thought that analysis would rip the children wide open. These fears were explained as the outcome of her own hostile feelings.

She saw the children today briefly, and everything went fine. She thinks that if she doesn't stay with them too long she won't do them any harm.

I suggested that the radio announcements might be an idea in her mind — she looked very startled. Then I asked whether it is frightening to think that all these ideas might be in her mind — she said no, on the contrary, it would be a great relief.

At the end she asked whether she was getting any better. I asked her what she thought; she said "I'm feeling better." I agreed.

Today she confided that last week she had become angry when I said that she wanted to be a baby, but did not feel it at the time. As she came in the building today, there was a "flurry" because the people in the house were going to protect me from her. I interpreted that I am to be protected against her hostile wishes, and again explained the difference between a wish and an action.

I explained the voices to her as reproaches; she is bawling herself out all the time. I went into the mechanism of how such a reproach becomes a voice. She has been working in her room. A voice says, "You can't work in your room." I explained this as a reproach.

During the night one of the women in the place where she lives opened the door around 2 or 3 o'clock, evidently discovered it was the wrong room, and went away. She feels bad about living there. I interpreted this as a fear of her homosexual wishes.

After leaving here yesterday, there was a great commotion, voices talking all over the place. It lasted so long it couldn't be a hallucination. I showed her that it was.

Yesterday she went to Fountain House; it was all right. She spoke a little, did some lace work. Some people looked worried.

Last night she had a strange experience — a ringing in the ears. She seemed fogged, in the process of closing up. I interpreted this as an exaggeration of bodily sensations.

She thinks I don't understand the seriousness of her situation fully. (What makes you feel that?) She may be doing harm, particularly to children, without me knowing about it. She went into the fact that she does have an effect on other people — if she looks distracted or worried, they notice it. I said that she exaggerates their normal reactions in her hypersensitive state. We discussed her friendly feelings, and the difficulties she had with them in this state, which makes her want to do harm.

She is wondering about the cause of the relapse. She thinks it is because she was coming to grips with living alone.

I suggested we get at this relapse by comparing it with

what happened three years ago: Then she did not hear voices, nor did she have such terrible tension, but was strained by fantasies, sexual and whipping. Now these have disappeared. She thinks maybe subconsciously she was affected by her husband's remarriage. After all, she had a sex life for twenty years and now she had to give it up. I explained how this led to feelings of unworthiness and ideas of doing harm.

Lately she's been experiencing some smells — coffee is expecially strong, and laundry. Voices say, "You stink." I explained the difference between fear and reality.

Occasional voices and fears remain. She now realizes that she was much sicker than she thought.

She went to the Met, yesterday, and felt that people were talking about her. Her fears are greater than yesterday, which I tied up with her coming back to life and going to the movies and the Met.

She hears voices calling her "clinker" and "that B. woman." For the first time she revealed that her mother's first name was the same as Dr. B's. She had tremendous admiration for Dr. B. I pointed out that Dr. B. is like a mother.

This session she produced a dream for the first time since the relapse. It occurred last night:

"I'm in an office with an oblong desk; I go in and out a number of times. The children are mixed up in it somehow or other. Then my father comes in and he is perfectly all right."

The dream was merely used to get whatever associations she cared to make. She remembered that three years ago she was overcome once by the fear that her father had died.

On the way here she heard "She is a clinker" and "Look at that B. woman." People looked at her and saw that she was a peculiar person, but she is able to force herself through these fears and do things now.

She feels terribly isolated, nobody to have friendly sensations about. She feels nothing — this has been going on for some time, though she cries a little.

She feels terrible because she had a relapse. She had

come so far, and then suddenly changed — she does not understand it really. I told her it was tied up with her ideas of doing harm, the self-reproaches, and the wish to make me a mother, but she could not understand the explanation.

She feels awfully guilty about spending her husband's money and not getting better. She was getting so well and then suddenly she has a relapse. I said, "How do you help yourself by feeling guilty?" She could not see that.

I explained how all her life she has been reproaching herself for things which are an exaggeration of normal occurrences. She said, "I don't want to reproach myself."

At the end she wanted to take an empty cigarette box along; I laughingly urged her to leave it.

The next session she came in terribly frightened. These voices are not hallucinations, she insisted; there's some reality to them. Last night there were musicians in the courtyard who were there just to mock her. Army planes fly over and clink her. That incident with the police that time was real — they did call her a clinker.

I inquired what had happened to frighten her so. Yesterday when she left, she said, there was a silly grin on my face, and she knew that she had upset me. If even an analyst cannot get along with her, what was the use? I reminded her of the cigarette box incident — she said yes, she was afraid that she had done me harm.

I reminded her that a week ago she realized that all these things were hallucinations. That, she said, was because she hadn't been around so much. Now she's been around, and knows that they're real.

I pointed out the cigarette box incident, that the day was Sunday, and Fountain House was closed — all this made her so terribly afraid.

She was not convinced; there is an element of reality, she kept on repeating.

Much better than yesterday. In spite of everything yesterday, she went down to Fountain House.

The voices were again discussed, particularly clinker and clinking. Today she associated drinking to it, but there is still no great clarification.

The highlights of the next few months can be briefly indicated. The hallucinations and delusions were treated as experiences of anxiety so far as possible. Where she could not grasp the explanations no matter how often they were repeated, the subject was either dropped or environmental manipulation resorted to.

She revealed that when she was sick she had the fear that she was a radio antenna, and that her head was made of ravioli; no associations could be obtained. Now she thinks that there's cotton wool in her head and feels closed up.

The present-day material could be related to her childhood for the first time. She had heard a voice say "apple tree." When asked for her associations, she recalled that when she was four or five years old she ate a crab apple and it was sour, added that an apple a day keeps the doctor away, and that she is a sour patient. The voices could thus be seen as stemming from the childhood feeling that she was a bad or "sour" girl.

She reported another dream:

"There is a girl at a lecture. The lecturer looks like my Uncle C. They move from room to room. The lecturer is talking. The girl gets up to say something; he waves her down. Finally, she gets up and says, "I'm leaving." She leaves with seven or eight people. I watch all this and become angry with her, but repress it."

The dream was used to help her to see her anger at me, caused by a previous interpretation. The difference between her angry wish to destroy and events in the outside world was again emphasized; e.g., the day before she had reported that there was a tremendous explosion in the subway, for which she thought she was responsible.

More childhood material came out. She was brought up by grandparents and her grandmother was deaf. She had to take a nap in the afternoon when she was six years old. Grandfather had an ear trumpet. She thought of herself as a brutal little girl; when she was six she once pushed another little girl down the steps. After eight, she remembers herself as sullen and angry. She could see the parallel between her feelings of being a brutal little girl as a child and her fears of upsetting people now.

She reported that she had awakened at about six in the

morning hearing voices across the hall. Then she realized that it was a hallucination and experienced great relief.

The working-through process continued. Voices, delusions, neologisms, and other material were consistently analyzed. Since there was now some material from her childhood, the present could be connected with the past; for example, she sees herself as a "marked" woman now; in her childhood she felt marked out from other children because her grandparents were so old.

At the end of the eighth week after the acute outbreak, she was well enough to skip a day.

More of why she felt peculiar as a child came out. She was kept home from the time she was six until the time she was seven, and forced to take naps and be quiet. She was suffering from some illness, but does not know what. She was a tomboy. She was also peculiar in that she went to her own father's wedding. (He remarried when she was nine.)

She spoke of some sexual feelings. The next session she reported a dream:

"I entered a boat at the invitation of a strange middle-aged man. It was a small, open boat, and we both stood in it. It was night, and I was talking to him, relating a strange occurrence in the sky that had happened in the previous part of the dream. Suddenly the moon shone, abnormally clear and bright, seeming very close — almost frighteningly close, and I pointed to it and said, "Like that." In a moment or two it changed to resemble a globe of the world, still retaining a brilliant light around it in the dark sky. Then another boat, open at the stern end which was toward our craft, came toward us very rapidly. I was frightened and jumped overboard. The men in the other boat seemed menacing, and I jumped from fear."

The luminosity and fear were tied up with her sexual feelings. However, any efforts at sexual interpretations and any attempt to let her talk more directly about her sexual feelings met with such violent resistance that I did not persist. Earlier, she had once spoken of a feeling in her breasts — they rose, occasionally. When I asked her more about it, she said, "Do you want to drive me completely crazy? Do you want the radio broadcasting such things?"

She came out more directly with some hostile feelings toward me. She said that the children (who had met me once for a few moments) did not like me as much as they had the previous therapist; I was not as warm.

After this release of feeling, she had a sexual dream:

"I'm in an old house; there are children outside playing and laughing. A man is there. He is joking and talking. He lies down on the bed and invites me to lie down too."

She denied anything sexual about this dream. The man she recognized as an old bachelor from her home town; he looked somewhat like me.

Around this time I had already decided on my summer vacation plans. Although it was still six weeks off, preparations were made to transfer her to another therapist while I was away, and her reactions to the vacation and shift were discussed. I was going to be away for six weeks. In order to make the separation easier, the frequency of sessions was cut down to five, then four, then three a week. After I left, a social worker was also retained to see her three times a week socially, because of the continued shakiness of her reality adjustment.

She was again noticeably upset. She thought she was marked out, knew that these things were real, heard a voice say, "We'll tweak you in the vagina," wanted to know if I was familiar with her entire history, if I had been in touch with her previous therapist, etc. I interpreted her anxiety in terms of my vacation, which she vigorously denied.

She expressed the feeling that I had really understood her for the first time with an interpretation I had given her about her guilt about her grandfather's death.

Another dream:

"Three trees stood on a sandy plain and not much life around. Suddenly all three trees fall as if in an explosion, though there was no sound and no signs of such."

To the trees she associated herself and the children. To the explosion she associated one which had occurred at a friend's house when she was in her teens, and for which she thought herself responsible. The explosion was interpreted as her anger, and the dream as a fear of what her anger might do.

In a sense, this dream was quite similar to the one which had preceded the recurrence of the psychosis, in which she touched her cousin and shriveled him up. In the meantime, the fear of doing harm had assumed delusional forms, and then diminished gradually, though a number of the delusions were still present at this stage.

During the session I burped. She expressed the feeling that she gave me indigestion and caused me to burp.

She said that she wanted to get a radio for her room. She still heard names she knew on the radio, and said that she heard my name a lot. I said I thought it best that she should not have a radio, and she complied.

There was some increase in anxiety shortly before I left. At one point, she even expressed the thought that she should go back to the hospital. I discouraged that idea, and interpreted her fears in terms of her reaction to my vacation.

The switch to the vacation therapist occurred without incident. When she arrived at his office, his electric clock had temporarily stopped, and she felt responsible; she also told him that she withers flowers. However, she established a satisfactory relationship with him, and weathered the summer without any noticeable storm.

Psychodynamically, the hallucinations generally lent themselves to analysis, though the degree to which she grasped the explanations remained an open question. Eventually, the cries of "dink-tink-rink" were related to stink, and a feeling of slight loss of bowel control. One sequence, which was worked out much later, related to the idea that when she came into a room there was a "flurry" of people talking. It came out that she thought she created an odor, and people were too polite to tell her, so they talked more loudly to cover it up. The cries of "That B. woman" embodied both a reproach for sexuality (Dr. B. was a gynecologist) and a wish for her mother (Dr. B. had the same name as her mother). The feeling that children especially laughed at her and saw her as marked and peculiar was tied up with memories of her own childhood, and reproaches felt because of her inability to take care of her children.

Although she seemed to have improved considerably as a result of the intensive analysis, the amount of insight acquired was small. When she did not hear voices, her explanation was that the outside world had changed, so that there were no voices to be heard. The idea that her fears could lead to hearing voices remained totally incomprehensible; she said, quite logically, how can fears inside me produce voices outside? Yet, there were some glimmers of understanding, and several times an insight jelled after many years of intensive denial on her part.

Upon my return from vacation, I found the patient in substantially the same condition as when I had left.

The analysis was resumed three sessions per week. The social worker continued to see her on alternate days, three times per week, so that some therapeutic contact was available six days per week. Naturally, this also helped me to get a first-hand version of her behavior away from therapy.

An attempt was made to enlist the aid of friends or relatives to give her more of a social life, since she was extremely isolated. A number of possible contacts turned out to be either psychotic (hospitalized) or to have been psychotic at some time in the past. One such interested relative was found, an unmarried woman in her fifties. She allowed the patient to share her apartment. After six months, however, the relative had to be rehospitalized. Thus, no real emotional help from the family was ever available.

In this period Beverly's therapeutic time was dominated by two particularly strong fears: that others knew what was happening to her and that she forced others to conduct conversations. These fears did not lend themselves either to clarification or to a ready therapeutic resolution and remained prominent for a number of years.

The extreme fear and clinging dependency on me which she had displayed at the time of the acute psychosis from March through June now began to give way to a variety of negative transference manifestations. She had always compared me unfavorably with the previous therapist, Dr. A., to whom she had felt much closer. At one time she even expressed the thought that maybe the relapse was my fault.

After the vacation she also began to compare me with the substitute therapist. She also found him much warmer and much more understanding. Curiously, this led to a strengthening of her tie to me. Now that she knew one of my friends and he was so nice, I could not be so bad and she could place much more faith in me.

For a long time, the negative transference centered around three questions which were repeated over and over again: (1) What objective reasons did she have for placing confidence in me? (2) Was I taking care of her properly? (3) Why didn't I provide her with a third person to talk to and handle her affairs, one who was closer to her family? This last demand, of course, was for the restoration of her family.

The transference phenomena were handled by a combination of release, reassurance, and interpretation. Naturally, here she had a chance to release hostility towards me without suffering the consequences, and every effort was made to help her to see that.

Apart from the transference, the major focus of the analysis in this year was placed on the life history, and its connection with her illness. No hostility could ever be elicited against any of the major figures in her life, however. Even the idea that her father could have taken better care of her was vigorously denied. He was a poor man, he had to work, if his work carried him to Puerto Rico that was unavoidable. Of course, at this point in the therapy she was greatly preoccupied with her own adequacy as a mother, and to blame her father would have meant to invite blame for her own conduct, which was too much for her to handle. Thus, the denial mechanism served to reinforce the crushing superego formation, and erected a formidable barrier against the therapeutic effort to lighten superego pressure.

A good deal of time was devoted to her father's remarriage, which occurred when she was nine.

The therapeutic attempt to understand her life met with increasing resistance as time went on. She would harp repetitively on certain fears or preoccupations, such as whether we could not arrange for a third person to handle her affairs, what she could do about the children, or money, which were extraordinarily difficult to handle therapeutically. The situation was unduly complicated by the all-encompassing solicitude of the previous therapist. I felt that it would be wisest to urge her to seek more real-life contacts.

The relative who has been mentioned (the woman who shared her apartment with the patient) arranged for an inter- view with an employment agency and then contributed a small sum to allow an educational institution to employ the patient, who, of course, did not know that her employment was subsi- dized.

Though she felt very peculiar, she managed to go to work regularly and to do what was assigned to her. The main symp- tom that appeared at work was the feeling that she created a peculiar impression on others. Some of this was an obvious, disguised expression of homosexual wishes, but no interpretation at that level was ventured.

She had now progressed sufficiently to get along without a substitute therapist during my next vacation, which lasted three weeks.

In the fall she struck out for a job on her own, and suc- ceeded in obtaining employment a level below her prewar em- ployment, but still using many of her abilities.

The social worker was discharged. Roughly fifteen months after the acute psychosis had subsided, she was able to work and manage her affairs. Naturally, she was still quite disturbed and in need of much intensive therapy.

She stayed two-and-one-half years at her new job. A new problem now dominated the therapy for most of the period of her employment. Her new boss was a woman, Susan, in her late twenties. The patient developed a strong crush on Susan.

At first she was quite certain that Susan had some homo- sexual leanings, and thought about the possibility of an affair with her. Susan was married, mother of one child, and a short time later became pregnant again. The patient reported nothing that pointed to Lesbian tendencies in Susan, but the patient could not be shaken from her conviction. As she (in a sense quite reasonably) argued, how could I know that Susan was not homosexual; I did not know the woman.

No attempt was made to act out the homosexual side of her transference to Susan, but she did try to make a mother of her. She wrote her letters, asking for an opportunity to discuss personal problems with her. In Susan she saw the possible "third person" whom she had dreamed about so long. Since Susan was also a mother, she wanted particularly to discuss the children with her, since she was so troubled by the thought of being a bad mother.

Susan insisted on keeping the relationship on a purely business level. Eventually, Susan's continued rejection, my persistent interpretation of the whole fantasy as search for a mother, and her own slow but gradual growth, served to keep the crush within reasonable bounds. Characteristically, however, she never really gave up the conviction that Susan would respond to her, given the proper circumstances.

Most of the earlier complex of symptoms, particularly the hallucinations and delusions, disappeared in the course of time. More exactly, whenever they appeared, they were systematically analyzed in the manner indicated above, and yielded to the analysis.

One triad of symptoms, however, persisted many years after all the others had vanished. When she became anxious, she could not recognize the feeling but complained (1) that somebody had entered her room and disarranged objects there; (2) library books were marked up by some unknown person; (3) people, usually children, were laughing at her.

No amount of interpretation could convince her that this triad was not part of reality. After all, I wasn't there. How did I know that people did not enter her room?

In view of her obduracy, these symptoms, when they occurred, were encapsulated and separated for her from the rest of her functioning. I explained to her that whenever she became upset these symptoms would appear, and that it was important to bear that in mind even though she could not see the connection. By this method the symptoms would come and go, and she learned to handle them, even though she could not grasp what was happening.

Some two years after the acute psychotic attack, we reached an impasse. The patient complained bitterly that she was overworked, always tired (her physician found her in satisfactory health), and could not manage to come to therapy three times a week. I felt that we had gone about as far as we could, and allowed her to cut down to two sessions a week. From here on, the treatment became almost completely supportive. She had come a long way for a woman with her history, and I did not want to risk another break. By the fall of that year she had cut down to one session per week and in the next spring once every two weeks.

The treatment was not terminated completely; she was encouraged to come back and see me whenever she felt the need to. I functioned mainly as an adviser, although on rare occassions it was possible to offer her some usable interpretation.

In this supportive period, I found it possible to handle symptoms by merely ignoring them. Once she said that six-year-old children were laughing at her at 11 o'clock at night outside her window. At another time she complained that somebody had entered her room and cut a hole in her bathrobe. Both of these symptoms disappeared without further consequence. Evidently she could have hallucinatory or delusional experiences and simply get over them, just as the ordinary person has a blue spell and gets over it.

The follow-up period since then occasionally necessitated more intensive therapy. In nine years she had roughly eighty sessions.

Her capacity to tolerate rejection was remarkably good. In these years she passed through a number of experiences which could easily shake a normal person. Her roommate broke down in her presence and had to be removed to a mental hospital. Her father died. An old friend's son committed suicide shortly after she had seen him. She was fired from her job. She witnessed one man beating another to unconsciousness in the street. Her novel was rejected by a number of publishers. Her daughters married and she acquired two grandchildren. Her family consistently refused to help her, in spite of numerous pleas; usually they blamed her for not taking care of herself.

As we know, any one of the above incidents might set off an acute episode in a schizophrenic personality. That none of them did shows that her ego was strengthened considerably by the therapeutic process.

An important source of ego gratification for the patient was the novel she wrote about her hospital experiences. A few chapters had been written before she started with me. When the acute episode broke out, she put it to one side, and I discouraged her from taking it up again for several years thereafter. Finally she did get back to it, and completed a manuscript of some 180 pages. The book is a starkly realistic account of one patient's reactions to a mental hospital. It brings out the fear, monotony, and isolation she experienced as a patient. It is a moving document, but she has yet to find a publisher.

Anyone seeing her in her later years would have no inkling of the tremendous storms she has passed through. She lived the life of a normal spinster in her fifties. Her basic financial needs were taken care of by the alimony from her ex-husband, but she obtained work occasionally and supplemented it, although consciously her main source of worry was money.

She became a quiet, rather soft-spoken woman. Her clothes were unpretentious, but adequate. She preferred to dress in a businesslike way; to some extent this was due to her lack of money. Much of her time was spent alone, reading or working on her novel, or later attempting other kinds of writing. Occasionally she visited with her ex-mother-in-law, then in her eighties, and some friends; at times her daughters came to see her. As time went on, she looked more and more cheerful, no doubt because the fear which was so dramatically stamped on her face for so many years had gone. Her health is good. It has been many years since any of the severe psychotic symptoms have bothered her.

THEORETICAL COMMENTS

In reflecting on my therapeutic techniques, I would stress three in particular:

Intensive Contact

As soon as the acute psychosis reappeared, the frequency of sessions was stepped up to one a day, on occasion two. This contact served to gratify the increased dependency needs, and helped me get a more rounded picture of what was happening to her.

That intense contact is *per se* therapeutic has been noted by a number of observers. Even the most regressed schizophrenics may respond to prolonged human concern shown by another person.

The situation, however, is not as simple as "Provide contact and the patient will improve." If too much love is given the patient may regress further and become more inaccessible.

Had I offered to see my patient seven times a week when she first came to me, she would probably have protested and refused to cooperate. It was recurrence of the illness which made her accessible to the offer of maternal care on my part. There is a timing factor: the therapist must gauge when the patient's psychic economy is prepared to accept the increased contact.

The signal here came as an overwhelming increase in anxiety, which I handled both theoretically and actually as a cry for the mother.

Alternation of Gratification and Interpretation of Oral Needs

The patient's symptoms were explained to her as a regression to an oral level (naturally in language she would understand), particularly with regard to the longing for a mother and the loss of ability to distinguish between inner and outer reality.

Most of the symptoms make sense when looked at theoretically as the infant-mother relationship: both the previous therapist and her husband were mother-substitutes; when she lost them, it revived the memory of the loss of her own mother. She tried to restore the mother by magical means. But the mother rejected her; she told her "You're a stinker." This enraged the patient, and she wished to destroy everybody. The wish was not recognized as such; she attributed magical destructive powers to herself.

The auditory hallucinations for the most part represented a wish for the mother, and the reproach that she is bad if she has such a wish; i.e., the ambivalent mother, good and bad. Badness also took in much symbolism from the anal level. The hallucinations about "dink," "rink," "tink," all ending in "ink," seemed to be versions of "stink." Thus, when the police car pulled up and said "clink," it was first a hallucinated wish that mother (the police) was coming to her and simultaneously the reproach from mother: "You stink." When she entered a restaurant (food = mother), she thought she stank; the patrons (mother) wanted to say, "You stink," but were polite and merely talked louder.

The most persistent of all symptoms was the idea that her library books were marked up; it lasted long after the other hallucinations and delusions were gone. Later, we did trace it to the fact that the previous therapist, Dr. A., had on several occasions loaned her some books from his own library; those books he had heavily marked up with red pencil. The delusion was thus a disguised longing for Dr. A. In addition, in view of her lifelong love of books and preoccupation with them, books must always have been a mother symbol to her.

As I have indicated, the therapy did not proceed on purely analytical lines; it was also necessary at times to gratify her dependency needs. This varied with her psychic state; at times, I made many decisions for her, at times, few. The shift from gratification to analysis and back, the determination of how much she could handle at any particular time, and of what had best be avoided, represented by far the most difficult part of the therapist's task, and yet the most important.

Persistence in Interpretation in the Face of Denial and Incomprehension by the Patient

This is one of the most puzzling and most trying features of the analysis. Throughout she verbalized almost no insight. When the hallucinations disappeared, it was because the outside world had changed. When the delusions of doing harm vanished, it was because she no longer had those powers. To the repeated explanations of the difference between a wish and an action, she usually countered with the statement that she could not see how her wishes could influence the outside world.

In the absence of confirmation from the patient, I relied on my own subjective conviction of correctness. Whenever I could fit together pieces of the puzzling mosaic, I tucked them away in my mind and presented them to her when a suitable occasion appeared.

Nevertheless, the fact remains that although in terms of

her own verbalizations she grasped almost nothing, she continued to make progress. A skeptic might say that the interpretations were all a waste of time, and that she got better by accident (spontaneous remission), or because I paid attention to her. Neither of these explanations is particularly convincing.

Negative transference was probably at play here. Similar phenomena, though not on such an extensive scale, are often seen with neurotics. One sometimes sees the statement that in analysis an interpretation is not really effective unless the patient first denies it.

Thus, with one part of her mind she could accept the interpretation, while with another she would push me away. This is the same kind of ambivalence displayed in her hallucinations. After all, the mother (analyst) whom she imagines is always calling her a stinker causes her to think that she had better be wary of everything she says.

The discouragement of the therapist has been noted by many theoreticians as one of the primary countertransference problems with schizophrenics. Even before the large-scale advent of psychoanalytically oriented therapy, Bleuler set down as his principal rule that "No patient must ever be completely given up."

In terms of her ultimate adjustment, some comments are in order. In the course of the years, she eventually left her family, husband, and children, and adopted a rather solitary mode of life. Her adaptation shifted to a rather infantile level; she is the baby who is taken care of by the world, though as time went on, she showed more signs of wanting to be independent.

We have mentioned that the limits of the therapy were reached when sexual material began to come up. She could handle the oral phase, but human relations were too frightening. This would explain another baffling feature of her adjustment, the abandonment of homosexuality. Of course, in the period with Susan, the homosexual urges were strong, and were analyzed as a wish for a mother. Since then no trace of them appeared. The maternal need involved in homosexuality was analyzed. The bodily needs, like the heterosexual ones, were repressed. No doubt age also plays a part.

In view of the existence of spontaneous and physiologically induced remissions, the question may be raised as to the nature of the effectiveness of this therapy. The answer, I think, lies in the way in which the patient gets over the illness. Since her treatment, as mentioned above, she has lived through a variety of traumatic experiences which frequently affect even fairly normal people adversely; yet she has shown no reaction. We can assume that, as a result of the therapy, the ego has been strengthened to tolerate more anxiety, and to handle it differently, while superego pressure has been considerably reduced.

The persistence in interpretation must have meant to her that there was a stable figure in her environment who would not change or leave, no matter what she did, even to the extent of accepting her hostility. No such figure had ever existed in this woman's life before: sooner or later she had been abandoned by everybody, including all her previous therapists. For this reason, the insistence by the therapist that he was available for the rest of her life was important. Any indication that the relationship was terminated once and for all might conceivably have precipitated another crisis. The whole experience makes any crisis situation less threatening to her.

If we put these facts together, we get to an inner-dynamic change which could not be duplicated by any other method currently at our disposal.

Some theoreticians have raised the question as to whether a procedure of the type adopted here should be called analysis. I believe that it should be, since there is a working through of transference and resistance, a release and interpretation of unconscious material, and a reorganization of the ego structure.

Frank,
The Man Who Made
a Pact with God

Frank, a twenty-four-year-old unmarried clerical worker, came into analysis with a variety of troubling complaints. Primarily, he suffered from what he himself called "anxiety attacks," a term which he had learned during some six months of supportive therapy several years earlier. In these attacks he would be overcome with fear, panicky about what to do or where to turn. During one of them some time back he had made his pact with God. He had said to God, "If you get me over this attack, I will never have sexual intercourse before I marry." The attack subsided, for which he gave God credit. Frank had kept his part of the bargain by refraining from sexual intercourse. In fact, at twenty-four he was virtually a virgin, having had sex only once or twice while stationed with the U.S. Army in Germany. For sexual gratification he relied on heavy masturbation.

Apart from the anxiety, which troubled him, and the sexual abstinence, which did not, he had a variety of other problems. There was a severe fear of subways and elevators, which placed considerable restrictions on his movements; he was particularly panicky at the thought of being in a subway car which was stuck in a tunnel. To avoid such a catastrophe he carefully eschewed any subway line which went through a tunnel, always finding some alternate route, even if it meant lengthening his trip by an hour. He also said that he had "delusions of grandeur," referring to his conviction that he was a genius, a conviction going back to his earliest days in school. Nothing in his life substantiated such a belief, yet he felt that sooner or later his real talents would blossom. From time to time other symptoms of anxiety appeared, such as a persistent eye-blink and frequent blushing.

LIFE HISTORY

Frank was the youngest of three children. The oldest, Jerome, was about ten years older; the middle child, Sue, was about four years older. The family was full of the most marked psychopathology.

Mother was an extremely depressed woman, whom Frank remembered chiefly as sitting around the house crying. "Ich starbe aveg" was her most common expression (Yiddish for "I'm dying"). Apparently, in spite of this perpetual gloom she did manage to help her husband out somewhat in his store, and to take minimal care of the children. She died of cancer at fifty-two, when Frank was about sixteen. One of the most painful memories he had to digest was the story that when she was on her deathbed in the hospital, she refused to see Frank, saying "I don't want him. I don't care for him."

Father seems to have been the healthiest of the lot emotionally. He was remembered as a cheerful, gregarious storekeeper. He had a small truck for deliveries; when Frank was a child father frequently took him along in this truck. The family lived at a lower-middle-class level.

When his wife died, father began seeing other women, which made Frank jealous. About a year later he remarried, a woman by the name of Jennie. But shortly thereafter (perhaps a year or so) he had a heart attack. From this first attack he recovered, only to succumb to a second heart attack about six months later. After his death, Frank and Jerome continued to live with Jennie, whom they called "mother." Sue was already married.

Jerome, the older brother, had a history of two hospitalizations with a diagnosis of schizophrenia each time. After release from the hospital he returned to a solitary, isolated existense with his stepmother. Virtually devoid of friends or acquaintances, he would just about maintain himself at work as a physicist for one of the top-name companies. Since Jerome was a college graduate, Frank looked upon him as an intellectual, a kind of person whom he regarded with the greatest of ambivalence. Apart from his role as brother, Jerome was of about the same age as I was, and bore a marked physical resemblance to me, according to Frank, which gave Jerome an exceptionally significant part in the analysis. Through the years Jerome's adjustment remained essentially unchanged, although in more recent years he managed to take up a hobby as a bird watcher, which at least provided him with some social contacts outside the family.

Sue, the sister, likewise had many emotional problems, though not quite so severe as Jerome's. For a while she suffered from a fear of the streets which made it impossible for her to leave the house. An early hysterectomy at thirty-one exacerbated an otherwise unhappy sex life, and since her husband likewise had grave sexual difficulties their sex life was virtually nil. For a while I saw her in once-a-week therapy, but the transference became so sexual and so painful to her that she stopped abruptly. There seemed to be some slight improvement in her condition in later years.

As far back as he could remember, Frank was an anxious, frightened little boy. His earliest memories were of his mother crying and his fearful and confused reactions to her despair. Among his reactions was a persistent inability to be toilet trained. Having bowel movements in his pants continued well into his ninth or tenth years. At school he recalled trying to hide the smell of his shit when he defecated in his pants. At this, of course, he was unsuccessful, and he was frequently sent home, with further shame and embarrassment. When he was about four, his mother once wiped him after a BM in his pants with a little girl friend present; this created further shame and resentment.

Throughout childhood he had many nightmares, which usually led him to travel into his parents' bed. They objected, but allowed him to stay there. The only nightmare he remembered, from about the age of five, was:

"I'm with my family on a ship in the ocean. The ship breaks in two. The half I'm in breaks off from the other half, leaving me all alone in the ocean. I wake up terrified, screaming."

This dream graphically highlights the terrible isolation and separation with which he had to struggle all his life. A real-life memory along the same lines came to light at one point: when he was about seven he went to the movies once with his sister. In the crowd he got lost, leaving him crying in panic.

From about this age, seven, he also dated his first knowledge of sex. A little girl friend of his told him that her father peed into her mother's behind; this shocked him beyond measure. Among other things, this memory served to reinforce the confusion of sex with anality, and his later sexual difficulties.

Somewhat later, when he was about eight, another vivid memory emerged which he chewed over and over in the analysis: he walked in on his father and mother taking a bath together. He was particularly struck by their "black bushes."

In spite of a handsome, good-sized build, he was so ashamed of his body that he could not fight with the other boys. Early signs of the homosexual-masochistic development which was to play such a prominent part later appeared in a nightmare from about the age of ten: he dreamt of a big transport plane crashing into the playground. A few years later, at a family party he once got drunk and kissed his father. Consciously, of course he had only the greatest revulsion against homosexuality.

With the onset of puberty, he became obsessed with various forms of castration anxiety. One, quite literal, was the fear that his left testicle would crumble away (why he chose the left one never became entirely clear). Another, more persistent, was a fear of VD. He could fantasize about a girl's sucking him off, but since the only girls he could think of who would do such a "dirty" thing were prostitutes, he could not let himself try it because he might get VD. Prior to the pact with God, especially when he was with the Army in Eurpoe, there was a constant preoccupation with the wish to be sucked off and the fear that VD would result. After the pact with God, at least this conflict was spared him because premarital sex was not permitted; however, other conflicts took its place.

Although he was sure that he was a genius, his grades in school did not live up to this self-image. When he was about sixteen, around the time of his mother's death, he was called upon to give a verbal report in one of his classes. It was then that he had his first attack of blushing. This embarrassed him so much that he dropped out of school.

As has been mentioned, his father had a heart attack about a year after his remarriage. Some six months later, when Frank was about nineteen, he had his first anxiety attack. As worked out in the analysis, it was set off by smoking a cigar, in imitation of his father. The physical reactions of rapid heart beat, perspiration, and profuse vague sensations all over his body were similar to what he saw in his father.

For about six months the symptoms were quiescent. Then when his father died, they returned, and continued more or less unabated until they were resolved by the analysis. Repeated physical examinations were always negative.

When he was about twenty, after his father's death, he was drafted into the service. As mentioned, in Europe there were a few sexual experiences, the first and, prior to analysis, the only ones in his life. One, with a German girl, was very frustrating because he could not get an adequate erection. Mostly, however, he confined himself to masturbation and the obsessional preoccupation with VD.

Upon discharge from the Army, he found a job working at a low level for a newspaper. Here he again fantasized himself the smartest man on the paper, only to find that he was fired in one cutback.

Since the anxiety attacks continued, he decided to try therapy. A friend gave him the name of a man whom he called Art, a very directive, supportive therapist. As so often with supportive therapy, the transference was strong but unanalyzed. An early improvement soon disappeared. Discouraged, he went to Miami, where he took a job as a taxicab driver.

In Miami, things again took a slight turn for the better for a while. Then one day he had another anxiety attack, and called his therapist in New York. The therapist had no time for him, and merely recommended that he come back to New York, which he did.

Upon his return to New York he had the most severe
attack of all when a subway train he was in was stuck in a tunnel. He became so panicky that when the train finally started up
again, he rushed out to the street to ask for help from the near-
est policeman. When no help was forthcoming, he made the
pact with God, whereupon his anxiety was dissipated. It is to
be noted that he had no deep religious convictions which would
make the pact intelligible; if anything, he was more or less ag-
nostic, like most young people of his generation.

Temporarily he took a clerical job, to tide him over. When
he returned to his former therapist, Art felt that he needed
more intensive analysis. He was sent to a low-cost referral
service, through which he eventually reached me.

COURSE OF ANALYSIS

The analysis lends itself to a chronological arrangement
because of a severe regressive epidode after about three years of
treatment, the working through of which proved to be a significant turning point. Prior to that Frank had had many "insights"
but made little change in his real-life behavior. Once the regression was past he was able to find a reality resolution to his sex
problem, and to develop himself in various ways at work and
outside work. He became an excellent writer, and was even able
to achieve semiprofessional status at it. Unfortunately, his new-
found health led to a premature marriage, which the analyst was
unable to prevent because a personal illness of his own had
forced him to cut back somewhat on his schedule. The marriage
was followed by an untimely termination. Eventually he returned to analysis, and made further dramatic progress with his
problems. In spite of the inopportune interruption, the analysis eventually achieved a good result.

Only the early analysis is presented here. The frequency of
sessions varied from two to five per week. This period lasted
six years.

Period of Initial Insights

For the first three years of the analysis there was a series of dramatic insights which, however, led to no appreciable change in Frank's behavior. But it is clear that the liberation of so much unconscious material helped to carry the day in the difficult regressive period that followed.

The period of insights does not lend itself readily to any further compartmentalization. Certain themes were naturally repeated over and over, but in no clear-cut order. At times one would predominate, at other times another. The material can best be presented in chronological order.

From the very beginning the transference was markedly ambivalent. His first demand was that he be given a Jewish analyst from the Bronx; when I said that I was one, he seemed surprised and relieved. All too soon this was followed by the assertion that psychoanalysis just didn't work, and that sooner or later a drug would be discovered which would resolve problems like his by chemical means. When he was feeling particularly angry he speculated that the drugs would drive all analysts out of business, and that I would be in a particularly bad position. This "drug resistance" came up on and off throughout the entire analysis. His treatment was conducted in the early 1950s, before the days of the tranquilizers, so no medication was attempted. But even today it would probably be best to treat him without drugs.

An early dream brought out his frustrated strivings for masculinity, a recurrent theme.

> "I'm in the Navy. I'm trying to get into my pants but don't succeed; I try again and don't succeed. I'm bawled out."

Since he had actually been in the Army, the Navy had a special meaning for him. To it he associated the tight Navy pants, and the fears of homosexuality which had plagued him for such a long time. The bawling out is a transformed homosexual wish.

Initially the resistances were intermingled with feelings of improvement. On the one hand analysis costs too much money, he complained. He would rather have a car and a lot of girls. I didn't understand him as well as the other therapists, yet he admired me because I gave him interpretations which were omitted by Art. Yet still he felt I didn't take enough of a personal interest in him, or sympathize with him.

In the discussion of the attacks he mentioned for the first time that they started shortly after his father's heart attack. He recalled the incident from the age of thirteen when he had kissed his father while drunk. The first explanation offered was that the attacks were in some way connected with mixed feelings about father. This made a lot of sense to him and brought him some relief. Yet he was still so frightened that when his hours were late in the evening he would go home after work and then come downtown again; it was too dangerous to spend several hours in the city on his own.

At this point another recurrent theme emerged: two of the fellows in his office were making fun of him. One he admired, the other he despised, but both terrified him. The fellow he admired was Henry, the other Joe. Each thrust of theirs hurt him deeply, and he would spend hours of analytic time complaining bitterly about what they were doing to him. For example, one day a girl in the office came in wearing a rather flimsy blouse. He remarked to her, "You look transparent." Whereupon Henry said to him, "You're the transparent one." This remark pained him for weeks thereafter.

Initially there were a few hesitant efforts to make contact with girls. Two dreams bring out the dynamic factors which still made the superego prohibitions so strong.

> "I'm in a train, sitting with my mother.* On the other side are my sister and Shirley. My mother pushes me to go over to Shirley, but I'm afraid. She pushes me. I resist her. Sue comes over and says, "You see it's perfectly all right, come on over." I refuse. My mother pushes me. I grab her wrist and shout, "Stop pushing me". . . . The scene changes and I'm in a bus with Shirley. I talk to her. She gets out near the 100's and 9th Avenue. She passes by a building on which C is marked. There are men marching towards the building, all with C on their chests. She walks towards the Hudson River."

This dream brings out a number of recurring symbolic motifs. Mother and sister push him towards Shirley, the first

* Unless otherwise noted, he always referred to his stepmother as his "mother" and to his biological mother as his "real mother."

girl he worshiped as a child; he wants them to push him, but at the same time he does not want to leave. It leads to his grabbing his mother by the wrist, a combination of aggressive and incestuous wishes. The train, a source of one of his most important phobias, is revealed as the place where he gets sexually excited.

In the second half of the dream he finally reaches Shirley, but she spurns him for other men. The river and bridge are repeated symbols of freedom on the other side. For a long time in all his sexual fantasies he could only imagine himself having intercourse away from New York; in the city he was confronted by too many menacing father figures. Clearly, this is a variation of his Oedipal conflict; only by putting a great distance between himself and father could he escape father's wrathful prohibition against sex. It is already obvious that the pact with God is a pact with father.

"The company sends me on a trip to Florida with a car. I leave the car there and take the train back. When I come back I remember with horror that I left the car in Florida double parked in front of a bar. I'm frightened silly that the secret will be discovered. . . . One of the executives, a relative of mine, comes in and says are you ——? I don't understand why he doesn't know my name?"

Although no women as such appear here, the Oedipal theme is again predominant. Florida, a bar, and a car represent sexual freedom. To the secret he associates stealing from a candy store when he was four or five. Also he revealed that he was frequently tempted to steal things from my waiting room after I went inside with the next patient. The last part of the dream brings out the defensive pattern for fear that sexual and anal secrets will be discovered.

After the discussion of these two dreams he experienced a good deal of relief. But no sooner had he felt the relief than the other side of the ambivalence came to the fore. Suppose, he rightly argued, that he gave other associations, would I then not offer other interpretations? The fact that he had given precisely those associations did not impress him.

New fears came out. He was afraid of the occasional conferences in his office, when he would be called upon to say something. A habit of squinting, which had first occurred several years before, reappeared. This was related to a girl in the office with big breasts; he liked to stare at her breasts but was also afraid to do so. He felt some homosexual attraction for an anti-Semitic Irishman in his office. Yet then again he would say, "You stress sex too much. Sex can't be that important. It is something in my nerves, and some day they'll discover the right drug for it."

These critical remarks alternated with feelings of deep insight on his part. A blushing attack at the office and fear of an attack on the subway when the train accidentally slowed down were both connected with homosexual feelings. His fears of being transparent are just another form of anxiety, which he has been having all his life in one form or another. He decided that he was a "normal neurotic." All his fears of being immobilized — of suddenly losing power in his voice, legs, or eyes — were fears of castration.

One dream brought out a number of masochistic fantasies.

> "I come home and there's a big crowd around the house where I live. I ask what is the matter and a girl says some girl's brother has been stabbed and is bleeding. They've called an ambulance, and are taking him away."

In association to this dream he mentioned a book about a girl in an isolated country spot, who gets back her long lost brother, for whom she has a lot of affection. This association had stimulated him to masturbate with a fantasy of his real mother; he did it, even though he was afraid. At another time he had seen his sister in the shower, which also became a masturbation fantasy. The stabbing in the dream brought up fears of being penetrated, which he called castration fears. He cannot stand anything in his rectum. VD is especially horrible because the treatment involves putting a needle into his penis and draining everything out of it.

This was immediatley followed by one of his grandiose dreams which brought out many feelings about father.

> "I'm General MacArthur's enlisted aide. We are sleeping on two cots in the same tent. Before we go to sleep he starts telling me dirty jokes. I urge him to stop because I want to go to sleep. The next day enlisted men are

passing by. General MacArthur says, "Did you get that thing I did for you?" Each says yes but shows no gratitude. I think it's terrible that they show no gratitude."

MacArthur was one of a long line of famous men he dreamt about; they were father figures who gratified his need to be a great man. About MacArthur himself he felt somewhat ambivalent. In association to the two cots he was reminded of sharing a hotel room in Paris during his Army days with his friend Irving. This room had two beds; he slept in one, while Irving got himself a girl and had sex with her in the other. The two cots also reminded him of the room he shared with his brother, about whom he occasionally had sexual feelings.

During this period he still made sporadic efforts to date girls. One pattern was to visit dance halls — "I know all the dance halls in New York" he said at one time. Since he was physically attractive, girls were quite willing to start up a relationship with him; but as soon as he had dated them once or twice he would drop them. He could see no psychological factors in this pattern; it was just that they were all "dogs."

In one session a fifteen-minute tirade against his brother-in-law (sister's husband) was followed by the insight that his anger was due to jealousy. This incident was followed by a thinly veiled incestuous dream about his sister:

"Sue and I go to the movies. A fellow appears on the screen, short and stocky [a man he admires]. A whistle blows and he goes toward the river; it is a symbol of his failure. It blows several more times, this time for victory. Now I'm the man. I step down, and get a job from a mechanic who is walking along the street with his wife. His wife is thirty-five. I find her terribly attractive and want to have sex with her. I feel her up publicly. She is quite willing, but says not in public, not where we can be seen."

In association he describes the man as his hero, strong and rich. The river is again symbolic of crossing over to an area where sex is permitted. The man's wife is Frank's sister. Thus the dream *in toto* becomes another Oedipal fantasy: he defeats his brother-in-law, reaches his dream status, and has sex with his sister. After all these insights, as so often happens, he suddenly blurted out, "I don't know if all these explanations are right; it seems simpler to me."

Shortly thereafter he learned that he was being groomed for a more important job in which he would have direct contact with the public, which had not been the case up to then. This both excited and frightened him. He also started to argue that Horney was much closer to the truth than Freud, another dodge to escape his sexual conflict.

Fantasies about getting closer to girls continued. In one dream:

> "I'm in a group of people. There is a young girl of sixteen or seventeen who is intelligent as well as pretty. I'm on the outside of the group. . . . I'm crossing a bridge in Upper Manhattan. I slide down the bridge on my bare ass and crash on the Bronx side."

The bridge is again the crossing from childhood to adulthood, from anality to sexuality. Here he crashes back in the Bronx on his "bare ass," obviously, regressing to anality. The girl reminds him of a girl his father had been interested in shortly after mother had died. Thus it is again an Oedipal dream: his impotent inability to get father's girl.

Shortly thereafter he had a dream that a single-seater fighter crashed into his childhood home, which reminded him of a childhood nightmare that a big transport plane crashed into his playground. This dream had many determinants, among them the early thoughts about parental sex in which the plane is his father, the house-playground his mother.

After that he had his first unequivocal transference dream:

> "I'm in your office with Jennie. I point out to her what a handsome, distinguished-looking man you are."

On the one hand this brought out the Oedipal fantasy of restoring the family with me as the father. On the other it re-emphasized once more his extreme stress on appearances, part of his whole exhibitionistic complex. What counted above all was that the analyst should *look* right, just as in early puberty what counted most for him was that he should *look* masculine. At the same time, this was accompanied by a feeling of discouragement because all the insights did not help. When the boys at the office kidded him, he still blushed and felt terrible. It is to be noted that his negative feelings referred to his not feeling better, and not to his sexual abstinence, which troubled him little at this point.

A dream shortly thereafter brought out the sadistic side of the exhibitionism: he had to make a display of great strength to other people. This was part of his identification with the powerful father. Material about father was accompanied by renewed feelings of despair, resort to drugs, and some preoccupation about his pact with God. Then came a dream in which he replaced father:

> "I'm driving along in a car; my father is seated next to me; my cousin L. is in the back. I come to a red light, start pumping on the brakes to stop the car, but I can't stop it in time. I almost hit a cop, then go by and come to a stop. A second cop comes up to give me a ticket. My father tells me to lie and say I didn't see the red light, but I argue with him, say no."

To the car he associated father's truck and the childhood wish to drive father around instead of being driven around by him. Pumping meant masturbation, with its attendant conflicts. Cousin L. looks down on him intellectually, thereby resembling brother and analyst. To the ticket he associated an incident when he was driving with his mother. A cop stopped him to give him a ticket, but mother's pleading succeeded in getting him off. This in turn reminded him of a number of incidents from childhood where his real mother interceded with father not to punish him, one of the few good memories he had about her.

This dream led to some questioning of his pact with God. Why didn't I state my opinion and urge him to have sex? (At a later period when I did doubt that God would punish him for sex he replied, How do you know what God would do?) To get me to commit myself he gave me a terrific build-up, asserting that everything I said was well-considered, unlike Art, who was quite impulsive, like Frank. I merely interpreted his wish to turn me into an idealized father.

Shortly thereafter he had another dream in which he could let himself go because it released all his aggression.

"The third world war breaks out. They want especially young men. I feel very good because I'm important. I go riding in a car. Again the brakes fail, and I go through a red light. But I don't care because I know I'm important."

This was precipitated by a date with an Oriental girl, Stella, who let him feel her up. He came in his pants, but it didn't matter because as usual he was never going to see her again. The loss of control here leads to a sense of importance because he can join in the conquest and possible destruction of the world in the third world war.

For several sessions he was high, telling me how good I was, how much good psychoanalysis had done him, what a pity other members of his family had never been analyzed, etc. Then an incident with Henry, who had made fun of him on some trivial pretext, set him off again. Once more he was down in the dumps, hopeless, looking for drugs, etc. The concealed homosexuality in his continual sense of denigration by Joe was brought out in another dream:

"I'm in a bus; then I'm in a subway. The power fails; everything stops. Everything goes out of control. It starts up again slowly; my brother and I are in the last car. Another train is rushing toward us from the rear. I tell Jerome "Come on, let's get out of here"; he doesn't want to go."

The recurrent theme of being in a subway which goes out of control receives new elaboration here. It is related to his fear of attack from the rear (penetration of the rectum) which had come up before. At the same time there is a need to hold on to the brother, at least to cushion the attack to some extent, which shed light on his need to live at home, where he shared a room with Jerome.

Shortly after this dream he had one of his worst attacks. He had been on his feet all day; Joe in the office had again made some derogatory remark. This upset him so that he had to change subways several times before he got home. Once he was home he went to bed right away. Finally he managed to calm down.

Around this time he became interested in a girl, Linda, whom he had known years before. She had dropped out of sight for a long time; recently he discovered it was because she had been in a mental hospital. He thought that since she had been out of the running for such a long time he had a chance with her. Still she was used to professional men, so even with her he anticipated the worst. Actually, the relationship with her turned out to be full of odd, unexplained actions on her part.

No sooner had he contemplated another relationship with a girl than ideas of death pushed into the foreground. He dreamt:

> "Jane and I are walking along; we are walking to my bris [circumcision]. The baby is born dead. After the bris it comes to life. Then we go in to see my mother. I'm afraid that she will be sloppily dressed, but she's not."

In association he recalled several friends of his who had died in childhood. The circumcision is painful to the infant; he had seen two recently. His recurrent fears of castration are now seen as part of a death and resurrection fantasy; this also relates to the pact with God. The fear that mother will be sloppily dressed is part of a wish to see her in the nude, for which he also expects punishment (death).

> "John D. is driving along. He gets into the railroad tracks; it is very exciting and I ask him to slow down; I'm afraid that he's going to crash in the river."

John D. is looked upon as the office bully. In the dream he is showing Frank how to be aggressive, including sexually (driving along the tracks), which frightens Frank enormously.

For quite a while he continued this seesaw, alternately thinking of dating a new girl, and then retreating from the experience in panic after one or two dates. Frequent attacks occured in response to the ordinary kind of joking that went on in the office, and he took every remark as a mortal blow. Then came another exhibitionistic-incestuous dream about his sister:

> "I'm out in the park or an African jungle with Sue and Mary [her girl friend]. There are snakes all around, but if you don't bother them they won't bother you. Ely [brother-in-law] comes along and just to show him I go to get a rifle to shoot the snakes. I go to the car where my father and [real] mother are. I stand by our car

waiting for Sue and Mary to come back. But they decide to go off in another car with some strange men."

The snake symbolism was of course obvious to him; he wants to show his penis off to his family, especially sister. But then again there is also the ambivalent wish to drive her away, so that he will be the only child with father and mother.

For a while there were many fantasies about Mary, his sister's friend, and Linda, whom he dated on rare occasions. Mostly the material in this period related to homosexuality and voyeurism. Then came another celebrity dream, emphasizing his grandiose and destructive wishes.

> "General Eisenhower is making a speech on war, pointing out how horrible it is, and that it should be avoided at all costs. He shows a map of Frankfurt, and that it has been 75 percent destroyed. Then somehow he shows a map of the Bronx around where I live, and says the fires may extend there. . . . Then we go inside where there is a reception for Eisenhower, MacArthur, and many other dignitaries. They take my picture."

Here he wants the horrors of war to extend to his own home, i.e., to destroy his home. This sadism, as before, is coupled with the exhibitionistic wish to have his picture taken. The grandiosity was soon followed by a river-bridge dream (crossing over to sexuality).

> "I'm in Paris, but can't find any accommodations. I'm walking along the Seine, past the Eiffel Tower, cross the river on a slippery log which is separated from each shore by one foot. When I get across I see people admiring me because of my GI uniform. . . . I'm kissing a girl; she touches my penis, and I let her make me come."

The day residue for this dream was the funeral of the father of one of his friends, which brought back many memories of his own father. As in real life, once he is three thousand miles away from father (who retains his prohibitive superego powers even though dead) he can cross the river, be admired, and have sex.

Nevertheless, as mentioned, all the insights had not produced the slightest change in his sexual behavior. One or two dates and he would drop the girl. Then would come months of total sexual inactivity, masturbation, anxiety attacks, and a general atmosphere of gloom and doom. Through all this, however, he stuck religiously to the analysis, never missing a session.

One day when he was in the toilet with Joe and Henry he had an attack of anxiety and blushing. That night he dreamt:

"I'm in Randolph Field; it is very much like where I work. I'm terribly afraid of being bitten by snakes. One fellow shows me a snake he's caught; it is 3 feet long and about 4-5 inches in diameter; he killed it. Somebody comes upon me from behind, and buckles me at the knees."

Randolph Field is a park where sports events are held; it reminds him of his interest in sports. The snakes and the attack from behind are recurrent fantasies of homosexual attacks.

Still, while he agreed with the interpretation of a homosexual conflict, it did not stop either the blushing or the anxiety. Again he felt desperate; what could he possibly do, unless they discovered a drug?

One of his favorite pastimes was to go to the library and read psychiatric and psychological literature. I did not attempt to restrict his reading, but did ask him to discuss anything that seemed significant. One book stated that early sex experiences are important. Accordingly, he wanted to tell me that when he was very young at night he used to become frightened and jump into bed with his parents, even though they objected strongly.

Shortly thereafter he had another significant transference dream:

"I'm near the store we had when I was a boy, but somehow I'm a veteran. There's a horse outside which is groaning and suffering; we take it inside, but inside it is a different horse. You come in and I start telling you all about my cavalry exploits in Europe. . . . You come to my home. I show you my family, and show them what an extraordinary person a psychoanalyst is. Then I take you to my room and show you an album with pictures of all the girls I've been out with; I show you how pretty they are."

To the suffering horse he associated his mother, brother,

and himself. The contrast between outside and inside, as well as between veteran and little boy symbolizes his confusion about his self-image, as well as his surprise that despite all his inner tortures he can still function in the real world. The need to boast to me about his cavalry exploits in Europe, and all the girls he's been out with, is part of what he called his phony self-image which he constructed to handle his conflicts at puberty. Part of the intense shame attached to the kidding he took at the office derived from the shattering of his self-image. The surprise expressed at "what an ordinary person a psychoanalyst is" is associated with his continual astonishment that I do not boast more about myself or put up more of a front.

After this dream he began to boast of how well he was doing. Then he realized he hadn't gone one tenth of the way as yet. Still, he began to fill up with what he called "superiority feelings." In his work specialty he was the best in the company. For his age he's the best writer alive (at this point he had as yet written nothing for publication). This led to another sexual-Oedipal dream.

"Outside my building Joan is sitting, completely naked, with me. I take her to my apartment. On the way in my brother comes out in his shorts. We go into the bedroom and Jennie shows me Bill R. lying on the bed. He looks cheerful, but is really dying of an incurable sickness."

Joan is an Irish girl in his office who is very cheerful but sexually unattractive because she is flat-chested. To brother in his shorts he associates showing off to him that he, Frank, has a girl while brother does not; in sexual terms, his penis is bigger than his brother's. Bill R. is the chief of another department whom he once thought highly of but whom he now despises: he reminds him of his father. Thus, the dream depicts the wish for beating out the men in the family, and gaining mother: Jennie shows him the dying father, and permits him to have sex at home, while brother is displayed "with his pants down."

For some time after this the predominant theme in associations and dreams was how good he was, his superiority feelings. He fantasized or dreamt about defeating everybody. Again a clear Oedipal dream brought out the underlying dynamics of this fantasy.

"My father is crying. He is sitting next to a woman, who is a combination of Mary, a prostitute, and an aunt of mine, and it's just been announced that he's going to marry this woman. My stepmother is sitting nearby and she's crying. I take her side and become angry with my father."

The dream brought out many feelings about the women father had seen shortly after mother died, but not about Jennie, whom Frank idealized. It also led to the release of much anger towards the therapist. He accused me of being a snob, interested in cultural matters like his brother rather than in baseball, like a real he-man. Still, when a holiday forced the cancellation of one session during one week, he was annoyed that he could not see me.

This led to a discussion of his fears of being too dependent on me, which explained why he read so many books to clarify the analytic process. On the one hand he was checking up on me with acknowledged authorities. Since anyone who wrote a book thereby became an authority, this often sidetracked us into discussions of useless or bizarre theories. E.g., at one time he read about a theory of "aggressotoxin," which postulated the existence of a specific toxic substance, biochemical in nature, which accounted for all the aggression in people. He demanded to know why I didn't isolate this toxin, rather than work on psychological conflicts. Anger of this kind would frequently last several weeks.

In spite of his sophistication, shame about analysis was still strong with him. A characteristic ambivalent transference was:

"I'm on a farm in upstate N.Y. with you and a woman who's your mother or aunt. I leave and come back to N.Y. I meet Jack, who is with Murray and another fellow. He tells me he's going to a farm in upstate N.Y. which is run by a fellow by the name of Reuben Fine and invites me to come along. I think I'd love to go, but sooner or later it would come out that I know you, and then they would know I was going to an analyst, and I don't want that; I don't know what to do."

Jack and Murray were two fellows at the office whom he

was eager to impress. To the farm he associates another kind of home, a different environment from the one he had. Still he projects to me here his own form of sexual adjustment, living with a mother or an aunt. The dream brought out particularly the deep sense of isolation he felt from his fellow workers and, in fact, all human beings, and the urgent wish to break out of this isolation.

A date with a new girl brought on for the first time a demand for the solution of his sex problem; up to that point he had been rather lackadaisical about it. Now he became dramatic. He cannot wait any longer to have sex. If he cannot have sex he will kill himself. In fact, if it were not for his sister he would have killed himself a long time ago; it would set a bad example for her. But the pact with God is still in force, so it will not be easy to resolve the problem. In his dilemma he regresses to a wish to be mistreated by mother:

> "I have a cold. My mother tells me to put eardrops in my nose. I say, "How ridiculous! How can you put eardrops in the nose?" She says do it and I do."

To the eardrops he had a number of associations. He had been reading about Van Gogh and his self-mutilation by chopping off his ear. Joe, the envied co-worker in the office, had eardrops which he used occasionally. As a child Frank had often been afraid of having parts of his body chopped off, including the ears and nose. His fears of being penetrated have been mentioned before. The dream is essentially a wish to be castrated and attacked sexually by mother; this also sheds light on his lifelong fear of penetration, which is really a homosexual, masochistic wish to submit sexually to the powerful parent, both mother and father. It also brings out his confusion about the nature of sexual intercourse (how can you put eardrops in the nose?).

The consistent effort to make contacts with girls, in spite of the pact, dominated the analysis for the next year. In reality he continued to be unsuccessful. At the unconscious level he brought out the three main conflicts which interfered with his real-life efforts. These were the incestuous wish for sister, regressive homosexual trends, and repetitive anger towards me.

Although he had always had occasional incestuous fantasies, they became much stronger at this period. To some extent they were precipitated by a worsening in his sister's condition, which led her to seek out therapy at this time. Shortly after she began he dreamt:

> "I'm in bed with Sue. We are having intercourse. My mother walks in and we stop. . . . I'm off in a big room; Ely [Sue's husband] and Stan [a friend] are there. Ely says, "Why didn't you come to see me when Sue was in the country."

He felt rather happy about this dream, because the intercourse with his sister was actually acted out in it. At the same time he falls back on her husband when mother prohibits the sex. Stan was a friend who had been discussed a good deal in the analysis; he was in pretty much the same life situation as Frank. As might have been expected, there was a strong homosexual attraction between the two, which had come out in various ways. Mostly they joined in commiserating with one another, and in rejecting girls, as at dances. As his interest began to move strongly towards girls, and the homosexuality was brought out into the open, the friendship with Stan began to disintegrate.

Since he still saw me as a sexually forbidding figure in his unconscious, it was understandable that his anger towards me increased as his sexual drive became stronger. At one point he dreamt:

> "There's a group therapy session with Henry, Joe, and a fourth fellow. They say Dr. Fine is coming to lead the session. You come and take us all out driving. Joe starts attacking you. You don't answer and I'm very disappointed."

To group therapy he associates the recent information that his admired Joe is now going to a group. The fantasy is that in a group he can attack me more easily. He is also trying to make me responsible here for his poor relationships with other men.

Immediately thereafter he again had several incestuous dreams about his sister, and a homosexual one.

> "I'm with Jennie and Sue in bed. I play with Jennie and screw Sue."

Here there is the additional element of being in bed with both mother and sister. This is in contrast to the earlier dream in which mother holds him back from sister.

"I'm kissing Sue's vagina."

The idea of kissing a girl's vagina was one which horrified him at the conscious level; he is trying to break out of his inhibitions. Too soon; for immediately comes a homosexual dream:

> "I go up to a high floor of a building. There is Paul R. in the apartment. We go into the bathroom. There is something in the bathtub covered up. He pulls off the cover. It is a fellow with an erection. . . I get into a bathtub with another fellow; we go flying off, see all the girls through the windows."

The high floor is part of his network of phobias. Another dream from this period highlighted the regressive trends:

> "I'm working in a garage [near my home] on the second story. It's a rainy day and they let us out early, around 3 o'clock. I walk out with Henry. I go to look for my car but can't find it."

To 3 o'clock he associates the end of the school day. The second story means that he is less exposed. Rain brings back memories of one of his first jobs, shortly after he got out of school.

The dream is a wish to regress from his search for girls. In reality his car was out of commission for a while. He used this as an excuse to avoid women, since he needed the car to impress them.

In spite of the regression, or perhaps because of it, he felt better for a while. Insights began to come thick and fast, particularly into his homosexual impulses. It became easier for him to spend time with the fellows; he was less angry, and could let go with some of his aggression towards them. On the job he became more ambitious, working hard for a promotion to the next rung on the ladder. He wrote a piece for the house journal; much to his surprise it was accepted. Now that he was an established author, he could let his imagination go again about his talent. Still, the angry feelings towards me remained. He dreamt:

"You and Joe are in a group. Joe starts attacking you; you can't reply."

Noteworthy here is again how he puts me in an immobilized attacked position, the one he has so often complained about in himself. A few sessions later he made me into a woman in a dream, a type dream which has been described in several other men.

"I go to an optometrist for my blinking. It turns out to be a woman. She has been psychoanalyzed and we can discuss it at great length. She leans right up against me and I get an erection."

This dream brings out the wish to look me and other people in the eye as one element in his blinking. It also highlights the homosexual wishes towards the analyst.

By this time he was able to handle his anxieties in daily life to some extent by self-analysis. Accordingly, with the insights and the changes in his well-being, he felt that the analysis was getting somewhere. Still he was making no headway with the girls. Another incestuous dream about his sister came up:

"I'm on a couch with Sue. I get on top of her. She sees somebody behind us and gets panicky."

To the somebody he associates father. Consciously he was now obsessed with insights about the homosexual feelings, but the blinking persisted. He was also terrified of bridges at this time, fearful that he would lose control of the car whenever he had to cross one. Finally another bridge dream came along which helped to resolve this aspect of his phobia.

"I'm riding in a car with Fred. We go up to the East Bronx, near the river, and walk around. There's a bridge to an island in the river."

Fred was a man who could not control his anger. The spot in the river reminded him of a place where he had once taken some girls; he could have had sex with them there but didn't. The bridge is the transition to release of his sexual-aggressive feelings. Many other sexual memories also came up in association to this dream.

He continued in this way for quite a while, seemingly getting better, both behaviorally and internally. At one point he even revealed another great secret, that he had never in his life brushed his teeth.

Then, after about three years of analysis, he went into a severe regression.

The Great Fear

At first his regression took the form of increased argumentativeness, which did not seem so different from his previous behavior. He began to deny his sexual problem (which he had done before); it was not the sexual conflicts that led to blinking, but the blinking that led to sexual conflicts.

Then, without warning, came a new symptomatic obsession: his legs were going to collapse. He could not go to work because his legs would collapse. Then he'd have to be carried out, he'd lose his job, and be the laughing stock of the whole company. Maybe he should go to a hospital, as his brother had done.

The frequency of sessions had to be increased; for some time he came in five times a week. He discussed the same material that had come up before, but uppermost in his mind was the wish for reassurance that his legs would not actually collapse. Without such an assurance the whole analysis was a waste.

Most of the time the transference was negative in this period. He redoubled his tirades against Freud and sex; all that had nothing to do with it. It was something physical, some day a drug would be discovered to cure such conditions, which would put all psychoanalysts out of business, etc. Yet one day he came in drunk on a Friday, the last session of the week, and said that he loved me.

In real life he abandoned the effort to find girls, and almost all social life. He went to work, came to analysis, and went home; there was virtually nothing else.

Almost every session he demanded some reassurance that no harm would befall him. Since this demand was handled analytically, he frequently left angry. Much dynamic material, besides the obvious castration fear, came out in this period. His legs were dirty; the collapse would expose this dirt. A childhood habit of kicking the couch to annoy his parents was one which had led to endless quarrels, during which he would at times fantasize killing either one or both parents. And finally the collapse embodied his constant fear of loss of control, including bowel control.

Most important in his own self-analysis was what he called feminine feelings. Really he wanted to be a girl; the demands made on a man were simply too great for him. His exaggerated pose as a he-man since adolescence merely covered up his wishes to be a woman. Women had it easier.

All of this had come up before. The alterations in the analysis that are hardest to convey are the greatly increased fear, amounting to panic at times, and the virtual ultimatum, repeated several times a week, that he was going to crack up.

For a while it was indeed necessary to advise him to stop working; fortunately this lasted less than a month. Otherwise it was possible to handle the whole episode by systematic interpretation. With characteristic negativism, he would reject every interpretation. Yet in spite of all his defiance, something seemed to remain.

Gradually, after about a year the worst of the anxiety began to disappear. Reassurance was no longer so urgent: imminent collapse no longer seemed so near. He began to formulate in his own words the interpretations which he had previously rejected so vigorously and even, at times, so bitterly. Two dreams in which he would talk again about his sexual problems seemed to mark the end of the severe regression.

> "I'm in a girl's dormitory or school. Mary and Gerty are are there. I'm in my underwear."

This was mainly a wish to have a harem with a lot of women. He is still thinking of Mary, his sister's closest friend.

> "Mrs. K. is much younger. I like her breasts."

Mrs. K. was the mother of an acquaintance; he is coming back to the positive wish for mother.

The First Sexual Experience

Finally he seemed really ready to tackle the sexual problem.

But there was still that uncomfortable pact with God. When I doubted God's intentions, he rebuked me sharply, saying I did not know what God would do. At the same time there seemed to be some doubt in his mind that anything would really happen.

The dreams had shown a persistent pattern for a while that if he had sex in New York father would punish him, while if he went out of town father would not. I had interpreted the pact as a fear of father, but as yet this had seemed to make no impression on him. Accordingly, he conceived the idea that maybe if he went out of town, and did it with a prostitute, God would not strike him dead.

Full of trepidation he took off for a vacation trip to Florida. There he paid a bellboy to send a girl to his room, Sherry. While he did not tell Sherry his problem, she sensed that he was practically a virgin, even though he was then twenty-eight years old, and treated him with a certain amount of tenderness. Fear of VD was handled by using a condom. The only drawback was that Sherry had specified in advance that she had only half an hour to give him; after that she had to go to another "client." Still, it went well in spite of everything, and he succeeded in having intercourse.

Yet upon his return to New York the phobia and the pact with God were as strong as ever. He could date girls much more, and in ordinary social encounters he did much better. But, he insisted, "good girls don't want sex." He did not want to frequent prostitutes, he wanted to have some meaningful interchange with a girl. The problem remained.

Since he was now seeing girls much more, and confronting the past directly, I tried a kind of Talmudic approach.* I said to him, "Let us see if we can test out your theory about God. When you dance with a girl, your penis is, say, four inches from her vagina. Obviously at that distance, God does not strike you dead. At what distance will he do so?" Put in this way, it made sense to him.

There were a number of girls with whom he could experiment. One, a schoolteacher by the name of Estelle, seemed

* Nowadays this might be called a form of behavior therapy, though the idea that behavior therapy has any real value has yet to be proved.

particularly suitable, since she had indicated in various ways that she was attracted to him and might be willing to have sex with him. The thing that troubled him about her was that if he did have sex with her, and did not marry her afterwards, she would be terribly hurt. I urged him to take this chance; if she were hurt, it could be worked out later.

Accordingly he undertook to have sex with Estelle, inch by inch, as described above. As had been surmised from what he had said about her, she was more eager than he. Estelle was probably puzzled by the cautious way in which he approached her, but perhaps she rationalized it by the fact that they always fooled around in his car. He literally reduced the distance between penis and vagina inch by inch, coming to the analytic session after each step closer for reassurance and understanding.

Finally he was able to penetrate her. Even then, he only went in a quarter of an inch, and stopped, to see what God would do. When nothing happened, he went in all the way. At this point he experienced no sexual difficulties (they did appear later).

After she had had intercourse with him three times, Estelle, much to his surprise, told him that she was dropping him for another fellow. There were no tears, no demands for marriage, no guilt on her part. It was all rather matter of fact. He did not offer her enough, so she was moving on; the sex did not matter to her. It is quite possible that she was experimenting with him sexually, to seduce and reject him, but there was no definite information available.

Among other things the sexual success gratified his wish to get closer to me. He dreamt:

> "I'm in your waiting room, which goes into the rest of the house. You take me in and put me on the couch, which is reversed. Your wife comes up and makes me feel comfortable. There's a movie shown about monkeys and I'm supposed to guess which sex is which. A group of psychiatrists is sitting in back, applauding me."

Thus he brings out his wish both to come into my family and to be my favorite patient, on favorable display to a whole group of colleagues. He also wants me to teach him more about sex.

Once the initial barrier was broken, he was now able to have sex with other girls. But soon a new problem emerged: the guilt that he had projected to Estelle became stronger and stronger in him, and he began to feel obligated to marry one of the girls with whom he had had sex. This led to the next stage.

Premature Marriage

A few months after his experience with Estelle he met a girl, Cora, whom he responded to quite warmly. Cora had been married and divorced, so initially she welcomed the sexual release with him (later she changed). The earlier preoccupations with anxiety attacks, blushing, homosexuality, the pact with God, etc., had all gone. Instead, now he was preoccupied with the harm that he did to women by having sex with them. It was his duty to marry them, particularly Cora. In one dream it became clear that the fear of doing her harm was a wish on his part:

> "I'm up high on a bridge, with Cora and Sarah [her girl-friend]. I start pulling for Cora with Sarah. Cora falls down and I see her body shattered in little pieces."

The little pieces were described in great detail. The bridge, a recurrent symbol, appears here again. Now it is clear that the bridge is a crossing over to aggression and destruction, the sadistic side of sex, as well as tenderness and love.

Together with the sexual release went improvement in other ways. He took to writing letters to newspapers and several were published. On his job he received another promotion, because of his increased ability to deal with the public. He also became interested in acting, doing very well in a preparatory course. But he did not try to make the grade in acting professionally.

Unfortunately, the pressure to marry Cora continued to mount. Over my objections, he married her after they had been going together for about six months.

No sooner had he married than problems in the relationship began to appear. She was really cold in bed and would often refuse him sex. He could not stand her looks, especially her hair. Other girls began to interest him, but he would not get himself to see any. It was as though he was doomed to remain in an unhappy marriage.

Unsatisfactory Termination

On top of everything else money troubles now appeared. Cora objected to his analysis, asking him to spend the money on her. Too weak to withstand her, and filled with guilt about the anger he felt towards me, he stopped treatment. This portion had lasted in all about six years.

LATER REANALYSIS

About ten years later Frank applied for more analysis. The problems that had plagued him initially had all disappeared. He was secure in his job, had published a number of pieces in newspapers and house journals. Unable to have children, they had adopted a boy.

But his marriage was an exceedingly unhappy one. Sex was bad. She was a nag, who disapproved of all his ambitions. Her mother, who had come to stay with them for a while, was a source of constant irritation. Cora's disapproval, and the money problem, had prevented him from coming back to analysis before, but now he could not stand it any longer.

He was referred to another analyst, who saw him for a period of five years. The marriage broke up, and after a number of attempts he was able to find a woman with whom he could have a better love relationship. The lessons of the first analysis gradually became more and more meaningful to him as time went on.

DISCUSSION

This analysis presents several puzzling features. The problems that Frank came into treatment with all cleared up, yet a number emerged in the course of the analysis which remained unchanged for many years, in fact until they were altered by further analysis. Is the first analysis then to be considered a success or a failure?

In order to answer this question it is necessary to examine

the process of growth in Frank in more detail. When he first came to treatment he was preoccupied with problems that had disturbed him all through his life — severe anxieties, self-depreciation, inability to function sexually, overattachment to his home, various phobias.

To evaluate his situation the background from which he came must also be considered. Mother was a lifelong depressive who rejected all her children. The older brother had been hospitalized twice for schizophrenic pathology. The older sister had numerous problems, which culminated later in a severe agoraphobia. Only father presented some semblance of mental health.

A brief experience of supportive therapy for about six months had yielded no real results. At the start the picture looked bleak indeed, especially since it was complicated by the odd pact with God. At that time he could have been considered a true borderline, who might easily have become an overt schizophrenic with no treatment or poor treatment of the kind (drugs, shock, directive therapy) so often sanctioned by the profession.

Under these circumstances the resolution of the original problems, carrying along with it as it did the definite avoidance of a psychotic break, must be considered a positive step in his growth. The various phobias, including the sexual, were dissipated: the pact with God disappeared. His work situation was solidified at a level roughly commensurate with his abilities. He developed an ability, writing, which he was able to put to professional use (as a free lance) which had always been pure fantasy before. His self-esteem rose considerably, even though it still left much to be desired. Physically, he was able for the first time to leave home and set up an independent household.

On the negative side, what emerged was an unhappy marriage, which in turn was reflected in much internal misery. Why did he, in spite of the gains made by analysis, leave it to enter an unhappy marriage, with its attendant heartaches, especially inadequate sexual gratification? Clearly, there was a tug-of-war in his mind between Cora, his wife, and the analyst. At bottom this represented the battle between mother (Cora) and father (the analyst). It is not surprising that with his background the unhappy mother won, as she had so often won in the past. The balance of psychic forces at that point could only be tipped away from the suffering mother after he himself had gone through more years of suffering.

From the transference point of view, what was decisive was the intensity of the negative transference. It has been difficult to convey how he could go on for weeks or months berating the analyst for some alleged mistake or other. For example, his preoccupation with a new drug was not merely an ephemeral fantasy but a persistent conviction that carried with it the equally strong conviction that the drug would put all analysts out of business. His determination to destroy the analyst-father was both powerful and unrelenting. After it became apparent that the marriage was a failure, he even commented, "Here you are trying to remake a human being and I go off and get married. You must be angry at me." While he was aware of his vindictiveness against father-analyst, he did not realize how deep it was, nor that he would even go to the lengths of hurting himself in order to gratify his revenge.

Thus the negative side of the transference is primarily responsible for the unsatisfactory outcome. While the analyst was quite prepared to continue working on the negative transference, to the patient it was subjectively too uncomfortable. Further, it seemed to him (though this, of course, was entirely untrue) then that the analyst's request that he should not marry was just another sexual taboo. The pact with God had disappeared, but the guilt associated with sex outside of marriage had not.

The most dramatic aspect of his original pathology, the pact with God, was unconsciously an agreement with father to ward off the castration punishment for his Oedipal desires. In view of the extraordinary tenacity with which he stuck to his incestuous wishes, especially for his sister, it is not surprising that the anticipated punishment should have been so severe.

Frank's life history reminds one of Freud's observation that the most common ways of handling neurotic disturbance are physical illness and an unhappy marriage. His sister had chosen the former; he picked the latter. Yet it is necessary to add that the marriage remains unhappy primarily because of the vast residual hatreds carried over from the original family.

The later analysis, in which he was finally able to resolve the unhappy marriage, showed that the dynamic insights acquired in the first analysis had been absorbed to some extent, in spite of his negativism and vehement denials. Evidently, what is important is that the analyst should continue his interpretations, even in the face of vigorous opposition.

PART III
Discussion

A Review of the Ten Cases in the Light of the Analytic Ideal

In the major portion of this book each case has been reviewed and evaluated in its own terms. Now we can proceed to more global summaries by means of a systematic comparison of the results achieved with the various components of the analytic ideal. As clarified in the introduction, once therapy is underway, it comes to be formulated in these more human terms. No perfect solution is possible; nor is one attempted. What can be evaluated is the degree to which people do move closer to the ideal as a result of their analytic experience.

LOVE

In all cases there was a substantial growth toward love. But considerable differences existed in the significance attached to love by each person, and in the kinds of love relationships achieved.

Holly, Jim, and Harvey had almost idyllic love experiences, even though some of these (particularly Jim's) could be interpreted at an unconscious level as compensatory fantasies for the mother. But however love may be defined, the fact is that these three people reached love relationships they had never reached before, and felt very happy in them.

Peter's love for his second wife was genuine and fulfilling, but he was still so troubled by many residual problems that he could not enjoy it to the fullest. In any case, it represented a considerable advance over his first marriage.

Likewise Alice had a much warmer feeling for her second husband than for her first, and was much happier with him. But she was not a very passionate person, and her overall adjustment left less room for the transports of joy which some of the others experienced. To some people peak experiences are less important than to others.

Gloria and Sally, both self-centered women who had gone through periods of great promiscuity, reached a *modus vivendi* with their husbands, but never any great feeling of love. It may well be that if the analysis had come earlier in their lives, they would have left their husbands. At the same time the wild love fantasies which each had gone through with another man were seen to be self-destructive repetitions of childhood. Gloria maintained a real love feeling for the analyst, while Sally remained quite self-involved.

Frank's love for the woman whom he married was an obvious consequence of his crippled sex life. It was the classical idealization of the mother figure who is admired but with whom sex is unsatisfactory or forbidden. Yet, in spite of that, it still represented a step forward from his previous avoidance of all women other than the mother figure (stepmother) proper. Thus it was a partial advance, which had to be buttressed by much subsequent analysis, until he could experience a more mutual kind of love.

Beverly experienced no obvious growth in love in the course of her therapy. Except for the analyst, she did not relate to any man, and has not related to any other man in her subsequent life history.

Nevertheless, there was still a change in her love life. What she went through was a growth in self-love, which finally permitted her to get over her self-image as evil incarnate and to function in ordinary social situations. That this did not extend to love for other people is as much the consequence of external conditions as of internal.

With Sheldon, since he was a child, a different kind of evaluation must be used. The description of his therapy centered around the growth in his ability to communicate. This derived from an increase in his self-love, in that he shifted from a combination of panic and magical grandiosity to one of normal anxiety coupled with a more realistic self-appraisal. In interpersonal terms this manifested itself primarily in his relationship with his peers, secondarily in giving up some of the violent hatred of his father which lay at the root of his megolomaniacal fantasies.

PLEASURE

All patients experienced some increase in the capacity for pleasure and in the kinds of pleasure that they could allow themselves. As might be expected, this varied considerably, depending very heavily on past experiences.

However, none of these people developed into devil-may-care hedonists who pursued every impulse of the moment regardless of the consequences. Rather, what is most apparent is the *reduction in pain*. All, without exception, suffered much less at the end of treatment than at the beginning. In fact, it is surprising how little suffering there was in their lives when they discontinued. No doubt this was one factor in their decision to terminate. Follow-up material, which is available on all for a minimum of ten years, indicates that no prolonged period of suffering occurred in their lives after termination, with the exception of Frank. He did, however, return to analysis later, and worked out much of the conflict which had remained at the time of his first termination.

SEXUALITY

At the beginning of treatment, none of the patients except Sally had a satisfactory sexual adjustment, and hers was based on the shifty sands of promiscuity. Peter, Gloria, and Sally were married, the others not. By the end of treatment, sexual pleasure was markedly increased for all except Beverly (and again, except for the child, Sheldon, whose development has to be considered separately). But again, as with the love growth, the amount and quality of the sexual pleasure varied considerably.

Alice, who had started with the symptom of painful intercourse, overcame her symptom entirely, and emerged orgastic.

Holly had the most gratifying love relationship of all, and became completely orgastic. Sally always described herself as orgastic; her sexual advance lay in the increased capacity to enjoy herself with her husband and the ability to give up the vindictive forays with other men. Gloria derived more pleasure from sex, but remained satisfied with anal-clitoral gratification rather than vaginal. Beverly became completely asexual.

Among the men, Jim and Frank, who before analysis had virtually nothing to do with women, now enjoyed regular intercourse. Later Frank developed some premature ejaculation, but this too was corrected in the subsequent analysis.

Harvey had had a reasonable sex life even before analysis. The change in him lay in his new capacity to combine tender and sexual feelings for one woman, who reciprocated his feelings.

Peter's use of the drug had frustrated, and often blocked, adequate intercourse with his first wife. When he was able to give it up, this symptom disappeared, and he too could for the first time combine sexual and tender feelings for one woman. However, many neurotic residues remained with him, interfering with full enjoyment of sex.

Sheldon had revealed nothing of his sexual preoccupations in this therapy. However, there was the oral habit of chewing his shirts to the point of destroying them, which cleared up with the analysis. In later life, he was able to move on to an apparently satisfactory sex life with various girls. Eventually he married, and on the surface at least his marriage seemed satisfactory. At any rate, in adolescence, when he was still being followed up, his sex life seemed to be as good as that of his close friends.

FEELING

Towards the ideal of a rich feeling life, all patients made progress, though again in varying degrees.

Beverly was able to enjoy her children and grandchildren, though she still spent long periods of time "resting" from fatigue of undisclosed origin. Alice broke through her previous anxieties, made changes in her defensive socialization, and found herself experiencing more feelings than at any previous time in her life.

Sally, Gloria, and Frank retained a certain amount of anger, which spilled over on various occasions. Peter still held on to a good many anxieties, especially about his children and the fear of a return to the drug.

Holly, Jim, and Harvey experienced perhaps the greatest expansion of their feeling lives. The one change that could not be effected in Harvey was in his inability to get angry; however, he could no longer be pushed around in the old "schlemiel"-like manner.

In the realm of feeling Sheldon showed far-reaching changes. Where before treatment he was a sad-looking, withdrawn, angry, and frightened little boy, afterwards he was outgoing, cheerful, interested, and communicative. The extraordinary change in him was noticeable to everybody.

REASON

Without exception, all the patients at the end of treatment felt that their lives made more sense. They felt that they were operating rationally, not carried away by blind extremes of emotion, as had so often been the case in the past. Further, they all felt a sense of purpose which had previously been only dimly perceived, or had been completely lacking.

FAMILY ROLE

Before therapy, Peter, Gloria, and Sally were married, all unhappily. After therapy, Peter gave up his old marriage, entering upon a new one which was much more gratifying. Gloria and Sally diminished considerably the conflicts which had been disturbing their marriages. Alice, Holly, Jim, and Harvey all married either during or shortly after analysis was finished. All made very happy marriages.

Frank terminated his analysis to enter upon an unhappy marriage. After years of suffering, in the course of a second analysis he was able to give up his masochistic attachment and make a much better relationship.

Beverly never related to another man. But she did get back to her children, later her grandchildren. Thus she too returned to a family role which provided much gratification.

Sheldon's problem in the family was to adjust himself to being one of two children. The therapy was quite successful in this respect.

SOCIAL ROLE

In this area the results were quite divergent.

Some of the patients were content to live quiet lives, uninvolved with people other than close friends or family. Beverly, Peter, Gloria, and Frank fall into this category.

Alice had always been too active socially. Part of her change was to give up the social front, and achieve more happiness in her intimate relationships.

Holly, Peter, Jim, and Harvey all moved out into the wider world as a result of their therapy. Freed to a considerable extent from their personal problems, they now had the energy to devote to others. Interestingly, most of them became involved with activities relating to mental health.

Sally for a number of years devoted herself to her husband and two children. Then she went into a business where there were numerous social contacts, which she enjoyed very much.

Sheldon got away from his life as a loner and developed a set of friends, some of whom remained important to him. Since he came from a family of social revolutionaries, it was to be expected that he would also move along these lines. However, his own ideas seemed to be more down to earth than his parents'.

SENSE OF IDENTITY

The sense of alienation which had been so strong in all these patients at the beginning of therapy was virtually gone at the end. Some had blamed it on the confused, turbulent social scene, but once they found more personal happiness they came to see the social problems in a different way. By the end of therapy all knew with considerable clarity what they wanted and where they were going in life.

COMMUNICATION

By teaching the patient how to understand his unconscious,

analysis leads to an enormous increase in the capacity to communicate. Some people react to this by confining themselves to other analyzed people, claiming that these are the only ones with whom they can communicate. Some theoreticians have even made self-analysis and the capacity to communicate with others a desideratum for termination.

None of this occurred with any of the patients in this sample. Although all were "good" patients, in that they produced a lot of the kind of material that is helpful in analysis, once the analysis was over they paid scant attention to it. This shows that the capacity to communicate depends to a considerable extent on the existence of a person to whom these communications can be made. When no such person is present, the communication tends to recede into the background or disappear entirely.

What did become apparent in all the patients, however, was a vastly increased capacity to understand the communications of other people. An incident which occurred after the end of Holly's analysis can illuminate this point most clearly. Shortly after moving to another city, she found some diary notes of her husband in which he wrote about his attraction to other women. At first she was horrified and wanted to call me long distance to discuss it. Then she reflected on her own life, especially the sexual aspects, realizing that she had been attracted to a number of men and still was. When the question came up with her husband she asked him whether there was any specific woman (she knew quite well that there was not). When he assured her that there was not, she was able to forget the whole matter, resuming her warm, loving attitude to him. This is the kind of episode that in unanalyzed people frequently becomes the opening wedge in years of conflict and quarrel.

CREATIVITY

The need for some kind of creative outlet, and the consequent turning to some kind of creative activity, was noted in six of the ten patients. Beverly returned to her writing. Sheldon became editor of his school newspaper. Frank turned to writing and acting. In writing he was quite successful. At first he wrote letters to the editors of local newspapers; to his surprise some were published. Then he went on to do free-lance stories; these too sold. Eventually he became a writer for the company which employed him, as well as a free lance. He also had some success in acting school, but did not pursue that.

Holly and Harvey turned to art, in which they had had some previous experience. Gloria also got back to her music, making considerable strides beyond where she had previously been.

The creativity could be tied up with the need to communicate. Analysis releases so much inner life that some longing to communicate what is going on remains with many people. If it cannot be done directly to an analyst, it can be done indirectly via some acceptable art form. Few people have sufficient interest or ego strength to maintain a self-analysis after the professional contacts have been finished.

In the case of Sally a negative effect on her creativity was noted. Before analysis, in addition to being an artist, she had had a hobby of buying up old tables, renovating them, and then selling them. In the analysis what came out was that the table was herself. As a result she gave up the restoration of antiques, and the painting as well. In her case the art represented an aspect of her narcissism which had to be given up if she was to relate to her family.

WORK

In this area the analysis was signally effective. Even though a number of the patients had had rather severe work problems before analysis, particularly Jim, Harvey, Frank, and Gloria, all these problems cleared up entirely in the course of treatment. At the end all the patients were quite satisfied with their vocational choices, except Frank. As mentioned, he later became a writer.

On the other hand, as with creativity, no extraordinary new talents were uncovered in the course of the analysis. It was rather a matter of developing the talents that had been there before but had been blocked by a variety of neurotic conflicts.

PSYCHIATRIC SYMPTOMATOLOGY

Here, too, success was outstanding. Most of these patients

had been suffering from fairly severe psychiatric disturbances at the time treatment began. Beverly was openly schizophrenic. Jim seemed to be on the verge of another breakdown, as did Frank. Peter was a drug addict. Sally was suicidal. Harvey was about to run away to nowhere. Sheldon was threatened with expulsion from school.

It is striking that in this area considerable improvement was found in all patients, without exception. Nor have there been any serious relapses after termination, as continued follow-up has shown.

Six of the patients described had had nonanalytic treatment before coming to see me, or superficial analytic treatment. One (Beverly) had been immensely helped, but the psychiatrist, for personal reasons unknown to Beverly, had had to flee on three days' notice; she relapsed.

In no case could the previous treatment be said to have had any lasting effect on the patient. The success achieved in the present analytic treatment is therefore all the more noteworthy.

SUMMARY

In sum, when the present sample of patients is evaluated along the lines of the analytic ideal, it is found that their love lives improved (though in varying degrees); they had much less pain, though not many more peak pleasure experiences; sexual adjustment improved; they experienced more feeling; life made more sense; they acquired a family role, or strengthened one that they had had; some but not all moved out into the wider social world; all had a vastly improved sense of identity; they could understand the communications of other people better, but did not feel the need to communicate their own inner world; more than half turned to creative outlets, which had generally been present to some degree before analysis; all made dramatic changes in their work lives; and all were dramatically freed from psychiatric symptomatology, including a number who had tried nonanalytic approaches before.

THE MOTIVES FOR TREATMENT

What brings people to treatment? One sociologist, rather

baffled, has suggested that there is a circle of Friends of Psychotherapy, which gathers ever more people into its clutches, but he could not explain why new people would join the circle. Certainly, it is true that most patients come to therapy through the urging of friends who have been through the process and benefited from it. But the urging must touch off some deep inner need within themselves, otherwise they would not respond.

Turning to the ten cases described here, the reasons for coming to treatment were highly varied. Many of the patients had had the name of the analyst for a long time, some for years, before they made the first call. In fact, on looking over these cases, such a delay is more the rule than the exception. In the general atmosphere in which psychotherapy is available, everyone sooner or later hears about it. They make casual inquiries or are merely told by a friend or acquaintance of the names of analysts. Some had heard about therapy from college instructors.

In this climate, in which it is known that psychotherapy is possible, they generally wait until some crisis erupts: abandonment by a boy friend (Holly), or the break-up of a marriage (Alice), or rivalry with the husband (Gloria). Almost always there is the loss of some important person, or the threat of a loss. The analyst in the beginning then serves the function of buffering the person against the loss.

More generally, these cases seem typical of those that I have seen. Freud's remark that the two most common ways of handling a neurosis are to make an unhappy marriage or to focus on some somatic illness seems to hold for most of our patients today as well. Since medicine has advanced mightily, perhaps the somatic illness is less frequent than before. But the dependent, unhappy relationship as an escape from neurotic suffering is seen everywhere. It is primarily when the suffering in these relationships becomes too intense or when the relationship breaks up that the person seeks out an analyst. This process, observed in the present patients, would appear to hold generally.

It is noteworthy that medical referrals are rare from the present cases. All of the patients had their own personal physicians and attended to their somatic needs, but in no case did a treating physician refer them for psychotherapy. Even the physician/addict resorted to all kinds of medical manipulations before seeking out a psychiatrist. Jim, who had had some brief therapy while he was in the service (where he had been hospitalized for a while), was not urged by his physicians there to follow up with more intensive therapy on the outside.

Thus, it would seem from this sample that psychotherapy has grown up and flourished outside the area of general medical practice. It is of course true that a large number of therapists are physicians. But once they become analysts they necessarily lose contact with general medicine and move on to the problems of the soul. There is much talk in the air of psychosomatic unity, and in theory this is certainly correct. But in practice persons who treat the body are in one category, persons who treat the mind in an entirely different one.

It is also clear how psychotherapy has continued to grow and develop. Once patients start coming to a psychotherapist, sooner or later they recognize that their problems are not particularly different from those around them, either in their immediate family or in their social life. As a result of the positive transference and the therapeutic benefit derived, they then begin to urge others to seek out therapy. The others are often impressed with the changes they have observed. Thus they too start. Then the same process repeats itself; therapeutic benefit and positive transference impress other people as well.

The problems that bring people to treatment are universal: fears, work blocks, unhappy marriages, poor relationships, addictions, and so on. It looks as though it is only necessary for competent therapists to be available to call forth a stream of patients who clamor for help. What happened to these people before therapy, or what happens to them if they do not go to therapy? The answer has already been suggested: compromises of one kind or another, unhappy relationships, somatic illnesses.

Thus, the therapeutic population grows by the spread of knowledge of the analytic ideal and the availability of therapists. This last is particularly important, since it is known that therapists tend to congregate in large cities; therapists are also not available in totalitarian countries. The whole process is a gradually growing awareness of the realities of the world, outgrowing the fourth of July clichés that have kept individuals confused and miserable.

RESISTANCE AND REALITY

While resistance to therapy can take many different forms, and does vary widely, through it all there is one consistent thread: the patient blames reality rather than his inner psyche. Every one of the patients in this book hesitated a long time before going to therapy because of their image of reality.

Therapists have often been faulted for the length of time that therapy takes. Unfortunately, whatever they do, the patient takes his own time. And over and over a great deal of the time required for therapy is taken up with the patient's image of reality.

Sometimes the fight with reality takes almost ludicrous forms. Take, for example, the incident of Jim with the bank. He went there every day, even two or three times a day, to deposit or withdraw small sums ($5-10, sometimes less), until the bank, in disgust, asked him to switch his account to another bank. *Per se* this whole incident seems to be of no consequence. Yet it took up several months of therapy time before he realized that he was trying to make the bank the ever-giving mother, and the bank wasn't having any of that.

At other times, the fight is seemingly irrelevant. Frank insisted that the analyst looked like his brother, which does in fact seem to have been the case. Yet common sense would tell you that this accidental similarity had nothing to do with the therapy as such. Still Frank went on, hour after hour, month after month, berating the analyst because he looked like his brother.

It is the accumulation of these seemingly senseless and irrelevant incidents that makes it so difficult to convey the flavor and reality of the therapeutic situation. In another case, not discussed in this book, a woman, being seen once a week, suddenly got up in the middle of the session and walked out. Nothing could hold her back; nor would she return that session. The next week she did come back. Then she explained that suddenly the analyst's face had taken on the contours of her first lover, whom she still hated because he had rejected her in favor of another woman. Rather than verbalize these feelings she fled.

The reality resistance must be broken through to some

extent for the patient to come to analysis at all. Then the initial battle, and in part the battle all the way through, revolves around convincing the patient that his problems are essentially intra-psychic, not the result of reality. Until the patient really acquires this conviction, interpretations are of no value; if anything they may boomerang.

THE NEUROTIC COMPROMISE

Every patient comes to treatment with some compromise worked out in his mind. On the one hand he is obsessed with how realistic his fears are; on the other he has managed to find some *modus vivendi* either to rationalize them or to handle them. Usually it is only when this compromise is threatened that he comes to therapy at all, but even so the compromise maintains itself for a long time.

A typical compromise, although at a pretty infantile level, is Frank's pact with God. Frightened of sex and too timid to leave his home, he remained with his stepmother, whom he referred to as "mother." This was rationalized by the pact with God, as a result of which he did not have to face his feelings about girls. In his case the compromise was threatened by the increase in anxiety which raised the possibility that he might lose his job, and thus remain completely dependent on mother. There was further the example of his brother, who had been hospitalized twice for schizophrenia, and who also lived at home, isolated from other people, which made him feel that the compromise infantilization was of dubious value. At the same time he vigorously resisted any encroachment on this compromise solution, such as a suggestion that he might move out and try to be on his own.

THE PREOCCUPATIONS

The compromises are maintained by preoccupation with certain types of material, different for each patient, yet at the same time characteristic for him. These preoccupations wield tremendous power over the individual, and he can no sooner get rid of them by an act of will than he can get rid of his dreams.

It is here that the inner world makes itself felt. To the outsider these preoccupations seem harmless or banal; he is apt to say, "Forget it," or "Get over it, it's nothing." But the insider is stuck in this way of looking at the world. A patient, symbolizing this experience, once dreamt that he was frozen into a glass spoon; his whole body could be seen inside the glass, yet he could not move either inside or outside; he was totally immobilized. It is this frozen posture which is incorporated in the preoccupations, and which has to be freed and worked out in the course of the analysis.

The preoccupations may range from the mild to the delusional. Usually it is only when they approach delusional proportions that they become noticeable to the outsider, but they are always there. In this sense there is also a continuum from the healthy to the sick, in that everybody has some kind of preoccupation which takes up much of his thinking effort.

In the cases discussed here, Beverly and Peter both had delusional preoccupations. One was clinically a psychotic, the other a severely disturbed drug addict. Beverly was convinced that police were "clinking" her, that children were "riffling" her, that people in restaurants turned their noses away from her, that her name was being broadcast on the radio as a "public woman," and the like. To her these were all part of reality; in order to work them out it was necessary to show her that they were not.

The direct attack on a delusional preoccupation is, of course, useless; this is what turns people away from psychotics in the ordinary social situation. Therapy instead works on the transference preoccupation(s). Here the most significant for Beverly was the feeling that somehow she was going to destroy my practice; here too she was "evil incarnate." As this was talked out and worked out, the other preoccupations fell by the wayside, or eventually responded to rational elucidation. Even then, however, she argued that things had simply stopped happening to her; she still could not see that there had been an internal change.

With Peter there were several deep-going preoccupations. One was the conviction that he had several serious concealed illnesses, particularly colitis and pneumonia. Many people have such fears; most often they relate to cancer. Peter suppressed his medical knowledge in such a way that rational discussion, or reassurance from some other physician, could not break through his conviction. The second significant preoccupation was the "third-night anxiety," the fear that something awful would happen to him on the third night after drug withdrawal. It was the working out of this preoccupation, really a delusion, that took up most of the analytic time in the second year.

In this case the transference reaction was one of deep dependency mingled with deep distrust. This combination could eventually be traced back to his earliest relationships, especially with his next older brother. The dependency remained as long as he was taking the drug, but once he had given that up, the distrust took over and he left treatment prematurely. His social adjustment was good, but many of his inner conflicts remained.

With Frank, the man who had made the pact with God, there were many preoccupations. The most prominent, of course, was this religious agreement with the Deity, which seemed to have come up out of the blue, since his religious background was minimal. It served to keep him a good little boy clinging fearfully to the mother from whom he could not separate.

In the transference, however, an entirely different preoccupation came to the fore: the physical resemblance between the analyst and his brother. Not that he hated his brother that much; they were just miles apart emotionally. But why did the analyst have to look like his brother, why did he have to be approximately the same age, with similar intellectual backgrounds, and so on? Frank went on and on in this vein seemingly interminably.

The average person, when told about this situation, is apt to laugh at its incongruity. But it is essential to take it in deadly earnest. It is precisely this kind of incongruity, different in each case, which makes therapy so enormously difficult and complicated. One could easily say, granted it is true that the analyst looked like his brother, was of roughly the same age, and had a similar intellectual background, of what relevance was all that? Frank was there to get over his fears, not to change the analyst's appearance or background. Yet it was only the patient application of the transference principle, extended over several years, that eventually shed light on this situation for him.

With Sheldon, the frightened genius boy, the preoccupation was to get rid of his father. In his play this was what he did, discarding the old man and becoming the ruler of the universe, if necessary a new world where he could reign undisturbed. Hour after hour his play went on with these fantasies. Mostly they were disguised, and he did not realize that anybody could see what he was trying to say.

In the transference a gradual attempt at communication took place. It slowly dawned on him that here, unlike at home, was someone who knew what he was talking about, reacted sympathetically yet did not go along simply with his destructive wishes. Then came the period of bridges and tunnels, when he was trying to open up an avenue of communication. Eventually this succeeded. Here too, however, the noteworthy fact is that even with a child it took years of patient exploration to break through the barriers.

Holly and Gloria both had milder preoccupations, both sexual in nature. With Holly, who came because of a rejection by her boy friend, it took the form of picking men up. In one fantasy she would seduce the man next to her in the theater, in another the man next to her in the subway. Brought up as a good girl, these sexual wishes terrified her. Even though on the surface she was fairly solidified, she could allow herself to reveal the fantasies, whereupon they lost their force and eventually disappeared. They were, as she came to see, primarily signs of her low self-esteem, in that she did not have the feeling that she could attract a man in a normal way; the initial rejection meant rejection by all men. In a sense the analysis hinged on making this one point clear to her: she was rejected by one man, but accepted by many others.

With Gloria there were two main sexual preoccupations. One was that when she was on the podium the students could look up her skirts, the other was that someone would discover the "bumps" on her behind which were the residue of the treatment for syphilis (which she had surprisingly contracted from her husband). Throughout her life manipulation of feared situations was her favorite weapon, and at the start of the analysis the same kind of manipulation prevailed. In the transference she

was able to fall in love, for the first time in her life since adolescence. It was this love that carried her through and eventually
led to enough self-love to avoid her old manipulations, though
these naturally persisted for a long time.

TRANSFERENCE AND INTIMACY

It has already been stressed in the introduction that in the
treatment process a transference is formed which is essential to
success. Yet what is this transference in more ordinary terms?

To begin with, it is an attachment to another human being.
The analyst becomes the all-important figure, the center of the
patient's life. There may be a strong love feeling, or at times a
strong hate feeling; what counts is the intensity of the feeling
more than anything else. When there is no response, either positive or negative, the analysis tends to grind to a halt because the
patient lacks the drive to seek out the analyst. Sooner or later
the patient drifts away, as in any indifferent relationship.

How is the transference similar to and how is it different
from other life situations? Dependency or attachment is true of
the great majority of human relationships. Children attach
themselves to parents, parents to children; followers to leaders,
leaders to followers. The matching of love pairs is often a mystery to outsiders, yet the two partners cling to one another with
extraordinary tenacity.

Thus, as an attachment, transference does not differ from
what happens elsewhere. The difference lies only in what the
analyst does with it. For usually if somebody becomes very
dependent, the other person will sense the hold he has, and
exploit it accordingly.

Exploitation of the dependent individual has been elo-
quently described by many writers. Somerset Maugham's book
Of Human Bondage is one of many classics that come to mind.
Regardless of what the exploiter does to his victim, no rebellion
takes place. A common instance is that of the pimp with his
prostitute; he beats her, takes her money, scorns her, abandons
her for other women, and through it all she loves the terrible
mistreatment to which she is exposed.

Every analyst in fact knows how difficult it is to separate

a suffering dependent individual from his or her idol. As a rule of thumb, it is wise not to attempt any such separation in the beginning; it is only after a relationship with the analyst has been securely established that the attempt can be made. The transference in other words serves as a way out of a slavelike subservience.

This highlights one of the major differences between the transference attachment and the real-life attachment. The attachment is of the same kind, but the analyst behaves differently. He does not exploit, he does not beat, he does not reject; he merely tries to help the patient understand his or her extraordinary dependency needs.

Freud once remarked that no matter what the analyst does, the patient will respond with transferences. If the patient has strong dependency needs, they will be brought into the analysis, regardless of how the analyst behaves. And once brought in, they may last for a long time. The problem of the excessively dependent patient has been one of the central problems of analytic technique from the very beginning.

Yet the attachment and fear of separation demonstrated in the analytic situation, are easy enough to understand, since they do not differ so much from what happens in everyday life. Much harder to grasp, and yet in a certain sense even more important, is the kind of intimacy that develops between analyst and patient. This experience of intimacy, which has no exact parallel in ordinary living, is a large part of what makes the analytic process such a complex problem.

There are many paradoxes attached to this analytic intimacy. There is no physical contact, even though the word "intimacy" in the average situation carries the connotation of either sexual intercourse or other physical closeness. The patient only sees the analyst at most for a few hours each week, in the most intensive kind of analysis five or six hours a week, in less intensive therapy sometimes only once a week. Also, intimacy in the ordinary situation suggests time, large amounts of time, endless time, for many. As a rule the patient knows very little about the analyst. Even those analysts who believe in sharing more of themselves with their patients in the nature of the case still hold back most of what is going on in their lives.

In addition, the patient knows that the analyst has other patients, like him or her, again a radical difference from ordinary intimacy where there is an agreement or pledge of exclusiveness which ties up with fierce jealousies if thwarted. And, finally, the patient has to pay the analyst a fixed amount of money, the kind of transaction which ordinarily makes people extremely jealous and as distant as possible. Yet with all these paradoxes and obstacles the analytic intimacy is like nothing else encountered in life. This is really the greatest psychological puzzle of all. How is it possible?

To see how it is possible it is necessary to examine each of the paradoxes mentioned. First of all, physical contact. While sex, properly pursued, is one of the greatest of all pleasures in life, the trouble is that it is not as a rule properly pursued. Consider, for example, the patients in this book. They divide broadly into two classes: those who have a great deal of sex and those who have very little. Sally had had literally hundreds, perhaps thousands of sexual encounters, yet none had had any meaning for her until love entered the picture. It had been an exercise in showing how desirable she could be to men — a conquest, seduce, and reject, and the more she could seduce the more she could reject.

Sally's marriage was a matter of convenience. She traveled from New York to Florida, mainly having quick sexual encounters, while her husband, who stayed in New York, did the same thing at home. They were like two planes in the night, moving in opposite directions, hurtling along through space at tremendous speeds, occasionally stopping to throw one another a nod.

These two people were highly destructive of one another, yet, and here is another peculiar surprise, they were also protective of one another. Separated, each would have deteriorated much further, perhaps ending up in mental hospitals, or addicted to drugs or drink. As long as they knew that the other was around some place they could keep going.

What upset Sally and brought her to treatment was that she fell in love. For the first time she had to admit that she needed more than a zipless fuck, that life really had to have more substance for her than one unidentified penis after another.

There had to be some feeling for another human being, so that she could finally get off the ever-moving elevator (in her symbolism).

In the transference Sally of course tried to seduce the analyst; what else was there to do in life? Outwardly distant, she secretly concocted one scheme after another to break through the analyst's reserve. None of this worked. Finally her dream brought out the meaning of her actions: she dreamt that the analyst approached her, put his arms around her, and kissed her, whereupon she turned around, said the analysis is over, and left. Seduce and reject was the leading theme of her life. This had to be given up, as the analysis helped her to do, before she could make further progress in her growth.

A contrary pattern was displayed by Beverly. To her, human contacts were terrifying, and especially terrifying was any degree of physical intimacy. An ironic situation arose at one point when, in the midst of a severe delusional and hallucinatory state, she came in to relate that she was having some sensations in her nipples. When I responded that perhaps she was beginning to have some sexual feelings again, she indignantly cried, "What are you trying to do, drive me completely crazy?" Like the witches of yore, to be sexual was tantamount to being condemned as evil incarnate.

Sartre in his play *No Exit* has portrayed these two opposite kinds of women beautifully: the nymphomaniac and the Lesbian. The man is caught between the two: the woman who wants him only as a conquest and the woman who doesn't want him at all. What Sartre does not describe is the deep despair that underlies the behavior of both of these women.

In the transference an opposing set of patterns emerges, if Sally and Beverly are compared. One tries to be sexual to cover up her destructiveness, the other is overtly destructive in order to cover up her sexuality. The analysis brings out the hidden feelings, and restores a sense of balance.

Nothing has ever been discussed more vigorously throughout the history of psychoanalysis than why the analyst cannot permit himself to have sex with his patient. It is well known that a surprisingly high percentage of therapists (not analysts) do allow themselves some physical intimacy, although not necessarily sexual intercourse, with their analysands (on rare occasions even homosexual intercourse between therapist and patient has been described).

By engaging in sex, or some physical contact, the analyst shifts from the analytic intimacy to the more ordinary kind. Thereby he moves into a new conflict area, the same as that seen in the ordinary love affair. If (assuming the most common case, of a male analyst with a female patient) he continues, sooner or later the question of marriage will come up. If he does not continue, she will feel rejected. In either case, the real analytic work, pursuing a different kind of intimacy, will collapse.

Physical contact may take forms other than sexual intercourse as well. Janet and Jim, a couple in their early twenties, prided themselves on being free of conventional bodily taboos. She sucked his penis, and swallowed his semen without compunction. Both would take pleasure in looking at the bowel movements of the other before they were flushed down the toilet. With all this she was extremely depressed, and had attempted suicide a number of times, while he was unable to work, and spent much of his time masturbating and fantasizing about other women.

In another case a girl went to a Reichian analyst, who instructed her to sit on a table and kick her legs, so that she could generate some sensations in her vagina and genital area. She followed his instructions dutifully, and sure enough began to acquire more and more genital sensations. At the same time she was crying throughout, miserably unhappy. Pleasure *per se* and orgasm cannot be equated with intimacy.

A second aspect of intimacy for the average person is time; to be intimate with someone means to spend time together. Usually, the more time two people spend together, the more they are considered to be intimate. Compared with the amount of time that lovers or friends spend in one another's company, the total number of hours involved in an analysis is minuscule indeed.

The problem with time as a measure of intimacy is that it fails to consider the quality of the interaction. Gloria and her husband spent an enormous amount of time together. Prior to the analysis in fact he had not gone out alone for *seventeen years*, in deference to her fear of being in the house alone. Yet their relationship was horrible.

A comparison of the various patients in this book shows that intimacy cannot be measured in quantitative terms. Gloria did not part from her husband for seventeen years, while Sally spent almost as many years flitting from one man to another, yet both were equally distant from their husbands. Frank spent every night with his mother and brother, while Beverly spent almost all her time alone, and again both were isolated emotionally from human contact.

It is always the quality of the intimacy that has to be evaluated. When Sally got close to someone she would fly into terrible temper tantrums, storm, yell, and eventually break up the relationship. Many people in fact become so terrified of closeness that they flee from it in one way or another, either physically by spending a lot of time alone, or psychologically by retreating into themselves. Thus, what passes for intimacy in many everyday situations is really a defense against being alone or a way of concealing one's innermost thoughts.

The concealment of thoughts brings up another aspect of psychoanalysis: making the unconscious conscious. Most people live unaware of their unconscious motives. When they enter analysis, these motives begin to come to the fore, under the guidance and expert interpretive skill of the analyst. As the unconscious motives are brought out into the open, the gratifications derived from an infantile kind of intimacy, such as that with Gloria and Frank, become less tempting. Hence the relationships change.

Analysis is a penetrating procedure. It is safe to say that in every case that goes beyond the superficial, the quality of the close relationships will undergo a marked change. Since so many relationships in our culture are based on infantile needs, most often the close relationships are strongly endangered; many times they break up. This is frequently brought up as a weakness of the therapeutic process, since it does not attempt to maintain a relationship at all costs. It should rather be seen as a strength.

An analogous situation occurs in marriage and divorce. When there is no practice of divorce, marriages often tend to deteriorate into arrangements of convenience because the only way out is "divorce Italian style" (murder or death). When divorce is possible, people make a much greater effort to derive happiness from the marriage, since if they do not the spouse will simply walk out. One common instance of that on the current scene is the great frequency with which women abandon husbands who are sexually inadequate, something that even a generation ago almost never happened. Thus, paradoxically the possibility of divorce makes marriages a much more viable institution. It derives from the shift from "glue" intimacy of the old style to emotional intimacy as urged by psychoanalysis.

A third paradox of the analytic intimacy is that the patient knows so little about the analyst, in contrast to the usual life situation where each party knows a great deal about the other. Further, the patient is usually extremely curious about the analyst; the slightest tidbit of information may come to have extraordinary meaning.

Many attempts have been made to break through this kind of ignorance, felt by many patients as extreme coldness and distance. Yet these attempts fail more often than they succeed. For instance, a patient in great distress made an initial appointment with an analyst, who said over the phone that he was setting aside a full hour for the initial interview, as was his custom. The patient arrived on time, the analyst was late. The analyst came after five minutes, and announced that he had to go to the bathroom. When he came out, he proceeded to tell the patient why he had been delayed, because of the heavy traffic (at this point the patient could not have cared less). The patient was so indignant at this inability to listen to him that he left early, and refused to pay the fee.

This example highlights what the patient is looking for and why knowledge about the analyst is superfluous. He wants someone to listen to him and help him sort out his troubles. What the analyst reveals about his own life is completely secondary to this main purpose.

An exception comes about with analysts who stick too ridgidly to this rule of nonparticipation. This is so often experienced as a rejection that a certain amount of flexibility is in order. But even under the best of circumstances, the analyst is after all a paid expert who is there to help the patient, not a buddy in a ball game.

A fourth difference from ordinary intimacy lies in the fact that there are other patients who share the analyst's time, attention, and affection. In this respect the situation becomes more similar to children with parents, which in fact it does resemble very much. The conflicts that occur are quite similar to jealousies among siblings. Should the analyst actually show any partiality toward one patient over another, the results may be devastating.

In one case an analyst raised his fees from $15 to $20 per session, to cover the increase in the cost of living. This is customary in long-term analysis. It arouses some resentment, understandably, but that can almost always be worked out. One patient, however, demurred against the raise, requesting that it be deferred because of heavy expenses that he was carrying; a compromise was reached at $17.50 per session. Several months later another patient accidentally discovered this compromise. Feeling that he had been slighted by the analyst, who he was certain preferred the other patient, he abruptly discontinued treatment.

There is hardly ever an analysis where the patient does not fantasize or dream of being the only patient. Yet when this happens in everyday living, the person is often dissatisfied as well. It is similar to a tired intimacy, where there is exclusiveness but qualities of freshness and excitement are lacking. Eventually it may reach a stage such as that in Eugune O'Neill's play *The Iceman Cometh*, where one character, tired of his wife's extreme submissiveness, finally shoots her.

Finally, the element of money would ordinarily spoil any intimate realtionship, yet the exact reverse is true in analysis. The money creates the necessary barrier so that the analyst and patient can see how the patient handles realistic demands in life.

Actually, if the fee is omitted, as happens from time to time, a new question crops up: why is the analyst devoting so much time to this patient without any ostensible reward. Fantasies may then arise about love feelings on the part of the analyst, or unreal expectations, such as demands set up by parents on their children, which create entirely new conflicts.

Besides in actuality the analyst is not as a rule in a position to dispense free or very low-cost treatment, so that his own handling of the situation becomes utterly unrealistic.

Inasmuch as the analyst is generally in a high-income bracket, a certain amount of resentment toward him is inevitable. Nevertheless, this resentment should not be allowed to obscure the psychological meaning of money to many people. For example, Beverly in the present series of cases could not afford to pay the full fee. I allowed her to pay part of it and gave her credit for the remainder. However, I did insist that she should pay the part agreed upon. This payment served to bolster her self-esteem considerably, since it showed her that she was not a weak, helpless creature who had to be supported entirely by others.

In our culture people often use soothing phrases and flattering words to cajole others into giving away their money. Hence, a certain amount of distrust of the analyst exists, as in all situations where money is demanded. Frequently it takes a considerable amount of time to overcome this distrust. The analyst should make it clear that the fee is necessary for his or her own economic well-being and not to punish the patient.

This comparison of analytic intimacy with ordinary intimacy can help to make clear where the problems lie. Ordinary intimacy is interfered with by unrealistic expectations, repressed hatreds, unsatisfied (and often unsatisfiable) sexual fantasies, stubborn idiosyncrasies, and many other psychological factors. Because of the strength of the unconscious, attempts to alter these conflicts or to straighten them out by rational means usually fail. Monologue replaces dialogue. In this sense, one of the major goals of analysis is to restore rational dialogue and do away with irrational monologue.

COUNTERTRANSFERENCE

"Countertransference" refers to the transference of the analyst to his patient. Every patient necessarily reminds the analyst in greater or lesser degree of some person from his past. It is in the nature of human affairs that conflicts are diminished but not fully resolved. So these figures from the analyst's past still serve to arouse or rearouse in him the conflicts once experienced. No matter how thorough the personal analysis, some of this is bound to remain.

Countertransference can interfere in several ways. First of all it can blind the analyst to the patient's real problems, instead leading him to focus on what was true of the transference figure years back. Thus a woman like Sally might be seen as a bad mother (and one consultant did actually characterize her that way) rather than a severely depressed little girl looking for the father she never had. And second it can bring back the conflicts that existed in the past, thereby upsetting the analyst and preventing him from functioning effectively.

A third, more general, aspect of countertransference is that the analyst fails to perceive the analytic situation as a dialogue between two human beings. Trained in one of the mental health professions, he tends to fall back on some standard diagnosis because it is too threatening to experience the give-and-take of the analysis. Basically, after all, the analyst has or has had problems similar to those of his patients; he is merely (or at least should be) further along with them. By attaching labels to his patients he creates an artificial distance between them which is death to the free flow and spontaneity of the analytic dialogue.

In my experience the last is the most pernicious form of countertransference of all. Because of the way in which training has developed, it is also the hardest to eradicate.

There are two aspects to this distance which are especially damaging. One is to exaggerate the meaning of any symptom and immediately dub the patient "schizophrenic" or "borderline." For many analysts this comes to serve as a convenient alibi: if the patient gets better, the therapist has quite an achievement to his credit; if the patient does not get better, well, after all, nobody can do much with these "very sick" people.

In the present series Beverly is perhaps the best example. Her symptoms were indeed severe, yet they were manageable. Even the hallucinations, when they existed, did not occupy her mind all the time, and within certain limits she was still able to function as an isolated individual. Previous therapists had generally dismissed her with a curt diagnosis, or some harmful form of physical treatment.

There is still another aspect of countertransference worth discussing. From Freud on, analysts have been hard workers — fifty, sixty, even seventy hours a week is not uncommon. One reason for this is the enormous gratification derived from the work. The analyst not only sees another human being grow, mature, and become a person, he has a chance to deal with many of his own conflicts. Many times, for example, patients are superior in certain areas to the analyst, who can learn from them. Or again the analyst is forced by the circumstances to abandon the conventional reaction of anger to an insult. By thus giving up his anger he has a chance to come to grips with deeper reaches of the personality, as well as to achieve a greater degree of maturity.

"WORKING THROUGH" and the THERAPEUTIC PROCESS

The notion that psychotherapy can be finished in a few sessions is another of those easy myths that people have to give up as they mature. Neurotic problems go back a long way; they persist and they resist change.

To explain how the change can take place, the term "working through" is used. It refers to the fact that one interpretation as such will have little or no effect on the patient. It is only the cumulative effect of a number of interpretations over a period of time that leads to permanent change. It is this need for a cumulative effect that accounts for the length of analysis.

PSYCHOTHERAPY AND LOVE

Every case is so different, the circumstances of each individual's life vary so much, the material discussed in each patient's case so divergent, that there seems to be little consistent thread to the process of psychotherapy. Yet the thread is there, if the surface appearances are penetrated. Love is always the *goal* of therapy, while making the unconscious conscious is always the heart of the *technique*. It is the confusion of goal and technique which bewilders the individual trying to comprehend the course of a case history.

It is at this point as well that theory and technique converge.

For theory has reached the conclusion that the heart of neurosis is excessive hatred, while technique has devised a variety of ways to help the person overcome this hatred.

The excessive hatred may turn outwards, where it will appear as sadism or cruelty, or it may turn inwards, where it will come out as masochism or excessive suffering. In our culture, for the most part, those who come to therapy have a stronger masochistic component, so that the accent of both theory and technique has been much more strongly on masochism than on sadism. The sadist unfortunately often finds a victim on whom to let out his rage rather than coming to a therapist. Underneath, however, he is just as sick and disturbed as the masochist.

Analytically, working out the hatred involves a number of different steps. First and foremost the patient has to become aware that this is a problem. Here already a strong resistance makes itself felt. For nobody likes to admit that he carries around any hostile feelings: they are always denied and rationalized or both. Here another error has supposedly become "common knowledge." It is supposed to be bad to hold back one's anger. Therefore the function of the analysis is to let the patient release his rage and not be afraid of the consequences.

In some cases this release of rage may provide temporary relief. It also often shows timid persons that they need not really be so afraid of the anger of others. But apart from temporary relief, the release of anger serves no constructive purpose. Ultimately, the roots of the anger have to be overcome so that the individual is really less angry inside.

Since the anger is so often transformed beyond recognition, it is the analyst's job to unravel this transformation and help the patient confront his angry impulses directly. But this, as can be seen from the case histories, is a long, tortuous, and difficult process, which many times succeeds only partially.

Among the cases in this book consider, for example, Frank's pact with God. On the surface this indicates an intense fear of women, rather than anger at them. Yet when this was gone into more deeply, what he brought out was his feeling that if he had sexual intercourse with a girl before marriage and then dropped her, which was what he wanted to do, the resultant rebuff would shatter the girl. This image of the shattered girl he held on to tenaciously, unable to see that it was here that his hostility was incorporated: it was not that the girl would be shattered but that he wanted to destroy her.

Likewise, in the transference for years, as we have noted, Frank was angry at his analyst because of his resemblance to Frank's brother. This transparent rationalization covered up his deep-seated fear of intimacy with the analyst, a fear which could be traced back to the unhappy experiences of childhood, especially the mother who was always complaining of being on the verge of death. Yet to Frank the anger was very real and very justified. Hence it took a long time to overcome.

The intensity of the hatred explains why some people are more easily treated than others. When the patient is very disturbed, he is more apt to make a negative transference, in which feelings of rage and hatred toward the analyst will be paramount. Since these feelings are very real to him, and not readily explainable at least in the beginning, such patients are much more apt to stop treatment prematurely, with little or no therapeutic benefit. Furthermore, when these hateful feelings arise, there is no alternative to bringing them out in the analytic situation, and working them out, which is both a long and a difficult process. Since it is so uncomfortable subjectively, many patients get to feel discouraged and drop out.

In extreme cases the hostility acquires a delusional form, making it completely unamenable to rational discussion. That was the case with Beverly. Since rational discussion cannot possibly succeed in such a case, the rage has to be avoided until the patient is ready to handle the necessary interpretations.

That mature love is the goal of analytic therapy creates a peculiar paradox. Those patients do best who before analysis have had some kind of gratifying love experience; Holly and Alice are good examples. But they must first learn that what they felt as love was really some kind of neurotic compromise, a step in the right direction, but not the full solution. This is difficult to see and even more difficult to handle once it is seen. Yet it becomes an unavoidable part of every analysis.

Peter, for instance, was in love with his wife when they were married. She was psychologically a real mother figure, more of a mother than he had ever had. Like a mother, she took care of him, tended to his needs, encouraged him in his ventures, consoled him in his failures. Then, like many mothers, she became overly demanding and clutchy, out of touch with his more mature needs. Love flew out of the window. Yet the fact that he had once been able to love a woman sustained him throughout his darkest period, and he could then go on to love another woman.

What love is has been hotly debated for centuries, with no clear-cut agreement. My own definition is that love is a combination of mutuality and pleasure with the other person: the more mutuality and the more pleasure the greater the love.

Our society is not one in which love experiences are encouraged. Quite the contrary: it could be called a hate culture rather than a love culture, since the predominant mode of relatedness between people is closer to hatred than to love.

In a hate culture such as ours, love becomes an oasis in which people can feel some surcease from the constant battles raging outside. Hence it becomes extremely possessive, ringed with ferocious jealousies, lest the beloved go off somewhere else, and gradually the source of an increasing amount of suffering rather than the joy that it should bring. Should the love relationship break up, the person is again exposed to the relentless hatreds and struggles that existed before. When that happens, it is not surprising that a depression of varying degrees of severity sets in. Holly and Beverly are both good examples.

By contrast, in a love culture, in which the predominant mode of relatedness is loving, the experience of love is entirely different . There is no need for extreme possessiveness, since other love objects are readily available. Thus the parental clutch on the child, so prominent a feature of our society, becomes totally superfluous: both parent and child have many other sources of love gratification after their relationship breaks up for normal reasons, i.e., as the child gets older and moves on to his or her own world. Similarly, jealousy does not have to be so painful, although some desire for exclusiveness may always be there. The jealous partner is fearful that if deprived of his partner he will be totally lost. When the world is different and there is no such danger, jealousy loses its hold. Already one modern country, Denmark, has moved in this direction by removing adultery as a cause of divorce.

Mature love has been defined as a combination of mutuality and pleasure. It must be mutual, in that both parties derive some gratification from the relationship and participate in it. It must give pleasure, since otherwise it is a form of sacrifice rather than love. In some cases self-sacrifice is called for to some extent, as when the beloved is ill and requires special care, but this self-sacrifice should not be confused with the essence of love.

Most people are confused about love. They throw their hands up in despair — *"Che cosa e amore?"* (What is love?). Their love relationships are driven by deep, unconscious, compulsive strivings. If they should happen to work out, the people are lucky; if not, they persist in their unhappiness.

In any intensive form of psychotherapy the love life of the individual is accorded serious scrutiny. How did it arise? How long has it lasted? What satisfactions does it bring? What sufferings does it entail? As all these questions are examined at length, the patient builds up a much better image of the way his life has gone.

Different kinds of love experiences are appropriate at different stages in life. For the infant there is only physical clinging, literally to the breast or a breast substitute. Later comes a warm secure feeling from being with another. Then in the preschool years there is a period of admiration. This is followed by the mutuality of peer relationships in the school years. After that comes the sexual adventures of adolescence. These are followed by a warm genuine intimacy with one other person, usually marriage. Finally, there is the parental stage, in which the individual returns to his or her identification with the parents.

It is against this background that the love experiences of the patient have to be evaluated. The basic approach of therapy is that mental or emotional illness results from immaturity. The love life is appropriate to an earlier age, not to the age where he is now.

Many common distortions of love can be understood in this light. Thus the marriage of a very young woman to a much older man is obviously a daughter-father attachment, frequent enough in our culture where women still have a hard time making a go of it once they leave the paternal home. The attachment of the man to a sick woman, as in the case of Peter, represents the attachment to mother, so prominent in his life, and his wife was almost a perfect replica of his mother. Frank could not relate to other women at all but instead remained at home with his stepmother, like a little boy; his brother did the same thing. Alice's love problem was the lack of sexual gratification, just as when her father in childhood had suddenly withdrawn from physical contact with her.

Apart from the element of immaturity, the greatest enemy of love is hatred. In its ultimate goal psychotherapy seeks to help the person to love. But in its everyday workings psychotherapy has to uncover the hatreds which dominate the patient, and assist in overcoming them. Again, this discrepancy between goal and technique baffles many people, and takes a long time to make clear to the patient.

One of the most common complaints in psychotherapy is that "there is nobody to love" and "nobody will love me." These feelings result from the excessive hatreds present. The vast majority of people suffer from a lack of love in their lives. If someone comes along who offers them love, they grasp at it eagerly. Then the world opens up for them, and seemingly out of nowhere all kinds of possible partners emerge.

Jim is an excellent example. At thirty-eight he was still seething with rage at mother and all women. He spent his time alone, masturbating, or going to the movies, or going to the bank (another substitute) three or four times a day to withdraw small amounts of money. He had already had a breakdown, when he spent several months crying his heart out.

The good relationship with the analyst led to a considerable lessening of the hatred in a little over a year. In a very real sense he had come to love the analyst, as he had never loved anybody in his life before. With the diminished hatred and the increased love, he was ripe for a love relationship with a woman. Almost out of the blue he found one. That he could remain so happy with her for such a long time would actually not have been anticipated at the beginning; one would rather have expected him to break off, try it with others, and after many ups and downs finally settle down with one. But to a certain extent human beings are unpredictable. He found love and happiness with remarkable rapidity.

Anothor major obstacle to reaching mature love is the myriad of pseudolove relationships that abound in our society. Homosexuality is a good example. Homosexual love is always full of tension, on the verge of breaking up, and serves as a cover for deep-seated feelings of hatred and revenge. It comes out of a childhood environment in which the love feelings for the parents were deeply frustrated. So the person caught up in such homosexual love affairs, even though he may appear to be living a happy life (the "gay" crowd), remains deeply dissatisfied underneath.

Another common type of pseudo-love realtionship is that of the young girl for the drug addict. Often the girl supports the man, lives with him in defiance of her parents, and endures all kinds of misery and humiliation. Underneath, such love affairs are generally an expression of anger and resentment at the parents, particularly in homes where the early controls have been excessively strict.

The cases described show how love is reached in varying degrees by different people. A great deal depends on how strongly motivated the individual becomes to straighten out his or her love life. All too often some shallow compromise is reached, as long as it makes a good impression on society. But love always remains the central human experience and in one form or another always remains the central theme of all psychotherapy.

THE EXPERIENCE OF BEING AN ANALYST

It is difficult to compare the experience of being an analyst to anything else in life. In some ways it is similar to being in organic medicine, but in most ways it is strikingly different. Part teacher, part parent, part physician, part friend, the analyst should be looked upon as a person who teaches other people how to love.

We have indicated above that while love is the goal, making the unconscious conscious is the technique. And in this process an enormous mass of hatred is invariably discovered. The experience of being an analyst involves accepting this hatred without becoming vindictive or discouraged. It is by no means an easy task. It is in fact so difficult that it takes many years of training to reach a state where the attacks of the patient no longer take their toll.

Apart from the anger, the analyst must allow the patient to live through a tremendous amount of discouragement, an inevitable aspect of every analysis. It is at this stage that many analysts themselves become discouraged, resort to some psychiatric diagnosis, and declare the patient "untreatable." The whole history of psychoanalysis shows that there are very few untreatable patients. It is essential for the analyst to be able to handle all the depression, apathy, and discouragement with which he is faced.

In addition to the negative feelings, the analyst must be able to handle the positive ones, especially the sexual ones. These may be even harder to manage than the anger. Many analysts become so excited by this constant sexual stimulation that they cover up their feelings, and deny that they have any reactions at all, in somewhat the same manner as a gynecologist. The trouble is that such a denial makes the patient feel much worse because, say in the usual case of a female patient with a male analyst, it is felt as a deep rejection, and in fact it is a deep rejection. The analyst must learn to enjoy his sexual reactions to the patient without acting them out or becoming upset by them.

The tasks set for the analyst are formidable indeed, so it is not surprising that many fall by the wayside. Actually, the number of fully trained analysts is surprisingly small. Many persons enter the training programs, and then, discouraged by the emotional storms aroused in them, are deterred from completing their training. Usually they drift off into one of the easier forms of therapy, such as primal scream, or transactional analysis, which make fewer demands on the analyst, but which unfortunately are also less effective as therapy.

Freud as the pioneer engaged in a long self-analysis, the first successful one in history. At first he thought that any reasonably intelligent person could do what he had done, then he came to the conclusion that no one could do it. Instead, from about 1930 on, analysts have been required to go into personal analysis, which is in every respect just as difficult and demanding as the analysis of their patients. Actually, in many ways the analysis of the analyst is even more demanding. Nevertheless, no practical alternative has ever succeeded. Anyone who has not had a deep analysis which effected significant changes in his attitude toward life, cannot practice analysis adequately.

Once he is practicing, the analyst is forced to engage in continual self-analysis to understand his reactions to his patients. Thus the experience of being an analyst involves a never-ending growth process which is extraordinarily stimulating. It goes so much deeper than most of what is encountered in life that many analysts discover that the practice of analysis is one of the most gratifying and rewarding of all human occupations.

CURE AND IMPROVEMENT

The analogy of medicine, with which most people come to view the field, leads to the image of the cure of an illness. Both analyst and analysand have to unlearn this view and take an entirely different tack. What the patient is suffering from is difficulties in loving, inability to work, trouble in communicating, and the like. We have formulated this as distance from the analytic ideal, which is quite different from the conventional view of normality.

The changes produced by analysis are subtle and far-reaching. Since they involve such essential life experiences as love, imagination, alienation, sense of identity, and the like, they are extremely difficult to qualify. Who is to say how one person's pleasure measures up against another's, or whether one person's dreams are superior or inferior to another's.

Thus the philosophy of analysis has shifted from cure to improvement. Within the experience of psychotherapy, analysis operates as a philosophy of living that will promote more happiness for the individual. And as Frederick the Great once said, "In my kingdom everybody finds happiness in his own way." No set formula can be applied to the analytic kingdom: each one finds a solution best fitted to his or her style of life.

Glossary

Glossary

Anal: the anal period or stage is the time when the child is toilet trained, usually about one to three years. If this toilet training is too severe, it has effects on later personality formation.

Ego: the part of the personality that deals with reality. The *tripartitie structure* assumes that there are three major psychic structures, or instances: the id, the ego and the superego.

Genital stage: final stage of development, after the oral, anal, phallic stages. The major hallmark of the genital stage is emotional maturity.

Hysteria: One of the two major forms of neurosis, the other being obsessional neurosis. Hysteria is characterized chiefly by bodily symptoms, and excessive emotionality.

Id: the reservoir of the impulses. See also ego and superego.

Latency: the latency stage or period is roughly the school-age period. There are three major phases in psychosexual development: infantile sexuality, from birth to about five years, latency, from five to puberty and adulthood, from puberty on.

Masochism: the tendency to prefer suffering to pleasure. Originally used to describe a sexual perversion that is rarely seen today, in which the individual had to have some form of punishment in order to enjoy the sex act.

Neurosis: milder form of emotional disturbance. The two major neuroses are hysteria and obsessional neurosis.

Obsessional neurosis: one of the two major forms of neurosis. In the obsessional individual there tends to be a marked emphaisis on obsessional ideas, compulsive actions, excessive rumination and withdrawal from life situations.

Oedipus complex: central conflict of childhood, in which there is a clash between the feelings about the two parents. From about three to five years of age. After the Greek hero Oedipus, who married his mother and killed his father. The feminine equivalent, of Electra complex, has never gained wide popularity.

Oral stage: earliest stage of life, in which the infant relates primarily to the mother. Usually thought to comprise the first year of life.

Phallic stage: last stage of infantile sexuality, from about three to five years. In this stage the penis is the primary source of concern.

Projection: a defense mechanism in which one's own feelings are denied and attributed, or projected to some outside person or force. Most often seen in paranoid individuals.

Psychosexual development: course of human development in which the person is conceived as going through different stages of sexual emphasis. In the earliest, the stress is on oral gratification, then anal, then phallic, and finally in puberty the love experience, in which there is a union of tender and sexual feelings toward a person of the opposite sex.

Psychosis: most severe form of mental illness, in which there is a break with reality. Popularly called "insanity."

Regression: a defense mechanism in which there is a falling back, or regression, to earlier levels of development.

Repression: a defense mechanism in which a wish or event is pushed out of consciousness ("repressed").

Resistance: the fight against the therapist in the therapeutic situation. Some resistance is always found in any treatment situation.

Sadism: the wish to be cruel or hurtful to another person. Originally described as a sexual perversion, in which another person had to be harmed for the subject to experience sexual pleasure; the perversion is seen less often, but the feeling is quite common.

Schizophrenia: the most severe form of mental disturbance (sometimes used interchangeably with psychosis). Literally "split mind".

Splitting: a defense mechanism in which a feeling or experience is split off from others with which it would normally be associated. E.g. love may be split off from hatred. Characteristic of the more severe forms of emotional disturbance.

Superego: internalization of the parents, often referred to as the unconscious conscience. Third of three aspects of psychic structure, the other two being the id and the ego (q.v.).

Transference: emotional relationship between the patient and the therapist. Transference and resistance form the core of all psychotherapy.

Working through: process of working out the various psychological mechanisms uncovered in the therapeutic process. Usually takes a long time, and has to overcome many resistances. Working through is an essential part of every therapeutic undertaking.

Index

Index (to significant
psychological motifs)

The entries in this index include the major significant psychological motifs found in the case histories and discussion. It may be used most profitably by comparing and contrasting how these motifs work out in the various individuals discussed.

Abortion, 45, 69, 123, 164, 177
Acting Out, 206, 208, 213, 218
Adultery, 302
   See also extramarital affair
Aggression, see hostility, rage
Aimlessness, 106, 108, 276
Alienation, 103, 277
Ambivalence, 30, 33, 35, 42,
    49, 63, 111, 126, 134,
    237, 177, 178, 198, 219,
    237, 241, 245, 247, 254,
    257
Anal, 43, 44, 63, 66, 79, 121,
    148, 163, 172, 174, 180,
    190, 192, 205, 223, 228,
    235, 241, 247, 250, 255,
    263, 292, 308
Anal intercourse, 56, 121, 129
Analyst, experience of,
    304-306 See also

countertransference
Analytic honeymoon, 58, 168
Analytic ideal 10, 12, 14, 19,
    272-280, 282, 306
Anger, See hostility, rage
Anniversary response, 101
Anxiety, panic, 9, 12, 16, 31,
    25, 55, 60, 83, 91, 105,
    106, 118, 136, 144, 149,
    155, 160, 165, 167, 168,
    173, 178, 179, 181, 183,
    185, 191, 195, 198, 203,
    204, 211, 224, 225, 226,
    228, 229, 239, 242, 243,
    244, 245, 255, 260, 261,
    262, 263, 264, 266, 268,
    273, 276, 286
Artistic gifts, 25, 29, 58, 83,
    107, 244
Beatings, 40, 56, 73, 83, 110,

119, 120, 123, 154, 163, 217, 218, 225
Behavior Therapy, 264
Bodily symptoms, (somatization) 27, 31, 63, 69, 119, 144, 146, 170, 191, 192, 195, 203, 240, 243, 258, 262, 285
Borderline case, 210, 268, 297
See also diagnosis
Brain damage 4, 11

Castration, 67, 90, 93, 127, 152, 172, 194, 242, 245, 258, 262, 268
Character structure, 12, 178
Communication, 8, 151, 156, 158, 160, 273, 276, 277 287
Compulsivity, 12, 36, 57, 79, 114, 148, 302
Countertransference, 296-298
Creativity, 278
See also artistic gifts
Crying, 106, 120, 135, 148, 166, 240, 241, 257, 292, 303
Cunnilingus, 34, 98, 163, 194, 201, 260
Cure, 306

Defenses, 4
Delusions, 217, 219, 220, 225, 228, 232, 240, 285, 286, 300
Denial, 230, 236, 270, 305
Dependency, 34, 116, 192, 210, 218, 229, 234, 236, 257, 281, 288, 289
Depression, 27, 35, 45, 51, 122, 128, 132, 146, 166, 167, 171, 183, 189, 202,

210, 240, 255, 268, 292, 297, 305
Diagnosis, 297
Dreams, 15, 29, 60, See also tranference dreams
Drugs, 16, 17, 189, 195, 210, 211, 245, 248, 251, 252, 255, 262, 268, 275
Drug Addiction, 8, 189, 290, 304
Drunkenness, 162, 187, 194, 244, 290
Dynamic Inactivity (of analyst) 17

Ego, 12, 188, 215, 233, 238, 279, 309
Ego structure, 12, 210, 213
Exhibitionism, 38, 170, 172, 174, 250, 251, 253, 254
Extramarital affair, 7, 38, 86, 103, 165, 199, 278
See also adultery

Family, 13, 35, 47, 55, 61, 83, 106, 119, 135, 145, 146, 164, 167, 189, 207, 216, 230, 240, 265, 276-77
Feeling, 275-276, 277
Fellatio, 66, 70, 79, 123, 194, 242, 292
Fighting, 40, 73, 85, 109, 118, 126, 133, 165, 174, 181, 242, 262
Freud, v, 4, 5, 11, 17, 250, 262, 269, 281, 289, 298, 305

Genital stage, 310
Grandiosity, 151, 153, 156, 240, 243, 254, 256, 273, 287

Guilt, 28, 41, 52, 79, 103,
    123, 126, 150, 175, 186,
    194, 224, 227, 265, 266,
    267

Hallucinations, 219, 222, 224,
    225, 226, 228, 229, 232,
    235, 297
Hatred, 37, 94, 132, 187, 205,
    269, 283, 288, 299, 300,
    301, 304
    See also rage, hostility
Homosexuality, 7, 28, 52, 56,
    61, 65, 69, 92, 99, 106,
    107, 127, 164, 176, 180,
    192, 201, 212, 217, 218,
    222, 231, 237, 242, 245,
    248, 252, 254, 255, 258,
    259, 261, 266, 202, 304
Hostility, 67, 83, 93, 116, 126,
    153, 182, 208, 222, 227,
    230, 238, 300
    See also rage, hatred
Hysteria, 66, 166, 183, 185,
    186, 308

Id, 178, 188, 308
Identification, 27, 52, 59, 80,
    175, 181, 251, 263, 302
Identity, 80, 103, 277
Impotence, 29, 119, 126, 131,
    142, 250
Improvement, 306
Incest, 68, 79, 101, 122, 142,
    162, 166, 169, 173, 177,
    179, 193, 206, 212, 247,
    248, 249, 253, 258, 259,
    260, 261, 263, 269
Inner image, 13, 177, 284-285,
Insight, 196, 202, 206, 212,
    229, 244, 245, 249, 254,
    260, 261, 270

Insomnia, 194
Interpretation, 284
Intimacy, 288, 291, 292, 293,
    294, 295, 300, 302
Introject, see inner image
IQ, 7, 150, 166
Isolation, See separation

Jealousy, 97, 132, 174, 189,
    240, 249, 290, 295, 301
"Jewish Mother", 55, 109

Latency, 308
Lay analyst, 189
Lesbian, 291
    See also homosexuality
Love, 9, 11, 12, 25, 57, 85,
    117, 118, 138, 139, 141,
    142, 164, 217, 262, 267,
    272-274, 275, 288, 290,
    295, 298, 301, 303, 304
Love affair, 23, 64, 85, 122,
    125, 141, 199, 294
Lovers, 33, 57, 86, 119, 124,
    283

Marital Discord, v, 23, 39, 56,
    82, 170, 171
Marriage, v, 26, 56, 86
Masochism, 58, 59, 60, 78, 84,
    123, 131, 135, 142, 176,
    192, 199, 202, 203, 209,
    215, 242, 248, 258, 276,
    288, 299, 308
Masturbation, 74, 106, 107,
    114, 149, 155, 158, 175,
    182, 193, 239, 248, 251,
    255, 292, 303
Methadone, 8
    See also drugs
Mood swings, 35, 166
Motives for Treatment, 280

Narcissism, 137, 176, 184,
    210, 273, 279
Neuropathologist, 5, 6
Neurosis, 9, 298, 309
Neurotic Compromise, 284,
    310
Nightmares, 35, 38-39, 127,
    171, 192, 241, 250
Normality, 3, 83, 102
Normal patient, 10
Nymphomania, 293
    See also sexuality,
    promiscuity

Obsession, obsessional neurosis
    164, 213, 262, 311
Oedipus Complex, 36, 45, 47,
    83, 84, 87, 93, 100, 123,
    124, 131, 141, 145, 160,
    176, 185, 247, 249, 250,
    256, 269, 309
Omnipotence, 112
Oral stage, 46, 55, 78, 83, 147,
    160, 187, 189, 220, 235,
    237, 275, 293, 309
Orgasm, 76, 117, 128, 129,
    136, 175, 182, 184, 201,
    274, 275, 292
Orgies, 32, 70, 78
Overintellectualization, 83, 91,
    94, 96, 111, 190

Paranoid, 180
Passivity, 17
Penis envy, 90
Personality theory, 13
Phallic stage, 184, 309
Pleasure, 79, 274
Premature ejaculation, 130,
    167, 170, 185, 275
Primal scream, 305
Projection, 65, 129, 142, 181,
    186, 188, 309
Promiscuity, 6, 26, 51-52, 129,
    131, 163, 185, 273, 274
Psychiatric patient, vi, 5, 9, 10,
    12, 107, 130, 138, 145,
    195, 198
Psychiatrist, 4, 5, 6, 9, 10, 19,
    81, 107, 167, 180, 182,
    189, 206, 207, 216, 217,
    218, 255, 265, 279-280,
    282, 305
Psychoanalysis, v, vi, 9, 10,
    14, 18, 75
Psychologist, 5, 6, 166, 190,
    197, 255
Psychosexuality, 149, 311
Psychosis, 106, 180, 187, 203,
    218, 219, 220, 228, 229,
    231, 234, 268, 285, 309
Psychotherapy, 4, 11, 145,
    158, 165, 168, 185, 189,
    220, 259, 281, 282, 298

Rage, 25, 26, 28, 62, 67, 73,
    79, 84, 91, 99, 127, 150,
    154, 162, 171, 173, 219,
    225, 227, 235, 254, 257,
    259, 260, 262, 266, 276,
    285, 293, 298, 299, 303,
    304, 305
Reality, 283-284
Reason, 276-277
Rebellion, 84, 106, 109, 119,
    152, 154, 288
Reduction in pain, 274
Regression, 77, 152, 210, 212,
    215, 218, 220, 235, 244,
    250, 258, 260, 262, 309
Reichian "analysis", 67, 292
Rejection, 7, 41, 58, 67, 84,
    114, 115, 118, 125, 143,
    165, 174, 192, 217, 232,

233, 249, 265, 281, 283, 287, 290, 292, 294, 305
Religion, 9, 18, 110, 181, 239, 242, 244, 257, 258, 264, 265, 268, 286
Repression, 84, 115, 160, 170, 203, 309
Rescue fantasy, 131, 142, 198
Resistance, 15, 18, 87, 108, 111, 132, 167, 168, 178, 190, 238, 145, 283-284, 299, 309
Revenge, 39, 42-45, 52, 62, 99, 114, 168, 171, 269, 275, 304

Sadism, 251, 254, 299, 310
Schizophrenia, vi, 10, 160, 167, 168, 169, 180, 185, 213, 217, 233, 234, 237, 240, 268, 280, 297, 310
Seduction, 30, 169, 265, 290
Self-analysis, 261, 263, 278, 279, 305, 306
Self-image, 4, 6, 26, 35, 53, 58, 80, 98, 113, 120, 129, 132, 143, 180, 210, 243, 256, 268, 287, 296, 305, 307
Separation, 83, 160, 175, 216, 227, 258, 286, 289
Sexuality, 7, 8, 11, 12, 16, 24, 42, 61, 70, 79, 82, 85, 88, 106, 122, 128, 139, 146, 162, 163, 164, 169, 175, 177, 182, 184, 185, 193, 200, 206, 223, 226, 239, 241, 254, 258, 262, 263, 268, 274
Shame, 32, 41, 52, 85, 119, 124, 126, 131, 147, 186, 241, 256

Social role, 277
Social worker, 6
Speech, speech therapy, 8, 148, 157
Splitting, 25, 32, 38, 98, 131, 310
Suicide, 29, 32, 36, 37-38, 51, 64, 95, 165, 185, 203, 211, 217, 233, 258, 273, 294
Superego, 13, 46, 62, 66, 88, 111, 115, 129, 176, 183, 185, 186, 187, 188, 199, 211-215, 230, 238, 246, 254, 310
Supportive therapy, 213, 218, 232, 239, 243, 268
Symbolism, 29, 47, 48, 60, 62, 67, 69, 76, 94, 94, 98, 100, 102, 134, 135, 152, 156, 173, 235, 246, 249, 254, 266, 291
Syphilis, 165, 168, 175, 180, 287

Temper tantrums, See rage, hostility
Transactional analysis, 307
Transference, 15, 31, 43, 49, 59, 74-77, 78, 87, 88, 93, 96, 98, 100, 101, 111, 112, 131, 139, 142, 156, 157, 168, 173, 179, 187, 188, 197, 212, 215, 218, 220, 229, 230, 237, 238, 241, 243, 257, 262, 269, 285, 286, 287, 297, 310
Transference dreams, 66, 78, 112, 113, 128, 133, 171, 173, 174, 250, 255, 261, 265, 291
Treatability, 305

Trial period, 106

Unconscious, 14, 79, 83, 100, 127, 142, 152, 169, 188, 211, 223, 238, 245, 258, 272, 277, 293, 298, 302, 306

VD, 8, 242, 243, 264
Voyeurism, 254

Withdrawal, 106, 111, 146, 168, 180, 191, 195, 206, 211, 276

Work, 13, 80, 119, 122, 165, 192, 231, 268, 279

Working through, 71, 92, 98, 116, 173, 226, 238, 244, 298, 310

Index (to case histories)

Alice   7, 82, 103, 273, 274,
        275, 276, 277, 281,
        300, 303
Beverly 9, 216-238, 273, 274,
        275, 276, 277, 278,
        280, 285, 291, 293,
        296, 297, 300, 301
Frank   9, 16, 19, 239-270,
        275, 276, 277, 278,
        279, 280, 283, 284,
        286, 293, 299
Gloria 8, 162-188, 273, 274,
        275, 276, 277, 279,
        281, 287, 292, 293
Harvey 6, 54-81, 272, 275,
        276, 277, 279, 280

Holly   7, 19, 118-143, 272,
        275, 276, 277, 278,
        279, 281, 287, 300,
        301
Jim   7, 19, 105-117, 272,
        275, 276, 277, 279,
        280, 282, 283, 303
Peter   8, 189-215, 272, 274,
        275, 276, 277, 280,
        285, 300, 303
Sally   6, 23-53, 273, 274,
        275, 276, 277, 279,
        280, 290, 293, 297
Sheldon 7, 144-161, 273, 274,
        275, 276, 277, 278,
        280, 287